EXECUTION!

Kim angrily shoved the U.S. Army people away from the others and grabbed an AKM from one of his men. He cocked it and opened fire on the astounded soldiers. They scattered in all directions but died running for cover as Kim emptied one clip, then jammed in another and emptied that one as well into the prostrate bodies of his victims. He threw the weapon at his men and screamed.

"Beginning now, we will kill all army personnel! Do you understand? Kill them!"

His tirade over, he led his men toward the Range Command Building—the center of anti-ballistic missile missions for the Kwajalein Missile Range.

Other Avon Books by
John Campbell

RAID ON TRUMAN

SUB ZERO

JOHN CAMPBELL

AVON BOOKS ◆ NEW YORK

SUB ZERO is an original publication of Avon Books. This work has never before appeared in book form. This work is a novel. Any similarity to actual persons or events is purely coincidental.

AVON BOOKS
A division of
The Hearst Corporation
1350 Avenue of the Americas
New York, New York 10019

Copyright © 1996 by John Campbell
Published by arrangement with the author
Library of Congress Catalog Card Number: 95-94924
ISBN: 0-380-78061-5

First Avon Books Printing: March 1996

AVON TRADEMARK REG. U.S. PAT. OFF. AND IN OTHER COUNTRIES, MARCA REGISTRADA, HECHO EN U.S.A.

Printed in the U.S.A.

RA   10   9   8   7   6   5   4   3   2   1

To Carol,
my hero, my love, my life

Acknowledgments

As usual, a host of people have helped make this novel possible. First among them is my brother, Chris, who helped greatly with the research needed for an accurate depiction of Kwajalein Atoll. Bruce Landis helped a great deal with technical details, along with John Nuttall, Clara Han, Judith Wang, Greg Cream, Eric Sudano, and Bob and Kathy Campbell. Roxanne Luebeck of the Marple Public Library helped me thread the maze of information that exists in my local library system.

Finally I thank my agent, Elizabeth Pomada, and my editor, Tom Colgan, for doing their usual stellar job on my work.

In Memoriam

Let us not forget the deaths of two American officers in the uneasy cessation of hostilities that exists among the United States, South Korea, and North Korea. Major Arthur G. Bonifas and Lieutenant Mark T. Barrett were murdered by North Koreans in August 1976. This work was based in part upon that disastrous incident.

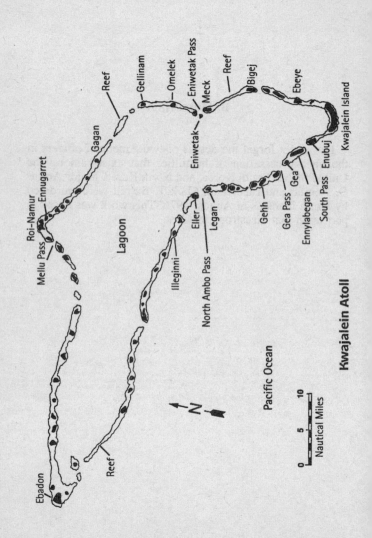

Kwajalein Atoll

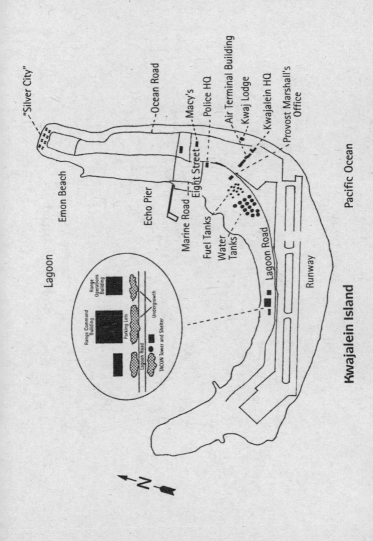

"Silver City"

Ocean Road

Macy's

Police HQ

Air Terminal Building

Kwaj Lodge

Kwajalein HQ

Provost Marshall's Office

Emon Beach

Lagoon

Echo Pier

Marine Road

Eight Street

Fuel Tanks

Water Tanks

Lagoon Road

Runway

Pacific Ocean

Kwajalein Island

Range Operations Building

Parking Lots

Range Command Building

Undergrowth

Lagoon Road

TACON Tower and Shelter

N

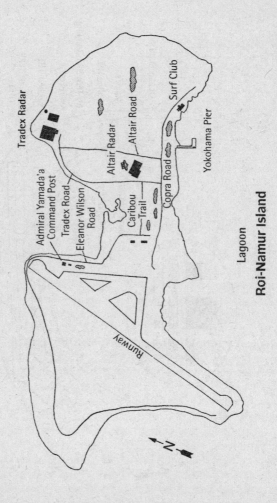

Pacific Ocean

Tradex Radar

Admiral Yamada'a Command Post

Tradex Road

Eleanor Wilson Road

Caribou Trail

Altair Radar

Altair Road

Copra Road

Surf Club

Yokohama Pier

Lagoon

Runway

Roi-Namur Island

N

PROLOGUE

Northern Surprise

George Tucker was a spy.

The building he worked in was nondescript and constructed of plain brick. Its location on the East Coast of the United States in the suburbs of a large metropolitan city hid its true worth in the U.S. Department of Defense scheme of things.

The structure was set toward the end of a large parking lot which doubled as the parking area for a line of stores on the opposite end of the lot. The building's plain vanilla wrapper with no company name on the outside was purely intentional. With no name to attract attention, people never realized that the building housed the employees of a large aerospace firm. The people who worked in the building were not at all different from the average white-collar workforce anywhere else in the country, except that they were whiter and more male. A step inside the entrance would reveal a guard who had the opportunity to get just as bored as most security people do.

Deep inside the building, George Tucker sat at a desk in a top secret vault. He kept one eye on the documents in front of him and one eye on his "buddy," the other engineer in the vault with him. Security rules stated that at least two people had to be in the vault when it was occupied. One person in the vault would create a security problem. The theory was that each person would keep an eye on the other, thereby making it impossible for one of them to copy the sensitive documents in the room.

Tucker smiled slightly as he thought of the word *impossible*. Truly nothing was impossible if enough effort was expended to find a solution. He flipped over the page of the document in front of him and put his left hand, on which he was ostensibly resting his head, a little closer to the page. The complicated diagram had some small print. He slowly moved his left hand from left to right to scan the page, allowing the lens at the end of the fiber-optic cable in his hand to get a complete view of the diagram. The fiber-optic cable ran up his sleeve, down the trunk of his body, ending in his pocket, where a miniature video camera translated the captured light into electrical signals. The signals were fed into a very small video recorder which was constantly running in his pocket.

After an hour of taping, he left the vault with a hurried men's room explanation. His "buddy" screwed up his face in annoyance—he had to leave as well, and the vault had to be resecured, necessitating the activation of a host of locks and alarms as well as a call to the central security station. Inside the men's room in one of the stalls, Tucker replaced the tape. He hurried back to the vault, where his companion was waiting outside, and apologized profusely. His friend just sighed and silently went through the rigamarole of reentering the vault.

Tucker signed out another document, entitled "ROK TBMD—Capabilities and Vulnerabilities—An Assessment." His control agent hadn't asked for this one by name, but it seemed that this particular document would interest them very much. How much would this document be worth to them? He had his eye on a small two-seat Mercedes Benz in a local dealership. It was maroon, and it had real leather seats. The smell of the genuine leather had hit him the first time he had sat in the car, and it had stayed with him. The car wasn't quite as good as sex, but pretty damn close. He risked another smile and gave his buddy a half glance. The other man had his nose buried in his own top secret document.

Tucker sighed and opened the bright red document. Now let's find out all about South Korea's new present from

Uncle Sam, he thought, a theater ballistic missile defense, or TBMD in the DOD's short language. He paged through the document in a steady stream, viewing each page for the same short interval. There was no need for him to read the document. If his masters wanted to read the page, they could just stop the videotape, or even make a series of still photos from the tape and turn the stills into a book.

Tucker had been at this for almost a year. The initial agonizing fear of being caught was long gone, and the rapture of great wealth was constantly with him. He had long resolved not to make the mistakes that Aldrich Ames and his wife had made. The FBI would not catch on to him because of his lifestyle as they had with Ames, one of the most celebrated and vilified spies within the CIA—celebrated by the KGB, vilified by the CIA. The elevation of his standard of living would wait until he left the country and was where the United States couldn't touch him. Meanwhile the money just accumulated in a foreign bank account until it had reached dizzying heights, and Tucker's smile grew broader as he sold away U.S. missile defense secrets to the interested parties of the world. Once in a while Tucker would make an exception to his stringent lifestyle. After he got the money for the highly desired information in front of him, he would buy that Mercedes Benz, and the FBI be damned.

He finished his scan of the document and glanced at his watch. Almost quitting time. He got his buddy's attention and pointed to his watch. The other man glanced at his watch and nodded. They left the vault and went through the elaborate securing procedure and then went to their respective offices.

Tucker gazed out the window at the parking lot below and smiled again. As a senior systems engineer working for the defense contractor who was responsible for integrating the TBMD program, the offspring of the now canceled Strategic Defense Initiative, he was in a unique position to know how the U.S. missile defense worked. He must be a godsend to whomever was getting his information. Twice before he had held up the transfer of the top secret information until he had gotten more money. They had threatened to get rough with him, but he knew they were bluffing.

The money had come through, obscene amounts of it. He went over to the office door and locked it quietly. He opened his attaché case, being careful to avoid activating its internal security devices, and deposited the day's tapes into a concealed compartment in the bottom of the case. All employees had to open their attaché cases, packages, or pocketbooks so that the guards could see inside, but a real search was never made.

Tucker left the building among a crowd of other employees, the semibored guards giving each opened package a cursory look. After the guards' "search," Tucker absentmindedly activated the attaché case's security system by pushing three buttons concealed in the lining in a specified sequence, and then walked out of the building. He approached his car, which was parked in the same general location every day, and a feeling of unease came over him. He pulled out the keys and slipped them into the lock, and immediately saw rapid movement in his peripheral vision.

Two men pressed him against the side of the car while a third lurked behind him out of sight. The third man spoke quietly.

"Get in the car quickly," he whispered in Tucker's ear. A fourth man turned the key in the lock and threw the door open.

"Look, if you want the car—" Tucker began as fear rippled through him. The men said nothing and shoved him into the backseat. They sat on either side of him, crowding him so he couldn't move freely. Tucker looked down at the hand of one of the men seated next to him. It held a very large automatic handgun that was pointed at Tucker.

"Don't say a word," the man said. He looked down at the attaché case next to Tucker's feet, then gazed intently at Tucker's face. Tucker wanted to hold the man's stare but couldn't do it.

The other two men jumped into the front seat and quickly started the car. Tucker looked around quickly to see if any of his coworkers had seen the event, but no one was visible. He licked his lips and couldn't seem to catch his breath. Must be the adrenaline, he thought. He forced himself to calm down and was only partially successful, and he stared at each of the men in turn. They all had Oriental features.

Something told him that this was no ordinary carjacking. The five of them sped out of the parking lot and down an empty street.

The man in the front passenger seat turned around and looked Tucker over. He mumbled something in a foreign language. The man next to Tucker nodded and passed the attaché case up to him, ignoring Tucker's horrified reaction.

"No," he tried to say calmly. "Don't open—" The man next to him swung the butt end of the handgun and struck Tucker a smashing blow to the mouth. Tucker's head flew back and bounced off the top of the rear seat. Through a fog he heard the latches pop open, first one, then the other.

"No!" he shouted as loudly as he could, his bloodied mouth distorting the sound. The man next to him gritted his teeth and swung the gun barrel toward Tucker's face. The blow never landed.

Two phosphorus grenades hidden inside the attaché case detonated simultaneously, turning the inside of the car into a flaming tomb. Tucker's scream hit the white-hot phosphorus that filled the air and died instantly. Tucker's final action was to hysterically inhale the incredibly hot chemicals, which instantly burned his mouth, throat, and lungs away. Tucker's brain shut down in sudden shock and blessed death came seconds later.

The explosion caught the three agents in the following car by surprise. They gaped in shock as flames poured out of the blown-out windows and they stared horrified as the car slowly went out of control and ran into a line of parked cars. The wreck slammed to a stop and in a matter of seconds was completely consumed in flames. The driver of the trailing car slammed his foot on the brake in a panic, bringing the car to a screeching halt. All of them stared, their Oriental features contorting with the intensity of the conflagration before them.

The driver put his hand on his door handle and jerked the door open. The man in the front passenger seat grabbed him by the coat sleeve.

"No," he said. "There's nothing we can do now." He gave a quick look around as the sound of a siren was heard above the crackle of flames from the devastated car in front of them. "Let's get out of here!" he ordered.

The driver reluctantly slammed the door and began to back up to turn around.

"Looked like a phosphorus bomb," said the man in the backseat.

"Yes," said the man in the front passenger seat. "That just about confirms it. The only agency that would use a phosphorus bomb to keep its covert targets a secret is the Liaison Bureau. Our friends from North Korea are intent upon stealing missile defense secrets from the Americans." The leader of the trio groaned. The bomb was a surprise, but he should have known that the North Koreans might use something like that. They had done so before in cases of extreme importance. Ballistic missile defense, especially when deployed in their hated neighbor to the south, would be of the utmost importance to their Communist neighbors. Four of his good agents dead because of his negligence in briefing his people.

"At least the Liaison Bureau didn't get whatever secrets Tucker had with him," said the man in the back. The leader turned and gave him a long look. The man in the back apologized with his eyes and the leader turned back around.

It's true, the leader thought after a few moments. Our masters in the Guojia Anquan Bu, the Ministry of State Security in Beijing, will be happy about that.

CHAPTER ONE

Arrival and Confrontation

Kwajalein Atoll
Marshall Islands

Ken Garrett shaded his eyes with his left hand as he stared at the horizon to the east. The plane would come from there, he thought, as he fixed his gaze on one spot in the distance. The tropical sun beat on his head and neck and made him squirm in discomfort. He decided after a moment to go inside the terminal building to get out of the intense heat. The terminal building wasn't air-conditioned, but at least he would be out of the direct sunlight.

Garrett glanced at his watch and shook his head with impatience. It was 12:03 P.M. and the flight from Honolulu had been due at 11:50 A.M. The flight was a few minutes late, and he didn't want to think of what the passengers would go through if they had to ditch at sea. He suddenly broke into a wry smile. Nancy had always told him he was a worrywart. Maybe she was right. Maybe she was right about a lot of things. His smile faded.

He lifted his sunglasses enough to get an unshaded view of the horizon and flinched against the unrelenting glare of the sand around him and the brilliant sparkle of the sea before him. He could feel the heat from the sand through his shoes, and he was sweating profusely even with the constant breeze of the trade winds in his face to keep him cool. He decided for the fifth time in the last five minutes

7

to go into the terminal building; then maybe he wouldn't sweat so much. It wouldn't do for Nancy to see him soaking wet after such a long time. Suppose she wanted to hug him. Suppose she wanted to kiss him . . .

He let out a sigh and stared at the horizon one last time. He blinked his eyes a few times in quick succession, and yes, there it was, the spot on the horizon. He watched it grow bigger, and in a few moments it grew into a full-size aircraft. The plane flew past the island and swung into a wide turn to approach the airstrip from the west.

Ken started to jog up the beach toward the terminal building, but then thought better of it and slowed to a fast walk. Not that it would make much difference, he thought. He would be sweating enough either way. He got to the terminal building just as the Air Micronesia 727 was slowing to a stop near the building. A few minutes later, the rear door of the airplane swung down and the passengers began to disembark onto the tarmac.

Garrett stared into the group of people, trying to pick out his wife. She was the green-eyed redhead and had to be the prettiest woman on the plane. Suddenly she was in view and headed with all the other passengers to the little room where dogs sniffed their luggage for drugs. After filling out some papers and showing security people their "orders," or their authorization to travel to Kwajalein, they would be given a temporary ID and let go to get a permanent ID card later. Ken stared at her to catch her eye, but she looked neither right nor left as she walked purposefully to the security room. At least it was air-conditioned in the room, he thought. He went into the terminal building and stood near a wall to escape the highly active children, who, he guessed, were restless from the heat. He also guessed that the children belonged to some of the people waiting for disembarking passengers.

The ceiling fans did little to ease his discomfort as he glanced intermittently at the door leading from the security room. He hated to admit it, but his inability to catch Nancy's eye disconcerted him. Normally people look around for the ones they are expecting to meet. Nancy hadn't done that. He hoped it didn't portend an ominous future.

He idly watched the people exiting the security room and

the people in the terminal building greeting their guests, some with a formal handshake, some with hugs of unconcealed joy. One man caught his eye. He was tall, thin, bald, fiftyish, had a gray mustache, and looked like a English gentleman. Garrett caught sight of his eyes just before the man put on his sunglasses. He had eyes that didn't miss anything. Probably some DOD bigwig, he thought. Nancy was the next person to leave the security room. He took a deep breath and walked toward her.

Nancy spotted him quickly and gave him a warm smile. Some of the tension eased within him. He quickly enveloped her in a close embrace. She seemed a little surprised but didn't object to his thinly veiled enthusiasm. He kissed her lightly on the lips and grinned from ear to ear.

"I missed you," he said softly.

She nodded almost sympathetically but didn't return the sentiment. Ken noticed it with disappointment.

"How have you been?" she asked lightly. She flipped her head to rearrange her long hair and gave him a close look.

"Fine," he said, and screwed up his mouth to convey just the opposite.

She smiled quickly at his implied discomfort and began to fan herself with impatience. "God, is it hot here," she mumbled.

"Yeah, it takes some getting used to," he replied. He wanted to launch into a discussion of their relationship and their life together but restrained himself. Time enough for that later, he thought. Don't bombard her ten minutes after she leaves the plane. He decided to change the subject.

"That tall, older guy who left the security room just before you did," said Ken, "who was he?"

She shrugged. "I don't know. He was just another passenger on the plane." She thought for a moment. "You know, they didn't put him through the same security baloney that everyone went through." She gave him a curious look. "He showed some guy what looked to be an ID card, and the guy just let him through after a phone call to somebody."

"Some DOD brass?" he asked.

"Or security," she said. "With this upcoming mission,

this sandbar will be crawling with all kinds of people like that.''

Ken did a quick, obvious look around to tell Nancy that she shouldn't be talking about their mission, especially with a lot of uncleared personnel about. She caught his meaning and dropped the subject.

They went outside to the checked baggage area and picked up her luggage after a rather tired-looking beagle finished sniffing it. Only two suitcases, he mused. She'd never make an actress or a rock star, he thought, and smiled.

"So where is this place called the Kwaj Lodge?" she said and smiled at the rhyme.

"The Kwaj Lodge is full. You'll have to stay with me," he said, and held his breath.

"It's full? But they told me—"

"Like you said—this sandbar is crawling with all kinds of people," he replied quickly.

Nancy gave him a semiannoyed look, as if she thought he was lying, but she let it go. "Well, as long as you have an air conditioner," she replied, and fanned herself to make the point.

He grinned at his small victory and at her. "Best air conditioner on the island."

She gave him a sideways glance to tell him that she didn't believe him, but she smiled in spite of it. They got in the bus and Ken told the bus driver that their destination was Silver City. The bus driver smiled and nodded. Only people who were thoroughly familiar with Kwajalein called the trailer park by that name. The bus started up, immediately pulled onto Ocean Road, and quickly passed the Kwaj Lodge. Nancy gave the beige-colored building a lingering look and turned toward him.

"Are you sure it's full?" she asked.

"I'm sure," he said. "I'm very sure."

Ocean Road ran along the southern coastline of the island past lines of impossibly skinny palm trees and various facilities, such as the swimming pool, two clubs right on the beach, and one tan, multistory building that caught Nancy's eye.

"Macy's!" she said in surprise. "Kwajalein Atoll has a Macy's?"

Ken grinned. "And you thought you were going to rough it." She laughed out loud.

The bus rolled on for another ten minutes until it pulled up to a structure with tarnished silver sides.

"A trailer," she said in a flat voice.

"I know the outside doesn't look like much, but it's comfortable," he said. They got off the bus, and Nancy stood looking around as Ken retrieved her luggage. He walked over to stand next to her and couldn't resist another smile. Smiling was getting to be a habit today, he thought.

"So, any nightlife around here?" she asked in a depressed voice. His smile faded.

They entered the trailer, and Nancy gave a yelp of joy at the cool interior. He had put the air conditioner on high before he left for the air terminal. He dropped the bags and got them both some iced tea, then they sat at the kitchen table while he quietly regarded her. She was beautiful as always, but she looked worn out from the twenty-four-hour trip from the States. The seven-hour difference from Eastern Standard Time would play havoc with her days and nights for a few weeks.

"I think I'm going to sleep late tomorrow," she said in a weary tone.

"You don't work tomorrow?" he asked in surprise.

"Do you?" she asked while raising her eyebrows.

"Yeah, tomorrow's Monday," he said.

"Oh, I forgot. We crossed the international date line, didn't we," she replied in disgust. "I leave on a Thursday, travel all day Friday, and get here on a Sunday." She gave him a sideways look. "By the way, where do I sleep?"

The ten-trillion-dollar question, he thought. He pointed down the narrow hall. She leaned out of her chair to see what was obviously his bedroom. The door was open, and she could see some of his clothes hanging on a stand by the bed.

"Let me rephrase the question. Where are you sleeping?" she asked as she turned back around. He pointed down the hallway in an identical manner as before.

She nodded. "I'll sleep on the couch."

He couldn't keep the disappointment off his face. "Do you want a divorce?" he asked quietly.

"I don't know," she said, and shook her head in real indecision. "Do we have to talk about this every second that we're together? I just want to take a bath and go to bed for a few hundred hours."

"We have to talk about it sometime," he replied.

"You know how I feel," she said lamely.

"Yes. That thing in New York. It's always that goddamn New York business," he retorted.

"It's why you came out here, isn't it?" she asked suddenly, as if she had made a great deduction.

He gave her a sharp look. "I came out here because of the opportunity this program represented," he said in an exaggerated tone of patience. He raised his eyebrows to form a question. "You never did anything because of the opportunity it represented?"

Nancy twisted her mouth into a line of disgust. "Why does the woman always give up opportunity just to follow the man around? I had the chance to do some real design work, work that was mine and mine alone." She stared at him with an intensity he had never seen before. "And I wanted that chance." She dropped her gaze to play over the kitchen table. "And I took that chance."

"You sure did," he said. "And now this next mission will pit your design against my design. Your PENAIDS against my tracking radar. It's funny that a woman would design penetration aids," he said with a leer.

Nancy rolled her eyes. "You crude bastard," she said. He started to speak again, but she interrupted him with an upraised hand. "I know, I know. Men are better at penetration than women. I've heard all this shit before. Do you always get crude when you're threatened?"

Garrett wanted to bite his lip, but he restrained himself. Why had he said that? How stupid could he be? Was she right about his feeling threatened by her accomplishments? She had just asked the same—and he thought silly—question that women had been asking men for years now. He thought he was above it all, and that men and women had advanced past that particular bit of provocative rhetoric.

But did she have a point? Was he jealous of her engineering talent? This upcoming mission, did it mean more to him than it should? Suppose her PENAIDS confused his radar and allowed the test warheads through the missile defense? Would he be devastated by it? His marriage, if one could call it that, had degenerated into an engineering competition.

"Yes, but it all comes down to those three men in New York," he said in a bitter tone. "I wish we had never gone to see that goddamned play."

"If you had only helped that man . . ." She left the rest unsaid.

"The other two guys could have had guns," he replied with anger in his voice. "You're so damn naive, Nancy. You think that nothing happens to the good guys who come to the rescue of the helpless. Life isn't some damn Arnold Schwarzenegger movie. Ever ask yourself why the cops have guns?"

"Maybe those two men didn't have guns," she said.

"I called the police, didn't I?" he shot back.

She sat silently, and the unholy incident in the streets of New York City hung between them. She finally spoke, but he knew what she was going to say before she said it.

"That helped the guy a lot, didn't it?"

CHAPTER TWO

Yi's Departure

Cha-ho, North Korea

Captain Hong Il Choi's eyes swept the horizon as his submarine, the *Admiral Yi*, slid quietly on the surface toward the waters of the Sea of Japan—or the East Sea, as the Koreans call it. He commanded one of the most capable submarines in the North Korean inventory, a Russian-made Kilo-class sub, one of the few purchased from the Russians in recent years. Most of the North Korean subs were now being built from Russian plans by the North Koreans themselves.

The North Koreans had been distinctly lacking in the submarine department—to the relief of the American, South Korean, and Japanese navies—but that was beginning to change. The Kilo-class sub, although diesel powered, could stay submerged for twenty days, and it provided a substantial threat in shallow waters. When running on batteries, the Kilo could be disturbingly quiet and hard to detect.

Captain Hong's Kilo-class submarine bore the proud name of Admiral Yi Sun-sin, who had defeated hordes of Japanese invaders in the late sixteenth century by using armored "turtleships" which destroyed hundreds of enemy vessels. The turtleships were completely enclosed to protect the crews and allow them to survive as the Japanese rained down shells upon them.

Captain Hong took one last look around and ordered his boat to dive. The alarm went throughout the ship, and his crew, one of the best in North Korea, jumped to their duties with enthusiasm. A feeling of satisfaction went through Hong. He and his men had trained long and hard for this mission. The fate of his nation could very well rest on them.

His deck crew cleared the bridge quickly, leaving the captain alone for a brief moment. He stared, mesmerized by the sight of the seawater washing over the bow and sweeping up toward the superstructure. The hull completely disappeared under the sea, and Hong knew it was time to go below. He took one last look at the sky, then hurried over to the open hatch. He knew he wouldn't see the world again for ten days as they wound their way fifty-five hundred kilometers across the sea to their distant goal.

Hong jumped through the hatch and slammed it shut. A sailor next to him spun the hand wheel to seal the hatch while Hong strode to the control room.

"Diving Officer, make your depth twenty-five meters," ordered Hong in a loud voice. The order was acknowledged quickly, and Hong could feel the boat tilt under his feet as the diving angle increased.

Hong's submarine was crowded. Normally the crew's complement on a Kilo-class boat was thirty-seven men and eight officers. In addition to that normal complement was a group of frogmen and a section of missile engineers who would do an evaluation of the intelligence gathered on the mission during the journey home from their target. His boat normally carried eighteen torpedoes, but this number had been reduced to two to make room for the extra personnel. Every spare cubic centimeter was used to store equipment. Hong's own cabin, while not spacious by any means, had quite a few sonobuoys jammed into the corners. The normally confined nature of life aboard a submarine had become claustrophobic in the extreme.

Hong knew there was one parameter that would make all the difference to him and his crew, and that was morale. He had never seen it higher. There was a light in the men's eyes that he hadn't seen before. A secret mission with their country's future hanging in the balance had greatly inspired his men. He suddenly felt a presence beside him.

"It is good to be finally under way, is it not, Comrade Captain," said a voice next to him.

Hong turned and eyed his second in command, Lieutenant Kim Il Kwon. The lieutenant was ramrod straight, thin and wiry. His eyes had a squint to them and a hardness that was difficult to endure. The entire crew immediately looked away when he stared at them as if it were painful to have Kim's eyes bore into them. Captain Hong had found himself doing the same thing, and with a force of will had commanded himself not to turn away. It wouldn't do to have a subordinate stare down his superior. And there was something else in Kim's eyes, a light that the rest of the crew didn't possess. The light wasn't generated by enthusiasm or even patriotism, as would be true for the rest of his men. The light was generated by something deeper, more long lasting, something from his soul.

Hong had seen his share of fanatics during his multi-decade career, but Kim's brand seemed different. Hong had scrutinized Kim's record for an excuse to drop him from this mission, but could find none. Hong's superiors had handpicked the crew, and the captain knew he had to have a very clear excuse for dropping one of the chosen ones. Hong had given up in the end but had resolved to keep a close eye on his next in command. One thing he didn't need on this mission was a lunatic who wanted to engage the enemy in combat. His orders were for strict stealth and to avoid contact at virtually any cost. The intelligence target they were after would lose some of its value if the enemy knew that it was in the hands of the North Koreans. Hong turned his attention to the matter of getting to his destination undetected and with all possible speed.

"Left standard rudder. Come to course zero, four, five," ordered Hong. The helmsman acknowledged the order. Hong knew the Americans were paying a lot of attention to his country lately due to the possibility that North Korea could make or had made at least a few nuclear weapons. In spite of the recent treaty with the United States, ostensibly giving up North Korea's nuclear program in exchange for nuclear reactors from the United States, all the world speculated if and when North Korea would produce a nuclear weapon. Even Hong didn't know what the status of his country's nuclear program was. He didn't have the need to know, and the exact status was a closely guarded state secret. With all this controversy, Hong had to make sure that his mission looked like a routine patrol in the East Sea.

Hong was acquainted with at least some of the methods that the Americans used to detect and track submarines. The U.S. attack subs presented a formidable problem. The underwater sonar arrays permanently attached to the ocean floor were another big obstacle that he had to overcome. Hong would use the very quiet characteristics of his sub while running on batteries to solve one problem and the presence of other ships to solve the other. Apparently the Americans had the ability to detect submarines from space via satellites. Hong knit his brow in thought. How did they do that? Some of the theories were wake detection and heat detection. So the answer was to go low and slow until they were out in the open ocean. Then it would be very difficult for the Americans to detect his sub.

An hour on his current course would allow any U.S. subs that might be tracking them to get the idea that his boat was on a routine patrol. At the same time they would be in a deep part of the East Sea, over two thousand meters deep, and with plenty of room to maneuver. Hong also knew that there was an inversion layer at about one hundred meters down from the surface. He had gotten a report from a North Korean ship that was in the area just for the purpose of taking temperature readings at depths down to three hundred meters, which was Hong's boat's test depth. Hong would dive below the inversion layer, which reflected sound, and any noise his boat would make would be largely reflected back down and away from any lurking U.S. submarine. Hong would send the *Yi* to nearly max depth and slow down. He would then change course to go southwest through the Korea Strait and the dreaded underwater passive sonar arrays. Any U.S. subs tracking them would be caught unawares and would spend a lot of time searching the East Sea for them.

And Hong and his crew would be long gone.

U.S.S. Topeka

Sonarman Ernie Menago suddenly sat up straight in his chair. "Sonar Supervisor, I have a high-speed contact—" He looked up at the waterfall display in front of him. "Bearing two, eight, zero relative."

Chief Sonarman Stan Geller was next to Menago in a second. "What is the designation?" he asked.

"Sierra One Five," responded Menago.

"What's the prelim classification?" asked the chief quickly.

"Preliminary classification is submerged hostile!" said the sonarman loudly. Geller picked up a microphone and informed the Officer of the Deck in the conn.

"Okay, now get on him and see what we've got," he said to Menago as he stared at the waterfall display in front of them. A line of bright green dots amid a sea of dull green dots meant a contact. Menago rolled the tracking ball on the console in front of him to put a cursor above the ragged line on the waterfall display. The tracking ball controlled the direction of a hydrophone, and placing the cursor over the contact line on the waterfall display allowed him to hear in the direction of the contact. Chief Geller allowed Menago to listen for a few moments to the contact. Menago was new; it was his first patrol, and Geller was taking him along gradually.

The IMC squawked into life: "All hands man your battle stations, battle stations torpedo!"

Chief Geller nodded to himself. The captain wasn't taking any chances. They never do. Geller didn't have to scramble to any other location—his General Quarters station was right where he was. He felt the boat sway under his feet; they were changing course to go after the contact. The line on the waterfall display changed its path down the screen until it was almost vertical. Geller gently took the earphones off Menago and put them on.

"Let me listen for a while," he explained to Menago.

"Sierra One Five has been redesignated Master Three," said Menago. Chief Geller nodded in acknowledgment. Their computers had analyzed depth, speed, and sound signature and had determined that the contact was hostile. Geller got on the microphone to inform the OOD.

Captain Fred Worden came into the sonar area and looked straight at the waterfall display, then he glanced at Chief Geller. "What have we got, Chief?"

After a ten-second pause, the chief replied, "Sounds like a six-blader. He's busting ass, too. But he's at extreme range, maybe fifty thousand yards." Geller took the head-phones off and offered them to Captain Worden. The captain put them on and listened for a bit. The chief took out a book with laminated pages and studied it while alternately looking at a display over the shoulder of a sonarman who was seated next to Menago. Chief Geller matched the sound profile on the display with a profile in the book and grunted with satisfaction.

"Kilo-class signature," said Geller quietly.

The captain nodded quickly and took off the headphones. "Must be that new Kilo that the North Koreans bought from the Russians recently." The captain had Menago punch a button that gave compass readings on the waterfall display and studied the screen that gave the bearings of the contact over the last few minutes. Geller could almost hear the wheels turning in Worden's brain.

"Came out of Cha-ho, didn't it?" concluded the captain.

Chief Geller was certain that if he plotted the movements of the *Topeka* and the movements of the contact over the last few minutes he would find that the contact's original bearing was in a direct line to the North Korean submarine base at Cha-ho. That job would take Geller a minute or two, but it had taken Captain Worden about ten seconds. Geller shook his head in wonder. There wasn't anyone bet-ter on the planet at visualizing two moving bodies in three dimensions than Worden.

The captain seemed distracted by thought. He handed the headphones back to the chief, who gave them to Menago. The young sonarman put them back on and continued to listen to Master Three.

Captain Worden beckoned Chief Geller away from the immediate vicinity of Menago and spoke in a low voice. "Is Menago the man to handle this?"

"I know he's inexperienced, sir, but I'll keep a close eye on him. He's gotta learn sometime," replied Geller.

The captain hesitated, then nodded. "Okay, Chief, but make it a *real* close eye on him," said the captain.

"Aye, aye, sir," said the chief automatically. The captain left the area and went back to the conn while the chief cast a worried glance toward Menago. He walked up to stand behind the young sonarman. "If anything changes with that contact, anything at all, you tell me, ya hear?" said Geller to Menago.

The young man squirmed around to glance at the physically larger chief petty officer. "Okay, Chief," he replied.

The chief sat down in his chair behind the sonarmen and Menago settled down to study the contact.

Five minutes later, Captain Hong on the *Admiral Yi* made his move.

Admiral Yi

Captain Hong glanced at his watch. It was time.

"All stop," he ordered. His crew knew what was coming and quickly obeyed his orders. "Diving Officer, make your depth three hundred meters."

The diving officer put downangle on the boat, and the *Admiral Yi* slid quietly into the depths of the Sea of Japan.

One more order to give, thought Hong. "Silence in the boat!" he said sharply.

U.S.S. Topeka

The mesmerizing watery thrumming noise in Menago's headphones suddenly ceased. Menago frowned and tapped his headphones as if to correct an intermittent connection.

"Oh, no," he muttered out loud.

Chief Geller suddenly was next to him. "What is it?" he asked.

Menago shook his head. "Lost him."

Geller took the headphones from Menago and gave a quick glance at the waterfall display. The ragged line representing the North Korean sub had degenerated into a jumble of green dots that blended into the background noise. The chief rolled the tracking ball slowly from side to side to pick up the sub. There was nothing but the background hiss and the sounds of marine life that existed in the sea around them.

Geller took off the headphones and cursed under his breath. He picked up a microphone and called the captain in the conn.

"Captain, we've lost contact," said Geller. He couldn't keep the disappointment out of his voice.

Admiral Yi

"Depth is three hundred meters," said the diving officer quietly.

Captain Hong nodded. "Ahead dead slow," he said in a low voice. "Right five degrees rudder. Come to course one, nine, five."

The sailor on the engine order telegraph slid the indicator from STOP to SLOW and dialed in five knots. The sailor on the control yoke nodded and silently complied with the order. The *Admiral Yi*'s single screw began to slowly rotate.

Hong sank deep into thought. With any luck he would avoid the omnipresent American subs in the East Sea. His next trial would be the Korea Strait between South Korea and Tsushima Island. He would have to come up in depth until he was well past the western edge of Japan. Hong decided to hug the bottom and ride it up into the Korea Strait. He would then make his depth only thirty meters and wait for a commercial freighter to come by. The freighters traveled at about ten knots and Hong could easily slide underneath them. Hong would keep close to the ship to mask the sounds from his own sub in order to get away from the underwater sonar arrays that the Americans had deployed on the sea bed. While staying only a few meters from the surface ship's hull, he would tiptoe his way past those arrays.

Once out in the Pacific, he could then afford some speed. His mission and the remote destination demanded it.

U.S.S. Topeka

Captain Worden huddled over the plot board with his senior officers.

"We lost contact with Master Three when it was right here." Worden's stubby finger jabbed at a spot on the chart in front of them. "Now, why would they suddenly go quiet?"

Lieutenant Commander Martin Riley, the *Topeka*'s XO, spoke up. "To change course."

"Right," agreed Worden. "The North Koreans know we're out here, and if they want to hide their movements, they slow down, change depth, and go below an inversion layer. After that, they change course. We've seen them do that a dozen times." The captain twisted his mouth up in disgust. "I *thought* we were above the inversion layer and had our towed array below it to be able to listen to both areas, but we were traveling too fast and the array popped up above the layer." He shook his head. There was a pause as the officers waited for a chewing out, but the captain already had his mind on other things. Worden raised his eyebrows in an unspoken question.

"Right here," said Riley as he read the captain's mind. He pointed to Korea Strait. "That's where they're headed."

Worden nodded. "Yeah. I think so too." He straightened and looked at each officer in turn. "That's where we're headed as well." Worden pulled out the message that he had been given just ten minutes ago. "We've been ordered to follow it to see what it's up to."

The officers nodded, telling Worden that the contents of the message were expected.

"Gentlemen, we will follow Master Three around the world if that's what it takes," he said quietly.

Admiral Yi

Hours later, the crew of the *Yi* sat dead in the water and silently waited for the expected commercial ship passing through the Korea Strait. In the months prior to this mission, the North Korean navy had kept a close eye on commercial traffic through the Korea Strait. Ship departures in the Far East were correlated against actual times, and schedules were scrutinized to pick out the best time for the *Yi* to sail. The timing had to be right—the *Yi* could not afford to wait a long time in the Korea Strait.

Hong stared at the ship's chronometer. The entire plan and its timing had been worked out long ago, and Hong had the expected time for contact with the commercial ship memorized. But any number of things could delay a ship—weather, balky machinery, even paperwork. Hong knew them all and fretted over every one. His contact was ten minutes late.

Hong noticed sudden movement from one of his phone talkers. The young sailor nodded solemnly to answer Hong's questioning stare as the captain swiftly left the conn to go to the sonar room. He entered and was immediately handed a set of earphones. Hong put them on and was treated to the joyous sound of the expected commercial ship lumbering toward them at ten knots. Hong waited until he judged the noise to be overhead and walked quickly back to the conn.

"Ahead standard. Make your speed ten knots," he ordered gruffly. His crew silently jumped to the task. "Helmsman, make your course two, two, five."

The helm acknowledged, and the *Admiral Yi* quietly picked up station slightly behind and thirty meters below the *Asakaze Maru*, a freighter outbound from Japan to a port in eastern China with a load of rice.

CHAPTER THREE

Guairen

Kwajalein Atoll
Marshall Islands

Mike Sprague leaned back in the deck chair on his boat and let the tropical sun fry his face for a few moments. The intense light penetrated his eyelids and made him squint even though he had sunglasses on and his eyes were closed. After a minute, he reached down and picked up a wide-brimmed hat, which had earned him the nickname "Indiana" in recent months, and plopped it on his head to alleviate the effects of the beating sun. The constant breeze moderated the heat, but in the rare moments when the breeze let up, the heat became claustrophobic.

Sprague's boat, the *Sea Dragon*, was anchored in the southern end of Kwajalein Lagoon near South Pass. He liked to go to a deserted spot in the lagoon, anchor the boat, and let the waves slowly rock him to and fro. The constant movement relaxed him, as did the constant flow of beer, he thought with a wry smile. He opened his third beer of the early afternoon, drank quickly and deeply, then set the can down on a nearby table. He folded his hands over his paunch and closed his eyes once more.

Sprague had the lazy thought that he might go diving on the *Prinz Eugen*, an old German World War II heavy cruiser that had sunk near Enubuj Island after the atomic bomb test at Bikini Atoll in the late 1940s. The cruiser had its heyday when it sailed with the pocket battleship *Bismarck* as it conducted legendary raids on Allied shipping during 1943. The *Prinz Eugen* had survived the war only to meet an ignominious end. The atomic bomb blast at Bikini had weakened the hull, which eventually opened to the sea, and when it was towed to Kwajalein to be inspected and decontaminated, it sank quickly. Kwajalein's occupants had dived on the wreck for years until two divers drowned when they ran out of air after they got lost within the huge ship. The U.S. Army authorities had forbidden any diving inside the *Eugen*, but some people, especially Sprague, were lured by the forbidden area and had gotten in some quick dives inside the hull anyway.

Kwajalein Atoll is a string of small islands, nearly a hundred in number, laid out in the rough shape of the state of Florida and creating a lagoon that covers almost a thousand square miles. Hawaii lies twenty-four hundred miles to the northeast, and Japan roughly the same distance to the northwest. The atoll had been the focus of the nation's Strategic Defense Initiative—or, as the media dubbed it, the Star Wars program. When Star Wars faded out of existence in 1993, the program continued under the guise of the Theater Ballistic Missile Defense program, or TBMD. The basic intent of the SDI had been to stop a Soviet strategic launch of ICBMs. When that was thought by some to be impossible, and by others to be too expensive, the mission was changed to stopping a smaller launch of missiles aimed at a specific theater.

The Persian Gulf War saw the spectacle of Patriot missiles taking off after Scud warheads launched by Saddam Hussein's minions. The Patriots did little but gave a psychological boost to the coalition arrayed against Iraq. Doubt still exists whether any Patriots hit the warheads, and instead many were thought to have struck the second stage as it headed toward the target behind the actual warhead. Refinements were made, and the Patriots made the headlines again when they were deployed to South Korea after North Korea refused to allow international inspection of its nuclear facilities.

Engineers knew that the Patriot would have a hard time against state-of-the-art penetration aids. Active and passive decoys, chaff to blind the radar, and electronic counter-measures, or ECM, to jam the radar, as well as launches of many missiles instead of just a few, would give the Patriot missile defense a rough time indeed. All the while the government shelled out millions and millions of dollars, and the people on Kwajalein tested each new improvement to the TBMD.

Finally a new system was fielded, and the first one was deployed to South Korea as a counter to the North's ballistic missile development. Everyone's nightmare was an attack by the North on the South using nuclear-warhead-tipped ballistic missiles. But the engineers, who always complain that a system needs more design and analysis, knew that there were some flaws, some subtle weaknesses in the new system that the right combination of penetration aids would overcome.

Thus the next mission, thought Sprague. They have to know how much chaff, what reentry angle, what speed, what frequency, and so forth would overcome the present design. Then the engineers on TBMD would fix the hidden doors in the defense. It's all in the PENAIDS, he thought. And some of the aids were pretty damn cheap. Chaff was nothing but strips of aluminized Mylar that was ejected by the ICBM. The chaff would give a large radar return and effectively blind the ground radar as to the exact location of the warhead. Passive decoys were just blow-up balloons that were supposed to give the same radar return as the real warhead. The ground computers would then have to decide which radar return represented the real thing and vector the limited number of missiles at their disposal toward the right target. Those two categories of PENAIDS were extremely cheap to implement. The joke would be on the Defense Department if five dollars worth of aluminum and balloons could defeat the multibillion-dollar TBMD system. However, the engineers had worked on those problems for years and thought they had effectively solved them.

Active decoys that provided the same electromagnetic signature as the real warhead were much more sophisticated, as well as any radar jammers that rode along with the ICBM. Even so, jamming ground radar was a lot easier than what the missile defense radar was trying to do, discriminate between decoys and a real warhead in the presence of jamming and chaff. So the active decoys and jammers would also be a lot cheaper than the missile defense system. The possibility still existed that the much cheaper PENAIDS on the ICBM would defeat the exorbitantly expensive TBMD.

That made the upcoming mission crucial to the future of TBMD. An ICBM containing several reentry vehicles would be launched from Vandenberg Air Force Base in California toward the Western Test Range. The maneuvering reentry vehicles would approach Kwajalein Atoll at varying angles along with varying loads of PENAIDS to test the TBMD system. The reentry vehicles, all without nuclear warheads, of course, would splash down in an area north of Kwajalein Atoll called Area J, which was a particularly deep part of the Pacific, and some would land in the lagoon itself. The trillions of bits of data from the mission would take years to fully analyze. A subset of the data would be analyzed quickly to allow engineers to modify the TBMD system to make it as immune as possible to any reasonable set of PENAIDS.

A lot of great information would be forthcoming from this mission, thought Sprague. Information was his business. As a tech writer, he polished up the writing of the engineers for the voluminous test reports that each mission required.

Sprague sighed and popped open another beer. The lagoon was fairly calm today even with the stiff breeze. He should have convinced his friend, Ken Garrett, to go diving with him, maybe even sneak in a dive on the *Eugen*. However, Garrett was busy with his wife, who had come to visit for the next mission. She was a PENAIDS engineer, of all things, thought Sprague with a grunt. Now *there* was some information.

No, he thought, I'll hang around on the boat and just veg out. Maybe I'll catch one of those patented brilliantly spectacular sunsets that the Pacific is famous for. He had a thing for sunsets. He supposed it stemmed from his tour on Kwajalein in the mid-1970s, when the U.S. Air Force had seeded clouds with metal particles to simulate the effect of high-altitude nuclear explosions on their radar systems. The cloud seeding had the unexpected effect of producing the most mind-bogglingly beautiful sunsets anyone had ever seen. He had taken dozens of pictures and had hung them up all over his trailer. He still had a few hung up around the boat.

Sprague opened a lazy eye and looked toward the island of Kwajalein. He tried to imagine what it had been like during the air attacks by the U.S. fleet during World War II, when the Japanese had occupied Kwajalein. He had read accounts of the attacks from the U.S.S. *Enterprise* that had devastated ships in the Kwajalein Lagoon on February 1, 1942. Bombers from Air Group Six attacked the airfield on Roi, the largest island in the northern part of the lagoon, and later torpedo bombers swept westward between Meck and Bigej islands. They quickly were fired upon by the Japanese ships and ground antiaircraft guns. The American pilots' targets were ten ships lined up parallel to one another in a line from Enubuj Island in the southwestern lagoon to Ebeye in the eastern portion.

Sprague stared at the water, visualizing where the ships were and how the American planes swept across the lagoon waters. When the planes were within five hundred yards of the line of ships, they released their torpedoes, then flew low over their targets, their pilots praying all the while for the inaccuracy of the Japanese gunners. The torpedoes hit, with one ship taking six direct hits and many others damaged, but despite the claims of some of the pilots, apparently no ships were sunk by the American planes that day. It would be two years later to the day when American Marines stormed ashore on the then separate islands of Roi and Namur to capture them from the Japanese. Kwajalein was taken by U.S. Army troops and secured four days later. Sprague began to fantasize about being one of the American soldiers in the assault and imagined what Kwajalein Island had looked like and how desperately the Japanese had fought for it.

He imagined the tanks that spearheaded the drive along Lagoon Road after the landings on the western end of the island. The GIs had gotten about halfway across the island during the first two days, then met stiffened resistance. After clearing out a maze of pillboxes and machine gun nests on the third day, the GIs were treated to a night of confusion as the Japanese and Americans mingled together in combat with no clear lines of battle. Bugles were heard coming from the direction of the Japanese near Echo Pier, and soon afterward screaming Japanese soldiers mounted a headlong charge into the American forces. By morning, this attack was broken up, and the fourth day was marked by more clearing out of pillboxes, five-inch guns, and the like. But by 7:20 P.M. resistance finally ceased and Kwajalein was in the hands of American forces.

A beeper alarm went off below deck and a surge of adrenaline went through Sprague. His onboard satellite system was to be used for emergencies only—and this was the first time it had been used. He threw himself to his feet and cast the large hat to one side as he wedged his overweight figure through the hatch to go below. A message had come in and his standing instructions were to decode it immediately. He quickly got to a side compartment, which was supposedly a closed-off head, and fumbled with the keys for a moment. Seconds later, he was through the door and staring at the coded message that had just come out of the printer.

He looked up the date and the time and did a mental calculation. After running through it one more time to be sure, he retrieved a small electronic box from the engine compartment and plugged its power supply and signal cables into the satellite receiver. He punched a button and loaded the message data into the small box. Then he punched in his calculated number on the miniature keyboard that was on the side of the box. After a few seconds' delay, the decoded message rolled out of the printer.

He read it over and over again.

Message for Guairen

Agents of the Democratic People's Republic of Korea are attempting to steal U.S. ballistic missile and missile defense details. They must be stopped at all costs.

Shifu

The North Koreans were going to make an attempt here? On Kwajalein? thought Sprague incredulously. Who were they? How could he, one man, stop them?

He would have to keep alert in the upcoming days before this critical mission. Sprague eyed the decoded message before burning it. Why had they given him the code name Guairen? It was a foreign word and he had always meant to look it up.

He knew it wasn't Russian. He'd have to find a Chinese dictionary.

Admiral Yi

Captain Hong spun around in a circle while staring through the periscope at the dark world above them. Nothing. No lights. Hong checked with sonar one more time and received a negative report once again.

"Surface!" he ordered in a gruff tone. The diving officer, who had been looking at his superior, nodded his head quickly and turned to his diving crew. He repeated the order, and the submarine tilted upward until it broke the surface with a shudder. A sailor opened the hatch, and Captain Hong ran up the ladder to be the first one on the bridge.

The cool night air struck him in the face, and he inhaled deeply. What a pleasure after the last five days, he thought. The rest of the bridge crew scrambled up to their stations behind him and inhaled just as deeply.

It wasn't natural, thought Hong with some sadness, that human beings shut themselves up in a metal can for days at a time. The human body just wasn't made for that. Yet that was the career he had made for himself, to travel the sea in metal cans . . . and under the sea as well.

Hong's mission had gone well up to this point. The *Yi* was about halfway there, and it seemed that he hadn't been detected yet. His sonar crew hadn't heard anything even close to a combatant vessel, and after getting through the Korea Strait and past the American underwater sonar arrays, he had gone to flank speed to make his scheduled time of arrival at his distant target. This was the first time they had surfaced during the mission. He had done the mandatory turnaround, known to the American submariners as a "Crazy Ivan," named for the high-speed turn the Russian submariners made, to hear what was behind him, and had even backtracked for a while to see if anyone was following them. He knew the American submarines could hear him before he could hear the Americans. Hong and his crew had played cat and mouse for five days without even knowing whether or not there was a cat.

"Start the diesels," ordered Hong. His deck officer nodded and relayed the order to a phone talker, who then relayed it to Engineering. Seconds later, the diesels coughed into life and settled into a loud grumble.

"Ahead flank, come to base course," ordered the captain. Time to make some speed, he thought. "Let me know battery charge status every half hour." The deck officer relayed the order to Engineering and received an acknowledgment back.

At night, in the middle of the Pacific, thought Hong, the Americans would have a hard time detecting them now.

Seven hundred miles above the Pacific, the parent satellite and three subsatellites of a Whitecloud U.S. Navy Ocean Surveillance Satellite constellation flew with their communications, radar, and infrared sensors trained on the sea below. The infrared sensors easily detected the *Admiral Yi*'s diesel exhaust and turned on the radar transmitter on the parent satellite. Radar pulses traveled to the ocean below and reflected off the water and the *Yi* itself to produce complex signals in time and frequency. The three subsatellites in the cluster received the reflected radar pulses, each at different angles and each receiving slightly different pieces of the reflected pulse.

Navy computers on the ground would piece the different received pulses together and get a rough image of the submarine. The infrared signature would also help to identify the *Yi* as it made its way across the Pacific.

U.S.S. Topeka

Captain Worden sat in his cabin and read the message he had received just over twenty-four hours ago. His boat had been ordered into the west-central Pacific from his position south of Japan to make contact with a possible Kilo-class sub that was headed southeast.

I guess the patrol in the Sea of Japan has lesser priority than hooking up with this mysterious sub in the Pacific, he thought. He reviewed the embarrassment of losing the North Korean sub. He dearly would have liked to blame the new sonarman, but in the end it was his fault. He was the captain, and while rank had its privileges, it also had its liabilities. Taking the blame for everything that happened wrong on his boat was one of them. He should have made sure that his towed sonar array was below the inversion layer.

Worden frowned at the message again. This Kilo couldn't be the one he'd lost, could it? He shook his head. Nobody was that lucky. The intercom in his stateroom came to life.

"Captain, Conn. Sonar contact, Sierra Seven Four, possible Kilo class," said the OOD.

"Captain, aye," replied Worden after pressing the talk lever. He jumped to his feet and nearly ran to the sonar area.

Chief Stan Geller stood leaning over the middle sonarman of the three and stared at the display showing the noise profile. He called up the stored profile of the Kilo they had lost in the Sea of Japan and compared it with the one now on the screen. The two profiles were identical.

"I'll be damned," muttered the captain under his breath.

"Sometimes you can fall into a cesspool and come up smelling like a rose," replied Chief Geller while shaking his head and smiling from ear to ear.

"All right, people, listen up," said the captain in a loud voice. The sonarmen dutifully lifted one earphone away from their ears.

"We lost this bastard once before in the Sea of Japan," began the captain. "But we're not going to lose him again."

Worden received a lot of aye, ayes, then lapsed into thought. A North Korean submarine in the central Pacific was pretty damn unusual. What were they up to? Training cruise maybe, but the North Koreans didn't stray too far from home port. He strode to the conn.

"Give me contact course and speed," he ordered.

"Contact course is one, six, eight degrees true, and speed is seventeen knots," replied the OOD as the information came in to the conn.

Worden leaned over the chart table and plotted the line on a map of the Pacific. The North Korean was headed in the general direction of the Marshall Islands. But why?

Why would the North Koreans be interested in the Marshall Islands?

CHAPTER FOUR

Gea Transit

U.S.S. Topeka

"Kwajalein!" exclaimed Captain Fred Worden. "Why didn't we think of it before?" he added in frustration. He stared at his officers one by one as his mind raced.

"Shall we give COMSUBPAC another position report?" asked a junior officer.

Worden shook his head. "Not just yet. I don't want to take any chances that the North Korean would detect us."

All the officers nodded. Even though the chances of detection were slim due to the high-speed, short-burst nature of their communications, the captain was playing it safe, and no one could blame him. The North Koreans were obviously on some sort of intelligence mission, which they would abort if they knew the *Topeka* was in the area. At the moment, the North Korean sub was near the surface running on diesels through a snorkel to conserve battery power. All the officers of the *Topeka* had the feeling that Master Three didn't care whether it was detected or not.

"Once he settles down, and we've got a good idea where he's going to stay, we'll stand off a few miles and tell COMSEVENTHFLT and COMSUBPAC," said the captain. He paused to lend the next statement increased weight.

"We have got to be ready for any action that we're ordered to do, including offensive action against the North

Korean.'' Worden's words sobered up an already tense crew.

"Captain to the conn,'' shouted one of the intercoms in the wardroom. "Master Three is changing course!''

Worden jumped to his feet and jogged to the conn. The North Korean Kilo-class sub, redesignated Master Three, had been approaching Kwajalein Atoll from the northwest, and Worden and his officers had theorized that the North Koreans would go to periscope or communications depth and deploy some antennas to listen in on the sophisticated radar emissions from the Ballistic Missile Defense project on the islands. Worden intended to stick with the sub until she set up somewhere, then get some pictures of her antennas via the *Topeka*'s periscope.

Maybe that would salve the wound he'd suffered when he lost her in the Sea of Japan, he thought. Worden thought the North Korean sub would set up north of Kwajalein Atoll because most of the sophisticated detection radars were on Roi-Namur, on the northern rim of the atoll. Worden had guessed at a final position for the North Koreans, but he was wrong. Worden watched in dismay as Master Three ran right past his projected position and swung around to the east of the atoll.

For the next three hours, the *Topeka* shadowed the *Admiral Yi* as she wound her way down the east coast of Kwajalein Atoll. Worden's crew strained their minds to the limit to attempt to divine the North Korean's next move.

"Sonar says Master Three is coming about!'' said a phone talker.

"All stop! Rig ship for silent running!'' ordered Worden. Was the North Korean taking one more Crazy Ivan before doing something significant? And what would that "something significant'' be?

Worden leaned over a chart of the area. One of his junior officers obligingly pointed to their position on the chart. Master Three was just east of Gellinam Island, and the *Topeka* was approximately four miles north of it.

"Master Three turning,'' said a phone talker quietly. "Sound fading. She's moving away from us.''

"Ahead standard. Make turns for ten knots,'' ordered

Worden. He scratched his head and was annoyed that Master Three hadn't done as he'd predicted. Good thing this wasn't wartime, he thought with disgust. With all my screwups, I'd be dead by now.

What the hell was the North Korean up to?

Admiral Yi

Captain Hong kept his eyes on the chart.

"Position!" he demanded. He sensed a flurry of activity as his crew did the required calculations. His second in command, Lieutenant Kim, placed a mark on the chart in front of Captain Hong.

"Ten and a half kilometers due east of Ebeye, sir," he said quietly.

The captain nodded and deliberately stared into Kim's eyes. "This next turn must be done perfectly," he said in a disapproving tone, as if he thought Kim wasn't up to it. Hong had been resorting to devices like that to keep his subordinate on the defensive. Hong was successful as only a captain of a military combat ship at sea can be. Hong knew Kim would have to take anything he dished out, and Kim knew it as well.

Three position reports later, Hong came to the required spot.

"Watch, Comrade Kim, and learn," he said under his breath into Kim's ear. Hong turned to the crew in the conn.

"Secure diesels," he ordered. In a flurry of motion, his crew complied.

"Battery status!" he ordered.

"Batteries are at ninety-two percent!" shouted Kim. Hong stared at Kim for an intense few seconds. His meaning was clear—be calm, don't lose control of yourself.

"Secure snorkel. Periscope depth," said Hong. At periscope depth he ordered, "Up scope."

He walked over to the large round periscope cylinder and patiently waited until it was extended above the water. He folded the handles down and spun around slowly, taking in the horizon. Hong centered up on a northerly bearing and backed away from the eyeglass. He gestured for Kim to take a look.

Kim eagerly set up behind the eyepiece. A string of lights lay on the horizon in stark contrast to the night sky beyond. Kim could imagine the extremely flat island that lay underneath the lights. It probably wasn't even one foot above sea level. Kim turned to his superior.

"Kwajalein?" he asked.

Hong nodded and waited until Kim took a second look while a junior officer read the bearing from the periscope cylinder. Kim turned the scope over to Hong, who irritably slapped the handles up and growled, "Down scope." It was yet another reminder to Kim that Hong was in command.

Hong's orders came in a rush. "Right full rudder. Come to course three, one, zero. Make your depth forty meters. Ahead flank speed."

The torrent of orders surprised Kim, who still didn't know what their intelligence target was to be on this mission. None of the crew knew except the specialists who were sequestered in the forward torpedo bays. He desperately wanted to ask the captain what their destination was but resisted the impulse. He knew Hong took every opportunity to remind him of his status, and he chafed under the yoke of the chain of command.

Hong rubbed his chin, with his thoughts on the next turn and how quickly he would get to the next turning point. The next turn was the critical one. If he failed to execute it properly, he and his crew would wind up on a set of coral heads.

Or the American sub that was most likely following behind would very quickly and expertly send them to their deaths.

U.S.S. Topeka

"Sonar says they lost him, sir!" said a phone talker.

Captain Worden wasn't particularly concerned. He had already deduced that the North Korean sub was circling the atoll. He knew that they had to find out if any American subs were in the area before they set up to collect their intelligence on the TBMD effort on the islands.

Worden's XO gave him a worried look. "At our present speed, we'll make the turn to go north up the west side of

Kwajalein Island in an hour and ten minutes. Shall we speed up to get around Kwajalein as quickly as possible, Captain?''

Worden shook his head. "No, let's not run up his back. We'll find him on the other side of the atoll. After all, how fast can he go? Seventeen knots submerged?"

Admiral Yi

An hour later, Captain Hong stood up and made a startling announcement to the crew.

"Crew of the *Admiral Yi*, this is Captain Hong speaking. A few minutes from now, we will enter Kwajalein Lagoon. We will remain submerged and undertake recovery operations to retrieve an American reentry vehicle from the lagoon floor. It is imperative that electrical power be conserved during this time. All nonessential power will be turned off. I expect everyone will perform his duty for the People's Republic!"

A low-level buzz went throughout the boat. The crew's excitement was palpable. When Captain Hong turned to look at Lieutenant Kim, he knew what he would see. The light in Kim's eyes, which Hong had done so much to dim, burned with unimagined brightness. Kim is in heat, thought Hong. I must do my utmost to control him.

"Everyone stay alert!" commanded Captain Hong. He knew he didn't have to say it—his announcement had sent electricity through the entire crew. All he had to worry about now was overzealousness. He gave Kim another sideways glance. His boat came to the next point on the chart, signifying that they were just southwest of Gea Pass.

"Right standard rudder. Come to course zero, six, three!" he ordered. The man on the helm turned the yoke to comply and acknowledged in a loud voice. Everyone leaned against the boat's roll, produced by the turn at flank speed.

"Report bottom depth!" said Hong.

"Three hundred fifty-one meters!" came the quick answer.

Hong continued on that course for ten minutes as the tension within the crew rose.

"Bottom!" commanded Hong.

"Eighty-six meters!"

"All ahead standard, make turns for six knots," commanded Hong. After waiting a few moments for the vessel to slow down, he continued giving orders. "Periscope depth!" ordered Hong. The boat quickly changed attitude with a large up angle. "Lower your up angle! I don't want to broach," said Hong to the diving officer. The man immediately changed the angle accordingly.

Lieutenant Kim looked at the chart of Kwajalein Atoll. His calculations had them very near the island of Gea.

"Up scope," said Hong, and the periscope cylinder slid up. He slapped the handles down and stared into the South Pacific night. Lieutenant Kim got ready.

"Flashing green light every six seconds. Bearing!" said Hong. A junior officer read the bearing from the periscope indicator.

"Three, three, two!"

Hong could see the buoy when the light came on and called out the height of the buoy as seen on the periscope graticules. Knowing the actual height of the buoy, the number of graticules in height on the scope, and the magnification factor of the scope optics, the estimated range was calculated by using a circular slide rule operated by a junior officer.

"Range!" commanded Hong after a few seconds.

"Two, five, zero meters!" said the junior officer.

Hong whirled the periscope around and looked to starboard to find Buoy Number Two. "Flashing red light every"—Hong mentally counted off—"four seconds. Bearing!"

"Zero, two, eight degrees!"

Again he called out the graticular height and the junior officer got busy.

"Range!" said Hong.

"Three, five, zero meters!" replied the junior officer.

"Down scope!" ordered Hong.

Kim feverishly plotted their position on the chart. The flashing green light Hong referred to was Buoy Number One, on the left side of the pass, and the flashing red light was Buoy Number Two, on the right side of the pass. He did a hurried calculation, then looked up at Captain Hong.

"Gea Pass in one minute!" Kim said in a breathless tone.

Hong nodded in an overly somber way, then went over to the intercom. "Sonar, this is the captain. Have you acoustically acquired both buoys?"

"Captain, Sonar. Yes, sir."

"You will track them and give bearing updates every fifteen seconds. Is that clear?"

"Yes, Comrade Captain."

Hong secured the intercom and turned to an officer. "Bottom!" he said in a loud voice.

"Fifty-three meters!" said an officer.

"Ahead flank!" Hong ordered as the rest of the crew cringed at the thought of going at flank speed in so narrow a passage.

The reports from sonar came in to the conn every fifteen seconds as ordered, as the sonar operators tracked the clanking of the chains and the sounds of the bells on the buoys. Hong knew that if the bearing rates of both buoys were the same, then he was in the middle of the pass. If the rate of change of bearing was different, then his boat would be headed toward one side or the other. They would then slam into the reef at top speed.

Kim calculated bearing rate and plotted the *Yi*'s position quickly. He looked up and hesitated. All eyes were on him, but he saw only the eyes of Hong.

"Gea Pass!" he whispered.

Captain Hong leaned over and peered at the chart in front of Kim. Kim's latest position was clearly marked and placed them in the middle of the pass. In a few short minutes, they would be within Kwajalein Lagoon.

"Captain . . ." began Kim. Hong stared at him with an uncomfortable gaze. Kim pointed to two large coral heads just inside the pass that lay dead ahead.

"Our speed, Captain," said Kim.

Hong said nothing but continued to stare at Kim. Kim returned the intense gaze with his eyes hardening in the process. The exchange between the two was clear to both of them. Captain Hong had better know what he was doing or Kim was ready to denounce him to higher authority as soon as they got back to North Korea.

"We should use our active sonar, Captain, before we hit the reef," said Kim in a low voice.

Captain Hong knew Lieutenant Kim wasn't sure about the use of active sonar, or else he would have suggested it in a much louder voice. This superpatriot is easy to read, thought Hong.

"We will not use active sonar!" thundered Hong. He stared at Kim, savoring the lieutenant's reaction. Kim's eyes narrowed to thin slits and he began to seethe with rage. Hong waited for a moment to see if the lieutenant would make the critical mistake and lose his temper, but Kim managed to suppress his anger.

Hong stabbed a finger at the chart, indicating a position frighteningly close to the coral heads that were in line with Gea Pass and just inside the lagoon.

"Tell me the bearing and range to Buoy Number Three now, and again when we are at this point," growled Hong.

Kim lowered his head and got busy. Fifteen seconds later, Kim had the answers. "Bearing now is three, five, five. Bearing at point indicated is three, four, one; range is two, five, zero meters." Hong turned away and went back to stand next to the intercom.

"Sonar, this is the captain!" announced Hong. "Have you acoustically acquired Buoy Number Three? It is now at three, five, five degrees."

"Captain, Sonar. Acquiring now."

"Report bearing to Buoy Number Three every ten seconds and when it reaches three, four, one," ordered Hong.

"Yes, Comrade Captain," said the voice from sonar.

Forty-five seconds later, the intercom came alive. "Bearing is three, four, one, Captain!" said the sonar supervisor.

Hong turned to stare at Kim. "Right full rudder! Come to course zero, nine, zero!" The sailor on the control yelled acknowledgment and complied with the order. Everyone leaned against the roll.

Sweat broke out on Kim's forehead, and he cursed himself for it. Captain Hong had just transited a narrow, unfamiliar passage at top speed and had come perilously close to ramming a series of very large coral heads that extended up to within three meters of the surface. Kim glanced at the chart they were using. Kim could read some English and easily saw that the chart was an American one printed by the Defense Mapping Agency and sold through National Oceanic and Atmospheric Administration. A note on the bottom of the chart said that some of the areas inside the lagoon were swept in 1940 and 1945 to the depths indicated on the chart. That made some of the depths in excess of fifty years old. Some information was based upon Japanese information that predated World War II. Kim's anxiety increased.

The *Admiral Yi* charged along through the narrow passage as Hong's crew waited and sweated. Their ears strained at every sound sifting through the host of noises that were conducted through the metal hull. They all awaited the telltale scraping sound that would foretell their doom.

A few minutes later, Captain Hong picked up a microphone.

"Comrades, we are now inside Kwajalein Lagoon."

CHAPTER FIVE

Anticipation

U.S.S. Topeka

"Nothing, sir," the sonarman said apologetically.

Captain Worden bit his lip as his mind raced. He strode back to the conn and stared at the chart of the area. Where could the North Korean have gone? The *Topeka*'s hydrophones had a clear acoustic view of the western side of Kwajalein Atoll, and they had detected nothing. His XO had plotted where the North Korean could be since last contact—it was represented by a semicircle with a radius of twenty-six miles, with the eastern half of the circle cut off by the string of islands that formed the atoll. Each passing second increased the possible area the North Koreans could be in.

Another screwup? he asked himself angrily. His report on this patrol would make him look like a regular in the Keystone Kops. He decided to race up the coast to see if the North Korean was following his previous plan and hugging the coastline. Worden communicated his intent to his XO and let him give the specific set of orders to carry it out.

Several hours later, Captain Worden sat staring at the chart. They had searched 90 percent of the original search area and a good deal beyond that as well. He had deployed his trailing sonar array and had scoured the area as much as modern technology allowed. There was nothing. Master

Three had vanished. His eyes wandered over the chart once again. They had searched everywhere. His eyes widened as a new thought struck him. Everywhere but . . .

Captain Worden got a pencil and pad of paper and began to write quickly. After a few minutes to reread what he had written, he turned to the OOD.

"Communications depth!" he ordered.

Admiral Yi

Captain Hong Il Choi felt his boat settle gently to the bottom of Kwajalein Lagoon. The boat took on a modest list to port, but it wasn't anything to worry about.

"Secure engines," he ordered. Hong breathed a sigh and commanded his body to settle down. His body, however, didn't always obey like one of his subordinates. He had spent the last few hours deploying sonobuoys on the southern half of the lagoon. He had found out just how inaccurate the American chart of the lagoon was after bumping into several coral heads that were at shallower depths than stated. They had also smacked into a few that weren't on the chart at all. That, as well as the high-speed transit of Gea Pass, had left his heart pounding.

Hong had requested several GPS receivers, which would have given him the capability to determine his position to within thirty meters or so. The Global Positioning System was a constellation of American satellites that transmitted signals simultaneously. Position on or above the earth could be determined with great accuracy by receiving the signals and processing each to determine the distance to each satellite. Some geometric calculations done in the receiver's digital processor yielded the receiver's position.

The Liaison Bureau had promised to get some, but they never came. Hong would have dearly liked to have had them for that Gea Pass transit. And for this bumping around in the dark in the lagoon as well, he thought.

Hong was struck by the thought that he would have some room in his stateroom now that all the sonobuoys were deployed. He almost chuckled.

He heard the aft hatch open with a squeak. His divers were going out to deploy the camouflage net to hide his boat from above. Hong knew that the Americans flew back and forth from island to island, and he didn't want to be detected through the crystal-clear water by one of the American flight crews. The camouflage net didn't completely obscure his boat, but it did smear the outline of the *Admiral Yi* so that it blended in with the floor of the lagoon. He had purposely positioned himself next to an underwater cliff as well. Hong sighed again. They had thought of everything.

There was nothing to do now but wait.

The Pentagon

Admiral Albert Kern, Chief of Naval Operations, settled down into a chair in the National Command Center conference room and read the message handed to him by the command duty officer.

ZNR TTTTT

Fm: Commanding Officer, USS Topeka, SSN 754
To: COMSEVENTHFLT
Subj: Master Three Contact

1. Contact with Master Three lost at 1536Z11MAY.
2. Search of the area did not result in reestablishment of contact.
3. Master Three is likely within Kwajalein Lagoon.
4. This command will not undertake to reestablish contact within Kwajalein Lagoon due to limited maneuvering room.

Kern winced at the message's import, then looked up as the Chairman of the Joint Chiefs, General Stephen Barnes, U.S. Army, strode into the room.

"All right, gentlemen, let's get started," he said, and all eyes fell on Admiral Kern.

"Message from the *Topeka*, sir," said Kern as he shoved the message across the large table. "Apparently Captain Worden feels that the North Korean sub has entered Kwajalein Lagoon." A few jaws around the table went slack.

General Barnes got the message and read it over. He looked up and stared at Admiral Kern. "Let's assume for the moment that the North Korean is in Kwajalein Lagoon. Options? Do we send in the *Topeka* after it?"

Kern shook his head. "No, sir. Captain Worden is exercising good judgment by staying out. If he enters shallow water, the playing field becomes a lot more level that way, and he loses a lot of the advantage our subs have. I think Worden has got to stay outside the lagoon."

Admiral Kern gave the chairman a glance to see what his reaction was, but General Barnes only waited for him to go on.

"As far as options go," continued Kern, "we could get some P-3s into the area and attack it from the air—"

"Are we going to attack this sub?" asked the air force chief of staff.

"The National Security Council will address that question," replied General Barnes. "We have to be ready to recommend a course of action to them. If the decision is made to attack this sub, then we have to know how to do it."

A lot of heads around the table nodded in agreement. Admiral Kern took the opportunity that the interruption gave him and whispered to an aide to find out the location of the closest P-3s to Kwajalein. The aide quietly took his leave. General Barnes continued.

"The idea of a foreign submarine, much less a North Korean submarine, in Kwajalein Lagoon has enormous implications," said Barnes. "Should they be able to get significant intelligence from anything recovered from the lagoon floor, or receive signals intelligence about our radars used for TBMD, then they might be able to effectively counter the TBMD system we just deployed to South Korea. I needn't tell you people the consequences. Will that embolden the North Koreans to the point of attacking the South? Or will the unthinkable happen? Ballistic missiles tipped with nuclear warheads raining down on South Korean cities, and we are unable to stop them."

The room was completely still. Admiral Kern couldn't hear anyone even breathing. Maybe it's drowned out by the pounding of my heart, he thought. The Chiefs of Staff were acutely aware of North Korean progress with the Nodong missile development. The Nodong was based on the same technology as the Scud, which was the missile Saddam Hussein had used during the Gulf War to terrorize Saudi Arabia and Israel. The Nodong has a range of up to eight hundred miles, which is enough to hit Japan with warheads as well as blanket South Korea. The Nodong can carry a one-ton payload, which would be sufficient for a nuclear weapon, but its accuracy is only certain within one to two miles, which limits its military effectiveness even with nuclear warheads. The one ingredient missing in North Korea that would greatly increase accuracy was reentry vehicle technology. Another necessary technology, in the face of the American missile defense system in South Korea, was penetration aids. This bold move to steal technology from Kwajalein Atoll would get the North Koreans both technologies so they could threaten South Korea, Japan, or even China itself if need be.

"We don't need another incident like the one in the late eighties," said the army chief of staff. "We suspected that the Russians sent a minisub into Kwajalein Lagoon and retrieved a flight recorder from a reentry vehicle that landed on the lagoon floor. We sent out several search parties and they couldn't find the reentry vehicle. And then the press had to find out about that beach party one of the Russian trawler crews had at around the same time."

General Barnes nodded. "And to hear it on the evening news was worse yet." He referred to a CBS Evening News report on January 12, 1989, about the incident. CBS reported that DOD officials had some evidence that one of the Soviet ships in the area of Kwajalein had conducted a beach party on an uninhabited island in the Kwajalein Atoll. DOD officials further suspected that a flight recorder from an ICBM test was stolen from the floor of Kwajalein Lagoon by a Russian submarine on July 7, 1987. The beach party incident was cited by CBS News as a possible indication that the stolen flight recorder incident was true.

Admiral Kern's aide entered the conference room and silently sat down behind his superior. He handed the admiral a sheet of paper.

"We're in luck," said Kern. "We have P-3s headed

back to Pearl Harbor after dropping sonobuoys on KMR North, which is the Kwajalein missile range north of the atoll itself, an area used for the splashdown of reentry vehicles.''

"So why would the North Koreans enter the lagoon if the reentry vehicles splash down in the open ocean?'' asked the air force general.

"Maybe the joke's on the North Koreans,'' said Kern.

The army chief of staff spoke up. "We sometimes drop RVs in the lagoon itself.'' Everyone turned to look at him. "I was with USAKA a number of years ago,'' he explained, referring to the acronym for U.S. Army Kwajalein Atoll. The people around the table collectively nodded to themselves.

"Why were the P-3s dropping sonobuoys?'' asked General Barnes as he rubbed his forehead in an effort to think.

"I guess there's a mission today,'' said Admiral Kern.

The room suddenly fell silent. Seconds later everyone reacted at once with the noise level jumping several octaves. General Barnes waved for quiet and picked up the phone on the table in front of him. He punched a button for the operator.

"Get me Vandenberg immediately,'' he ordered. It took four minutes for the general to get to the commanding officer of Vandenberg AFB.

"General Talbot, this is General Barnes, Chairman, JCS,'' began Barnes. Everyone at the table could imagine General Talbot stiffening out of respect for Barnes's rank. "You've got a mission to Kwajalein Missile Range today?'' Barnes waited for the affirmative answer.

"Cancel that mission, General,'' ordered Barnes. Admiral Kern could hear Talbot's hesitation for a moment, then a hurried comment which he couldn't make out. The expression on General Barnes's face changed quickly from offense to resignation. Barnes hung up the phone and looked quickly in Admiral Kern's direction.

"A Peacekeeper missile, carrying five RVs and five PENAIDS canisters, lifted off two minutes ago,'' said Barnes.

CHAPTER SIX

Mission

Range Command Building
Kwajalein Island

Ken Garrett leaned over the A scope repeaters to view how the radars on Roi-Namur would see the imminent mission. The radars on Roi-Namur are called the Kiernan Reentry Measurements Site, or Krems, and are named after U.S. Army Lieutenant Colonel Joseph M. Kiernan, who headed a project dealing with electromagnetic signatures. Kiernan was killed in action in Vietnam in 1967.

The Altair radar, or ARPA Long-range Tracking and Instrumentation Radar, a long-wavelength, high-power radar, would be the first to spot the incoming RVs just as they came over the horizon nearly two thousand miles away and about three hundred miles up over Hawaii. Next to see the targets would be the Tradex radar, named for Target Resolution and Discrimination Experiments, which has a shorter range than Altair but has better resolution.

The tracking data from these two radars are used to point the other two radars on Roi-Namur: Alcor, or ARPA Lincoln C-band Observables Radar, and MMW, which stands for Millimeter Wave Radar. These last two radars have much better resolution than the tracking radars, and Alcor and MMW are used for imaging the targets and providing signature data to powerful computers that match signatures against stored data in an effort to pick out the real warheads from the decoys and chaff. It was this most difficult problem that Ken Garrett had addressed for the last two years, the last year of which had been spent on Kwajalein itself as he continually refined the massive computer programs that detected warheads out of chaff and debris.

This mission was the finale of his effort. Pass the test against the mixture of PENAIDS that his wife had come up with and his future was secure, his reputation would take a leap upward. Fail the test and he was in for more development, which normally he would like, except that he would get a lot of "help" from above him in the management chain. He would have to attend endless daily meetings to give detailed status reports to management, thereby insuring that he got nothing done. Fail the test and the fun would end and the pain would begin. Not to mention that South Korea would remain vulnerable to the right kind of PENAIDS.

Ken Garrett wondered if the North Koreans possessed that kind of technology. Maybe the Russians, he thought, but the North Koreans? Probably not, but how long would it be before they acquired it? A few years, shorter if the Russians sold them anything. It looked like anything was for sale in Russia these days, but still, to defeat the TBMD and his computer programs, the North Koreans would need just the right kind of PENAIDS in the right combinations. Like the kind Nancy designed. It would still take the North Koreans a few years to get the right mix even with Russian technology. And then they couldn't ever be sure that it was just the right combination. Ken's task was to eliminate the vulnerability to PENAIDS, or to narrow the window of vulnerability to PENAIDS to make it extremely difficult for an adversary to penetrate the TBMD.

A familiar scent floated around him. It was subtle and charming and made him a little weak, as it was supposed to do.

"Hi, Nancy," he said in a low tone without turning around. He knew it was her. There weren't many female engineers in this line of work, and almost none on Kwajalein.

"Hi, Ken," she said softly. "You knew it was me?"

"Yeah," he replied. "I smelled your perfume as we

brushed by each other this morning in the hallway of the trailer.''

Nancy didn't reply. Ken was sarcastic every time they talked. She sighed and moved a bit farther away from him. She hoped he noticed.

After a moment, she pointed to one of the scopes. ''Is this Altair?''

Ken eyed the label above the display which had the word *Altair* in inch-high letters. ''Yeah, it's Altair.''

''How will the radar returns be displayed?'' she asked.

''The horizontal axis here''—he pointed to the bottom of the scope where there was a graduated line like a ruler— ''is the range, and the vertical axis is amplitude. The returns will look like lumps and they'll move from right to left and from the bottom to the top as the range gets smaller, and the amplitude gets bigger as the RV comes toward us.''

''Oh,'' she replied.

Ken eyed the A scope. The noise was greater than normal due to the recent sunrise. His wife had thought of everything. She had even timed the mission when the sun was near the main beam of the radars that were supposed to detect the incoming reentry vehicles. The sun was a great noise producer at virtually all frequencies and would make it that much more difficult for his radars to do their job.

A loudspeaker came to life. ''We have a launch from Vandenberg. Mission WSMC-8786 is under way!''

Both Ken and Nancy knew that WSMC stood for Western Space and Missile Center at Vandenberg, and the complete mission name was WSMC-8786/PENA1, PEN referring to the radar penetration exercise. They didn't have a clue to where the number 8786 came from. Probably some Pentagon computer, thought Ken.

''Well, we'll find out what's going to happen in a half hour,'' said Nancy.

''Seventeen minutes,'' corrected Ken. He glanced at Nancy. ''So, what surprises do you have in store for me?'' The double meaning was apparent to both of them.

''Well, your radars are in for a few,'' she replied. She gave him a sweet smile. It was his turn to sigh.

Sparring, always sparring, he thought. Was any of this any use? In the ten days she had been on the island, she hadn't slept with him at all. What the hell kind of a marriage was that? And she didn't want a divorce. What was she waiting for? They had talked fitfully about their relationship, and she had wanted Ken to give her more time. Time for what? She had been away from him for nearly a year while he wondered what she was doing, who she was seeing.

"Where's the typhoon?" she asked.

He pointed to a surface radar display across the room. "You can see it to the left of those dots representing the islands. It won't get here in time to scrub the mission, and they think it'll go south of us, so we won't get the worst of it."

Nancy nodded and moved closer to him to view the A scope. Her perfume washed over him, reminding him of the pure ecstasy their life had been before that damned business in New York City. He shoved aside thoughts of that inglorious night and was determined to concentrate on the mission and how his radars would be exercised. Her scent stayed with him, though, and made him even weaker.

A chorus of voices intoned their status in the background, everything from missile launch status to the weather. This mission had an advanced Patriot missile battery located on Meck Island containing a much faster, more maneuverable missile than what had been initially deployed to South Korea in early 1994. It was hoped that Ken Garrett's software upgrades would be proven effective against PENAIDS in this mission. If they were effective, then they would be loaded into the radars that would be deployed with the Patriots. The Patriot missiles on Meck Island would have to get close to, or actually hit, an incoming RV for the mission to be a success. Ken had no idea how many RVs his radars would face or what mixture of PENAIDS Nancy had come up with. He had refused to ask her what her design was, and she hadn't offered it to him. Had that exchange of information occurred, it probably would have invalidated the test.

The A scope for the Altair radar caught his eye. The noisy radar returns suddenly picked up form and shape and grew in strength. The form didn't grow to its expected narrow line shape, but instead turned into a fuzzy lump of much greater width than a normal return.

"Altair has it!" said Ken. "But you deployed PENAIDS before it came over the horizon." He raised his eyebrows and looked at Nancy.

She smiled sweetly at him. "Can't make it too easy for you."

The chaff and decoys were flying along with the real reentry vehicles, creating not single definitive returns from each RV but many returns from each decoy and piece of chaff. That accounted for the fuzzy deep return on the A scope. Ken bit his lip. His software should do all right against this scenario, but he worried anyway.

Two other large, well-defined radar returns became apparent on the A scope.

"Must be the third and fourth stages," mumbled Ken. His eyes widened as he had a sudden thought. He stared at Nancy over his shoulder. "You're not going to do what I think you're going to do, are you?"

Nancy's smile grew wider. "Watch," she said softly.

The strength of the radar return from the third and fourth stages of the Peacekeeper dwarfed the return from the RVs and PENAIDS. The noisy return from the Tradex radar, the next radar to pick up the incoming RVs, began to show a less fuzzy rendition of the signals than on the Altair scope. The increased range resolution of Tradex would locate the blob of incoming targets with a resolution of about fifteen feet and hand off the locations to the Alcor and MMW radars.

Ken glanced at the mission clock. One minute to go before the RVs impacted around Kwajalein. Adrenaline rose in him. The end would come quickly—the last thirty seconds would tell the whole story.

A voice came over a loudspeaker. "This is Meck Launch Control. Missiles launched! I say again, missiles launched!"

This was it. His missiles were rocketing into the sky to stop the incoming reentry vehicles with their simulated warheads, just as they did against the Scud warheads launched by Saddam Hussein during the Gulf War.

The Alcor and MMW radars were heavy into it now, making digital images of the incoming crowd of targets in an attempt to discriminate between the chaff and decoys and the real RVs. The large signals from the third- and fourth-stage fuel tanks and rocket motors of the Peacekeeper suddenly split into hundreds of smaller signals, confirming Ken's fear. Nancy had sent the final two stages of the ICBM into the atmosphere first to disintegrate and create a myriad of targets for the computers to analyze to determine if they were the real RVs. It was an attempt to overload the computers. Ken hoped they were up to it.

Seconds later, the fuzzy radar return representing the chaff and decoys suddenly slowed its advance from right to left on the A scopes and seemingly stopped. Ken knew that the atmosphere had slowed the descent of the extremely light chaff and balloon decoys while letting the real RVs continue their hysterical advance on the atoll.

The radar returns of the actual RVs were seen for an instant until they disappeared into the cloud of debris left by the Peacekeeper final stages. Several thin vertical lines could now be seen advancing from left to right, in the opposite direction of the RVs. The Patriots were closing in on the RVs.

The RVs could briefly be seen emerging from the slower, final ICBM stage debris cloud, but an instant later the returns from the RVs turned fuzzy again.

Ken Garrett's mouth dropped open. More chaff and decoys!

The Patriots met up with the cloud of chaff and decoys and disappeared within. The fuzzy blob hung suspended on the A scope due to the slow reentry of the PENAIDS. Some quick peaks were seen in the return and Ken hoped that they were Patriots detonating on incoming RVs. Ken held his breath.

Two narrow radar returns came out of the left side of the wide PENAIDS return and quickly disappeared to the left of the screen. Ken blew out his breath in disgust. Two got through? He didn't want to turn to Nancy and see her smug reaction.

"Damn," said Nancy under her breath. Ken turned to her in surprise. She was frowning.

"Something always goes wrong," she said. She seemed disgusted as well.

"I think two got through," said Ken for something to break his silence. The simple statement also helped him face up to the fact that Nancy had beaten him. They both stood in silence for a moment.

"You ran the third and fourth stages of the ICBM into the atmosphere so that they would break up and cause a lot of debris to mask the location of the RVs," said Ken.

She nodded. "They were coming along for the ride, so why not use them?"

Ken smiled. "Pretty standard stuff." Ken and his team had been working on just such a problem for the last two years.

"We wanted to throw everything we could at you," she said. "That's what the enemy will do. The third and fourth stages were just for openers."

"I like that business of deploying chaff and decoys in the middle of reentry," said Ken. That was the reason two RVs got through, he thought. "How did you do that?"

"We blew up an RV that had a huge load of chaff and decoys, which created a cloud about halfway down. It's a new design."

It was her design, he thought, and his feelings started to change. He couldn't help feeling proud of her. Nancy's frown returned.

"But there were supposed to be three chaff-and-decoy deployments, not just two," said Nancy. "One of the RVs that got through probably has a complete load of PENAIDS in it."

Meck Island

Technician Andy DeLong leaned closer to the spectrum analyzer screen as some unexpected signals continued their fitful dance on the left side of the image on the screen.

Systems Engineer Dick Toomey noticed DeLong's

movement out of the corner of his eye. "What is it, Andy?"

"Some signals in the UHF band," mumbled DeLong.

Toomey smiled. "The Altair radar is UHF." He thought that would end the discussion.

"Yeah, but these signals are at a different frequency," said DeLong.

"Could they be spurs from Altair?" asked Toomey. He had turned completely around now. He referred to the transmission of frequencies other than the desired frequencies. Engineers commonly called these undesired frequencies spurious frequencies, or spurs.

"They never varied all through reentry," replied DeLong. "If they were from Altair, they would have varied in signal strength as the antenna swung around during reentry."

Toomey rubbed his chin. "True," he said under his breath. He leaned over the technician to view the signals.

Toomey and DeLong were in the RFI van on the newly reopened Meck Island. Their mission was to make sure there were no interfering radio frequency signals before or during the mission, hence the name RFI, for radio frequency interference. They monitored a large portion of the electromagnetic spectrum and recorded the signals on magnetic tape for playback later.

"You know, they look like sonobuoy signals," said Toomey. "You don't suppose that the navy missed KMR North and dropped a few into the lagoon?" He smiled at what it would take for the navy to make a huge mistake like that.

DeLong laughed out loud. "I wouldn't put it past the navy to screw up like that." They enjoyed the light moment for a few minutes.

"The signal level is pretty low, nowhere near the interference level," mused Toomey.

"So, what do you want to do about this?" asked the technician.

Toomey shrugged. "Let's make a note of it, then leave it up to the evaluation team."

DeLong readily agreed.

Admiral Yi

"Captain! We are receiving data from our sonobuoys that will give us the position of the American reentry vehicles!" said Lieutenant Kim in a loud voice.

Captain Hong turned around and leveled his eyes at Kim. "I am a lot older than you, Comrade Kim," began Hong. "But I still have my hearing up until now, no thanks to you."

A stricken look flitted across Kim's face which was then replaced by the same practiced hard face that Kim always had. "My apologies, Comrade Captain. You must forgive my zeal."

Hong raised his eyebrows. "I must?" he asked in a low voice, and stared at the lieutenant until the subordinate looked away.

"Shall we come to snorkel depth to recharge batteries, sir, prior to getting under way to recover the space vehicles?" asked Kim.

Hong clenched his teeth to convey firmness. "We will not recharge batteries yet, Lieutenant. After we have recovered the vehicles, we will recharge, then exit the lagoon by a different passage than we entered. Is that clear?"

"Yes, sir," was Kim's comparatively meek reply.

Once in a while I will have to prop up this Kim's ego after putting him in his place so often, thought Hong. Perhaps now would be a good time.

"Lieutenant, give the appropriate orders for periscope depth," said Hong. The order made Kim responsible for taking the *Admiral Yi* off the lagoon bottom and up to where they could view the outside world. The enthusiasm returned in Kim's eyes, and he gave the orders with gusto.

These superpatriots, thought Hong. They'll be the death of us yet.

Range Command Building

Ken Garrett was feeling better by the minute. The post-mission evaluation of the TBMD's performance wasn't as bad as he had thought. A large team of engineers analyzed the recorded radar returns as well as optical trackers—called RADOTS, or Recording Automatic Digital Optical

Trackers, and Super RADOTS, which were more powerful and had better resolution.

The Super RADOT on the island of Gagan had clearly shown that the advanced Patriot missiles had come within the kill radius of one of the surviving RVs, but for some reason the warhead hadn't detonated. Patriot warheads were not Garrett's responsibility. His radar had gotten the missile there and that's all that he was supposed to do.

The second RV that had gotten through was a near miss for one of the other missiles, leading to the conclusion that a slightly more maneuverable missile would have done the trick. Garrett resolved that his report would make that case very clearly.

"Whew," he said with a big grin. He beamed at Nancy. She couldn't resist a return smile. "Smart guy Charlie."

"Well, I wiggled out of that one, didn't I?" he said with alacrity. "C'mon, let's go outside and watch the chaff reenter. It's the damndest sight you'll ever see. Like an explosion in a tinsel factory."

Nancy nodded and smiled at him. He was like a kid at Christmas. Her smile faded as she thought of the strain he must have been under to make this mission a success for the TBMD. Now the strain was lifted by the good, but not perfect, showing of his radars.

They left the Range Command Building and walked down by the water's edge. The wind had picked up and was blowing very hard from the west. The sky was black with the approaching storm.

"I wonder if that typhoon is really going to miss us like they said," said Nancy over the noisy wind.

"Yeah, it doesn't look good, does it?" replied Ken as he stared into the western sky. "Sometimes these typhoons change course suddenly. I hope it doesn't happen now—" He looked at Nancy. "Now that we have the rest of the day off." He redirected his gaze to the east and pointed skyward.

Nancy looked in the direction he indicated and saw a bright cloud very high up in the sky. The cloud was too bright and its edges too regular to be a natural cloud. Nancy caught a glimpse of its three-dimensional shape and was startled to discover that it seemed to be in the form of a huge cylinder. She marveled at the well-defined form in a place where she had only seen random ones. She squinted at the chaff cloud and thought she saw it scintillating as the individual aluminized Mylar strips caught the early morning light. The gigantic scintillating chaff cloud high in the sky made a spectacular end to the mission.

"So that's what chaff looks like when it reenters the atmosphere," she said in a voice filled with wonder. They both stared at the sight for a few silent moments. The wind suddenly gusted, and they felt the first few drops of the impending storm.

"We had better get a bus back to the trailer," said Ken, "or we're going to get caught in this thing." Nancy nodded and they both ran to catch the bus.

Once on the totally deserted bus, they settled in their seats and watched the typhoon rapidly build strength.

"It's not going to miss us," said Ken with an air of resignation.

Nancy sighed. "We'll be stuck in the trailer. What are we going to do all afternoon?" she said innocently.

Ken smiled from ear to ear and stared straight at her. She instantly caught his meaning and rolled her head around in semidisgust.

"I left myself wide open for that one," she mumbled to herself.

"I have some computer games," he said in an innocent-as-a-newborn-babe voice. "They're real fun."

"Yes," she said in a deadpan voice. "Computer games." She screwed up her mouth and looked at him. "Your favorite is Strip Pac-Man, no doubt."

His smile grew broader. "I don't know how to play that. You'll have to show me."

Nancy groaned in good-natured humor. A thought suddenly came to mind, and she was grateful for the change in subject. "I can't help think that if the second RV had deployed its PENAIDS, then more RVs would have gotten through," said Nancy.

"Oh, here come the excuses," he said, laughing.

Nancy shook her head and couldn't think of a better outcome for this mission. Her PENAIDS and his radars—it was damn near a draw. Ken felt good about the radar performance, and Nancy knew she had stretched the TBMD performance to the limit. It's doubly good for Ken, she thought. He hasn't had anything to cheer about for a while. Still, she had to tweak him a little.

"Of course, we slowed the RVs down from their normal reentry speed by using maneuverable vehicles," she said with a half smile. She glanced sideways at Ken for his reaction.

He rolled his eyes in mock disgust. "Oh, sure. How slow did you make those RVs? From a normal Mach twenty-five to Mach twenty-four point nine?" He had a broad grin on his face again.

"We were trying to simulate a future North Korean threat," she replied seriously. "You got briefed about the ballistic missile development in North Korea, didn't you? The RVs would enter faster than the Scuds but slower than if deployed from a real ICBM."

"Okay, so you slowed them down," Ken said, giving in. "But we zapped them pretty good."

She gave him a look of admiration. "Yeah, you sure did," she replied in a quiet voice. She looked away from him and out the window of the bus as it rumbled along the road toward Ken's trailer.

Her mood changed from one of satisfaction to one of unease. Everything had worked except for the load of PENAIDS that didn't deploy. She couldn't put her finger on why the undeployed PENAIDS made her nervous. The RV had probably broken up, and the PENAIDS load was scattered among the waters of the lagoon.

Or the PENAIDS could be on the bottom of the lagoon if the RV was still intact. It was an unsettling thought.

CHAPTER SEVEN

Incident at the DMZ

Panmunjom, North Korea
August 1976

Kim Hak Hyun had been ordered to clean his rifle, and so he dutifully went over to a sergeant and picked up the cleaning materials and went to work. A half hour later, the rifle was shiny with Kim's work. Kim looked it over with satisfaction, then took a moment to look at his surroundings. Barbed wire formed a line in the distance with the Demilitarized Zone beyond. The wire and the Zone had been there for twenty-three years, a year longer than Kim had been alive. The South Koreans were on the other side of the four-kilometer-deep Zone and behind their own barbed wire. The Americans also were there.

Why were the Americans there? Why had they teamed up with the corrupt ones to the South and opposed the forces of unification of the Korean Peninsula? Had it not been for them, the North's leader would now rule over all of Korea. And would have ruled for the last twenty-six years. Kim's comrades hated the Americans so, and while not many realized it, race was a large factor in their hatred. The Americans had many races that made up their people, while the North Koreans had but one. Therein lay the superiority of the Koreans over the Americans, thought Kim.

A sergeant screamed at the men with Kim to get ready and to keep their rifles loaded at all times. There were no calm orders given to the lowest ranks in the Democratic People's Republic Army. They all stiffened to show proper respect, then relaxed slowly as the sergeant strode away. Kim reexamined his rifle and noted that he had done a good job of cleaning it. He looked down the sight and centered it on the barbed-wire fence in the distance. If it came to shooting, he would be ready. Kim was one of the elite group of soldiers that manned the unit at Panmunjom, the site of the Military Armistice Commission meetings. The meetings extended from 1953, the year the Korean War ended—or, rather, when the armistice began—to the present, over two decades, and had basically produced nothing. The North Koreans took every opportunity to insult the South Koreans and Americans to the point of spitting, name calling, obscene gestures, and even shoving the Allies around. American troops wore football-style athletic supporters in case the extracurricular activities got out of hand.

Kim stood and shouldered his rifle. He knew he had to be ready when the sergeant came back. The other men around him duplicated his actions. They waited for a few minutes until the sergeant strode back and surveyed them with anger on his face. He exploded into a flurry of orders and screamed at them to leave their rifles behind. The confused men hurried to comply. The quickly formed up into a column of twos and marched off toward the barbed wire.

Kwajalein Lagoon
Present Day

"All stop!" ordered Captain Hong.

Lieutenant Kim Il Kwon snapped out of his reverie. It was his responsibility to get the divers out on time and with the proper equipment. The captain had gotten them to the spot where one of the American reentry vehicles had splashed down, albeit with some difficulty. The old American charts they were using didn't show the increased coral growth over the intervening years, and this had caused many problems as they groped their way around the lagoon in search of their intelligence bonanza.

Kim made his way up to the forward hatch and sized up

the divers who stood ready to exit the boat. They stiffened at Kim's approach.

"Divers from the *Admiral Yi*," Kim began as his eyes lingered on the stark red stars in a circle of white on a red background that were painted on the sides of the divers' air tanks. Each diver had a small North Korean flag on his equipment. "You will now embark on the most important mission for our nation's navy. The intelligence windfall that you will bring to our forces will be so great that our victory over our corrupt southern neighbors and the Americans will be assured." Kim spoke on for several minutes as the divers grew restless, but no one dared look at a watch.

Kim finally broke off his long dissertation and abruptly sent them on their way just as the intercom came alive with Captain Hong's voice demanding to know what the delay was. Kim placated his superior and watched the divers depart by twos into the airlock. The inner hatch closed on the first team of two divers, and seconds later, they could hear the loud sound of water rushing into the airlock. The clanging of the outside hatch came through, conducted by the hull and water in the airlock, and Kim knew his first team was on its way.

The divers' work was dull and brutally repetitive until the actual reentry vehicle was found. After locating the RV, the tough work of excavating the vehicle from the bottom of the lagoon would begin. The work would be made worse if the RV had split into pieces. The divers would have to pick up as many pieces as they could find, and the technical people would be evaluating each piece as it was brought back to the boat. Some pieces would be useless, but some, he knew, would be priceless.

Lieutenant Kim went back to the conn after the last of the divers had left the *Yi*. Captain Hong was peering through the periscope.

"Typhoon," said Hong as he looked at his second in command. "The perfect camouflage. The Americans will not have anyone out looking for their reentry vehicles for quite a while."

Captain Hong smiled at Lieutenant Kim for the first time.

Panmunjom, North Korea
1976

The group of North Korean soldiers marched up to a waiting truck and were quickly ordered to load into the vehicle. They all expected that the engine would be started and they would immediately be taken to some area for a work detail. They sat in the vehicle for ten minutes without stirring.

The men were just starting to get restless when an unseen officer ran up to the sergeant who was standing outside the truck. Quick, loud orders were given which were immediately acknowledged. The truck's engine came to life, and they quickly started down the road at high speed. What was all this? Kim asked himself. Was this the beginning of his country's glorious push to liberate the South? Excitement rushed through him. Was this what they were all hoping for?

Kim suddenly realized that, without his weapon, the war would be short for him indeed. What was it, then? The officer had sounded very excited, even more excited than normal. Something was happening.

The truck rumbled on and the men watched the country-side roll by out the open back of the truck. Some of the more experienced men recognized the route and began to talk excitedly about going up to the DMZ. So, thought Kim, we're getting closer to the Americans. This will be very interesting indeed.

The truck screeched to a halt, and the men were ordered to get out immediately. Kim leaped to the gravel-covered road and gave a quick glance about. There were low curved walls lining the road on one side and trees on the other. The road led to the bridge, called the Bridge of No Return by the Americans, which had seen the vast prisoner exchange at the end of open hostilities in 1953. The sun was hot and beat down on the North Korean soldiers as they milled about for a moment.

Kim gaped in the direction of the bridge and stared at the first American he had ever seen.

The Pacific Belle
Present Day

Captain Peter VanHoeven leaned against the roll of the ship as another wave battered the windward side of his vessel. He had been on his approach to Gea Pass when the typhoon struck, and now he had no choice but to go through the passage in the reef and into the lagoon. To turn around now in order to ride out the storm at sea would be suicide in the narrow channel. The shipping authorities on Kwajalein had advised him that the typhoon was going to pass to the south of Kwajalein, but the unpredictable storm had taken a turn to the northeast and now was in line to run right over the island.

VanHoeven knew the approach to Kwajalein well, having made the journey from Hawaii to the Marshall Islands over fifty times. He had even refused the harbor pilot offered to him by the shipping authorities on Kwajalein. And now he was headed into the lagoon, which was no place to be during a typhoon. Too many ships and their crews had met their ends while anchored in a confined area like the lagoon.

This damn typhoon wasn't supposed to come up this way, he thought in a rage at himself. How could he have been so stupid! He knew from his many years at sea that typhoons are prone to sudden changes in course, and this one had done just that. Now he was approaching the neck of the channel, and there was no turning around. He'd have to go dead in the water to do that, and then he'd really be dead. The storm would throw his ship against the coral reefs and rip out its bottom, and it would be the deep six for his ship. Or maybe in these waters it would be the shallow six, he thought without mirth. If the ship sank, it wouldn't have very far to go before it hit bottom.

Peter VanHoeven was the master of a container ship that regularly serviced Kwajalein Atoll with supplies from Hawaii. His ship carried almost two hundred twenty-four-foot containers stacked in its hold and above decks. The ship was over three hundred feet in length with a fifty-foot beam, but it had only a fifteen-foot draft and a terrifying tendency to roll in a storm.

VanHoeven went out on the port wing of the bridge and stared aft through the pounding rain at his containerized cargo that sat behind the superstructure of his ship. None of it seemed to be shifting, and all seemed secure, although he wondered if another wave like the last one would jar some of the boxlike containers free to slide and break others loose. If that started to happen, he'd have a chain reaction that would easily destroy his ship—or cause it to capsize.

The ship pitched forward with its bow sinking and its stern rising up out of the water, the single screw suddenly screaming with speed as it momentarily left the sea. VanHoeven could imagine the engineers scrambling to close the throttle on the engine before it could damage itself. He scrambled to get back inside the bridge.

This is getting serious, he thought. Another kick in the butt from a wave like that and we all might collect on our life insurance. Sweat broke out on his forehead. At what point do I abandon ship? he asked himself. The Gea Pass was narrow, only about two hundred forty yards across at the depth he needed to safely transit the pass. One gust of wind and . . . He didn't want to think about it.

The bridge crew called out that Buoy Number One was on the port beam. That meant that he was about to enter the narrowest part of the pass. If he could hold course for a few minutes more and make the hard starboard turn to avoid the coral heads that waited for them inside the lagoon at the mouth of the pass, then they would be all right. VanHoeven leaned over the chart where his first mate was marking their course. Only twenty-five hundred yards to go.

The bridge lookouts called out the distance to Buoy Number Two. Five hundred twenty yards. Distance to Buoy Number Three was seven hundred seventy yards. Van-Hoeven glanced at the mark made by the first mate just as the lookouts called out the bearing to Buoy Number One: two, seven, zero.

They were to the left of the channel, almost on the reef!

"Right full rudder!" yelled VanHoeven. He rang up full speed on the engine annunciator. He quickly picked up a phone and called down to his chief engineer. "Give me everything you've got! We're almost aground on the reef!"

"Aye, Captain. But we haven't got a lot left, sir!" said the engineer.

VanHoeven groaned. Top speed for his freighter was about twelve knots. The ship was designed to run at a steady speed for a long time until it eventually got to its destination, not quickly accelerate in a typhoon. Van-Hoeven held his breath.

"Depth is coming up fast!" said one of the bridge crew with anxiety in his voice. "Twenty-five feet!" Seconds later: "Fifteen feet!"

The first grinding noises were heard two minutes later as the reef reached up to blindly rip at his ship.

"All stop!" ordered VanHoeven in a vain attempt to stem the damage. The grinding noise which had begun at the bow and worked its way down the port side of the ship diminished somewhat as the ship lifted in the sea when the push from the screws stopped. Thirty seconds later, the grinding began anew. The first mate flew out of the bridge shelter and into the teeth of the storm to assess damage.

The engine room crew called to report major flooding in their space, and minutes later the captain received a disastrous report from the first mate.

VanHoeven picked up a phone and called the engine room. "Engineer, get your people topside now!" He didn't receive any argument.

The *Titanic*, thought VanHoeven. Just like the *Titanic*, ripped from bow to stern. He went over to the ship's PA system.

"Abandon ship!" he shouted into the microphone, and heard his voice echo throughout the ship.

Panmunjom, North Korea
1976

Kim squinted at the collection of South Korean soldiers and a few American soldiers as well. Apparently the South Koreans and Americans had been escorting some South Korean civilian workers who had put ladders against a large poplar tree and were in the process of pruning it when the truck Kim had been in burst upon the scene.

All North Korean eyes, including Kim's, shifted to the senior North Korean officer. The look on his face was one of barely controlled fury as he stared at his sworn enemies. The officer swung his gaze around at his men.

"*Konggyok-handa!*" he screamed, and pointed at the Allies. "*Chukyo!*"

The order to attack and kill the enemy had an electric effect on Kim and the men with him. It galvanized them into immediate action. Kim turned toward the Americans and began running as fast as he could. He raced past his comrades, who were initially closer to the party than he was, and covered the twenty feet in seconds. He leaped at one of the Americans.

The American officer was half turned away from Kim and had not expected the North Korean attack. The two of them thudded together, with the American staggering backward from the force of Kim's assault and colliding with one of the South Korean workers, sending him to the ground. The American officer disengaged himself from Kim, took a step backward, and tripped over the outstretched foot of the fallen South Korean. Kim fell to his knees, then scrambled to his feet and saw an ax that had dropped from the fallen worker's hand. He ran over to it and grabbed it with both hands, unmindful of the direction the ax blade was pointing. He leaped over to where the American officer had just regained his feet.

The North Korean soldiers had joined with the South Koreans and Americans in a free-for-all. The North Koreans wielded ax handles, axes, and metal pikes in a frenzied attempt to fulfill their orders.

The American shouted something just before the flat of Kim's ax blade slammed across his back. The blow sent the U.S. Army man to his knees once again. Kim grunted with exertion and excitement as he readjusted the angle of the ax blade and got set for another strike. The American officer was halfway up when the next blow from Kim's ax sank the blade edge into his shoulder. Blood gushed from the American's open shoulder down his right arm. He screamed and fell.

Another North Korean ran up to the fallen American and stabbed him in the side with a metal pike. The American cried out in agony and rolled over on his back.

Kim, now a man possessed, with his breath coming in gasps and his system filled with adrenaline, lifted the ax for another blow to the fallen American's head.

Kwajalein Lagoon
Present Day

Lieutenant Kim Il Kwon brooded over the incident in the DMZ. He had thought of it often, and even imagined what he would have done if he had been there. He imagined the weather in August. His father had said it was hot and sunny. To be given a chance to strike at the Americans was something to be treasured, and his father had made the most of it, telling the story over and over as the years wore on. Kim had never tired of hearing of his father's one heroic moment, in August 1976. The elder Kim was certain he had killed one of the American officers, and he took every opportunity to boast of it. His comrades praised him for it, and his army gave him a medal for it.

Two American army officers, Lieutenant Mark T. Barrett and Major Arthur G. Bonifas, whose promotion to major had come through on that fateful day, were killed by the North Koreans, two more in a long list of dead from border incidents that marred the peace along the DMZ on the Korean Peninsula. However, the aftermath of the incident was disappointing to hawks on both sides. The North Koreans went on a war footing, a status that they were not far from at any time since 1953, and the U.S. sent some aircraft and the carrier *Midway* to the area.

The incident was defused, however, when Kim Il Sung, the leader of North Korea, sent a halfhearted apology to the United States calling the murders ''a regrettable incident.'' The United States, after some vacillation, called the North Korean leader's personal note ''a positive step.''

Kim asked himself the same question every time he thought of his father's heroism. Would he have obeyed orders so swiftly and so surely as his father had done? Yes, he was certain of it.

Given the chance, he would act just as his father had done some twenty years ago.

CHAPTER EIGHT

Belligerence

Admiral Yi

The hatch clanged shut on the outside entrance of the air-lock, and the expectant crew heard the rush of compressed air as it drove the water out of the chamber above.

Many of the crew crowded around, but the officers took no notice. They had been waiting and training for this moment for many months. The divers had found one of the reentry vehicles and had signaled that they were bringing it in. A special crane had been fitted into the airlock to lower the RV into the dolly that the technical people would use to wheel the precious cargo to its examination and storage space for the trip home.

The divers above opened the hatch with a pop of compressed air and the attendant spray of remaining water, and began to lower the American RV into the hold of the submarine.

The crew broke into excited chatter, and Captain Hong and his officers exchanged broad smiles. Hong stepped up to examine the RV and noted its size and shape. It was smaller than he'd expected, being only about five feet tall and two and a half feet in diameter at its base. The tapered cone shape of the RV was distorted, and Hong guessed that it was due to the impact with the water. They had been lucky that it hadn't broken up into a million pieces. This one was quite a find—it was completely intact.

What secrets did this nose cone have within it? Hong mused as the technical section huddled around the device. His superiors had risked this boat and the entire crew to get one or more of these American reentry vehicles. Yet it was worth the risk. Hong smiled again. His career would take quite an upturn with this victory in his record. Not quite the same as combat, which he would have preferred, but a tremendous victory nonetheless.

And now to the next task, he thought. Get the boat over to the second impact site and search for the next RV. Hong happily scratched his head, aware that most of the crew was watching him now that the RV had been wheeled away by the engineers for evaluation. He tried to wipe the smile from his face without success. The entire crew grinned back.

No matter what happened now, his place in the history of his country was assured.

Hong strode to the conn, then got on the intercom to tell Lieutenant Kim to inform him when the last diver was aboard. Hong went to the chart of Kwajalein Lagoon and noted that the second RV had impacted near Eniwetak Pass. His plan was to pick up the RV and exit via that pass, which was different from the one they had used to enter the lagoon. That would serve to confuse any American submarine that might have detected them prior to entering the lagoon.

Then he would make a run for home.

Kwajalein Island

The storm-driven wind howled around the trailer and periodically a particularly strong gust would shake the trailer from its roof to where its wheels used to be.

"It's getting pretty tough out there," said Ken Garrett to Nancy, who was seated on the living room sofa. He gazed at the storm-tossed water in the lagoon and watched fascinated at the bending palm trees as they swayed over with the wind. This particular typhoon seemed especially violent, and he suspected that the storm would leave quite a lot of damage behind.

"How long do these things usually last?" asked Nancy.

"A day maybe," he said, then had a thought. "Sometimes two or three," he continued with a smile.

She rolled her eyes. "I'm going to have to fight you off for that long?"

"Well, you don't *have* to fight me off," he replied with his eyebrows raised. She made a face at him, which made him laugh.

His campaign was stalled at the moment. While she wasn't running for cover every time he sat next to her, she wasn't exactly enthusiastic at the prospect of lovemaking either. There was one good thing about the afternoon—neither of them had spoken about the New York incident. Maybe they were all talked out, he thought hopefully.

All right, thought Nancy, when is he going to make his big move? More important, what am I going to do when he does make his move? This last ten days with him had been alternately painful, when they talked about their relationship, relaxed, and almost joyful, when they talked about the islands or even work. She was reminded why she'd married him, how cute he was when he twisted his head a certain way, and how funny he could be when he was in the mood.

She shook her head. They hadn't made love in over a year, and he hadn't demanded anything since she had arrived. He had been extraordinarily patient. She sensed that their relationship was coming to some sort of crossroads with her visit to Kwajalein, and the turning point could be this afternoon.

Ken dropped the window curtain and sat beside her on the sofa. He was near enough to be intimate, yet not close enough to crowd her. If she could have picked the distance between them, she couldn't have done any better. The distance perfectly mirrored their uncertain relationship.

They both stared at the TV, which had been on for most of the afternoon. The quiz program went off and one of those annoying public information programs came on which were generated by the army command on Kwajalein. This one was devoted exclusively to restating the dangers of going out during a typhoon. A thoroughly bored army officer ran down a litany of dangers from typhoons taken from a seemingly endless list.

The TV picture suddenly disappeared and was replaced by a white-dot-filled screen.

"They lost the transmitter," said Ken.

"In this storm they might have lost the antenna as well," replied Nancy. The wind howled around the trailer to make Nancy's point.

"Well, there's always Strip Pac-Man," said Ken with a smile.

Nancy laughed out loud at the reference to her joke on the bus about his supposedly favorite game. Ken got up to shut off the TV and had his hand poised to twist the volume knob when the TV died of its own accord. The one light they had on went off also.

"The power's gone?" asked Nancy incredulously.

"I'll be damned," muttered Ken. "This doesn't happen very often. Some storm." He sat back down next to her, a little closer than before, and hoped he wasn't being obvious. The living room was shrouded in gloom as the storm raged outside.

There he goes, she thought. He's got his head cocked in a cute way, and now he's making a joke about the storm. She laughed at his joke, her laughter coming easily and naturally. He must know somehow that that combination is damn near irresistible. How did he find out? I never told him. She knew what was going to happen for the rest of the afternoon.

She was not so surprised to find that she still loved him.

Admiral Yi

Captain Hong's smile grew broader as the technicians and engineers he had taken with him from North Korea excitedly explained what was inside the first RV they had retrieved from the lagoon floor. Crammed full of the latest PENAIDS designs from the United States, the stolen RV represented an incredible intelligence find. The engineers went on to explain the strategic importance of the RV, which Hong already knew, but there was no stopping them. Their excitement knew no bounds. They knew this would save North Korea many years of development and testing.

The technicians left and hurriedly went forward, where

the divers were bringing in the second RV. Hong had already received the word that this RV was in worse shape than the first. This one had split into three pieces, but the divers, through monumental effort, had recovered all three pieces.

To pick up both reentry vehicles! His country would be grateful to him and his crew indeed. In a few years, it would be Admiral Hong who would stare back in the mirror.

Yet he felt strangely unfulfilled, as if the mission hadn't been difficult enough to merit all the rewards his superiors would heap upon them. He had expected some sort of danger or resistance from the Americans. Even though his countrymen belittled the Americans, Hong knew better. The United States wouldn't be a world leader if the Americans were as stupid and decadent as many of North Korea's citizens believed.

Hong smiled again in the solitude of his cabin. He had achieved a truly glorious victory for the Democratic People's Republic of Korea.

Lieutenant Kim retreated to his cabin after his duties with the RV were completed and the technical people took over. The *Admiral Yi* would stay still until daybreak to let the engineers examine and store the second American reentry vehicle. Captain Hong wanted to transit the dangerous Eniwetak Pass in daylight.

Thoughts of his father filled his mind, of his heroism, of his great triumph. Not many people in North Korea today had engaged the enemy in combat and had come out a victor. His father had been injured in the battle with the Americans and South Koreans that day so long ago. A South Korean soldier had hit the senior Kim with an ax handle across the face and had broken his jaw. The jaw had set badly and permanently disfigured his father's face, but the elder Kim had worn the twisted jaw with pride. Everyone knew he had gotten injured in a fierce battle with the Americans.

Kim leaned against the bulkhead and felt the water's tepid temperature seep into him. The hull of the submarine had been cold during their long voyage across the Pacific, but now it was at the same temperature as the warm lagoon water.

Kim placed his fingertips to the hull and ran his hand lightly down the metal surface. The Americans were nearby. He could feel them. So close, and yet a world away. A world of discipline, training, and water separated him from the enemy. Kim desperately wanted to come back to North Korea a hero, as his father had two decades ago.

Orders had been given. No contact with the Americans. Avoid shipping lanes. No radio transmissions. Run submerged as much as possible. All of this ran contrary to every instinct drilled into him from his birth. His time near the enemy was coming to a close. In a few hours, the *Admiral Yi* would stir and grope its way toward the open sea.

In Kim's mind, they would go home without victory.

Captain Hong stared through the periscope into the dim morning's light. The typhoon had largely passed, leaving lead-gray skies and rough seas. Eniwetak Pass was more narrow than Gea Pass, three hundred meters wide, then narrowing to seventy-five meters, but Hong was determined to get through a different pass than the one by which they had entered the lagoon in an effort to confuse any American submarines that might have followed him to Kwajalein. He had spent the last several hours bouncing off coral heads as the *Yi* stumbled its way to the mouth of the passage. There would most likely be a strong current through the pass, and he would have to get his speed up to keep control of his vessel.

Hong knew he had only a few navigational aids for this passage. The only buoy was to his south and due west of Meck Island, which bordered the southern edge of the passage. He also had a red-and-white steel tower on the northern shore of Meck and a navigation pole on Omelek Island, to the north of the passage. He had realized long ago that he had to make the transit at periscope depth; there were no buoys lining the channel that he could track acoustically as there were in Gea Pass.

Hong prepared to order range and bearing readings to the navigational aids around the passage as he had done during the harrowing high-speed transit of Gea Pass just two days before. The chart of Eniwetak Pass had been seared into Hong's mind by endless memorization over the last year and again over the last twenty-four hours. He knew what the bearings to the navigation aids should be and at what time the bearing should occur. The bearing and distance readings had been memorized for all the major passes through the Kwajalein reef long ago. Hong squinted through the periscope at the flashing green light almost due south of the *Yi*.

"Bearing to Buoy Number One," commanded Hong.

"One, eight, five," said a junior officer in a loud voice.

"Range," said Hong after reading the height of the buoy from the graticules on the periscope.

"Thirty-six hundred meters," was the reply.

Hong went through the same procedure with the tower on Meck and the pole on Omelek, then nodded to himself in satisfaction. Lieutenant Kim was busy plotting the *Yi*'s position, and after fifteen seconds of intense labor pronounced the sub in mid-channel. Captain Hong knew without Kim's telling him. A few minutes later, Hong was ready for another set of readings.

"Bearing to Buoy Number One," ordered Hong.

"One, nine, six," replied the junior officer.

An alarm went off in Hong's mind, and he quickly read out the graticular height on the scope. "Range," said Hong quickly.

"Twenty-seven hundred meters," was the reply.

Lieutenant Kim got busy again, but Hong was ahead of him. "Left full rudder!" ordered Hong hastily. Hong wanted to order the engines ahead flank, but to do so would bend the periscope tube, making it impossible to retract the device. Hong swung the periscope around to line up on Meck's tower. "Bearing Meck tower!" he bellowed.

"One, five, five," replied the officer.

Hong read the height in a loud voice and demanded the range instantly.

"Twenty-two hundred meters," replied the officer, who gave Hong a worried look.

Hong went immediately over to Kim's chart. He unceremoniously shoved Kim aside and stared at the mark Kim had just made.

"Captain, we are to the extreme right of the channel!" said Kim in a very loud voice. "We are in danger of running aground!"

"I know that, you fool!" growled Hong.

Kim's mouth dropped open at the virulence of Hong's retort. He snapped his mouth shut and pressed his lips together into a thin line.

The helmsman was looking at Hong expectantly.

"Come to course one, one, zero," ordered Hong in a guttural voice. He berated himself mentally. He had forgotten to give the heading after giving the rudder orders. Captain Hong got back to the periscope and ordered another round of bearing and range readings to Meck's tower and the one buoy in the area. He was astounded at what he heard. The readings were virtually unchanged. They were making almost no headway!

Hong rubbed his forehead and visualized what was happening. An extremely large current was entering the pass, almost due west, then sweeping around and striking the *Yi* from the northwest, which was driving his boat toward the small island of Eniwetak, which sat almost due west of the passage. Nowhere was any mention made of this strange current. He went over to the chart once again, now unsure of himself. Hong peered at their latest position and noted that they hadn't lost any ground toward the reef which surrounded Eniwetak.

Captain Hong tried a different course and gradually over an hour they worked their way free of the peculiar currents of Eniwetak Pass. Hong breathed a sigh of relief and considered his next move. He leaned over the chart once again, ignoring Kim at his side. He went over it again and again, then straightened and shook his head. He came to the inevitable conclusion.

Gea Pass was their only way out.

Kwajalein Island

Ken Garrett lay on the bed in the dark staring at the ceiling of the bedroom of his trailer with his mind wandering over the events of the day. Nancy had finally fallen asleep after some particularly erotic lovemaking. All their pent-up desire had flowed out as they indulged themselves in passionate sex.

But what would it all mean in the end? Was this the new beginning he had hoped for in their marriage? Or would she remain resolute and still keep him at a distance?

He tried to shove all the questions away and think about his radar work, but his parents flashed into his mind. They were still alive, although his father led the existence of a vegetable. The circumstances of his father's condition were particularly painful, but now and again he found that he couldn't resist thinking about it, as if his mind kept reviewing it all, hoping to yet make sense of it.

His parents had been violent people. They didn't abuse Ken or his siblings, but they retaliated with extreme belligerence when they were wronged or even slighted by strangers. Ken's father, Lloyd Garrett, had an extremely quick temper, saving all his patience for his wife and children. Ken and his brothers and sister hated to go for rides with their father in the car because of the vitriolic abuses Lloyd Garrett would heap on other drivers for insults both real and imagined. Often Lloyd would threaten other drivers with a tire iron he kept just for that purpose under the front seat. When that would happen, Ken and the others would cry in fear at the sight of their maniacal father. Most of the time Lloyd's belligerence had the desired effect. Most people apologized profusely just to get away from the lunatic with the tire iron.

The local police knew the Garretts' tendency toward violence. Lloyd Garrett had been in jail and had defended himself in lawsuits enough times to be well-known to court officials and the local lawyers as well. The atmosphere of Ken's childhood was one of constant turmoil. His mother did her part also with actual fistfights with some of the other ladies in the neighborhood and a particularly violent assault on one of Ken's teachers who'd had the temerity to say that Ken wasn't working up to his ability. Ken hadn't seen his mother for a month after that incident as she paid the price to society with a stretch in jail.

As violent as his parents were to strangers, they were restrained with their children. Ken could remember some spankings when he was little but no more than that. He marveled at how his parents could be so irrational with strangers but so caring with their children. Maybe we were extracareful not to provoke our parents, thought Ken. We didn't want to be treated the same way they treated strangers.

As Ken grew up, he wondered when his father would overretaliate on the wrong man. The long-dreaded event came when they were all in the car traveling to a relative's house and Lloyd Garrett was attempting to merge onto a highway in a bumper-to-bumper traffic jam. People were patient. The cars on the highway were alternating with the cars on the entrance ramp, each car on the highway letting one car on the ramp go in front of it. To Lloyd Garrett, it was the only fair way to handle the situation.

Everything was proceeding well, much to the relief of the Garrett children, until someone in a Cadillac went around the line of patient people on the entrance ramp and tried to muscle in just ahead of Lloyd Garrett after he had merged onto the highway. Ken's father had seen the impatient Caddie swing out of the line in his rearview mirror and had begun cursing the driver as he anticipated what would happen next.

When the Caddie driver stuck his bumper in front of the Garretts' car, Lloyd Garrett swung the wheel quickly and pulled up very close to the car in front of him, effectively nudging the Caddie out. Only the Caddie driver would have none of it. The cars came closer and closer together until the Cadillac's bumper scraped the side of the Garretts' car. With Ken's mother urging him on, Lloyd Garrett leaped from the car with his tire iron in hand and ran around the front of the car to confront the other driver.

The driver of the Cadillac also jumped from his car—with a long silver object in his hand. Ken remembered the next events as a blur of motion accompanied by the clanging of steel against steel. The Caddie driver also had a tire iron and wasn't afraid to use it. In the general melee that followed, one or the other of the fighters, while swinging a tire iron wildly, smashed the side rear window of the Garretts' car, sending a shower of glass fragments over the Garrett children. Lloyd Garrett would later use that as an excuse for revenge.

The police pulled the two men apart and arrested them both, but Ken's mother wrote down the license plate of the Cadillac, thereby insuring that the battle would continue. After Lloyd got out of jail, he and his wife began to plot their revenge on the Caddie driver—who turned out to be one of the town's "fat cats" as they put it.

Ken Garrett, when he could get his parents' attention, pleaded with them to stop the fight, to just leave the other man alone. Lloyd Garrett gave Ken a stern lecture in return about the necessity of standing up for your rights and about the administration of justice to the unlawful.

They ignored Ken's pleas in the end and set fire to the offending Cadillac one night, and then laughed about it for the next week. When Lloyd Garrett woke up one morning and found that all four of his tires had been slashed, he knew immediately who had done it.

Nancy stirred next to him and mumbled something that he couldn't understand. Ken rolled toward her and kissed her lightly on the neck. She settled down again and her breathing gradually became slow and shallow, which told him that she had sunk into a deep sleep.

Ken's thoughts returned to his father's actions years ago as he feverishly tried to make sense of what had happened next. His father had gone to take revenge almost immediately, intending to set fire to the man's garage, which stored two other cars, both expensive antiques.

But the man was ready, and Lloyd Garrett's life was effectively ended by a shotgun blast.

CHAPTER NINE

Discovery at Gea

Kwajalein Island

Mike Sprague knocked again on the door of Ken Garrett's trailer. He heard no movement from inside so he transferred his pounding to the window glass, which made a distinctly sharper sound. A minute later, Ken Garrett was standing in front of him in a bathrobe and rubbing the sleep from his eyes.

"Oh, hi, Mike. C'mon in," mumbled Ken as he stepped aside. Sprague entered quickly, and Garrett knew something was wrong. The overweight Sprague never moved very fast.

Nancy walked down the hallway from the end bedroom pulling on her robe belt to tighten it around her. Sprague gave her a look and couldn't help but raise his eyebrows.

"Hon, this is Mike Sprague," said Ken.

"Hello," said Nancy.

"Pleasure to meet you, Mrs. Garrett," replied Sprague. He shifted his attention to Ken. "*The Lady N* dragged her anchor during the storm. I'm not sure where it is."

Ken rolled his eyes around. "Oh, no! I'd forgotten all about her."

"*The Lady N*?" asked Nancy.

"Where would she be?" asked Ken.

"What's a *Lady N*?" persisted Nancy.

"Ma'am, it's Ken's boat," replied Sprague. He looked back at Ken. "I think it's near Gea Pass."

"You've got a boat named *The Lady N*?" asked Nancy as she stared at the back of his head.

"Some of the other guys said they saw wreckage near Gea," said Sprague. "Let's get out there and see if we can find her."

Ken nodded quickly, now fully awake. "Give me two seconds to put on some clothes," he said as he headed down the hallway.

"You never told me about any boat," protested Nancy.

"We were both too busy preparing for the mission," said Ken.

Mike Sprague mumbled something and gracefully made his exit to wait outside.

Ken Garrett went into the bedroom and quickly threw on his clothes from yesterday and went to the bedroom door. Nancy stopped him with a single word.

"Ken," said Nancy. He turned to look at her. Her face was tense. "About yesterday afternoon and last night . . ." She hesitated. His lips drew into a thin line as he realized what was coming.

"I don't want you to get your hopes up," she said in a rush.

Disappointment swept over his face, and the half smile he'd worn since the previous afternoon disappeared. After a moment he said, "I'll see you later."

Ken went through the bedroom doorway and quickly walked down the hall toward the outside door, his pace quickening as he neared the doorway.

Nancy bit her lip with anxiety at yet another confrontation with Ken. A sudden thought hit her.

"*The Lady N*!" she exclaimed. "Wait a minute! Ken!" She heard the door open. "Did you name your boat after—" The door slammed.

"—me?" she finished in a low voice.

Admiral Yi
Gea Pass

"All stop!" snapped Captain Hong. The crew in the conn started with surprise. They had been expecting another exciting transit through Gea Pass at flank speed.

Hong stared through the periscope and tried to make sense of the outline that appeared just above the sea in the middle of the channel. Something was there. Floating or . . .

Suddenly the entire outline, including the part that was submerged, clicked into recognition in his mind. A ship had sunk in the narrowest part of Gea Pass! Hong uttered an oath, which was highly unusual for his tightly disciplined, ascetic nature. Hong could see the stern, which appeared to be hung up on the reef, and his mind filled in the rest of the ship's outline. He looked up into the expectant eyes of Lieutenant Kim.

"Get the divers out," ordered Hong in a level voice, his discipline already back in place. "A ship has sunk in the channel. They may have to blow the stern off the reef."

Lieutenant Kim gave quick assent and rushed to fulfill his orders. Hong walked over to the chart of Kwajalein Lagoon. He carefully studied all the other passes. Eniwetak had already defeated them. South Pass was only eight meters in depth while his boat was nine and a half meters tall. Bigej Channel was a mere six meters deep. Some other passes at the northern end of the lagoon might be deep enough, he thought, but he had no desire to grope his way through the lagoon for eighty kilometers, slamming into uncharted coral heads all the way.

Hong muttered another oath. A thousand meters away was the open sea, and he remained trapped in the lagoon.

The twin engines of Mike Sprague's cabin cruiser throbbed their powerful beat as he and Ken Garrett cut through the rough sea across Kwajalein Lagoon. Mike Sprague was following the reef on the southwestern side of the lagoon to Gea Pass. The wind drove the sea against the reef, setting up a cloudlike mist along the meandering coral sea bottom and making it easy for Sprague to follow the reef to the northwest. Ken stood near the bow and scoured the horizon for *The Lady N*—or its remains.

"Anything yet?" asked Sprague. Garrett shook his head while keeping his eyes on the horizon.

The sea was still racked by four-foot swells, the remnant of the recent typhoon. Garrett stared at the outline

made by the tips of the waves for anything irregular
floating on top, then scrutinized the sea between the
swells to pick out anything at all that might tell him the
fate of his boat. He had to take a break every few
minutes to wipe off the lenses of the binoculars to re-
move the spray kicked up by the wind and by Sprague's
bold advance through the choppy lagoon.

It was only about ten miles from where Sprague's boat
had been moored to Gea Pass, a trip time of about forty
minutes at Sprague's rate of speed. Garrett looked at his
watch. Thirty-five minutes since they had left Kwajalein
Island. Any minute now, he thought to himself.

His thoughts ran to his wife and their torrid afternoon
and night together. Pure ecstasy, he thought. But now she's
still unsure, and she had to say that their lovemaking might
not change the ultimate outcome of their marriage. How
could she make love to a man like that and then reject him
so soon afterward? How could that one incident in New
York so totally change her view of him? So what was it,
then? She loved him but didn't respect him? He slowly
concluded that it was possible.

He wanted to think that if the same incident happened
again, he would act differently and confront the muggers.
But he realized with a sinking heart that he would do no
differently the second time around. It just didn't make sense
to go up against two men who might be armed. He couldn't
outrun a bullet, could he?

But it was more than that. He always tried to apply logic
to the situation in New York, but what had ultimately
stopped him from helping the victim was the violence required and the horrific thought that he might become like
his father, an unreasoning, out-of-control lunatic ready to
deal violence to anyone who got in his way. He had promised himself that he would never become like his father.
He had tried to tell Nancy about his parents, but she hadn't
listened.

The water in the distance glistened with miniature rainbows, a telltale sign of oil on the water. Garrett's mind
snapped back to the search for his boat. His heart sank.
Was the oil from *The Lady N*? He surveyed across a wide

angle to measure the extent of the oil slick. It was large, very large.

"Mike! Oil slick dead ahead. Something sank," he shouted over the noise of the waves. Mike Sprague stood upright and stared into the distance. He picked up a set of binoculars and stared at the water.

"Yeah, something big," he yelled back to Garrett.

Ken felt better knowing that the oil slick couldn't have been created by his relatively small boat. He then had a pessimistic thought. If the storm had sunk a large ship, then what chance did his thirty-foot boat have?

"Watch out for debris," yelled Sprague to Garrett, who nodded in an exaggerated fashion to acknowledge the request. Sprague then had another thought. "Maybe the supply ship sank," he said. The supply ship that kept Kwajalein in food and other necessities made regular runs each month, and both Garrett and Sprague knew that the ship was expected any day now.

Garrett nodded again. "Yeah, probably."

He went back to scouring the sea in front of them and quickly made out a form rising above the sea at the horizon. He squinted and after a few moments he saw that it was the stern of a ship. Sprague had hit it on the nose. The supply ship had gone down in the middle of Gea Pass. He turned and yelled the fact to Sprague, who whistled in surprise and shook his head in sympathy with the ship's crew. Sprague got on the radio to let someone on Kwajalein know the ship's fate. He tried repeatedly but got no answer.

"No contact with Echo Pier!" shouted Sprague. Garrett nodded in acknowledgment.

Garrett glanced through the binoculars again and saw a jagged outline at the top of a wave which immediately disappeared into the trough between waves. Debris? he wondered. Two minutes later, he made out what was floating on the sea. Ken ran back to the pilothouse.

"Mike, take a look at that," he said, and pointed toward the horizon. He took the wheel from Sprague and allowed the big man to peer through the binoculars.

"Guys in a rubber boat?" Sprague asked incredulously.

Ken nodded. "Are the Navy Seals having an exercise there?" asked Sprague.

Ken shook his head. "This is an army base, remember?"

"Who the hell are they, then?" asked Sprague. He stared at the men in the rubber boat for a full minute and a half. "What the hell . . ." he mumbled to himself. Ken was surprised at his reaction. Sprague seemed overly concerned.

"Ken, keep her at least three hundred yards away from them," said Sprague. He then turned and started to go below.

"What? Why?" asked Ken, who was even more surprised at the order. Sprague didn't reply and went below in a hurry.

He went directly to the deck panels that allowed access to the engine compartment. He got the deck panels up in record time, flinging them aside with abandon, and jumped into the shallow space. Sprague reached under, opened a concealed compartment, and withdrew a rifle and a sight. He heaved himself up onto the deck again and quickly attached the sight and loaded the weapon.

Sprague ran up the ladder to the weather deck, unmindful of Garrett's surprise at the appearance of the rifle.

"Keep her as steady as you can," he shouted over the noise of the wind.

"What the hell are you doing?" screamed Garrett in reply. "You can't shoot those guys!"

Sprague ignored his friend and set up near the bow, resting the barrel of the rifle on the back of a deck chair. He peered through the telescopic sight and waited for the pitching of his boat to align the barrel of his rifle with the rubber boat so that he could get off an accurate shot.

Suddenly Sprague felt the barrel being lifted and nearly yanked out of his grip. He looked up angrily.

"Are you nuts?" shouted Garrett. He grabbed Sprague by the shoulder and held the rifle barrel up toward the sky.

"Ken, you stay out of this! This doesn't concern you!" shouted Sprague in return. He swatted Garrett's hand off his shoulder and yanked the rifle free from his friend's grip.

"I can't let you do this! You can't shoot someone for no reason!" yelled Garrett.

"Take a look through the binoculars. They're North Koreans!'' replied Sprague as he gestured angrily in the direction of Gea Pass.

Garrett shifted his gaze from Sprague to the horizon. "North Koreans?'' he said in astonishment.

The boat suddenly began to roll quickly to port. The boat, which had been heading into the waves, had been turned by the rough seas until the waves were hitting the vessel broadside.

"Damn it, man!'' yelled Sprague. "Get back to the wheel and straighten her out!''

Garrett ran quickly back to the wheelhouse and got the boat pointed into the waves once again. He picked up a set of binoculars and stared through them in an effort to verify Sprague's contention that North Koreans had invaded the lagoon.

He saw a patch of red on one of the diver's air tanks and squinted to make out the detail of the pattern in the field of red. He could see a circle of white with a blood-red star on it. Sprague was right! Garrett gaped at the divers as they prepared to go over the side of the rubber boat. What were they after?

Garrett had the answer in a flash. They were diving on the sunken supply ship! More questions occurred to him. But why?

The crack of Sprague's rifle made him jump. Garrett put down the binoculars and fine-tuned the boat's heading to give Sprague a steady platform. He then picked up the binoculars and peered through them once again.

The North Korean divers were looking about frantically to find the source of the gunfire. Another crack and the divers all stared in his direction. Garrett heard a third crack from Sprague's weapon.

One of the divers disappeared in a cloud of mist. The bullet from Sprague's rifle had shattered one of the divers' air tank, sending shards of metal flying in all directions. The mist was quickly blown away by the wind, and Garrett again had a good view of the North Koreans. Of the four divers Garrett had seen, only one seemed to be moving, and he was doing so lethargically. The remaining diver began to wave one blood-soaked hand back and forth, signaling someone in the distance.

Garrett looked about quickly but saw no one. Sprague suddenly was next to him and out of breath.

"We stopped them," said Sprague as he gulped some air.

Garrett lowered his gaze to the deck and tried to stem the shock of what had just happened. His friend had just killed three people.

Admiral Yi

Captain Hong stared at the spectacle through the periscope. He watched horrified as the rubber boat containing the three dead divers and the one wounded diver slowly lost air. The remaining diver's waving grew frantic as the waters of the lagoon closed around him. Hong stared at the spot where his last diver had disappeared for a moment or two, mesmerized by the working water, knowing that it had gobbled up his man in a mindless manner.

Hong rotated the periscope to take a second look at the boat containing the intruders who had killed his divers. He savagely shook his head. By the time he could surface and engage the boat, the boat would be long gone. He would then have given his position away to the enemy.

Hong had seen enough. He slapped the handles up and ordered the periscope to be retracted. Lieutenant Kim gave the captain a puzzled look. Hong knew what Kim desired above all else in the world. Some men are ambitious, some desire power, some lust after fame or women. Kim was consumed by the Americans. He wanted to get near them, to observe them, to see if they were really the superhumans the North Koreans had always feared they were.

Now it looked as if Kim would get his chance.

"Why are North Koreans here? Where did they come from?" asked Garrett to take his mind off the devastating vision of seeing men killed for the first time. His eyes flicked over the compass heading, and he gave the boat a little left rudder to keep it headed toward the island of Kwajalein.

"The mission," answered Sprague. "They're here to steal data from the latest mission."

Garrett nodded. It made sense. Years ago, the Russians had always tried to track incoming RVs and intercept their telemetry with their so-called trawlers that bristled with antennas and electronics. There were even rumors that the Russians had stolen a flight recorder from the lagoon floor. Now the North Koreans were trying their hand at stealing technical secrets.

"But where is their ship?" asked Garrett.

Sprague shrugged. "Submarine maybe." He gave Garrett half a glance to see his reaction to his suggestion.

"Yeah, submarine," said Garrett thoughtfully. He snapped his fingers after a few moments. "That's why they were diving on the sunken supply ship! They're stuck in the lagoon!"

Sprague sat upright and gave Garrett a penetrating look. "You're right!" he said excitedly. The big man sat in thought for a few seconds. He suddenly jumped to his feet in an explosion of movement. Garrett leaned back quickly and nearly let go of the ship's wheel.

Sprague made his way forward and began to set up an antenna. He went below and Garrett could hear a door opening, then closing.

"Hey, Mike! What's the antenna for?" he shouted in spite of the closed door.

Sprague pulled out his electronic encoding device and put in the key word based on the day and time. He composed a message and transmitted it through the miniature device to encrypt it, then set it up with his transmitter. He cursed and forced himself to settle down and transmit the message he knew had to be sent. He waited ten minutes, then twenty. The link came alive, and his printer spat out the coded response. He immediately set about decoding it, then sat and stared at the message, reading it over and over.

Message for Guairen

North Koreans must be stopped at all costs.

Shifu

CHAPTER TEN

Invasion

U.S.S. Topeka

Captain Fred Worden didn't like the last message he had just received from COMSUBPAC. He showed it to Lieutenant Commander Riley, his XO, who pursed his lips in a soundless whistle.

"Well, I guess our tracking mission is kaput," he said as he handed the message back to the captain. "I don't know why these landlubbers can't take care of themselves."

"I guess the Pentagon is getting flak over the loss of communications with Kwajalein," replied Worden. "Everything must be out to get them this upset. The damn North Koreans could spot us when we surface."

"You never know, Captain," said the XO. "We could get lucky. Maybe the North Koreans are not in a position to see us when we send out the landing party."

Worden rubbed his forehead and gritted his teeth. "I hope so. I don't like the idea of tracking an enemy sub for over two thousand miles and then losing it. Then, before we can pick it up again, our mission is aborted."

"Yeah," said Riley. "All because some of Kwajalein's antennas are knocked over in a storm." He shook his head in frustration at his superiors' decision. He lifted one eye to give the captain a glance. "Still want to send Lieutenant Eckman, Captain?"

''He's the weapons officer,'' said Worden, and shrugged. The officer in charge of the Weapons Department normally led landing parties. ''I know he's inexperienced at landing parties, but who has experience? Besides, he'll have Chief Stevens with him to keep him out of trouble.''

''Standard weapons, sir?'' asked the XO.

''Yes, let's play it by the book,'' replied Worden, then he smiled. ''Maybe they'll tangle with a half-mad, drug-dealing sand crab.''

The XO tilted his head back and laughed out loud.

Lieutenant Mark Eckman tried to suppress the butterflies in his stomach. So what's the big deal? he thought. It's only a landing party to check up on some civilians who lost a comm antenna. Then why am I so nervous? He picked up his bulletproof vest and slung it around his short frame. After pulling it snug, he smashed the Velcro belt to the body of the vest and checked the fit. In the heat and humidity on the island, he'd be soaking wet in ten minutes. He put the life jacket on over the vest and felt hot already.

So why do we need all these weapons? He shoved a nine-millimeter automatic into a shoulder holster and eyed the rest of the landing party as they checked out their M16s and shotguns. Chief Petty Officer Ike Stevens orbited the men and gave sharp commands to each of them to square away their equipment. Normally Chief Ike would have been chomping on an unlit cigar, but with their departure imminent, he had been forced to do without one. He seemed strange-looking without the cigar, like just some mere mortal instead of the god of knowledge that he was.

Lieutenant Commander Riley strolled up and looked over the fourteen-man landing party and their diminutive leader, Lieutenant Eckman.

''You ready?'' asked Riley.

''Just about, sir,'' replied Eckman.

Riley nodded. ''You might want to give the weapons a low profile so we don't get the civilians all riled up.''

Eckman smiled. ''Aye, aye, sir.''

Lieutenant Commander Riley returned the smile. ''Should be a piece of cake.''

Eckman tried to continue smiling. "Yes, sir, it should be."

An hour later, the *Topeka* surfaced off the southwestern coast of Kwajalein Island, and Lieutenant Eckman, Chief Stevens, and the rest of their party scrambled out of one of the boat's hatches and inflated their rubber boats. Ten minutes later, they were headed for Kwajalein's southern beach. Eckman scoured the coastline with his binoculars for any sign of trouble but there was none. No one was in sight either. Eckman was puzzled. Surely he should see someone.

Lieutenant Kim Il Kwon stared at Kwajalein's north coast and tried to pick out any movement as the rubber boat he was in bounced on the still-choppy lagoon water. The effort was in vain. Things can be so quiet after a storm, thought Kim. What were the Americans like? His father had described them as very large, a whole head taller than the senior Kim. Kim grunted to himself. He was taller than his father, so what did that make him with respect to the Americans?

Kim's government had taken an officially arrogant line and looked down upon the Americans and their South Korean allies as inferior beings. Yet everyone knew, without saying it, that the Americans and South Koreans were extremely powerful. The American nuclear weapons were always in the back of everyone's minds. Kim smiled with the near certainty that the North Korean nuclear power program had evened the odds by producing some nuclear weapons of its own. Even though the United States had concluded a treaty with the Democratic People's Republic to stop North Korea's nuclear weapons program, Kim speculated that the program still went on in secret with nuclear material purchased from greedy scientists in Russia.

Yes, the Americans had substantial weaponry, but what were the people like? Were they the supermen that everyone feared? His father had proven years ago that they died like anyone else. Perhaps that is why he was hailed as such a great hero. Kim grinned to himself. Perhaps I will prove it again, he thought.

He pulled out a map of Kwajalein Island and looked it

over once again. He and his men would land at Echo Pier and drive inland to the police headquarters. Kim's mission was to prevent any interference with the *Admiral Yi*'s divers in their second attempt to blow up the ship that had sunk in Gea Pass. Kim shook his head slightly in consternation over the supposed twenty-five hundred people on Kwajalein Island itself. He looked back at the three rubber boats with twelve men in each of them. Counting himself, there were thirty-seven men to control twenty-five hundred Americans.

To succeed in this mission, he had to control the weapons, boats, and the police. With speed, surprise, deadly force, and hostages, Kim was certain he would succeed. He only had to keep the Americans at bay for a few hours while the divers got ready, surveyed the wreck, and blew it up. His men were heavily armed with AKMs, the descendants of the notorious AK-47 that had accrued fame in Vietnam. Some of his men had grenade launchers as well.

Kim looked over at his second in command, Junior Lieutenant Park San Hoon. He was already surveying the boats which could be seen on the horizon and determining whether to sink them or not. There were a lot of boats toward the western end of the island, and Kim had given Park orders to ignore them and instead destroy the boats near Echo Pier, which was close to the police station. He didn't want the security force on the island to follow them if he and his men had to make a quick exit from the island.

Kim nodded to himself with satisfaction as he thought of Junior Lieutenant Park. Park felt much the same way he did about the Americans. Anxiety at their weapons' capability but total certainty at the superiority of the North Korean in face-to-face combat, where all the American fancy weapons didn't come into play. Hadn't Kim's father proven that years ago?

Kim's boat and one other broke away from Park's boat, which was dispatched to survey nearby boats for destruction if necessary. The boats were in pretty sorry shape, some half sunk, others capsized by the violent storm. Park quietly would take care of the boats that were in good condition without using their automatic weapons or grenades, then join Kim at the police headquarters and the provost marshal's office, which was their next destination. Kim didn't want any shooting until they were set up near their two strategic targets.

Kim looked over Echo Pier as they rapidly approached and studied the two tug boats that were tied up to the pier. They had white superstructures that contrasted with their dark gunwhales, which were lined with old tires on the sides to protect both the pier and the tugs themselves. One tug was down by the bow, obviously damaged by the storm. Kim decided to let Park destroy the other.

He bit his lip as the boat pulled up to Echo Pier. Did Kwajalein have an armory? Where were the weapons stored? How many and what kind did they have? Kwajalein was a U.S. Army base, and they would have a cache of weapons somewhere. He shook his head again slightly and tried to shove the questions from his mind.

Kim's boat pulled parallel to the pier, and Kim nimbly jumped up on the deck. His men followed, and Kim silently waved his arm as a signal for his men to spread out. He turned toward the island with its palm trees bent over in homage to the stiff wind. Curious, no one around, he thought, as his insides fluttered at the thought of coming face-to-face with Americans. He spotted two catamarans tied up at the base of the pier. They looked to be very fast and in good condition after the storm. Kim reached for his radio, then thought better of it. Now was not the time to break radio silence. After the first shots were fired, he would tell Lieutenant Park to destroy them, as well as the tug, when he came ashore.

Kim put his AKM at port arms and started off at a quick run down the pier toward the police headquarters.

Mike Sprague almost ran his boat aground in his haste to get ashore on Kwajalein. Ken Garrett had a small rubber raft ready. When Sprague came near Coral Sands Beach on the lagoon side of the island near the Kwajalein Range Command Building, Garrett flipped the raft over the side and tied the line to the deckrail so that the raft wouldn't float away while Sprague set the anchor. They had both decided to get back to the Kwajalein Range Command Building as fast as they could, rather than go back up to the marina near Echo Pier. They had to tell someone in authority about the North Korean invasion of the lagoon.

Garrett and Sprague jumped into the rubber raft, let go the line, and started paddling for the beach, thirty yards away. Garrett noted that Sprague had taken his rifle with him. He had even offered Garrett a handgun, which Garrett had refused. Sprague had then jammed the pistol into his own pocket. Garrett wondered why Sprague had weapons which were illegal on Kwajalein. And what was all that business with the message he had sent? To whom did he talk? Garrett had pestered Sprague with questions, but the most that the large man would say was that he was "working for the good guys." Sprague was some kind of intelligence agent? Could he be CIA?

Sprague had clammed up after that, even under a barrage of questions from Garrett.

They reached the beach and ignored a few people who braved the still-raw weather to stroll along the sand. They regarded the two men curiously but kept the slow pace of people with no place to go. One or two of them frowned at the sight of Sprague's rifle, but the others just assumed it was some kind of army or security exercise.

Sprague and Garrett started off at a fast jog toward the Command Building, but Sprague slowed to a walk almost immediately. He gasped for breath as Garrett looked at him incredulously. Mike was that out of shape? He looked about as he waited for Sprague to catch up to him, to see if there was anyone in authority to tell of the North Koreans.

He gaped in the direction of the runway. Coming across the airstrip in what looked like full combat gear were U.S. military men!

Kim squinted his eyes and watched the police pickup truck work its way around several fallen palm trees that blocked the road. Kim had hurriedly gotten his men out of sight behind a building on Marine Road halfway to Eighth Street and intended to let this lone policeman go on his way. Surprise in attacking the police station was paramount. This single policeman would present no problem if his headquarters were destroyed.

The police truck abruptly came to a halt when it ran into

a palm tree that totally blocked its path. The driver, a civilian protective agency employee, quickly got out of the truck and surveyed the obstacles in front of his vehicle. He cursed at the tree and bent down to try to slide it out of the way.

Kim brought his field glasses to his eyes and studied the man's uniform. It was black, with long pants and no hat. Kim's gaze centered on the man's right hip, where he immediately saw a revolver. They really were police and not regular military, thought Kim. A revolver wasn't much of a weapon when compared to the North Korean AKMs. The rate and accuracy of fire was ridiculously one-sided in Kim's favor. Kim suspected, however, that when the shooting started, he and his men would see more formidable weapons, M16s and the like.

The policeman suddenly straightened and kicked the fallen tree in frustration at his inability to budge the huge log. He put his hands on his hips in disgust and looked around, surveying the area for anyone to help him. Kim could sense his men shrinking back behind their cover. Above all he did not want to be detected now before they could sneak up on the police station.

The policeman suddenly stopped his survey of the area and took his hands off his hips in a sign of alarm. Kim put the field glasses to his eyes quickly. The man was staring at the other end of the building which was being used for cover by Kim's men. He had seen something!

The policeman leaped over to his truck and reached for the microphone on his two-way radio. Kim whirled to the men beside him.

"Kill him now!" he shouted.

The men ran around the side of the building and set up to fire. The policeman keyed his microphone. The call sign died on his lips as automatic weapons' fire slammed into the truck, piercing the door and entering the man's back. The policeman slumped forward and lay bleeding and barely alive on the front seat. One of Kim's men ran forward a few paces and fired a grenade into the truck. The round neatly entered the front window and exploded in the driver's seat.

* * *

Lieutenant Eckman's head whirled around at the sound of the explosion as it rolled over Kwajalein Island.

"What the hell was that, Chief?" he asked.

Chief Ike Stevens chomped down hard on his unlit cigar and stared in the direction of the sound. Smoke, driven by the stiff wind, was visible above the trees.

"If I didn't know better, I'd think that was a grenade goin' off," he said almost under his breath. "I think we'd better check it out, sir."

Eckman rubbed his chin. "I think we should stick by the plan and get over to the Command Building and talk to the authorities. They have security forces here. Let them check it out."

Chief Stevens's eyes grew wide in disbelief and he began to argue in a low voice so that the other men couldn't hear him. He hadn't gotten far when they heard a shout in the distance. They turned and saw a man running toward them at top speed. He ran up to them and stopped only when Lieutenant Eckman held up his hand for him to halt.

"Hey! Who are you guys?" asked Ken Garrett.

"Identify yourself, please," said Eckman in a formal voice.

"Ken Garrett. I'm a radar engineer here on Kwajalein," replied Garrett. "Where are you guys from?"

"We're a landing party from the U.S.S. *Topeka* sent here to help Kwajalein reestablish contact with the United States," said Eckman.

"The *Topeka*?" said Garrett, his eyes searching the horizon in vain.

"It's a submarine," replied Eckman.

"You guys are navy? U.S. Navy?" asked Garrett excitedly.

Eckman nodded impatiently. "You have to show us where the Command Building is. We have to contact the authorities there."

"Forget that! Listen to me!" said Garrett. "There is a North Korean submarine in the lagoon. I think it's trapped there by a supply ship that sunk in Gea Pass during the typhoon." Garrett stopped for a second to gulp some air.

Eckman and Stevens exchanged quick, shocked glances. Eckman took a step closer to Garrett.

"You saw this submarine?" he asked the engineer.

"Well, no. But we saw divers who were near the sunken ship in Gea Pass," replied Garrett.

"How do you know they were North Korean?" asked Chief Stevens.

"They had North Korean flags painted on their air tanks," answered Garrett. "Mike and I—" Garrett turned to look at his friend and found that he was nowhere to be seen.

"Chief, get on the radio and tell the *Topeka*," ordered Eckman. "And tell them that it's an unconfirmed report. Also request further instructions."

"Aye, aye, sir," replied Stevens, and quickly complied with the order.

U.S.S. Topeka

Captain Worden scratched his head and couldn't contain the excitement building within him. The North Korean had gotten undetected into the lagoon! He walked quickly over to the charts of Kwajalein Lagoon, dragging his XO with him.

Lieutenant Commander Riley shook his head after a moment's thought. "Captain, I don't understand. If Gea Pass is blocked by a sunken ship, then why doesn't the North Korean go out by a different pass?"

"Well, take a look at the depths of some of these passes," replied Worden as he pointed to the chart in front of them. "South Pass is only nine meters, and he's got a solid reef from Kwajalein to Bigej Pass on the eastern side of the lagoon. Bigej Pass is only six to ten meters deep, and a Kilo needs about ten meters to stay submerged."

"But he could go north," protested Riley, "and use one of the passes near Roi-Namur." Riley searched the chart for a pass that would fit his theory. He straightened and pointed at the chart near the island of Roi-Namur. "They could take Mellu Pass. It's about twenty meters deep."

Captain Worden grimaced and shook his head with doubt. "It's fifty miles north of here, and he's probably thinking he has to stay submerged to avoid detection. He'd be bumping into uncharted coral heads all the way. It'll take him forever to get out of here."

"He might have orders to stay submerged while in the lagoon," mused Riley. "The best intelligence operation is getting good information and keeping your enemy from knowing you have it."

"We know that they're there, and we could give a pretty damn good guess at what information they have after the mission yesterday," said Worden. "I think if it was me, I'd at least survey the wreck in Gea Pass with some divers to see if it could be easily cleared. That's probably what our North Korean captain was doing when his men were spotted by the Kwajalein people." Then Worden nodded his head, showing his XO that he had come to a conclusion. "Gea is the deepest pass—it's periodically dredged for the large supply ships that go through it—and it would be the easiest for a sub to go through."

"So, we go to Gea," said Riley.

"Yep, but first we've got to tell the boss," replied Worden. "Raise the BRA 34 and let's get a message out to COMSUBPAC, CINCPAC, and the CNO. Tell them we're rendezvousing at Gea Pass with the North Korean sub. And request instructions."

"Track him, capture him, or—" began Riley.

"Or sink him," finished Worden.

CHAPTER ELEVEN

Murder

Kwajalein Island

Lieutenant Kim and his men turned east on Eighth Street from Marine Road and double-timed to the police station. A few curious people looked at them from a distance but had no idea what was actually going on, and had they seen a North Korean insignia, they wouldn't have believed it.

Kim had ordered the Democratic People's Republic flag, which had become increasingly known throughout the world in recent years due to the embryonic North Korean nuclear weapons program, concealed until after they had taken out the police headquarters and the provost marshal's office. Then they would flaunt their nation's flag in the faces of the defeated Americans.

The corner of Eighth and Lagoon Road came into view, and Kim knew he was near his first objective, the police station. A section of his group broke away and ran down the road toward Ninth Street and the provost marshal's building. Kim wanted to take both buildings at the same time.

The police headquarters seemed quiet, and the area outside the building was lined with police trucks similar to the one they had just attacked. Lieutenant Kim fervently hoped that the policeman they had killed hadn't gotten a message to the headquarters they now approached. Kim and half his remaining men took up positions across Lagoon Road on one side of the library while another group of men set up behind the police station on one side of the building adjacent to the police headquarters.

Kim waited impassively as he listened to his portable radio, which he had pressed to his right ear. After an impossibly long three minutes, Kim got the word from his group that was assigned to attack the provost marshal's office. One guttural word grunted over the radio link sent a thrill of anticipation through his body. Kim put his hand on the shoulder of one of his men who had a grenade launcher.

"Fire," he said calmly to his man.

The man squinted through the sight and squeezed the trigger. The grenade was launched with a sharp report and traveled through the air, leaving behind a thin trail of smoke which was quickly swept away by the stiff breeze. The grenade smashed through a front window and disappeared inside. A half second later the grenade detonated with a booming noise, sending glass and wood debris, followed immediately by flames, from all the first-floor windows.

Kim's men got ready, and Kim could see in his peripheral vision the AKM gunbarrels steadying up on the police building. Seconds later, the police officers who had gathered for a shift change began pouring from each doorway. Kim's men opened up on the unsuspecting officers and sent a brutal stream of lead into their ranks. The men grunted, screamed, and died, dropping straight down to lay in the parking lot and on the road.

A small group of men got behind some police vehicles and began to return fire, their pitiful revolvers no match for the North Korean AKMs. Kim's men shredded the vehicles that the policemen were using for cover, the hail of bullets sending pieces of metal and glass flying in all directions. A grenade slammed into a vehicle and exploded instantly, destroying the truck and all who were hiding behind it.

Kim ordered his men to cease fire. He could now hear the chattering of AKMs at the rear of the building. The firing slowed down until it tapered off altogether. His men at the rear of the building had completed their mission. A squad of men leaped to their feet and ran across the street and through the front door of the building. Kim could hear a few small bursts of gunfire within the building, then nothing. His men returned to the front doorway and waved to indicate all was clear.

Two quick explosions were heard a block away, and Kim and the men with him turned to look in that direction. Smoke driven by the wind worked its way through the palm trees. Kim knew that his men had taken the provost marshal's office. He looked over the bodies and counted the ones within his view. Assuming the same number in the rear of the station, Kim realized they had just taken out two thirds of the estimated thirty to forty security guards on the island. Kim gave a smile, then got on his radio to get an update from the group that was attacking the provost marshal's office. Kim gave another slight grin as he received the report he had hoped for. The attack on the second target had gone well, none of his men were injured, all U.S. Army personnel at that location were killed.

That was it, then, thought Kim. A few more details and they would have complete control of the island.

Lieutenant Eckman and Chief Stevens stared eastward down the runway toward the air terminal building. The island formed the flat underlayment for the ragged line of white buildings behind which palm trees bowed before the quick wind that came down from the lead-gray sky. The wind was blowing westward toward the landing party and driving smoke through the trees. Four explosions had occurred in less than two minutes. The first two were farther up the island, but the last two were at the other end of the runway.

"I think we ought to take a look at what's goin' on here, Mr. Eckman," said Chief Stevens as he rolled his unlit cigar around his lips.

"You just convinced me, Chief," replied Eckman.

Ken Garrett squinted toward the eastern end of the island. What was happening? Could the North Koreans have landed on the island? He turned and looked at the navy men and watched them move off up the runway to investigate the explosions. He counted them as they quickly jogged away from him. Fourteen men armed with M16s and shotguns, and backing them up was a nuclear attack submarine. Garrett knew he felt a lot better with the U.S. Navy around.

Garrett turned and started walking back the way he had come. Now where was his friend, Mike Sprague?

Lieutenant Kim and his group of men gave an appreciative eye toward the provost marshal's office. The building wasn't on fire, but all the windows were blown out and a host of corpses lay about. Kim stared at one of them. He was tall but skinny. He would have towered over Kim's five-foot, five-inch frame, but now he was dead. Just as I knew would happen, thought Kim. Take the fancy weapons away from the Americans and they were grossly inferior to his men.

He received a body count from one of his men and nodded with satisfaction. Fifteen servicemen had been killed. There weren't many U.S. Army personnel on the island even though Kwajalein was a U.S. Army command. The Liaison Bureau, North Korea's intelligence agency, had estimated thirty to forty army people, a number similar to the civilian police force. That made twenty-four policemen and fifteen army personnel disposed of, thirty-nine out of a total of perhaps sixty to eighty people who could make trouble for his landing party. Not a bad first twenty minutes.

Kim gathered his men around him. "Now that we have killed the soldiers, let us go after the senior commanders at the air terminal and at the control center. We will not immediately kill these officers, but we will take them hostage in order to keep others from resisting. They will be shot when we are ready to leave the island."

His men nodded in response and showed the enthusiasm that any commander could only hope for. The orders of his captain came to mind, and Kim remembered that Captain Hong had emphasized taking away the ability of the Americans to get into boats and attack his divers as they prepared to blow up the sunken ship in Gea Pass. Kim could see fuel tanks sticking up above the trees behind the provost marshal's building. He turned around in indecision. His men were ready to leave, and he didn't want to delay his capture of Kwajalein's senior brass, but he needed to blow up the fuel depot as well.

He quickly made a decision. Junior Lieutenant Park's group, which was headed for Kwajalein after disabling boats in the lagoon, would be ordered to blow the fuel depot. With the water tanks next to the fuel tanks, maybe Park could devise some way of poisoning the water supply as well. Kim brought his radio to his ear and contacted Park. He gave the junior officer the orders and broke contact. The tug and the two catamarans near Echo Pier would have to wait until later, he thought.

They heard a fire alarm go off, and Kim knew that the quiet island might soon be teeming with civilian onlookers and fire department personnel. Kim had a quick thought and ordered his men not to shoot bystanders as long as they weren't threatening his men. He didn't want the civilian populace hiding from his party. Right now, there was confusion in their minds, and Kim wanted to keep it that way. He divided his men into two groups. He headed for U.S. Army Headquarters in the air terminal building while his other group went to the Kwajalein Range Command Building.

"Mr. Eckman," puffed Chief Stevens, "I don't think it's a good idea to walk down the middle of the runway. A blind man could spot us ten miles away. We should get off to the side and circle around where those explosions occurred. You never know what we're goin' to run into."

Lieutenant Eckman nodded at the wisdom of the older man and headed for the southern edge of the runway. When all his men were off the concrete and among the scattered palm trees that lined the southern edge of the runway, he stopped and squinted at the buildings in the distance. He had thought they would be there in ten minutes or so, but they had been walking for more than that and they weren't even halfway there. Distances on these flat islands must be deceptive, and judging travel times between points was difficult.

Eckman took a deep breath and picked up the binoculars that dangled around his neck. He trained them on the white buildings at the eastern edge of the runway. He saw figures moving quickly toward the large building on the southern edge of the aircraft loading and unloading zone. Eckman shook his head. His group didn't have any maps of the island and he had no idea what the building represented. He took a second look through his binoculars and blinked a few times in disbelief.

The men now entering the building had automatic weapons.

Kwajalein Headquarters

Colonel Gary Descano listened to his civilian facilities manager give him the bad news.

"... so the power plant will be down for about a day. We've got three crews on it now, and the good news is that we have the spare parts, but it just takes a long time to fix this stuff," said the voice over the phone. "The Range Command and Range Ops buildings have auxiliary power from some generators we got going. So, it's not all bad news."

"Okay, what about communications?" asked Descano impatiently. He rubbed his forehead in anticipation of a migraine.

"We have emergency generators supplying power to the comm equipment, but the antennas have to be realigned," complained the facilities manager. "The damn typhoon ripped a hole in the radome and threw the antenna out of alignment. We also have some damage to the equipment itself which will only take about four hours to fix."

"Four hours?" replied Descano. "You've got to do better than that."

There was a hesitation on the line, long enough to convey to the army colonel that improving that time estimate would be tough.

"Okay, I'll kick a few butts," said the manager as if that would solve the problem.

"Well, do what you can," said Descano in a subdued voice. "At least the phones are still up."

"Not for long, Colonel," said the manager. "The phone system is on batteries right now and won't last but another few minutes."

"Oh, that's just great," said Descano sarcastically. "Listen, we've got a pile of engineers and technicians on this island. Put them to work.''

"All right, Colonel, I know a few guys we can grab in a hurry.''

"Good. Do it and keep me informed by radio if you have to,'' said Descano. "By the way, do you know what those explosions were a few minutes ago?''

"No, I don't. But the fire brigade is on their way. I'll let you know what they find out,'' answered the facilities manager.

"I'm going out there myself,'' said Descano. "One of them sounded pretty close by.''

Colonel Descano hung up the phone after bidding his manager good luck. His eyes wandered over to Master Sergeant Louise Mayfield's thick figure as she opened the safe on the opposite wall from his desk. She was busy at a time when no one else could get anything done due to the damage from the typhoon—except the power plant people and the fire brigade. Louise was always busy, and Descano knew better than to think that she did it just to show him how industrious she was. Louise got things done.

Descano leaned over to peer past Mayfield's head into the safe's interior. He could see the glint of the crome-plated .45 automatic his father had given him when he had gotten his commission seventeen years before. He had carried it with him to every duty station to which he had been assigned. This particular duty station had afforded him some time and a place off the western end of the island to do some target practice. He grunted to himself in amusement. He still wasn't as good a shot as his father, who had been a master sergeant in the army himself.

Descano heard quick footsteps in the hallway outside his office, and the explosions suddenly came to mind. He ran past his desk into the secretary's alcove with the intention of peering out the door to discover who was coming up the hallway. He feared that the people outside the door and the explosions were connected somehow, but his mind couldn't explore the possibilities before he had the answer. Five grim-faced Orientals exploded through the doorway and were in the alcove in a matter of seconds. The colonel immediately recognized the weapons they carried. A feeling of true helplessness ran through Descano. Either these men were terrorists or Kwajalein had been invaded by enemy forces.

"Who are you?" shouted Descano in a loud voice, then quickly thought that they wouldn't understand him.

One of the invaders jammed the rifle barrel into Descano's chest and acted as if he were going to shoot him. Descano's insides felt like they had turned to jelly. Another intruder jammed his rifle barrel into Descano's stomach, and together both North Koreans pushed him backward into his office. The colonel caught sight of Master Sergeant Mayfield out of the corner of his eye. She was holding something in both hands. Something large, something that reflected the light. His mouth dropped open in horror.

The thunderous report of Descano's .45 filled the office as Mayfield fired point-blank at the nearest North Korean's head. The large-caliber slug ripped through the man's skull, shattering his brain in a fraction of a second and dropping the sailor to the floor like a stone. Louise Mayfield brought the weapon down from its recoil and placed her gun hand in the palm of her other hand and aimed at the second North Korean. The second sailor swung his AKM around toward the master sergeant and had gotten within a few degrees of pointing accurately at Mayfield when she fired the second round. The bullet tore into the North Korean's chest and threw him backward to bounce off the wall and land in a heap on the floor.

The remaining three North Koreans set up behind Sergeant Mayfield's desk and opened fire with their weapons on full automatic. They sprayed the inside of Descano's office with lead, riddling the bodies of both Colonel Descano and Master Sergeant Mayfield. They both died quickly, slumping to the floor in pools of blood.

Lieutenant Eckman and Chief Stevens stopped in their tracks at the sound of automatic weapons' fire.

"I know what that is!" shouted Chief Stevens, and flung his cigar to the ground in fury. He whirled around to the sailors from the *Topeka*.

"Lock and load!" he ordered without waiting for orders from Eckman.

Eckman nodded in an absentminded fashion, agreeing with the chief's orders. He stared at the air terminal building, which was still quite a distance away. Something was going on here that he knew he wasn't going to like. He pulled out his sidearm and raised it into the air.

"All right men, double-time!" he ordered, and they all started off toward the building at a fast jog. Even at this pace, he thought, it will still take fifteen minutes to get there.

Lieutenant Kim was furious at the loss of two of his men. Kim had gathered his men and their hostages in the parking lot on the eastern side of the air terminal building, the side away from the approaching landing party from the *Topeka*. Kim's men were unaware of the presence of the U.S. Navy party, as the Americans were unaware of the presence of the North Korean party on the other side of the building. The navy men were still ten minutes away from the building when Kim got the news of the loss of his two sailors. He surveyed the group of ten men and women his men had gathered together as hostages. Half were U.S. Army personnel: four men, one woman.

He angrily shoved the army people away from the others and grabbed an AKM from one of his men. He cocked it and opened fire on the astounded army people. They scattered in all directions but died running for cover as Kim emptied one clip then jammed in another and emptied that one as well into the prostrate bodies of his victims. He threw the weapon at his man and screamed at the top of his lungs in fury.

"Beginning now, we will kill all army personnel!" he shouted at his men, who gaped at the berserk officer. "Do you understand? Kill them!"

His tirade over, Kim calmed down slightly and ordered his men to take the hostages with them to the Range Command Building, the center of antiballistic missile missions for the Kwajalein Missile Range.

Junior Lieutenant Park ran his rubber boat up on the beach near the fuel tanks which were his next objective. He ordered his men ashore and took cover behind some trucks that were parked in a sandy area between the fuel tanks and the beach. He watched a rare truck speed by on the road behind the fuel tanks toward the eastern half of the island. Other than the truck, there was no one around. Park suspected that the recent typhoon and what he thought was a loss of power had kept almost everyone indoors.

Park and his men studied the host of tanks before them. There were three large tanks in a row near the beach and several smaller tanks behind them. Park grabbed his man with the grenade launcher and ordered him to fire into the larger tanks. The man got set and jammed the butt of the grenade launcher firmly into his shoulder. He took aim and fired the first grenade at the rightmost tank. The grenade arched through the air and hit the tank dead center and detonated on contact.

The explosion ripped a hole in the side of the tank and detonated the fumes at the top of the fuel tank. The top of the tank peeled back with a frightening roar and shards of metal were sent flying in all directions. A large ball of flame flew upward, turning into a mushroom-shaped cloud reminiscent of a small hydrogen bomb. Flaming gasoline rushed out to spill on the ground, stopped in its furious advance only by the mound of dirt functioning as a safety bulkhead that formed a rectangle around each tank at ground level. Park gulped nervously and quickly ordered his men a safe distance away from the conflagration.

Park's man continued his work until the other two large fuel tanks were set ablaze. A siren suddenly split the air with its desperate sound. Park judged that the firehouse was nearby due to the siren's earsplitting noise, and he knew he would have firemen all over the area in a few minutes. The last orders he was given by Lieutenant Kim were to take hostages. The firemen would be his first hostages.

The bright yellow fire trucks rolled down the access road alongside the tank farm only a few minutes later. They screeched to a stop near the three burning tanks and the firemen jumped out to prepare to fight the fire. Park's men were waiting for them and leaped out from a wooded area near a building across the street. After Park's men fired a burst into the air to get their attention, the eight firemen fell into shocked submission.

Park and his men proceeded to destroy the rest of the fuel tanks with machine gun fire and grenades. The blaze generated heat that could be felt over half the island. Park and his men took in the spectacular sight and then moved down the road with their hostages toward their next objective, the water tanks. Kim had given Park orders to somehow poison the water supply on the island. Park counted the water tanks, fifteen in all. They were very large as well, not as tall as the fuel tanks but much greater in diameter. How could he poison so much water? Park scratched his head in thought.

The only way that came to mind was to destroy the water tanks as they had the fuel tanks. He gave the order to his man with the grenade launcher. The man nodded with a short smile and put the stock of the grenade launcher into his shoulder in preparation to launch a grenade at the nearest water tank.

Park heard a thud and the involuntary gurgle of a man dying. Before Park's mind could register what was happening, he was covered with blood, brain matter, and skull fragments. The man with the grenade launcher, who was standing next to Park, had just had his head nearly taken off by an unseen, unheard assailant. Park hit the ground next to the bloody body of his man and choked out some frantic orders for his remaining men to take cover. Park crawled behind a parked car near one of the water tanks with one thought on his mind.

The Americans were beginning to fight back.

CHAPTER TWELVE

Intel Harvest

Western Kwajalein Island

Ken Garrett glanced over at his pudgy friend, Mike Sprague.

"So, where the hell were you when I was talking to those navy guys?" asked Garrett.

Sprague shrugged. "I figured if they saw me with this rifle, they might shoot and ask questions later."

Garrett screwed up his face to say that he didn't believe him. An explosion on the other side of the island filled the air with distant noise. They both stood and stared at the rising fireball, which was suddenly bent over by the force of the strong breeze.

"What the hell is happening on this island?" asked Garrett in frustration. He suddenly gave Sprague a piercing look. "You don't suppose the North Koreans . . ."

Sprague gritted his teeth and nodded solemnly. "It would make sense. They would want to keep us from interfering with them blowing up that sunken supply ship and getting out of here."

"Oh, God. Nancy," mumbled Garrett under his breath. He had to get to her to make sure she was all right. She was probably still in his trailer, on the eastern tip of the island. He was about as far away from her as he could get and still be on the same island.

Sprague gave his friend a sympathetic glance and nodded

in agreement. "Okay, but let's give our North Korean friends a wide berth."

Garrett nodded quickly and gave his friend a quick, tense smile. They both started eastward on Lagoon Road, which led past the Kwajalein Range Command Building. When they were within a quarter of a mile of the Command Building, they spotted a group of what looked like soldiers marching down the road. They were in two groups, and there were some other people with them. Ken Garrett had the binoculars and raised them to his eyes. He let his breath out in disbelief.

"North Koreans! A lot of them!" he said in a tense voice. He lowered the glasses and gave Sprague a shocked look. "And they've got hostages!"

Sprague snatched the glasses away from Garrett and stared through them for a long minute. Sprague grimaced. "Landing party from the sub." He glanced at Garrett. "Looks like you were right."

They both took cover behind the few palm trees that lined the road. They cautiously worked their way forward, the last fifty feet flat on their stomachs. The North Koreans forced the captured residents to sit down in the narrow parking lot in front of the Range Command Building. The bulk of the North Korean party quickly entered the building.

Garrett grabbed Sprague's arm to get his attention. "Why are they over here?" he asked in a whisper. Sprague shrugged. Garrett asked another question. "Where are those navy guys?" Sprague shook his head this time.

Sprague leaned and put his mouth next to Garrett's ear. "Do you know any of those people who have been captured?" he asked in a hoarse whisper.

Garrett surveyed the fifteen hapless American civilians who sat in desperation on the hot asphalt of the parking lot. "I think some of them are maintenance people, but the rest I don't know."

"Any of them engineers who might be valuable to the North Koreans?" asked Sprague.

Garrett gaped at him in surprise.

* * *

Lieutenant Kim and his men had the few U.S. Army people in the Range Command Building cornered in the first-floor stairwell. He and his party had completely surprised them, and the Americans, having no weapons, surrendered immediately. This was going well, thought Kim, except for the two men he had lost in the air terminal building. He fought down the rage that leaped up within him. He would vent his wrath on the Americans later. Now he had to concentrate on taking this building.

Nancy Garrett sat reading a top secret document which summarized the PENAIDS design parameters for the just completed mission. The lights flickered quickly but stayed on this time. The power had been going on and off all morning. She looked over at Nate Jackson, who shook his head in semidisgust. Her "buddy" in the top secret area was also her boss, and he was studying mission results. Nancy was reviewing the design parameters for any improvement she might make to increase the reentry vehicle penetration probability. Now the lights seemed steady, and she dove into the technical subject with enthusiasm. Her design had just barely defeated her husband's radar, and she wanted to see where the parameter thresholds were, which of them were the values that were critical to penetration performance.

With nothing to do at Ken's trailer, Nancy had decided to go to work for a while. After a few hours, she would return to the trailer. Maybe then Ken would be back from searching after his boat, she thought. He had named it *The Lady N.* It was obviously named after her. She had a sudden, sinking feeling, then relaxed. His mother's name was Rita.

A rapid pulsing sound was heard through the thick, locked door.

"What was that?" asked Jackson. Nancy shrugged her shoulders in puzzlement. The sound was heard again, this time bringing Jackson out of his chair.

"If I didn't know better, I'd swear that was an automatic weapon," said Jackson in an incredulous tone.

What could be happening? Nancy's thoughts ran the gamut of the ridiculous to the deadly serious. Someone playing a practical joke? Or had a riot broken out, and the police were trying to quell it? She quickly shook her head. Both were ridiculous.

The quiet of the top secret chamber suddenly was shattered by a loud pounding on the door. Both Jackson and Nancy Garrett jumped with nervousness. The pounding started again and seemed more insistent.

"I guess we'd better open it," said Jackson. Nancy's heart seemed to pound against the walls of her chest. She had a very bad feeling about who was on the other side of the door.

"Nate," she said. He turned to look at her. "Don't," she implored simply.

He opened his hands in frustration. "Maybe they want to evacuate the building." He turned back toward the door and placed his hand on the doorknob. Nancy instinctively retreated until she had her back to a filing cabinet.

Jackson turned the doorknob, but the door around where his hand was seemed to explode, sending pieces of wood and the lock mechanism flying about the room. Jackson yelled with pain and staggered backward, gripping his right hand with his left. The shattered door flew open and two North Korean sailors stood in the doorway and sprayed the room with gunfire. Jackson cringed at the foot of the front wall next to the doorway, and Nancy leaped into a corner and desperately rolled herself up into a ball. They both miraculously escaped the gun blast from the two intruders.

The two men shouted something in a language neither could understand. When they remained where they were, shaking with fear, the North Koreans ran over and yanked them to their feet. Jackson and Nancy were shoved out the door with the invaders continually shouting incomprehensible phrases at the top of their lungs.

Kim stood with his hands on his hips as he surveyed the defeated Americans who sat before him in the parking lot. A surge of satisfaction ran through him. These Americans weren't so invincible after all, he thought. His father had proven that by killing an American officer in the DMZ twenty years ago, and he was proving that now on Kwajalein. How proud his father would be of him when he returned! He would be the cause of a great burst of patriotism in his country which was greatly needed since the

Great Leader died a few years ago. His country hadn't been the same since that awful event. His countrymen needed a boost to their morale, and he would be the one to give it to them.

A subordinate came up to him. "The buildings in this area are clear, sir. The last of the hostages are being brought out now."

Kim nodded, a small smile beginning on his lips. Two of his men came out of the front door driving a man and a woman in front of them. Kim's men brutally knocked them to the ground with rifle butts in the middle of their backs.

Ken Garrett's heart went into his throat. It was Nancy! He gagged with desperation at the thought of what they might do to her. Without knowing what he was doing, Ken Garrett slowly stood up from behind the foliage across the road from the Range Command Building. Sprague got up to his knees and dragged Garrett back down behind their cover.

"Are you nuts? They'll shoot you in a second!" hissed Sprague into Garrett's ear.

"They've got Nancy!" said Garrett in a plaintive tone.

"I know. I know," replied Sprague, and held his head in his hands. He could hear Garrett grinding his teeth. He grabbed his friend by the shoulders. "Listen! You're not going to do Nancy any good if you crap out on me. Understand?"

Garrett took a deep breath, then nodded. His insides felt like concrete.

After a minute, Garrett spoke in a wavering voice. "You asked if they had any engineers that could be valuable to the North Koreans. Well, Nancy's one of them."

"I know. I know," replied Sprague, and put his head back into his hands.

"Comrade Lieutenant," said a voice at Kim's elbow. The North Korean officer turned and looked at the man standing next to him. It was one of the technical people who had been included on board the sub to evaluate the stolen American RV. Moon Si-Bok was a civilian but had asked to be included in the landing party to gather any data he could on the American missile defense system. Kim had refused him, but Captain Hong had overruled the lieutenant. Just the mere presence of Moon represented a defeat for Kim. Kim gave him a disdainful look and said nothing.

"Look at this," said Moon, and held up a document that had a red cover. Moon read the title of the document, simultaneously translating into Korean. "Theater Ballistic Missile System Vulnerabilities to Various Penetration Aids."

Kim's eyes narrowed at Moon. The man was clearly excited.

"Do you see what this document represents?" asked Moon. He didn't wait for Kim to reply. "This tells how to defeat the missile defense system in South Korea!"

Kim slowly realized just how important this little man was who stood next to him. Moon could recognize things that, if captured by Kim, would be an intelligence bonanza to his country and a disaster to the Americans. How great a hero would Kim be if he brought back the means to defeat the missile system that the United States had recently deployed to protect North Korea's sworn enemies in the South? Kim began to smile once again at the thought of the great defeat he would hand the United States.

"You will safeguard this document with your life," said Kim as he put his hand on the smaller man's shoulder.

"Lieutenant, you don't understand," said Moon. "In the building behind us are *hundreds* of documents just like this! Documents on the design of penetration aids, on the design of reentry vehicles, radar signal processing software . . ." Moon went on and on, and Kim realized that he had hit an intelligence gold mine. Maybe fighting the enemy meant more than combat, more than killing, more than destruction of their facilities, thought Kim. Here was a way to truly damage the United States and render useless a system that the United States had labored over for decades and had spent billions to achieve.

"Comrade Moon, take ten men and gather up the most valuable of these documents," said Kim. "We will steal a truck and load the documents into it to get them back to the submarine.'' Moon nodded excitedly and ran off to carry out the orders.

Nancy Garrett caught a glimpse of the documents the invaders were taking out of the building. They all had red covers, meaning they were all classified. Nancy groaned to herself. The documents in the Command Building would be the most damaging ones on the island when in the hands of an enemy. Whoever these people were—she suspected that they were North Korean—they would reap the benefits of decades of work American engineers had done in the antimissile area.

Kim's radio crackled into life. He yanked it off his belt and acknowledged the call. It was Junior Lieutenant Park. One of his men had been killed by a sniper before he'd had the chance to destroy the water tanks. Rage boiled up in Kim but he forced it down. The young Park would need to know what to do next. He ordered Park to immediately join him down at the Command Building.

The sun started to come out from behind the clouds as the remnants of the typhoon began to slowly break up. The bright sun, usually the reason for an increase in morale on the island, brought no solace to the captured Americans even as the powerful rays washed over the nearby buildings and began to heat up the pavement in the parking lot.

Nancy Garrett dared a look around to see if there was any avenue of escape. She guessed that there were about twenty of the invaders in a ring that completely encircled the terrified Americans who sat or lay in the parking lot. Her back hurt from the blow one of the intruders had given her, and her insides quivered with fear. Who were these people? What did they want? Where were the police and the army? Why didn't they rescue them?

A glint of reflected light flickered in her peripheral vision. She turned slightly and stared across the road. Someone was moving in the brush.

''For God's sake,'' whispered Sprague. ''Stay still!''

Garrett obeyed his friend and trained his field glasses on the group of people in the parking lot. He lined up on Nancy, who was staring in his direction. He pulled the glasses away from his face to look at her without benefit of magnification.

"Don't look straight at me," he mumbled under his breath. He raised the glasses to his eyes again and saw her face change from one of puzzlement to recognition.

"She knows I'm here," he said with some relief.

Nancy's face changed from recognition to supplication, then rapidly to defiance. She rotated her head to look over the North Koreans, then stared back at him with the righteous look he had seen so many times before. Her meaning was crystal clear. *How are you going to call the police this time?*

The incident in New York City roared through his mind. Two men beating up a third, Nancy urging him to help the victim, he hesitating, she attempting to jump out of the car to help the unfortunate man herself, with him dragging her back into the car. He had jammed the car into gear and had sped away. Her words had cut into him: If you didn't want to help him, then why did you stop me? *I* would have done *something*. She had called him a wimp; he had called her a hopelessly naive child whose view of the world was taken from action-adventure movies.

When he and Nancy had returned to the scene with the police, the man was dead, his head beaten savagely with some blunt instrument. The accusation in Nancy's eyes had been clear and unrelenting. Just as it was now.

Garrett slumped back and exhaled with frustration. Mike Sprague looked at him with concern.

"What's the matter?" he asked. "What's happened?"

Garrett waved his hand in an attempt to dismiss his friend's concern. "Nothing. Nothing's happened." He grimaced at Sprague. "Maybe that's the problem," he added cryptically.

The idea struck Kim as he was carefully looking over his prisoners. If he could take documents, then why not take the people as well? How many more technical secrets were in the heads of the people in front of him? His countrymen had various well-honed methods of loosening people's tongues and exacting the most enthusiastic cooperation. Yes, he thought excitedly, the intelligence bonanza might well be in the people in addition to the documents.

Moon arrived at Kim's side to tell him that the documents were loaded in a truck. They had found the keys and had made sure that it could be started. Kim nodded and smiled.

"Now, Comrade Moon, you will find out if these people are here with us," said Kim as he pointed to the signature sheet on the top secret document he still held.

Moon gave him a puzzled look, then a slow smile began on his lips as he realized what Kim had in mind. He nodded quickly and stepped in front of the hostages.

"Americans, attention," said Moon in broken English. Some of the prisoners seemed startled that one of the invaders was addressing them in English.

"I will call name. You come," he said. Moon began calling names, mangling the pronunciation, from the signature list on the document he had with him. Kim, meanwhile, had some of his men run to the truck and get more of the documents.

Moon called name after name. No one stirred. Moon's voice grew louder and louder. Kim's patience hit its limit. He grabbed Moon by the arm.

"Check their badges," he growled to the smaller man. Kim pointed to the small rectangles of plastic that every one of the Americans were wearing.

Moon nodded quickly and walked among the prisoners while shuffling through the documents. He came up to Nate Jackson and bobbed up and down excitedly as he read Jackson's badge. Moon motioned to two guards and they quickly grabbed Jackson and dragged him to his feet. Jackson protested until one of the intruders punched him in the face. All the Americans cringed at the brutal act and winced in sympathy at the streak of blood on Jackson's chin.

Nancy was next in line. Moon peered at her badge and then at one of the top secret documents he had with him, one that she had written a few months ago while she was putting the finishing touches on the PENAIDS design. Her heart sank as the invaders roughly dragged her to her feet and dropped her next to Nate Jackson. What was in store for her if these people were successful in kidnapping her?

She knew but didn't want to face it. She and the others would be tortured for the missile secrets they all had in their heads.

Desperation welled up in Nancy. She had to get rescued! She immediately thought of her husband lurking in the brush on the other side of the road. No help from that quarter, she thought savagely. Just like in New York. Her anxiety hit a peak, then diminished as the North Koreans busied themselves with the preparations for moving out. They appeared to be waiting for someone. Maybe, she thought, if I can't save myself, I can save someone else.

Moon walked by looking over the select group of five American engineers he had separated from the rest of the prisoners. He had a smile of satisfaction on his face. Nancy raised her hand and caught his attention. He walked over with a puzzled look on his face.

"That man," said Nancy, pointing to Nate Jackson, who was looking the other way. "He doesn't know anything."

Moon scratched his head and pointed at Jackson as well with his puzzled expression growing deeper. He obviously didn't understand.

"Let him go," implored Nancy. "He just signed the document but doesn't know what it all means."

"Who write this?" asked Moon as he held up a document.

"Me. I did," replied Nancy. "Jackson doesn't know what's in it."

"Jackson not know?" asked Moon.

Nancy nodded furiously. She was finally getting through. "Jackson knows nothing. After all, he's only my boss."

"Jackson is boss?" asked Moon as his eyes widened.

Oh, no, thought Nancy. I've blown it.

"Ah, boss knows everyt'ing. Good," said Moon, and walked away with an even bigger smile on his face than before.

Nancy exhaled in disgust. She should have known that the North Koreans think that managers know every detail of an organization and the work within it. In the aerospace business, it was rarely true, especially in America.

* * *

Junior Lieutenant Park had his men spread out on either side of Lagoon Road as they moved slowly west toward the Range Command Building. In addition he had two scouting parties of two men each far in front of his men. He knew he was being very cautious, but he didn't want to lose more of his men to the sniper who had blown the brains out of one of his best men. If he lost any other men, Lieutenant Kim would be extremely angry with him when they got back. Park didn't need to have Lieutenant Kim as an enemy.

The only hostages he had taken at this point were the firefighters. Apparently the island's inhabitants had caught on to the situation and were hiding from his men. Park hoped that Kim would feel he had taken enough hostages. Park gave a nervous look around. Where was the sniper?

Petty Officers Song Kyung Won and Pang Ju-Rha picked their way along the southern side of Lagoon Road. They approached the helicopter hangar, which was about halfway between the air terminal building and the Range Command Building, and peered inside, but it was deserted. They didn't check every room in the building but moved past it to an area that was wide open and devoid of any cover. No trees, no buildings, no vehicles to hide behind. Song and Pang glanced quickly about them, paying close attention to the rooftops of the buildings that stood on the opposite side of the road. They looked back at the main body of the group led by Park. It was barely in sight among the buildings and the trees. Park was moving slowly since he had lost his first man.

Song's gaze swept over the runway and settled on the brush next to the runway farther down the road. Someone was moving in the foliage. He thought quickly. If Lieutenant Kim's men were across the road in the Command Building, then who was this in the brush? He motioned to Pang to crouch down as they approached the brush. There was a short tower with some antennas on it and a small building in between the two North Koreans and the brush. Song made a decision to set up on one side of the building for cover as they took a look at who was there.

Minutes later, Song and Pang got up to the northern side of the structure facing the road and slid along the shelter's wall to view the brush on the other side. They both peered around the corner and saw the exposed sides of two Americans as they lay facing the Command Building across the road. One of the Americans had a rifle pointed through the bushes.

Song whispered to Pang to get set to open fire. They both cocked their weapons and aimed carefully at the Americans. Song heard a thud, then a rustle, as Pang slid to the ground. Song looked around puzzled. Pang was lying at his feet with a large hole in the crown of his head. The smear of red that covered the wall of the building next to him hung ominously in his peripheral vision.

Song opened his mouth in surprise and raised his eyes toward the rooftops. He had heard nothing! The second bullet flew into Song's open mouth, shattering the back of his throat and ripping apart his medulla oblongata, causing instant death.

CHAPTER THIRTEEN

Orders

Range Operations Building

Jack Pearson rolled his thin frame to his left to quickly get the rifle out of view. He waited thirty seconds, then peered over the rooftop toward the two North Koreans he had just shot moments before. The two sailors were lying still in pools of blood next to the small building across the road. Pearson cautiously looked about, noting the positions of the North Koreans around the Kwajalein Range Command Building. They hadn't moved at all, and they didn't seem to know that he had just killed two of their number.

Pearson slid the rifle up next to his chin, his gray mustache tickling the wooden stock, and peered through the telescopic sight. The two Americans barely hidden in the brush next to the equipment shelter across the road hadn't moved either. Pearson let out his breath in a rush. His own position was still hidden from everyone else in the area. Pearson was on the roof of the Range Operations Building, which was adjacent to the Command Building. He had just had a nervous moment when the North Koreans had searched the building for Americans. Fortunately they hadn't searched the roof well at all. He felt a surge of satisfaction. He had personally taken out three of the invaders. Maybe it was an opening payback for the murder of his friend.

Chief Warrant Officer Dave Burgess had been in the provost marshal's office when the North Koreans struck. Burgess hadn't had much of a chance. He had been shot in the back of the head. Pearson had seen the North Koreans and had stayed out of sight, watching in horror as the North Koreans shot the occupants of the provost marshal's building and destroyed the vehicles that were parked around it. Pearson waited helplessly until the North Koreans were gone and then entered the building to count the bodies and find the corpse of his friend.

Pearson looked over his rifle and rubbed the barrel as if it were a lover. Jack Pearson and Dave Burgess had been snipers for the U.S. Army, and even though both of them, now in their fifties, had retired from that particular line of service, Burgess had somehow kept a 7.62-millimeter M21 sniping rifle complete with silencer. He had told Pearson that he had gone out to the small arms range at the western tip of Kwajalein Island several times to keep up his accuracy. And now he was dead, thought Pearson.

Pearson looked at the silencer that nearly doubled the barrel length and felt the hard metal cylinder. It was quite warm to the touch. A few more quick shots and it could be too hot to touch. He passed a hand over his nearly bald head and felt the heat from the tropical sun that seared him. I should have a hat, he thought aimlessly. So, I'll get some sunburn, and these people down below will lose their lives. Pearson grimaced. Not if I can help it, he resolved grimly.

He peered over the edge of the roof and through the tops of several palm trees toward the Command Building, and counted the North Koreans who were guarding the Americans in the parking lot. He could easily take out the five guards, but he worried about the lives of the rest of the hostages. They could run, but the automatic weapons of the remaining North Koreans would cut them down in an instant. He studied the movements of the North Koreans intently. They had loaded some documents into a pickup truck and a couple of Jeep Cherokees, and had separated some of the hostages from the larger group. All ominous signs. The North Koreans were preparing to leave, and the question of what the intruders would do with the hostages was uppermost in his mind.

Pearson caught a glimpse of movement out of the corner

of his eye. He slid his tall, thin frame across the roof and stared to his left. More North Koreans were coming down Lagoon Road headed toward the Range Command Building to join up with the group that was already there. Pearson bit his lower lip and cursed himself. He should have known that the group of North Koreans near the water tanks would meet up with the larger group here.

Pearson had killed one of them who was about to launch a grenade at the water tanks, then, worried about detection, had moved quickly away as all good snipers do. He had moved down toward the larger group at the Command Building. Now that he had killed the two North Koreans who were the advance party for the larger group, he should move to a new spot. He bit his lip again. He hadn't been spotted yet, and this was a good vantage point to see what was going on. He even had palm trees to hide his outline whenever he peered over the roof edge. He decided to stay for the moment.

Pearson quickly counted the second party and saw that there were nine North Koreans driving five Americans along. They appeared to be firefighters, judging by the yellow uniforms they wore. So, the damn North Koreans were going to let the island burn. And what would they do to the hostages?

He glanced over at the attaché case–size satellite communications equipment he had brought with him to the island. Pearson had sent a message to his superiors at Langley when he had assessed the situation. He could imagine the consternation with which his message was received. He couldn't envision a more outrageous invasion by the audacious North Koreans. He knew what the North Koreans were after, and their taking of the documents and the separation of the hostages were troubling indeed. What was in the documents? Details of the U.S. missile defense system?

Why were the hostages separated? Were the remaining Americans to be executed?

Ken Garrett strained his eyes to get sight of Nancy. He stirred to get a better view and got a quick restraining arm from Mike Sprague. His friend glowered at him with an obvious, unspoken message. Don't move. Garrett put his mouth next to Sprague's ear.

"I can't see Nancy," he whispered.

Sprague's face mirrored the conflict within him. He finally relented and nodded reluctantly. They slowly moved through the brush toward the small building at the edge of the road that was used to house the Tactical Air Navigation, or TACAN, equipment. Sprague, who was leading the way, suddenly stopped and pointed. Garrett looked over his shoulder and saw the smashed head of one of the North Koreans, obviously killed by someone nearby.

"It looks like we have an ally somewhere," said Sprague in a hoarse whisper. Garrett took a quick look around and gave a half sigh of relief. Maybe the authorities were gathering for a counterattack on the invaders.

Maybe they would be rescued.

Park studied the road and the buildings on either side of it as they moved slowly down Lagoon Road. All seemed still, but Park was extremely nervous. He had lost one man to the mysterious sniper, and he was in fear of losing another as his party slowly moved toward Lieutenant Kim's group at the Kwajalein Range Command Building. He had also lost his one and only grenade launcher. It had fallen under the man who had been killed by the sniper, and because the body was out in the open, Park had left the area without it. He decided that he would feel much better when the two groups of North Koreans joined up once again.

To his left was the vast flat expanse of the runway, and to his right was a small flat area that led up to some small buildings which seemed to be the communications center of the island, judging by the round shape of a white antenna radome that rose behind the buildings. Park could see that the storm had ripped a hole in the radome, and he could barely make out the figure of a workman on the inside of the structure attending to the antenna.

Park at first thought that his men should shoot him just in case he was the sniper, but after looking at him for a few moments through his binoculars, Park decided that the workman didn't know that Park's party even existed. Park decided against splitting his party just to kill the workman. That might embolden the sniper.

Park shifted his attention to the small building coming up on his right, beyond which was the Range Command Building and Lieutenant Kim. His advance party, which he had sent down Lagoon Road, had already checked out these buildings, but Park dispatched two men to make a circuit around the buildings just to make sure. His men came back after a few minutes and pronounced that all was quiet there. Park nodded to himself. His men had checked out the Range Operations Building twice, and it seemed unoccupied. However, they hadn't searched the building exhaustively, so there could still be someone hiding inside.

Or there could be someone on the roof, thought Park nervously. He licked his lips and let his eyes play over the edge of the roof. A perfect place for a sniper. He couldn't take the time to let his men check out the roof—Kim had wanted him to join up quickly. Apparently Kim was getting ready to leave.

Park swung his binoculars around and scoured the road ahead for any Americans. There was a small structure to the left side of the road up ahead next to a radio antenna tower. What he saw made his mouth drop open with surprise.

There were two bodies between the building and the road. They both were in North Korean uniforms.

Lieutenant Kim gazed at the hostages who remained in the parking lot in front of the Command Building. They were useless to him. He scowled at them, and they cowered in fear before him. They weren't worth bothering with. He made a quick decision. When they were about to leave, he would give the orders to have them killed. These people in front of him weren't able to play the game; they weren't able to keep up to the superior Korean abilities. They were unfit to live.

There was a stir at one edge of the parking lot. It was Park's group arriving from the eastern end of the island. Junior Lieutenant Park dutifully approached Kim and reported his status.

"We have five hostages," said Park. "But we have lost three men to a sniper, sir."

Rage boiled in Kim. The Americans were still resisting. A total of five of his precious men had been killed by these defeated Americans. These people were incredibly stupid—they didn't know when they were defeated.

"Take five of the hostages and shoot them in plain sight," ordered Kim with a shaking voice.

Park's eyes narrowed in surprise at the order, but he didn't hesitate. Park's men grabbed the nearest five men and shoved them out into a clear area of the parking lot. They took several steps backward and took aim at the puzzled Americans. The bursts of gunfire cut the air with ear-shattering noise and made the remaining hostages jump.

Both Garrett and Sprague jumped involuntarily as the automatic weapons' sounds shattered their nerves. Garrett stuck his head above the brush and gaped at the falling bodies in the parking lot next to the road.

"Oh, God—" he began. Sprague grabbed him and yanked him roughly to the ground.

"You idiot!" whispered Sprague. "Do you want to join them?" He jerked his thumb over his shoulder at the hostages.

"Nancy!" said Garrett. "Was she one of them?"

Sprague put his hand over Garrett's mouth. "Goddamn it! Shut up!" he said through grinding teeth. When Garrett calmed down a bit, Sprague slowly removed his hand. He gave a slow look around and determined that no one had heard his excitable friend. Sprague couldn't blame Garrett. If he had a wife like Nancy Garrett, he'd be upset too.

"They were all men," replied Sprague. He tried to put enough certainty in his voice so that his friend would calm down and not get both of them killed.

"Are you sure?" asked Garrett breathlessly.

"Yes, I saw them when they were shoved away from the others," said Sprague. The truth was that he had seen three of the five who were murdered. He fervently hoped that Nancy Garrett wasn't one of the other two.

"I have to rescue Nancy," said Garrett in a whisper. Sprague could hear the desperation behind the words.

"I know. I know," replied Sprague in a sympathetic way.

"You don't understand. *I have to!*" said Garrett in a passionate voice.

Sprague gave him a sharp look of surprise. Something else was driving him, he thought. This wasn't the normal male drive to protect women in general, a wife in particular. It was something else, something driving him to a near panic.

Garrett launched into a brief account of the incident in New York City, to Sprague's increasing compassion for his friend. When Garrett was done, Sprague shook his head in puzzlement.

"But they might have had guns," said Sprague.

"It didn't matter. Nothing mattered," said Garrett in a depressed voice. "If I don't do something now, she'll never forgive me."

Sprague rolled his eyes around. "Look, screw all that stuff about what happened in New York. The most important thing is to keep Nancy alive. We don't want to do anything that'll get her killed."

Garrett lowered his eyes and stared at the ground. He eventually nodded in agreement. A moment later, he lifted his gaze and stared Sprague in the eye.

"When we were at the boat, you offered me a gun," said Garrett.

Sprague instinctively touched the butt of the automatic which was jammed in his belt.

"I'll take it now," said Garrett.

Lieutenant Eckman turned to Chief Stevens in frustration. "More gunfire, Chief!" he said in an almost plaintive tone.

Stevens shook his head. "We seem to be two steps behind whoever is doing this."

"It's got to be the North Koreans," said Eckman. He fingered his automatic nervously. He desperately wanted to stop the killing that he and his landing party had seen at the air terminal building and at the provost marshal's office. Eckman's insides shivered with fear. Real gunfire, real killing. And the *Topeka* headed for Gea Pass. There would be no help from them. It was only his party that could help the people on Kwajalein. Eckman clamped his teeth together in a grimace. Whatever happened, he would do his duty. He raised his sidearm in the air to get everyone's attention.

"All right, men," he said in a loud voice. "Double-time!" Eckman turned and ran down Lagoon Road at a fast pace.

Jack Pearson groaned as he saw the five hostages drop quickly to the ground. He made an instant decision. If the North Koreans set up to murder more Americans, he would open fire. He couldn't hope to get all of them before they got him. They would find him eventually and kill him, but he decided that there were worse ways to die. At least I'll take a few of the bastards with me, Pearson thought grimly.

He got set in a comfortable position and peered through the scope to set the elevation of the rifle for the most accurate shot he could get. He heard a soft beeping sound and whirled around to see that his satellite communication equipment was receiving a message. He gave the North Koreans one last look in indecision, then reluctantly slid over to open up the flip top of the satellite transceiver. The liquid crystal display announced that a message had been received by the satellite equipment. Pearson typed in the commands to unscramble the message using the crypto gear integral with the satellite equipment. After a few seconds, the decoded message was displayed.

Pearson read quickly, then dropped his hands in dismay. His CIA superiors had gotten his message and told him that certain American personnel on the island must not fall into North Korean hands. He read on and groaned quietly at the incredible orders. Pearson hit the Page Down button on the small keyboard and paged through the three pictures and descriptions of the important Americans on the island.

The separated hostages! Pearson slid hurriedly over to the edge of the roof facing the side of the Command Building. A number of American prisoners had been shoved into vehicles for transport to a destination known only to the North Koreans. Pyongyang maybe, thought Pearson.

He looked through the scope and focused on the hostages

in the truck. Auburn hair caught his eye and he settled in to study the stunningly beautiful woman in his telescope. He knew who she was instantly. He had traveled to Kwajalein with her on the plane, and as most men do, he had surveyed all the women in view and decided that she was the best-looking woman there.

She was also number one on the list he had just received. Her name was Nancy Garrett.

CHAPTER FOURTEEN

Charge

Lieutenant Kim stood directly in front of Junior Lieutenant Park.

"You and I are somewhat alike," said Kim.

Park was flattered. Kim was easily the most belligerent officer on the *Admiral Yi* when it came to the Americans. Kim fit the ideal of a North Korean officer as Park saw it, and Park never tried to conceal his admiration and even his fear of the bellicose lieutenant.

"Therefore, I will give you a most important assignment," said Kim.

Park's chest swelled with pride. His career was assured.

"I will take the hostages in the trucks and the documents back to our boats, and you and your men will cover my movement," said Kim. "You understand how important these hostages and the documents are, don't you?"

"Yes, Comrade Lieutenant," replied Park enthusiastically. "Uh, the rest of the hostages?"

"Shoot them," replied Kim, and stared at his subordinate to discover any hint of reluctance on his part. Any flicker of the eyes, any lessening of the steel in his face, would reflect cowardice. Park knew and returned the stare.

"Do you understand your orders, Comrade?" asked Kim through clenched teeth.

"Yes, Comrade Lieutenant," replied Park.

Kim lowered his stare and nodded with satisfaction.

"The sniper, sir," said Park. "Please be careful."

Kim looked at Park curiously. Something bordering on affection from one of his men? It was unexpected, but pleasant.

"Maybe we can take care of the sniper right now," said Kim with a hint of a smile.

Jack Pearson stared at Nancy Garrett through the scope on his rifle. Add it up, he thought. The North Koreans had documents in the vehicles along with five hostages, Nancy Garrett included. It could only mean that they were being kidnapped to be brought back to North Korea. They would be tortured for the secrets they all had in their heads regarding the U.S. Theater Ballistic Missile Defense system. Should the North Koreans get that information, the fate of South Korea would be tenuous indeed. Would the North become confident because of the knowledge gained here on this island and invade the South? How many would die because of the information in the heads of the hostages in the truck?

Pearson groaned. And Nancy Garrett was the most valuable of the bunch.

He forced himself to concentrate on the mission at hand. His job was to prevent the hostages from being taken back to North Korea. If they couldn't be rescued, then he had to kill them. He knew all the arguments for completing his mission, but his heart stood squarely in the way. He mentally shoved the mission and his feelings aside and tried to think of the mechanics of being a sniper.

In the telescopic sight mounted on the top of his rifle, he could see two lines. These two lines, called stadia, represented points about thirty inches apart at one thousand yards when the variable magnification was set to ×3. Thirty inches is about the distance between the top of someone's head and his waist. Pearson lined the two stadia up on a North Korean who was standing next to the truck with the hostages in it. The two lines were beyond the Korean's head and waist. Pearson rotated the magnification ring to lower the magnification until the two lines rested in their proper places. This automatically set the correct elevation for an accurate shot.

Pearson flipped off the safety and shifted the rifle around

to view Nancy Garrett, who was only a few feet from the North Korean guard. He placed the crosshairs on her right temple. He took a breath then slowly exhaled.

Kim shouted to one of his underlings to send his technical expert to him. A half minute later, Moon Si-Bok ran up to him and bowed deferentially.

"Chief Nam said he found a bullhorn," began Kim. "Get it and get back here immediately." Moon nodded and ran off to do Kim's bidding. Thirty seconds later, he returned waving the bullhorn. Kim strode over to the area of the parking lot containing the hostages and yanked a man to his feet. The North Korean dragged the American toward the truck and shoved him out in front of him. Nancy gave an involuntary cry and held her hands to her face in fear. Kim pulled his sidearm from his holster and pointed it at the back of the man's head.

"Now, Comrade Moon, tell the sniper to give himself up or I will kill this man," snarled Kim.

Moon immediately put the bullhorn to his lips. He struggled to think of the English word for sniper, then quickly gave up. He had to say something now or he might face the considerable wrath of Lieutenant Kim.

"Give up now, or this man be shot!" said Moon over the bullhorn.

Pearson's mouth opened in surprise. He eased the pressure he had been applying on the trigger and looked around the rifle's scope to view the situation on the ground below. The North Korean, who was in obvious command, was hidden behind a truck, but Pearson could see the barrel of the man's handgun pointed at the hostage.

They're not bluffing, he thought. Moon's amplified words rushed up at him and seemed to echo between the buildings.

"Man who kill our comrades, come out, or this man die!"

Pearson swallowed and had a dry feeling in his throat. He would have to surrender to save the unfortunate hostage.

But surrender was out of the question.

* * *

Garrett and Sprague had slowly made their way along the side of the TACAN shelter facing the runway to get a better view of the North Koreans and the trucks they had loaded with documents. Garrett peered around the shelter and raised the binoculars to his eyes, focusing on the trucks. He glimpsed a flash of auburn hair, and he realized, with simultaneous relief and alarm, that Nancy hadn't been in the group that had been shot earlier, but instead was in one of the trucks. He told Sprague, who was staring at the proceedings intently.

Moon's ultimatum floated across the road to them, and they each held their breath.

"Oh, God, they want us to give up!" said Garrett in a hoarse whisper.

Sprague shook his head as if denying the situation, but in reality his mind was racing.

"We can't give up," said Sprague. "We'd only get shot, and then they'd shoot the rest of the hostages anyway. Besides, I think they're after our unknown friend."

Garrett gave him a pained, quizzical look. Sprague pointed around the corner of the small building toward the two dead North Koreans. Garrett nodded, then a moment later gasped with fear for the unknown hostage, who stood looking around the area imploringly.

Garrett jammed his eyes shut at the crack of Kim's weapon.

Pearson let his breath out in a rush as he saw the hostage's body fall quickly to the asphalt below. The man hit the ground and lay perfectly still with his head gushing blood. The pool widened in the few seconds that Pearson stared at it as the murdered hostage's blood pressure drove the life-giving liquid out of his body at a rapidly diminishing rate. Pearson shoved the horror of the scene aside and lined up the crosshairs in his telescope on the nearest North Korean he could see. His right index finger curled around the trigger and he inhaled and held his breath.

Pearson hesitated. If he killed another of the enemy, the North Korean in command would certainly kill more hostages, maybe all of them. If he did nothing, the officer might still kill more hostages. Or he might just take his people and go. If I surrendered, he thought, I'd be shot along with the rest of the Americans. Some choice, he thought.

It was the same choice the French Resistance had had during World War II, when they fought the Nazis. Surrender and die. Live and watch innocent people die. He had never appreciated what those people had gone through until now.

Lieutenant Kim savagely looked about the area for any movement, any hint that the mysterious sniper would give himself up. Kim's head darted back and forth as rage built up within him.

"These Americans! These fools! They will not be able to stop us!" screamed Kim. He realized swiftly that he needed something else to get this sniper to come out. A flash of dark red hair hovered in his peripheral vision. He turned and stared at Nancy, who gaped back at him from the truck. Kim ran over to the vehicle's door and yanked it open. He grabbed Nancy by the hair and dragged her out into the open. He shoved her in front of him and pointed his weapon at the back of her head in the same manner as before. He was targeting the American male weakness for protecting their women. The sniper will never let this woman be shot, thought Kim.

"Comrade Moon, tell the sniper he has thirty seconds to give up!" shouted Kim.

Moon was mortified. "Comrade Lieutenant, not this woman," said Moon in a tremulous voice. "She is a valuable hostage. She knows missile—"

"Do it now!" screamed Kim. "Before I have *you* shot!"

Garrett's jaw dropped in abject despair as Moon's words boomed out across the road. He could see Nancy in front of the gun pointed at her by the North Korean. She was half bent over as if in pain at the thought of her immediate death. She looked around wildly, then centered her gaze in the direction where he had been before, when she was in the front parking lot. She looked straight at her husband in the distance without seeing him. He could see her lips quiver as they formed his name. She was calling out to him in desperation. He wanted to say something to Sprague, but he choked on the words. He finally got out one word.

"Nancy!" he gasped.

Sprague took the binoculars from Garrett and stared through them for an instant to verify what the situation was. He gave Garrett a quick look of sympathy.

Garrett pulled the automatic from his belt and hefted it. "I've got to get in there. They might kill me, but I've got to try."

Sprague shook his head and said nothing to dissuade his friend. He quickly looked over his rifle and made sure the safety was off.

"I never thought I'd go out like this," Sprague said quietly.

Together they got ready to rush the North Koreans.

"Shit," mumbled Pearson to himself. The North Korean officer was going to do Pearson's job for him. But the middle-aged CIA man didn't like it. Pearson made an instant decision. He would kill as many North Koreans as he could. Who knows? Maybe I'll live through it all, he thought. Stranger things have happened.

Pearson centered the crosshairs in his scope on the head of the closest North Korean. He took a deep breath and slowly exhaled.

Pearson gritted his teeth and pulled the trigger.

"Let's go!" shouted Garrett as he leaped from behind the building and began to cross the road. His overweight friend was only half a step behind him. Their eyes feverishly searched the bushes and the line of palm trees on the other side of Lagoon Road for any presence of the enemy. Their shoes clattered on the asphalt road, setting up some worrisome noise that seemed to be reflected back toward them by the line of palm trees and foliage on the other side of the road. Run as fast as you can, thought Garrett in a panic.

Seconds later they both entered the brush and immediately fought their way to the other side. He pushed the brush aside and got a good view of the parking lot on the eastern side of the Range Command Building.

His eyes locked on to Nancy immediately. She was still standing, although she was bent over almost to the ground. The North Korean guard who had been standing next to the truck with the hostages had fallen to the ground, blood running down the front of his uniform. The North Korean officer who had the gun pointed at Nancy was looking about with darting glances in a puzzled fashion. No one had heard a shot.

Time seemed to slow down for Garrett as he realized that his wife was still alive and that someone had killed another North Korean. In his peripheral vision, he could see a North Korean turning to fire at both him and Sprague. Garrett struggled to whirl around to aim at the invader but instantly knew he would be too late. The North Korean would have his automatic weapon pointed at Garrett in less than a second.

Garrett heard a crack at his elbow. The North Korean's mouth dropped open in pain and his weapon went awry as Sprague's bullet smashed into his neck, severing his carotid artery. The North Korean went down in a cloud of blood.

Garrett dropped to the ground and pointed his weapon at two North Koreans who had just seen the two of them among the bushes. Garrett began to fire wildly at the Koreans.

They know we're here, thought Garrett. This is it.

"Take cover!" shouted Chief Stevens as he shoved Lieutenant Eckman over into the trees that lined Lagoon Road. Eckman set up behind a palm tree, then grimaced at the sound of gunfire, which seemed to be just around the corner.

The *Topeka*'s landing party had just approached the Range Operations Building, the same building that Jack Pearson was on, when they heard Sprague and Garrett open fire on the North Koreans in the parking lot. One of the sailors had seen Garrett and Sprague run across the road but didn't have time to tell anyone before the gunfire occurred. Eckman surveyed the area. Both the Command Building and the Range Operations Building next to it were set back off the road with parking lots in front of them. Between the parking lots and the road were bushes and trees.

Chief Stevens and Lieutenant Eckman crawled through the brush and got a clear view of the parking lot of the Range Operations Building. Some sailors filled in the gaps in the brush around the officer and chief petty officer. By craning their necks, they could see the hostages lying flat on the ground in the adjoining parking lot of the Command Building. The Koreans had set up around some vehicles and the corners of the Command Building, and were beginning to return fire at some individuals who were firing at the enemy.

"We've got to help them out," said Eckman.

Stevens eyeballed movement off to the right of the Command Building. "I think we've been spotted!" he said, and began shoving sailors back while yelling for them to take cover.

The North Koreans took ten seconds to take their positions, long enough for the American sailors to get behind cover. Some vehicles in the parking lot in front of them and several fallen palm trees from the recent storm provided protection. The invaders and defenders eyed each other across the Range Operations Building parking lot.

The North Koreans and the American sailors opened fire simultaneously.

Ken Garrett rolled to his right in a frenzy to get away from the automatic weapons' fire from the invaders. Bullets slammed into the ground in front of him, sending bullet fragments and pieces of asphalt into the crown of his head and his shoulders. He groaned with pain and kept rolling until he got to the base of a wide palm tree. He took cover behind it and shivered with fear as the gunfire began to shred the tree a foot above his head.

The gunfire let up for a moment, and Garrett risked a glance to his left to see where Sprague was. Garrett was relieved to see Sprague huddled behind another palm tree, frantically working the bolt action on his rifle between firing at the North Koreans.

With the North Koreans' attention on Garrett and

Sprague, the hostages began crawling toward the extreme western edge of the Command Building parking lot. Garrett could see that if they could get into the brush on the far side, they might be able to evade the enemy.

Garrett turned back to the two North Koreans who were keeping him pinned down behind the palm tree. They were behind a parked pickup truck and were almost done reloading their weapons. In seconds, they would send lethal blasts of lead in his direction. He lifted the half-empty automatic with his right hand and placed the butt of the weapon in the palm of his left hand. He aimed the gun as best he could and began squeezing off rounds in their direction.

He fired twice and saw where the bullets hit on the side of the truck, then adjusted his aim and fired twice more. One of the North Koreans grunted with pain and grabbed his leg while dropping his weapon to the ground.

I've hit one, thought Garrett. But where is Nancy?

When the gunfire began in the parking lots, Kim immediately turned to assess the threat. He got next to the truck with the hostages in it and peered toward the front of the Range Operations Building. He caught a glimpse of black and dark green.

The U.S. military is here, thought Kim. I must attack! The thought slowly faded as the priority of the mission came to mind. He had prisoners with highly technical information that had to get back to North Korea, as well as the top secret documents describing the U.S. missile defense system. That had to take priority over leading an attack on the Americans.

He whirled around, looking for Junior Lieutenant Park. His eyes rested on his tech expert, Moon, who had thrown himself on the female prisoner in order to protect her. He walked up to them and waved his pistol in their faces.

"Get her into the truck!" Kim ordered above the rattle of gunfire. Moon was all too eager to comply. He got up and gently ushered her into the nearest vehicle, the one with only documents in it. Moon had the fleeting thought that she might be saved somehow if she were separated from the rest of the hostages. Nancy, sobbing with relief, looked around wildly. Where was Ken? Was he all right? She got inside the truck and lay down alone on the floor along with the piles of top secret documents that were crammed into the backseat of the Jeep Cherokee.

Park ran up to his superior and saluted.

"Comrade Park, you will complete your mission," growled Kim.

"Yes sir!" replied Park, and went toward the parking lot to take charge of his men.

Kim's mind raced. The Americans had taken up positions between the road and the building next to them. If he could get the trucks on the small road that ran along the beach on the lagoon side of the island, he might be able to get past the American forces and get back up to Echo Pier, where they had left their rubber boats.

He thought of Junior Lieutenant Park, the young man who so reminded Kim of himself. Park would do his duty. But Kim had no illusions.

Park and his men were expendable.

Jack Pearson lined up the crosshairs on the back of a North Korean's head. They had all taken cover when the first North Korean fell, but this one couldn't keep his head down. He pulled the trigger, feeling the rifle jump and hearing the dull thump of the silenced gunshot. Pearson saw a burst of red in his scope and knew he had hit the man. He looked beyond his scope and viewed the scene below through the tops of palm trees that he used for cover. His target, now smeared with red, fell behind one of the vehicles, its white exterior spattered with his blood.

The North Koreans were getting ready to move out, and the U.S. Navy counterattack, which was being mounted in the front of his building, wasn't going to prevent it. He looked around quickly, trying to find Nancy Garrett. She was inside the truck but lying on the floor. He could see her leg, but otherwise he didn't have a good shot at her. Pearson felt relief that he couldn't complete his mission, but felt anxiety at the same time. What if they really did get her back to North Korea?

* * *

"Chief!" shouted Eckman over the gunfire. "We've got to flank them!" Eckman pointed to his right and made a motion to go around the corner of the building toward the lagoon and the road that ran along the beach.

Chief Stevens nodded quickly. "I'll take three men and see if we can get around them."

Eckman nodded, and the chief crawled off shouting men's names. He got three of the best shots in the landing party and they all wiggled their way to the extreme edge of the parking lot in front of the building. They jumped to their feet during a lull in the firing and ran to the far edge of the building. The four of them quickly ran down the length of the building and peered around the corner. The parking lot that Kim and his party were in was only forty feet away.

Stevens and his three men left the side of the building and took cover behind other smaller buildings that were behind the larger Range Operations Building. Stevens studied the scene in the parking lot and saw that the North Koreans were just starting to move out with five captured vehicles. The chief decided to wait until they got out onto the road to get a better shot at the invaders.

The sound of starting engines rolled across the parking lot to Ken Garrett and Mike Sprague. Garrett squirmed around to see where the remaining North Koreans were. The gunfire directed at them had stopped a few minutes ago, but it had picked up to Garrett's right. Two different sounds mingled together; one was the North Korean weapons, the other was different. Garrett imagined it was the U.S. Navy's M16s. Garrett took a careful look around and couldn't see any of the enemy. He looked to his left and noted with satisfaction that all the remaining hostages in the parking lot had gotten away. Garrett couldn't see Nancy and thought that she was in one of the captured vehicles. He slid over next to Sprague.

"Mike, I hear engines starting. The North Koreans are leaving, and they've got Nancy!" he said in a breathless tone. "C'mon, let's go!"

Garrett started off to his right, but Sprague grabbed his

arm and pulled him to the ground. Garrett gave him a fierce look.

"Ken, we've got navy guys to our right, and it sounds like they're really giving these bastards hell," began Sprague. "If you were the North Koreans, which way would you go?" Sprague pointed toward the gunfire. "Toward that? Or the other way?"

Garrett looked quickly both ways. He had to admit it. Sprague was right. They both cautiously moved to their left and made their way around to the western side of the Command Building.

Lieutenant Kim caught a flash of green near the edge of one of the small buildings in front of him. The Americans! They were here as well! His plan to go up the beach road eastward to get around the American force had to be scrapped. How many Americans was he facing? It could be anywhere from ten to a hundred or more. Kim, for the first time, felt panic.

Kim thundered out an order to the driver of his vehicle to turn around and head the opposite way toward the front of the Command Building and Lagoon Road. The driver obediently swung the vehicle around and stomped his foot to the floor, causing the Cherokee's tires to squeal in protest. They accelerated quickly and drove at high speed between the two buildings toward the front parking lot. Kim turned around and saw that the rest of the trucks had followed suit.

Kim slid down in his seat as they ran past the firefight between Park's men and the Americans. He nodded to himself. Park would hold them at bay.

Junior Lieutenant Park San Hoon paid little attention to the white vehicles that flashed by behind him as he constantly assessed the situation. The Americans were standing and fighting, not running, as he had always been told they would. Park shook his head. Soon his men would run out of ammunition, then what? Surrender? Never, he resolved.

Park summoned his courage, then stood up among the bullets that whined within inches of his head.

"Sailors of the Democratic People's Republic!" he

shouted at the top of his lungs. The firing went into a lull as they turned to look at him. The Americans took the opportunity to reload.

"Fix bayonets!" shouted Park. His men didn't hesitate. Shafts of thin steel appeared and were quickly fixed to the tips of rifle barrels. His men completed their task and looked at him expectantly. Their faces reflected fatigue, fear, patriotism, and shining idealism.

"Let's go, men," shouted Park in a quivering voice. "Charge!"

Park ran out into the open with his men following him, their long bayonets glinting in the sunlight.

CHAPTER FIFTEEN

Escape

Lieutenant Eckman snapped another clip into his handgun and suddenly looked up at the unholy noise that was headed his way. He looked without realization of what the line of men forty yards away represented, and his mind struggled for a instant to understand the scene.

The North Koreans were strung out in a ragged line across one end of the parking lot. They were screaming at the top of their lungs and running at top speed straight at Eckman's position. The rifles they carried out in front of them seemed too long, of ridiculous length compared to the short stature of the North Koreans. A gleam of reflected light off the metal tips of these too-long rifles suddenly jarred his mind into recognition.

A bayonet attack! Eckman quickly glanced to the right and left to assess his unit's condition. They were just finishing reloading after the brief hiatus in the battle. They looked up as one and gaped at the charging North Korean line.

"Pick your targets!" shouted Eckman to the right and repeated the order to his left. "Fire! Fire! Fire!" he shouted a second later.

The navy men immediately put their weapons to their shoulders and opened up on the rapidly advancing North Koreans. The air was filled with the chatter of automatic weapons' fire and the explosive thump of shotgun blasts. Expended shells flew from the M16s, and the men with shotguns pumped the handles as fast as possible, sending the red casings whirling away from them in a frenzy.

Three North Koreans dropped immediately, felled by the stream of lead from the sailors of the *Topeka*. The remaining seven Koreans kept coming in spite of the fire from the navy men. A shotgun blast hit one in the legs and he pitched forward to hit the ground on his face. Junior Lieutenant Park caught a quick automatic burst, which emptied half the clip of one of Eckman's men, across his chest and spun to the ground to land with his arms and legs at awkward angles. Seconds later, he died of his wounds.

The remaining five came on, with the *Topeka* sailors pounding away at them. Lieutenant Eckman fired rapidly, his nine-millimeter sidearm flinging rounds toward the attackers. He hit one in the abdomen, and the stricken man slowed to a stop and fell to his knees.

The charging North Koreans fired their remaining few rounds, and with ten yards left to go, they had the American sailors ducking behind their cover. Seconds later, the U.S. sailors peered around their vehicles and fallen palm trees to find the remaining four North Koreans on top of them.

Lieutenant Eckman cautiously looked over the hood of the truck he was using for cover to discover the horror of a bayonet coming directly at his face. He jerked to the right as the deadly shaft flew at him but raised his left shoulder in the process. The bayonet sliced through the life jacket, the strap of his bulletproof vest, and his uniform to reach his skin underneath. Eckman felt nothing initially except loss of strength on his left side. The pain hit him an instant later.

Eckman groaned and fell to his knees near the front of the truck. The North Korean lunged with the bayonet as far as he could across the hood of the truck, then stepped back and ran around the front of the truck to finish Eckman off. The lieutenant saw him coming and raised his weapon to fire at him, only to catch the barrel on the underside of the bumper of the vehicle. The enemy sailor raised his rifle and pointed the bayonet straight at Eckman's chest. Eckman saw the North Korean's face, which was twisted with the rage of combat, hover over the poised weapon.

The North Korean began his downward thrust just as

Eckman got the barrel free from the bumper. He pointed the gun at his attacker and fired as fast as he could. The first three slugs hit the Korean in the chest, the last two slammed into his face, sending him reeling backward in a final frenzied twitch ending in death.

The rifle, minus its master, continued on and the bayonet struck the ground an inch from Eckman's right ear. The rifle hung motionless with its stock to the sky for a moment, then fell across Eckman's chest.

Eckman looked around and saw that the battle was over. He staggered to his feet and saw with relief that Chief Stevens had returned from his abortive effort to flank the North Koreans. His concerned face stood a few inches away from Eckman's face.

"Lieutenant, are you okay?" asked Stevens.

Eckman nodded, jammed his sidearm into its holster, and grabbed his throbbing shoulder with his right hand. His legs felt rubbery.

"Chief, get the status," said Eckman.

Stevens eyed the blood dripping from Eckman's shoulder. "Okay, Mr. Eckman, but you take it easy now, and we'll get you patched up in a hurry."

The chief ran off to check out the rest of the landing party and to send over the one corpsman they had with them. Eckman decided to give in to his legs and sat down heavily on the pavement with his back resting against the right fender of the truck. He heard the cracking of gunfire in the distance and turned around to look across the Range Operations Building parking lot toward the far end of the Command Building parking lot.

Jack Pearson ran down the rooftop toward the front of the Range Operations Building. The North Koreans were moving out and this would be the last chance he would have to carry out his orders. He had been setting up for a shot toward the back of the building until the North Korean convoy had suddenly turned around and headed at high speed toward the front parking lot.

Pearson got to the front corner of the roof and knelt down at the edge. He propped up the rifle with his left hand and put his left elbow on his knee in a classic kneeling position.

He looked through the scope and quickly surveyed the five vehicles that were escaping toward the western end of the island. The parking lot below exploded with noise as Park and his men made their last charge. Pearson didn't even glance in their direction, but kept his concentration on the problem of the escaping North Koreans and the prisoners that were going with them.

In seconds, Pearson determined that it was impossible to see which vehicle contained Nancy Garrett, and he decided to try to stop the last truck in the line. That one seemed to have the most people in it, and he hoped they were the hostages. Maybe he could shoot the enemy driver and guards. Maybe the rest of the vehicles would just keep going. Maybe.

Pearson placed the crosshairs in the scope on one of the rear tires of the trailing vehicle.

Ken Garrett grabbed Mike Sprague by the shoulder as they rounded the corner of the Command Building on the opposite side of the building from the Range Operations Building.

"Mike! They're coming this way!" said Garrett in a panicked voice. Sprague whirled around and looked quickly toward the front parking lot. The five vehicles came into view and crossed the parking lot at high speed. They appeared to be headed to an adjoining parking lot of the small building to the west of the Command Building. Garrett thought that probably they would go out to Lagoon Road from there.

Garrett and Sprague both raised their weapons and thought of impossible shots to stop the fleeing vehicles. Garrett fired the last two rounds in his clip, and Sprague squeezed off a shot at the lead vehicle. Garrett's bullets hit the door of one of the vehicles, and Sprague's slug smashed the side window of the vehicle that contained Lieutenant Kim.

The line of trucks flew by, their speed unabated.

Pearson knew there was no time to adjust the elevation angle by using his scope so he quickly estimated the angle and fired three shots at the trailing vehicle's rear tire. The first bullet missed wide, the second hit the tire and punctured it, the third hit the rear bumper. The vehicle went out of control and skidded around sideways as the inexperienced driver made all the wrong moves to try to keep the vehicle pointed correctly.

The white Jeep Cherokee ground to a halt at the edge of the Command Building parking lot. Pearson gave a worried glance at the other four vehicles, but they didn't slow at all as they flew out toward Lagoon Road.

The North Korean driver leaped out, along with another North Korean who had been in the front passenger's seat, and they both frantically waved to their comrades in the fleeing vehicles, to no avail.

Pearson placed the crosshairs on the driver, who was the easiest shot at the moment, and pulled the trigger. The bullet hit him in the chest instead of the temple, which was where Pearson had been aiming. The North Korean grabbed his chest and fell to the ground.

Pearson swung the rifle around and aimed at the other North Korean. This one had an automatic weapon and was pointing it randomly at imagined enemies. Pearson raised the barrel to compensate for the inaccuracy of his last shot. His finger tightened on the trigger.

The North Korean suddenly opened his mouth wide, his eyes rolled in his head, and he staggered against the Cherokee. He slowly slid to the ground, his weapon sagging in despair, until he landed abruptly on the pavement.

Surprised, Pearson lowered his rifle and looked over the area. He hadn't yet pulled the trigger. Someone else had shot the North Korean. He looked down at the parking lot in front of his building. It was littered with bodies, and the U.S. Navy men below appeared to be picking up the pieces. It wasn't any of them, thought Pearson.

He looked back toward the disabled truck and saw the hostages cautiously exit the vehicle. He looked them over through his scope, and he recognized one face immediately. Nate Jackson, thought Pearson. One of the three engineers who must not be taken by the North Koreans. He counted the former North Korean hostages who stood in shock around the truck, then grunted with disappointment. Only four, he thought. The North Koreans still have one. They still have Nancy Garrett.

Lieutenant Kim squirmed around in his seat while brushing pieces of the shattered side window from his uniform. The Americans were coming at him from every direction now. He looked to the rear as they rumbled out onto Lagoon Road, and to his surprise, he counted only four vehicles including his own. He had lost one vehicle already!

Kim looked around wildly for attacking Americans. What am I to do now? The rubber boats were on the other side of the island. Do I have to fight my way through hundreds of Americans to get to the boats? Panic seized him momentarily, but with a great force of will he suppressed it. He looked out the right side toward the lagoon and immediately saw Sprague's boat anchored in five feet of water near the beach.

Kim grabbed the driver's arm. "Quickly! That way!" he ordered.

The driver immediately complied and yanked the wheel around, running across a lawn in the process. Kim looked back and saw the three trailing vehicles follow his lead. He settled in the front seat and stared at the rapidly approaching beach and the large boat near it.

Yes, it will be all right, Kim thought. If I can't get to my boats, then we'll steal one.

"Nancy's not with them," said Garrett under his breath as he looked over the four men who got out of the stopped truck. "I don't believe it. The goddamn North Koreans still have her!" He looked around in desperation. "C'mon, Mike, we've got to get a truck and get after them."

Sprague stared at the dead North Korean guard he had shot a fraction of a second before Jack Pearson could pull the trigger. He felt some satisfaction. At least that was one of the enemy they didn't have to worry about. He looked around at the rooftops. Someone had shot the driver. One of the navy guys?

"Mike! For God's sake, c'mon!" shouted Garrett, causing Sprague to jump.

Garrett's remark about getting a truck suddenly registered in Sprague's mind. "I saw a truck down toward the beach," he said.

They both ran as fast as they could along the side of the Command Building toward the lagoon beach. They reached the rear parking lot and ran toward the nearest truck. Garrett opened the door and reached for the ignition. He swept his hand over the ignition switch and felt nothing. He jumped out and slammed the door.

"No keys in this one!" he shouted to a huffing and puffing Mike Sprague as he straggled up behind Garrett. Sprague and Garrett spread out and checked all of the half dozen vehicles in the parking lot. There were no keys in any of the trucks. Garrett ran over to the line of bicycles that were parked in a line at one end of the lot.

"Mike! Get a bicycle and let's go!" shouted Garrett to his slow-moving friend. They grabbed the two bikes that seemed in the best condition, even though they were quite rusted, and pedaled off in the direction of the beach. Good thing no one was worried about anyone stealing bicycles on this island, thought Garrett. No one used bicycle locks on Kwajalein.

They left the parking lot and went along the road that ran parallel to the beach. The road curved up toward Lagoon Road with a few unpaved roads leading from it to other smaller buildings. Garrett looked around constantly to discover where the North Koreans had gone. He looked back to see where Sprague was and saw the overweight man struggling to keep up the pace.

Garrett suddenly spotted a group of vehicles in the distance near the beach. He jammed on the bike's brakes and skidded to a stop. Garrett put the binoculars to his eyes and saw the four trucks with North Koreans around them. He saw Nancy, her red hair and tall stature sticking out among the short, black-haired Koreans. She was being shoved toward the water. He had a feeling of dread.

The North Koreans had stopped, but why? What were they going to do to Nancy? Then he saw Mike Sprague's boat.

Lieutenant Kim surveyed the area. Yes, we have time, he thought. Not much, but only a few minutes will be enough. The boat they were going to use seemed to be in good condition; it had enough fuel, and it even had the keys in the ignition.

He counted his men and got only to eighteen. Rage flared up in him once again. He had lost half his men to the Americans! He glared at the terrified American woman he had nearly shot in the parking lot. She was being shoved toward the boat by one of his men with Moon following and fretting behind them.

Comrade Moon had better be right about these documents and this woman, he thought savagely. He decided to take an extremely unpleasant revenge on Moon if the documents and the woman turned out to be less than what the technical man had said. The deaths of half his men demanded such.

Kim eyed the boat critically. As large as it was, it wouldn't hold all the documents and twenty people. His men would be hanging off the side. He looked around the area and saw several other boats and was glad for the first time that he had hurried Park and his men along, effectively aborting their task of sinking all the boats in the lagoon. He called Chief Petty Officer Nam over and ordered him to pick out another boat to transport himself and ten men. He considered sending Moon along with Chief Nam but relented. Moon seemed to be able to control this woman who supposedly knew incredible secrets about missiles. He was able to control her without using force. It wouldn't look good if she were beaten senseless when he delivered her to the Liaison Bureau.

Kim looked her over carefully. In his mind, she was tall, skinny, and bony. He studied her face intently. She was also terrified. That is good, he thought. We will all keep her terrified for a long time. What would the trip be like on the way home with a woman aboard? She wouldn't have to worry about rape. He was sure Captain Hong would have none of that. The crew was disciplined, and upon orders from Captain Hong, there would not be any attempts either. Perhaps he should imply that she could be attacked by the crew. That might keep her in line.

Another thought struck him. Would the technical people on board want to start interrogating her on the way home?

Yes, of course. He, or some of his men, might be called upon to physically convince her to cooperate. Kim smiled. He wished he had some of the American male prisoners as well. He knew the male weaknesses much better than the female ones. He would learn the female pressure points, physical as well as mental—this reddish-haired stick of a woman would teach him during the long voyage to North Korea.

Multiple engines roared into life, first the two on Kim's boat, then the two on Chief Nam's boat. Kim took a last look around and noted that his men had finished loading the documents and were boarding the boats. He waded into the water, feeling the wetness seep through his boots to his skin. This battle was over.

The *Admiral Yi* was half an hour away.

CHAPTER SIXTEEN

Pursuit

Lieutenant Eckman breathed deeply and tried to make sense of the last fifteen minutes. His legs still felt rubbery, and his insides felt as if they would rattle apart. He had killed a man for the first time in his life, and the event stunned him into withdrawal. For the last several minutes, he had been reduced to staring at Chief Stevens as the senior enlisted man hovered around the men, getting them medical help and sorting things out.

The landing party from the *Topeka* had been lucky. The North Korean bayonet charge had wounded only three men, Lieutenant Eckman included. One man had taken a bayonet in the stomach and was in critical condition, and another had taken a AKM round in the chest but was saved by his body armor. The bullet had penetrated his chest enough to crack a bone and break the skin. Two North Koreans out of the ten who had charged into the U.S. sailors were still alive, although one appeared to have only minutes to live. Eckman was sure the other North Korean would be interrogated more than just thoroughly.

The island, which at times had appeared like a ghost town, suddenly came alive with the departure of the North Koreans. A crowd of people gave aid to the former hostages, who huddled on the western side of the parking lot of the Range Command Building, where they had fled during the gun battle. Others gave assistance to the wounded navy men. And some cried over the bodies of the murdered

Americans in the parking lot of the Command Building. The landing party, after seeing that their wounded shipmates were being taken care of, formed up under Chief Stevens's command and checked their weapons and ammunition. Chief Stevens walked slowly over to the lieutenant.

"Mr. Eckman, the men are ready," said the chief in a low voice. Eckman returned a doleful stare. "Sir, we've got to get after them," said the chief.

Eckman nodded. "Yes, we can't let them get away with this." He let out his breath in a huge sigh. "All right, let's get down toward the beach and see if we can find a boat to follow them." Eckman turned to move for the first time in several minutes, and winced with the pain from his left shoulder.

The chief spun around and marched the remaining ten men toward the beach past the Range Operations Building. Once on the beach, they all looked west and saw the two boats full of North Koreans head out into the lagoon. There were two men running along the beach in the distance headed toward some boats that had been tossed up on the beach by the storm.

"Okay, Chief, let's get down there and talk to those two men," said Eckman.

"Right, sir," agreed Stevens.

At Eckman's order, they began to double-time down the beach toward the two figures.

Ken Garrett and Mike Sprague ran breathlessly up to a twenty-five-foot cabin cruiser that had been washed away from its anchorage by the storm and had wound up near the beach on the western end of Kwajalein Island. One thought was on Garrett's mind. The North Koreans still had Nancy, and he would move heaven and earth to get her back.

Garrett got aboard first and immediately went to the wheel. Sprague, huffing and puffing as usual, dragged himself over the side in typically fatigued fashion.

"Any keys in it?" asked Sprague when he could catch his breath.

Garrett shook his head in disappointment. He had a quick

thought. "But there has to be a toolbox around here somewhere."

Thirty seconds and two smashed doors later, Garrett had a large pipe wrench in his hand. He swung it desperately at the ignition switch. Sprague was about to object, but stopped as he saw the wrench smash into the control panel next to the switch, putting a large ragged hole in the wooden panel. Garrett got a pliers and had the ignition switch free in another minute. He ripped the wires from the switch and stripped the insulation from the wires with a needle-nosed pliers. He wrapped the two wires together and noted with relief that ignition lights came on and the gauge needles moved. He quickly looked at the voltage gauge. It was normal. Thank God, he thought, that this boat ignition was a lot simpler than a regular auto ignition.

He hit the button to start the engines. The starters whirred frantically, then stopped as Garrett took his finger off the starter button. After a few more tries, the engines rumbled into life.

Garrett exhaled quickly. "Get the anchor up!" he shouted to Sprague. The heavy man was already headed for the bow with his eyes on the anchor chain. Garrett caught movement out of the corner of his eye. He turned around and saw a welcome sight. The U.S. Navy men, holding their weapons at port arms, were wading through the surf toward his boat.

Garrett ran back toward the stern and helped the navy men aboard.

"Am I glad to see you guys!" he exclaimed.

Eckman nodded seriously and recognized Garrett almost immediately. "We saw you on the runway, didn't we?"

Garrett nodded enthusiastically. "They have my wife, who's a reentry vehicle engineer, and they also have a load of top secret documents on our missile defense program. So, let's go get these bastards."

"Yes, well, that's what we had in mind," said Eckman. "The only trouble is . . ." His voice trailed off.

Garrett looked at Eckman with mounting unease. "What?"

Chief Stevens stepped up. "We can't take you guys. You're civilians. We can't risk your lives."

"Bullshit!" exploded Garrett. "They have my wife!"

"Yes, and we'll try to rescue—" started Eckman.

"Try! Try?" shouted Garrett. "Look, you're welcome to come along, but don't get in our way!"

"I haven't got time for this," said Eckman. "I'm sorry, but you have to leave now."

"You lousy goddamn—" began Garrett, but he was cut short when Sprague came up behind him and grabbed him around the chest, pinning his arms to his sides.

"C'mon, Ken, let's go," said Sprague, and started to drag him away toward the stern. Lieutenant Eckman gave Sprague, who had his rifle slung over his shoulder, a curious look but then turned away to make sure his men were ready to pursue the North Koreans.

"You assholes!" shouted Garrett in desperation. Sprague wrestled him over the side and pleaded with him to calm down.

"Take it easy, take it easy," said Sprague. "We'll just get another boat."

"Why the hell were you taking their side?" fumed Garrett at his friend.

"They weren't going to give in, and we were wasting time," replied Sprague.

"We'll waste more time looking for another boat," yelled Garrett. "That was our boat. Why didn't they get their own goddamn boat?"

Sprague opened his arms and gestured with his palms up in an effort to convince his friend to forget the incident. "That was the quickest way for them to get after the North Koreans. Besides, who has a better chance of stopping them? Us, or the U.S. Navy?"

Garrett ground his teeth but gave in to Sprague's logic. Sprague nodded, then immediately turned to the nearest boat that wasn't half submerged.

Delay, thought Garrett. More delay.

Lieutenant Kim surveyed the horizon for any sign of the *Admiral Yi*. It was early yet; they had been traveling in the boats for only ten minutes, which meant that they had an additional twenty minutes to go. He looked at the water as it slid by the bow of his boat and again tried to estimate their speed. Fifteen knots was the number that came to mind. It was about twice the speed they had made in the rubber boats when they had traveled toward Kwajalein Island.

He lowered his binoculars and turned to look at Chief Nam and the men in the second boat. They were following along dutifully, nicely keeping up with the larger boat's progress. Well, it was all but over. He, his men, the top secret documents, and this American woman would all be loaded onto the *Admiral Yi* within the next hour, and they would run the Gea Pass out to sea.

Kim thought over the battle he and his men had had with the Americans and wondered if there had been anything more that he could have done to save some of his men's lives. The force that they were up against seemed to be very large. Perhaps a hundred soldiers. Where had they come from? The Liaison Bureau hadn't told them of any force of that size on Kwajalein.

He thought of Junior Lieutenant Park and of his heroic attack on the American military men who had arrived when they were near the Command Building. Where was Park now? Probably dead, along with the rest of his men. Kim sighed. It was tough to lose someone you felt close to, but that was warfare. And Park was as expendable in their fight with the Americans as anyone. Park deserved to become a national hero, but Kim knew he would suppress Park's heroic last stand and enhance his own actions. Revision of the facts was always the prerogative of the survivors.

Kim spotted a dot on the horizon behind his boat. He raised the binoculars to his eyes as a feeling of dread filled him.

Lieutenant Eckman stared through his binoculars at the two fleeing boats filled with North Koreans. He saw one of the North Koreans looking straight at him through binoculars. Eckman quickly lowered his glasses and turned around to Chief Stevens, who was nervously chewing on yet another unlit cigar.

"Chief, see if there's an ensign aboard," said Eckman. "I want them to know who they're up against." The chief nodded and got another man to find the boat's ensign. The man came up with a large American flag.

Eckman nodded and ordered the man to hoist it on the aft flag boom. The sailor attached the flag and ran it up to the top of the short boom. The Stars and Stripes seemed to crackle in the sunlight. Eckman wasn't one for speeches but decided that now would be an exception, even though the speech would be a short one.

"Men, take a look," he said as he pointed to the newly raised flag. "In case you were wondering what we were fighting for. Take a good look."

The twelve men on the boat stared at the rippling red, white, and blue flag for a few seconds, then gripped their weapons with new determination and turned their attention to the upcoming battle.

So these Americans were not going to quit, thought Kim as he eyed the flag of the country he despised most in the world. That raising of the flag—they were flaunting themselves at him. But how many was he up against? How many soldiers could they fit into that boat?

Kim looked at his watch and gauged the advance of the American boat. He nervously looked at the position of the throttles near his wheelman. They were fully forward. He refused to ask the helmsman if they could go faster. That would convey weakness. He looked again at the advancing American boat. They would be on him in fifteen minutes, which was just about when they would be near the *Admiral Yi*. He couldn't let an enemy boat get near the sub, and he couldn't risk the loss of the documents or the woman prisoner. That left only one alternative.

Kim ordered one of his men to find the megaphone that Moon had used in the Range Command Building parking lot. The man handed Kim the instrument after a short delay. Kim ordered the helmsman to slow slightly to allow Chief Nam's boat to come alongside.

"Chief," said Kim into the bullhorn. Thirty feet away on the other boat, Chief Nam looked at him intently.

"Engage and destroy that enemy boat!" ordered Kim.

Chief Nam nodded immediately and saluted, then ordered a change of course to intercept the rapidly closing American boat.

Chief Nam and his men were expendable as well, thought Kim.

Lieutenant Eckman turned around to Chief Stevens. "They're coming about!" He leaned over to the helmsman. "Don't let him ram us!" The man nodded grimly.

Eckman looked over the rest of the boat as the anxiety of imminent combat was on him once more. Concentrate, he commanded himself. Concentrate on what has to be done. At Chief Stevens's orders, the men had taken every scrap of metal and had lined the sides of the boat with it. Metal trays, steel deck panels, metal chairs, and anything else that would impede a bullet were stacked up around the boat. Knowing Chief Stevens as well as he did, Eckman was sure that they had done all they could. He turned and squinted at the rapidly approaching boat. He estimated that they were headed toward one another at a combined speed of over forty knots. Would they attempt to ram his boat? That would be the North Korean style, he decided quickly as he thought of the bayonet charge in the parking lot. He had a sudden idea.

"Aim for the engines!" he shouted over the roar of boat's motors. "Shoot to disable the engines and the rudder!" The men on both sides of the boat nodded. The boat coming at them had powerful twin outboard motors that extended over the aft transom, and as a result were exposed to their fire.

The North Koreans opened up when they were a hundred yards away. The fire kicked up the water in front and on the side of Eckman's boat and sprinkled the vessel with bullets. The U.S. Navy men huddled behind the sides of their boat and tried to keep as much metal as they could between them and the enemy gunfire. Lieutenant Eckman lay on the deck listening to the sounds of bullets slap into the sides of the boat. He rolled over and eyed the helmsman. Brave man, he thought. He's in an exposed position, even though he's crouched behind the wheel and the firewall in front of him. Yet there's no complaint from him.

All of my men are like that. They haven't complained once since we started.

The helmsman peered periodically out the window to gauge the attacker's speed and direction. As the North Korean boat pulled to within ten yards, he gave the wheel a sharp turn to port and shoved the throttles wide open. The boat heeled over to the left, and Eckman could hear the sounds of the attacking vessel's engines and the splash of water caused by their bow wave as it hit the side of his boat. He waited another few seconds, then peered over the side. The North Koreans were charging by abeam of his boat and going in the opposite direction. His helmsman had successfully avoided being rammed by the North Koreans.

"Now, men!" he shouted, and brought his automatic up to bear on the other boat. "Fire! Fire!"

The sailors duplicated his action and a host of gunbarrels swung around to point over the side at the North Korean boat. The American military men opened fire with a deafening noise. The staccato sounds of the M16s mixed with the explosive thumps of the shotguns as they all fired at the stern of the boat. A wall of lead slammed into the two outboard motors, shredding the port side motor and ripping several large pieces of the cowling from the starboard motor.

The North Korean boat immediately slowed as the engines died and kept going only on inertia. The North Koreans scrambled to bring their guns to bear on the Americans while two men rushed over to revive the now dead engines and to put out an embryonic fire that had broken out. North Korean weapons began to appear over the sides of the vessel and from around the walls of the superstructure. The American sailors raked the sides of the enemy boat with automatic weapons' fire, and Eckman could see a few North Koreans slump over after being hit. The enemy gunbarrels were quickly withdrawn as the North Koreans jerked themselves down to take cover behind the boat's gunwhale.

Clips ran empty, and half of Eckman's men frantically began to reload, ramming fresh clips home and jamming individual shotgun shells into their weapons as fast as humanly possible. Eckman held his breath as he watched the gunbarrels reappear from around the walls of the enemy boat. The North Koreans opened fire and riddled the sides of the American boat with gunfire. Slugs penetrated the side of the boat and many also made it through the metal shields that they had set up as protection. Three sailors grunted, cried out with pain, and rolled over in agony from their wounds. There's no cover, thought Eckman as a bullet whizzed past his right ear. They can shoot right through everything.

The American boat kept going past the stern of the enemy boat and started to go up the starboard side. Eckman yelled to the helmsman to slow down, then turned toward Chief Stevens.

"Keep up a steady rate of fire, but don't shoot toward the bow," he yelled. The chief nodded. "I'm going to board them," shouted Eckman. He grabbed the nearest two sailors, one of whom had an M16, the other of whom had a shotgun. "You two are with me!" he ordered.

Eckman and the two sailors got onto their hands and knees and crawled up to the helm. Eckman got into a crouch and put his hand on the helmsman's shoulder.

"Take us alongside!" he ordered. The sailor nodded and expertly maneuvered the boat's port side along the enemy boat's starboard side. Eckman waved the two sailors to follow him and exited the boat's cabin on the starboard side away from the North Korean boat. Eckman could hear the furious battle rage on at point-blank range just yards from where he stood. He circled around in front of the boat's front windows and crossed the foredeck to get to the port side. The enemy boat was five feet away and Eckman could see out of the corner of his eye the exchange of gunfire from both parties farther aft.

Now is the time, he thought, while they're distracted by the firefight aft. Eckman stood up from his crouch with the two sailors on either side of him doing the same. The officer stared at the swaying deck five feet away and gauged his leap. A North Korean suddenly appeared on the opposite side of the enemy boat. He pointed his weapon at the three Americans as they jumped into the air between the two boats.

The North Korean opened fire quickly, moving his

weapon from left to right, sending a stream of lead across the three American sailors. His aim was high, the blast catching the first sailor in the head and putting two bullets into his face. The shotgun he was carrying out in front of him flew forward and clattered on the enemy boat's forward deck. His body, propelled backward by the impact of the bullets, fell into the water between the two boats. The next few rounds went into the space above Eckman's head. Due to his short stature, the burst from the North Korean weapon flew by above him. The last set of bullets hit the second sailor in the right shoulder and hit his bulletproof vest just under his chin, sending him spinning backward onto the American boat.

Eckman hit the deck of the enemy boat and fell flat, immediately aiming at the North Korean. He opened fire as the enemy sailor tried to readjust his aim. All three of Eckman's bullets hit the North Korean in the chest. The enemy's weapon wavered and fell, and his body slumped to the deck. Eckman took a frantic look around and spotted one of his men writhing in pain on the deck of his boat, but the other sailor was nowhere to be seen. Realization hit him that he was alone on the enemy boat. He looked at his handgun and saw with alarm that its slide had locked in its rearmost position. Not only was he alone, but he was out of ammunition.

He saw the missing sailor's shotgun and quickly picked it up, taking a second to make sure the safety was off. Eckman again looked at the boat with his men on it, and saw with disappointment that the boats had drifted apart and his boat now stood ten yards away. There was no going back now.

Movement in the cabin on the North Korean boat caught his eye. He lay on the deck near the bow not ten feet from the cabin and could see the tops of two heads as they continued the battle with the American sailors. The gunfight had slowed somewhat due to the mounting casualties on both sides, and the earsplitting sounds of automatic weapons had gone from a continuous barrage to intermittent short bursts.

Eckman crawled up to the cabin window and pointed the shotgun at the Plexiglas. He closed his eyes and fired a round through the Plexiglas into the cabin, sending pieces of plastic flying in all directions. The American officer pumped the handle to put another round into the firing chamber, and after opening his eyes a crack, put the barrel of the shotgun through the jagged opening in the window. He quickly pulled the trigger without worrying about aiming accurately.

Eckman frantically rolled to his right, then cautiously peered through a side window into the cabin. Two of the enemy lay on the deck. Chief Nam was lying very still with his head in a pool of blood, and the other man was gasping desperately while holding his neck. Eckman averted his eyes. He'd have no trouble from those two, he decided.

Flames sprang up from the outboard motors, and their unexpected crackle caused Eckman to look aft with a start. The small fire grew suddenly, fed by the boat's unexpended gasoline. He surveyed the situation. Only two North Koreans were moving and returning fire, the rest were lying still, scattered about the deck aft of the cabin. Miraculously, the remaining North Koreans hadn't seen Eckman kill their comrades in the forward part of the boat. They had been concentrating on the battle with the Americans on the other boat.

Eckman brought the shotgun up to bear on the nearest enemy. He pulled the trigger, feeling the powerful kick of the weapon on his shoulder and sending a lethal blast into the back of the North Korean sailor. The enemy sailor's body slammed against the side of the boat, then he slid down to lay quietly on the deck.

The second North Korean looked around in a panic, then swung his weapon about, firing as he moved. Eckman, who was in the middle of pumping another round into the chamber, scrambled forward with his legs flailing wildly. He slipped, the shotgun flying out of his hands and splashing into the lagoon waters below. He slid under the port side hand railing and nearly fell over the side, his hands desperately groping for any handhold. His right hand closed around something metal and gripped it desperately, preventing himself from falling into the water. He pulled himself up and wrapped his arm around the vertical portion of the side rail. The North Korean's blasts shattered the side cabin window and the wood surrounding it and began to chop apart the deck near the port side railing.

The North Korean gunfire suddenly stopped, replaced by what Eckman knew was fire from an M16. Eckman slowly pulled himself back aboard and cautiously peeked over the shattered wood and Plexiglas to determine the location of his assailant. Nothing but blood-soaked, torn bodies greeted him. He searched the human pile for his most recent assailant and finally saw that he was dead, lying next to his comrade whom Eckman had shot moments before. My men on the other boat must have gotten him before he could get me, thought Eckman.

He felt the shattered wood under him as he lay on the port side outside the cabin. This was where I was when the North Korean opened fire, he thought, then glanced back over his shoulder to the torn deck railing. His slip had saved his life.

Eckman's eyes flicked over the boat. The engine fire was increasing rapidly, and the aft deck was awash with seawater, making some of the bodies float in the mixture of water, blood, and gasoline. He noticed that the boat was going down by the stern. All the gunfire had opened the hull to seawater. The transom was almost down to sea level. In a few minutes the water would wash over the aft edge of the boat and the craft would be doomed.

Gunfire from his own men slapped into the starboard side of the boat and had Eckman ducking frantically to escape from being hit by ricocheting bullets. He slid over the port side of the boat into the water with the wetness piercing him with a start. He dully realized, as his life vest automatically filled with CO_2, that the apparent chill wasn't from the temperature of the water. It was from the sudden death that surrounded him.

Lieutenant Eckman swam over to the boat with the remnants of his landing party aboard and was pulled aboard by a grateful Chief Stevens. Eckman looked Stevens over and decided the chief was unhurt.

"There's only me and another guy who's not hurt," said Stevens.

Eckman's strength left him as he saw the results of the

gun battle with the North Koreans. His men lay about ooz-
ing blood, some crying out in pain, some lying with the
stillness of death about them.

"Three dead, five wounded," intoned the chief.

The North Korean boat, fully aflame, suddenly exploded
as the gasoline tanks detonated. Chief Stevens ducked instinctively, but Lieutenant Eckman ignored the blast of heat
and flaming debris that flew about them. His feelings were
frozen with the human consequences of the battle as he
turned away from the carnage on his boat to look over the
water around the two boats. The North Korean boat, with
its sides gone, rapidly slid beneath the waters of Kwajalein
Lagoon, leaving a flaming slick of gasoline and pieces of
shattered wood and equally shattered bodies. A red smear
lay on the water. The North Korean blood was mixing with
the waters of Kwajalein Lagoon.

A spot of orange hovered in his peripheral vision. He
turned and focused on it. It was a U.S. Navy life jacket
bobbing in the disturbed lagoon water. Inside it was the
body of one of the sailors who had attempted to board the
North Korean boat. His life jacket had automatically inflated when he hit the water.

Eckman gave an audible gasp and raised his arm in a
leaden motion to point out the body to the chief. The chief
let out an oath under his breath and ran forward to retrieve
the body from the sea.

Eckman sat down with his insides fluttering and tried to
settle himself. When the chief got the body alongside, Eckman went to help him. He tried not to look at the young
man's face as they dragged him aboard, leaving a trail of
American blood in the water. Eckman and Stevens laid the
dead sailor out flat on the foredeck near the bow and gazed
at him for a moment. Was it all worth it? Eckman asked
himself the question a few times, then gave up.

He stood, a bit more steady now, and looked into the
distance at the last fleeing North Korean boat. Chief Stevens handed him the binoculars, and Eckman obediently
put them up to his eyes.

The horizon swung shakily into view, and he saw a dot
which he thought was the boat. He also saw a long thin
vessel floating on the water next to the dot. He could no

longer mount any sort of attack on the boat, but it was a moot point. In a few minutes, they would board a submarine and slide below the waves and disappear.

The North Koreans were getting away.

CHAPTER SEVENTEEN

Opening Shot

Ken Garrett pounded on the wheel and tried to shove the throttles farther forward. Mike Sprague glanced at him and shook his head.

"Can't this thing go any faster?" asked Garrett in frustration.

"I doubt if we're going ten knots," replied Sprague. He lifted his binoculars and peered through them at the battle two miles off their starboard bow. "Those navy guys are really giving them hell."

Garrett blew out a puff of air in resignation. "Okay, okay, so I got a little carried away back there. Wouldn't you, if the North Koreans had your wife?"

Sprague shrugged. "I was never married." Garrett gave him a glare of annoyance.

"But I had a look at your wife for the first time this morning," Sprague continued. "Some babe. I can see why you go crazy about her."

Garrett grunted in semisatisfaction, then fell silent as he thought of where Nancy was at the moment and tried to block thoughts of what they would do to her when they got her back to North Korea. Or what they might do to her on the trip back.

"Listen, Mike," said Garrett in a subdued tone of voice, "I want to thank you for sticking with me in all of this. When we charged across Lagoon Road into that parking lot . . .'' His voice trailed off. Garrett was reluctant to reveal the emotion behind his remarks.

"Yeah, I thought it was checkout time," said Sprague. "We're damn lucky we're still alive." He sounded a little miffed.

"Yeah," replied Garrett, his voice conveying regret. "But I couldn't just stand by while that Korean son of a bitch shot Nancy."

"Yeah, I know," said Sprague. "Dying for the one you love isn't a bad way to go."

Emotion rose in Garrett. He felt his chest swell and began blinking his eyes quickly. He glanced sideways at his friend, who was studying the horizon intently. What did I do to deserve such a good friend as Mike Sprague? Garrett shook his head in reply to his own question. As an engineer he had been trained to approach things analytically and objectively. That was the only way to get things done in the engineering world. Emotions only got in the way.

Now, emotion was the chief driving force in him, and the bond between Sprague and himself had become infinitely stronger. He resolved that if Mike Sprague ever needed him, he'd be there for him.

Garrett also had the sudden realization that emotion was drowning out the promises he had made to himself about the conduct of his life. After his father had been nearly killed in an attempt to take revenge for a driving incident, Ken had vowed to renounce violence whenever he could and lead a totally nonviolent way of life. The police were getting paid for a reason. Let them enforce the law. Had Lloyd Garrett left the administration of justice to the civil authorities, he would still be a vital man today, and not the slobbering vegetable that he was.

Ken Garrett did not want to admit it, but he hated his parents for being irrationally violent. He especially hated his father for letting his rage take him away from the rest of the family. Every time he'd gotten a hit in Little League, he'd wondered what his father would have thought about it, whether he would have been proud of him.

That, and a lot more, had been taken away from him, and Ken never forgot or forgave. That business in New York, he thought. Was his response to the muggers' violence a result of the violence of his parents, or was it just common sense?

And now this, he thought. He squirmed at the feeling of the handgun under his belt. It was hard next to his stomach and an ever-present reminder of what he had done earlier in the day. Would the violence overwhelm him as it had his father?

Garrett took a deep breath and tried to shake the feelings and the questions with only partial success.

"Can you see the other boat?" asked Garrett. Sprague turned slightly to search for the second North Korean boat, the one that Nancy was aboard. It was easy to recognize— it was Sprague's own boat.

"Oh, man," mumbled Sprague under his breath. Garrett's head whirled around to look at his friend.

"The sub's there," said Sprague in a quiet voice that was almost drowned out by the engine noise.

U.S.S. Topeka

"Captain!" said Lieutenant Commander Martin Riley, the *Topeka*'s XO. Captain Fred Worden's head lifted from staring at a chart of Kwajalein Atoll.

"Incoming message from Lieutenant Eckman!" said Riley, and he flipped a switch on the intercom to allow Eckman's voice to fill the compartment.

"Black Knight, this is Lima Papa One, over."

"Lima Papa, this is Black Knight," said Riley into the intercom. "We read you five by five. Report status, over."

"We have engaged a large force of North Koreans and have suffered three dead, eight wounded," said Eckman in an out-of-breath voice. Riley gave Captain Worden an astounded look at the news from Lieutenant Eckman. The XO found himself at a loss for words. Eckman stopped talking and Riley and Worden suspected that the young lieutenant was struggling with his emotions. The captain leaned over to talk into the intercom.

"Lieutenant, this is the captain," said Worden in a subdued voice. "Please give us some details of the encounter." Eckman complied in a voice shaking with anger, frustration, and anxiety, betraying his shattered nerves.

When Eckman was done, Worden said, "Lieutenant, you and your men have done an outstanding job. Well done. Your mission now is to take care of your men. Get them the best medical care that Kwajalein has to offer. Over."

"Aye, aye, sir—and thanks," replied Eckman. "One more thing, Captain. The enemy has captured at least one engineer and has stolen a large number of top secret documents relating to missile defense and ballistic missile technology. Presently the enemy submarine has surfaced, and they appear to be getting on the sub. Over."

"What is the position of the enemy sub? Over," said Worden.

"Captain, it's . . ." began Eckman. "It's impossible to tell exactly. We're somewhere near Gea Pass. We're approximately five to eight miles south southeast of Gea Island with the North Korean sub about four miles due north of us. Over."

Riley had been looking at the chart of Kwajalein Lagoon and pointed out the spot to the captain.

"They're going to make a run through Gea Pass," said Worden. "And we'll be there to meet them."

Riley nodded. "But what do we do? Do we attack them or what? They've got an American prisoner aboard."

"All right, let's send a message to the Pentagon asking for instructions," said Worden. He keyed the intercom once again.

"Lieutenant, can you identify the American prisoner? Over," asked Worden.

"I don't know her name, Captain," replied Lieutenant Eckman. "But she's got dark red hair, and she's about five foot ten. Over."

Admiral Yi

"What have you done, Kim?" asked Captain Hong in a venomous voice. "Where are the rest of my men?" Hong expected another of Kim's arrogant stares that he had been subjected to during the long voyage to Kwajalein, but he was astonished when Kim avoided his eyes.

"I did what was necessary, Comrade Captain," Kim mumbled.

Hong grabbed Kim's arm in a fury. "My men! Where are the rest of them?"

"Dead, captured, I don't know," said Kim from behind dead eyes.

Captain Hong's eyes grew wide at the realization that twenty-nine of his men had been lost to the Americans. His head snapped around to search the horizon while keeping a viselike grip on his subordinate. He saw a plume of smoke in the distance from the burning North Korean boat and a speck that looked like a small boat heading toward them. Hong wrenched Kim around and pointed him toward the speck.

"Our men?" asked Hong with acid in his voice.

Kim shook his head. Hong let go of Kim's arm and rubbed his hands over his face. How could this have happened? Hong asked himself.

The captain straightened and stared at the sight of two of Kim's men forcing a tall woman through the forward hatch. "Who is that?" asked Hong.

"She is an American engineer," replied Kim. His voice reflected more confidence now that the captain was onto the subject that would save Kim from a firing squad. On the contrary, this subject would make him a hero, much as his father was over twenty years ago.

"An engineer?" asked Hong, rage barely contained in his voice.

Kim spoke quickly. "She knows missile secrets that we can use to develop our own missiles. And we have many top secret documents on missiles and the American missile defense system. This will be an intelligence gold mine for our country!"

Hong was livid. Kim had traded almost thirty of his precious men for a woman and some documents. Hong gritted his teeth as he saw five men starting to unload the documents from the stolen boat to be loaded into the submarine. Hong leaned over the side of the sub's sail and gestured angrily to the men on the deck below.

"You men, stop what you are doing! Get below immediately!" screamed Hong at the top of his lungs. The men stopped in their tracks and gaped in astonishment at the enraged captain.

"Captain! What are you doing?" asked Kim.

"Drop those documents and get below!" repeated Hong. The five men immediately dropped the documents and ran for the forward hatch, leaving a trail of white punctuated by a few red rectangles on the black skin of the *Admiral Yi.*

"Captain! Those documents will save our country many years of development—" began Kim.

Hong's face quivered with rage as he turned to face the lieutenant. "You will get below before I have you shot!"

Kim knew when to quit, and this was one of those times. A subordinate will always lose to an angry captain, especially in the North Korean navy. Kim quickly went down the ladder through the conn and went forward to see to the condition of his only remaining prize, the American woman engineer.

Hong watched Kim's hurried exit, then vowed to himself that Lieutenant Kim would pay a very high price for the slaughter of his men. Hong exhaled slowly to calm himself. He squinted into the distance at the slowly approaching dot. It looked more like a boat now with a readily definable wake. Who was on this boat? American military?

He glanced at his watch. Time to leave. The charges his divers had placed would go off in a few minutes, and he had to be ready to exit through the Gea Passage just after the detonation.

He looked at the documents that were scattered over the water. Had Kim been right? Were they that valuable? Too late now, Hong thought. It would take too much time to get a squad of men topside to get the remaining documents below.

Hong ordered the sub to dive, and looked at the approaching boat once again just before he went through the hatch into his metal world. The boat wouldn't get there in time to endanger him or his crew, he thought. This was the end of the encounter with the Americans.

U.S.S. Topeka

The shock wave hit the *Topeka,* catching the crew and the captain by surprise. The deafening sound had a metallic clang to it and rolled the boat from side to side.

"What the hell was that?" gasped the XO. Captain Worden glanced about quickly with alarm.

"Conn, Sonar," said a voice over the intercom.

The rattled OOD pushed the lever. "Conn, aye."

"Underwater explosion bearing zero, four, eight true," said the sonar supervisor.

"That's in the direction of Gea Pass," said the captain. He pushed down the intercom lever. "Damage Control, this is the captain. Give me a report from all areas on the boat."

"Damage Control, aye, aye, Captain," was the quick reply.

"What are the North Koreans up to now?" asked Riley.

"They blew the supply ship that sank in the channel," said Worden. "You remember what Eckman told us just after he arrived on Kwajalein? A couple of Kwaj inhabitants saw divers around Gea with North Korean flags painted on their tanks. They also said that the supply ship sank in the channel."

"Yes," mused Riley. "They really *are* going to come out Gea Pass." He shook his head and gave the captain a wry smile. "Sometimes you just luck out."

"Yeah," replied Worden. "Of all the passages through the reef, they chose to come out the one they apparently went in. And we're in position to pick them up again."

"Conn, Damage Control," intoned a voice over the intercom.

"Conn, aye," said the OOD.

"Watertight integrity is maintained in all areas. No apparent damage. Please inform the captain."

"Conn, aye," repeated the OOD. He turned to Captain Worden.

"I heard," said Worden.

"Conn, Radio Room," said another voice on the intercom.

"Conn, aye," said the OOD.

"Tell the captain we have a flash operational message requiring acknowledgment."

"Conn, aye," repeated the OOD. He turned again to Captain Worden.

"Okay, I'm on my way," said Worden. He lifted himself out of the chair and hurried to the radio room. He quickly went through the doorway and a radioman immediately handed him a printout of the message. Worden scanned the message, and his mouth fell open with surprise. He forced himself to slow down and concentrate on every word.

"I don't believe this," he mumbled under his breath, then looked at the radioman. "Acknowledge receipt?"

"Already done, sir," replied the radioman.

Worden dictated a short message formally acknowledging the message and stating that the orders would be carried out. Worden scribbled his signature on the quickly written copy of his dictated message and left for the conn.

Worden entered the conn in a rush, and immediately gestured for the XO to join him. He handed Riley the message as the lieutenant commander walked over to Worden's side. Riley read it and reread it.

"Holy shit," he said in a low voice, then gave the captain a look with raised eyebrows. "We let 'em get out through Gea Pass, then go to work on 'em?"

Worden firmly shook his head. He pointed to the chart of Kwajalein Atoll. "Get us to this point—" His finger stabbed a spot southwest of Gea Pass. "Then we'll line up to look right down the passage."

Riley's raised eyebrows got higher. "Captain?" he said to ask for more information.

"I don't intend to let this North Korean bastard get out," said Worden in a menacing voice. "They've already killed a number of Americans, our own men included. Now it's payback time."

Riley nodded and pulled himself up to his full height. "General quarters now, Captain?"

Captain Worden nodded, then glanced at the message one more time. He had sent a description of the captured American to his superiors in an effort to identify the prisoner. Sorry, Nancy Garrett, whoever you are, he thought.

But direct orders gave him no choice. Why did it have to be a woman?

Admiral Yi

Lieutenant Kim felt the submarine surge under his feet as they got under way toward Gea Pass. Kim knew they were going to get under way as soon as they endured the excessively loud blast from the charges placed on the sunken supply ship by the *Admiral Yi*'s divers. Normally he would be in the conn with the captain, learning as much as he could about handling the boat and about command at sea. Captain Hong, however, had made it very clear to Kim that his presence was not desired.

The captain was wrong, he thought. To waste the top secret documents like that was inexcusable. Kim planned to make the situation very clear to higher authority when they returned to the Democratic People's Republic. His thoughts ran toward the female American prisoner. She was the only prize he could claim at the moment, but she could give his country an intelligence bonanza in the missile area. He made his way aft toward where she was being held, driven by some need to insure that she was being treated all right.

Kim made his way toward the stern through the narrow passageways. Any of the men he met along the way deferentially scrambled out of his path by pressing themselves into small recesses in the sides of the passage. Kim could see a knot of men farther aft, and he squinted his eyes in an attempt to identify them. One of them was Moon. The woman must be nearby, thought Kim.

As Kim approached the small group of men, they noticed him coming and quickly scattered, revealing an open door. Only Moon remained, alternating his gaze between the approaching officer and the interior of the compartment.

"What is going on here?" asked Kim in his most arrogant tone.

"Comrade Lieutenant, the men had never seen an American before," replied Moon. "And they wanted to see the prisoner."

Kim leaned around the corner of the open door and

peered into the room. There, seated in a chair, was his intelligence coup. She was tied hands and feet to the arms and legs of the chair. She flicked her head to get a wisp of hair out of her eyes and stared at Kim with abject fear. Kim turned to Moon, his voice hissing with authority.

"Untie her, you fool!" said Kim. "She must be treated well! I want to deliver her in good condition to our friends at the Liaison Bureau."

Moon scrambled to obey, quickly deciding against telling the lieutenant that Kim's own men had tied up the woman. Kim stood with his arms folded and with a haughty expression on his face. He wondered what his father would think. Despite what Captain Hong thought, he had fought a great battle against overwhelming odds and had defeated the Americans. His father would be very proud, but would he understand that the greatest defeat for the Americans was in the person of this woman and the information she had in her head?

Moon got the rest of the rope free, and Nancy Garrett sat rubbing her wrists. She looked at Kim with a mixture of fear, gratitude, and hatred. The sub began to roll to starboard. Kim adjusted his feet to keep his balance, and Nancy grabbed the arms of the chair to steady herself.

Kim knew what the turn represented. They were entering Gea Pass.

U.S.S. Topeka

"It's pretty shallow in there, about a hundred and fifty feet," said Riley. His forehead was wrinkled. Captain Worden knew that when his XO's forehead was wrinkled Riley had doubts about their course of action.

"I can't see letting them get out into open ocean where they can maneuver and then maybe get off a shot at us," replied Worden.

"The torps might not work right in water that shallow and with a channel that narrow," protested Riley. His forehead was even more wrinkled.

"Yes, well, we'll just have to take care of that," said the captain. He turned to the OOD. "I'll take the conn."

"The captain has the conn, the OOD retains the deck," repeated the young junior officer.

"We're at Point Alpha, Captain," said the quartermaster as he eyed the navigation display, then made the appropriate mark on the chart which showed their position to be in line with Gea Pass but five miles to the southwest.

"Right standard rudder, come to course zero, six, three," ordered Worden.

"Rudder is right standard," said the sailor on the control yoke.

"Very well," replied Worden.

Seconds later, "Heading zero, six, three," said the sailor.

"Very well," said Worden. He looked at Riley, who was standing over the fire control party, a group of sailors seated at a set of consoles.

"Right now," said Worden. "We should be lined up with the Gea Pass."

Riley nodded but still seemed doubtful. Worden pushed the talk lever on the intercom.

"Sonar, this is the captain," said Worden. "Listen on this heading for our Master Three contact."

"Sonar, aye, aye, Captain," was the quick reply.

Worden hurried over to the chart and studied it. The North Korean sub had to come from the south and turn to port to avoid coral heads at the entrance to Gea Pass. A minute later Sonar came back on the intercom.

"Contact bearing zero, six, three. Slow speed screws, probable speed five knots. Preliminary classification: submerged hostile."

Worden acknowledged Sonar's information with his mind racing to visualize the next steps in his attack on the enemy sub. He'd turn the *Topeka* to port to block the noise of launch with the hull of his boat and fire one of his port torpedoes.

"Make tubes one to four ready to fire in all respects," ordered Worden in anticipation of confirmation of the contact's identity.

"Conn, Sonar. Contact is confirmed as Master Three," said the sonar supervisor. The OOD acknowledged Sonar and looked at the captain. Worden nodded to show that he had heard, then stepped up behind the fire control party, which was headed by the XO.

"Fire control and tracking party, I intend to destroy Master Three contact pursuant to orders from COMSUBRON2," said Captain Worden in clear, strong tones. His voice betrayed no weakness or doubt, even though he felt both to a degree he had never experienced before. "We will use torpedoes one and three and keep two and four for defensive purposes."

"Contact is turning to port," said a phone talker who was linked to Sonar.

There it is, thought Worden. The North Korean is making his final turn to line himself up with the Gea Pass.

"Left standard rudder," ordered Worden. "Come to course three, three, five."

"Tubes one to four are ready to fire in all respects," said another phone talker.

Worden received acknowledgment of the helm orders, then the sailor on the control yoke announced that they were on the ordered course. Worden gave a series of "very wells" to confirm that he understood the man.

"Captain, we have a firing solution," said Lieutenant Commander Riley.

"Ship ready?" asked Worden.

"Ship ready!" replied the XO.

"Solution ready?" asked Worden.

"Solution ready and loaded into tubes one through four," replied the XO.

"Weapons ready?" asked Worden.

"Weapons ready!" answered the XO.

"Select torpedo tube number one. Open outer doors," ordered Worden.

The noises of the torpedo tube outer door opening were conducted through the hull and were clearly heard by the conning crew.

"Outer doors open," said the XO.

"Stand by to fire," said Captain Worden.

A fire control technician grabbed the firing switch and shoved it over to the standby position. "Ready," said the XO.

"Shoot!" ordered Worden. The fire control tech flipped

the handle in the opposite direction from the enable position. New sounds filled the boat. After sounds of rushing air and sloshing seawater came a clunking sound and the noise of compressed air venting into the interior of the boat. The sudden increase in air pressure made the crew's ears pop.

Another fire control sailor steered the torpedo from its initial launch heading to a bearing that would send it down the center of Gea Pass. Captain Worden went over to the Geo Plot, which was a piece of paper that was placed over a light table and had the ship's position plotted on it along with a plot of the progress of the torpedo.

Bearings to the torpedo came in from Sonar as they tracked the noisy fish rapidly working its way toward the mouth of Gea Pass. Two junior officers busily drew bearing lines from the marker, called the "bug," that designated their own position. One of them quickly slapped down a piece of paper with lines predrawn on it, called a torpedo speed strip. The lines already drawn on it gave the distance covered by the torpedo in a given period of time. Worden watched, fascinated by the officers ticking off each speed line which represented his torpedo's relentless advance toward its rendezvous with the enemy submarine.

A thought struggled to the surface of Worden's mind. He had been fighting to keep it down, to deny its existence, but in a calm moment as they had now when the crew waited to hear a distant explosion, it had won its battle for recognition. Worden gave in to the thought and just let it happen.

Nancy Garrett.

CHAPTER EIGHTEEN

Maneuver

Admiral Yi

Nancy Garrett couldn't keep the tears from flowing. She had no hope now. The sub had submerged, and they were on their way to North Korea. What could she hope for? A quick death? How could anyone rescue her from the inside of a submarine? Complete, abject despair filled her as she thought of what they would likely demand of her. Could she hold out? What sort of torture would they perpetrate on her?

She was convinced that she was no hero, but she also knew that people who were under extreme stress could do amazing things. Was she one of those people? New hot tears ran down her face as she unleashed her anguish. She cried out loud in agony as she confronted the answer to all the questions she was asking herself. She knew what would happen. She would cave in at the first opportunity. They would ask her missile secrets, and she would give them all she knew, PENAIDS information, radar-signal-processing details, the entire missile defense penetration scenario.

It's so easy to be a hero when you're in the safety of your own country, in the comfort of your own home, she thought. But when you are actually confronted with torture and death, how many are the hero type? Well, she sniffed to herself, there's one less than I thought there was.

She began to rationalize her future actions to herself.

After all, she thought, the government couldn't expect her to withhold information under torture. They knew she couldn't withstand that sort of thing for long. After all, I'm just a wo— . . . Oh, God, what am I doing?

She squeezed her temples to stem her thoughts and forced her mind to listen to the sounds coming through the hull. There was the steady drumming of the screws and the rush of water past the hull. And there was something else.

A high-pitched whine getting louder by the second.

"Emergency dive!" shouted Captain Hong. He gave one of his officers a furious look. "How far is the bottom?"

"Fifty meters!" was the immediate answer.

"Make your depth fifty meters!" ordered Hong. His mind raced with the knowledge that an American submarine had been lurking just outside Gea Pass for who knows how long, and the devastating realization that it had just launched one of its extremely capable torpedoes at his boat. The channel was too narrow to maneuver in two dimensions and too shallow to effectively maneuver in the third. His only hope was to hit the bottom and try to duck the onrushing torpedo.

The men's relaxed faces had been jolted into imminent fear of death by the advent of the American torpedo. Some of them seemed frozen, others were breathing so fast that Hong feared that they would hyperventilate.

"Diving Officer, back off on your diving angle as we get near to the bottom," said Hong in a steady voice. "I don't want to stick the bow into twenty feet of mud."

Most of the men seemed to relax a bit upon hearing the calm voice of their captain. They'll be calm all right, thought Hong. Calm until we all die. He shoved the thoughts aside and tried to concentrate on the battle with the undetected sub and the single torpedo that could very well kill them all in the next two minutes. He eyed the depth gauge with its needle rapidly approaching the fifty-meter mark.

"All stop," said Hong as the needle swung past forty-five meters. The sub glided along for thirty seconds as Hong's men braced themselves for the collision with the bottom.

They heard light scraping along the hull, then the bow struck something hard and the sub ground to a halt with a shudder. The men bounced about, then came back to their original positions as the sub settled on the bottom of Gea Pass. The whine of the torpedo's screws was clearly heard through the hull. The crew in the conn all looked at Captain Hong.

"Its sonar hasn't started yet," whispered Hong's weapons officer with a hopeful tone in his voice.

Not yet, thought Hong. But soon.

U.S.S. Topeka

Captain Worden looked over the shoulders of the junior officers who were hovering over the Geo Plot. The position of his torpedo inexorably came nearer Gea Pass, which was sketched in pencil near one end of the paper. A bearing came in from Sonar which the officers quickly plotted with a hurried pencil line on the paper. It showed the torpedo at the entrance to Gea Pass.

"Enable Unit One," ordered the captain. The torpedo had been running with its sonar and its warhead disabled until Worden was sure the torpedo was close to his quarry. Worden felt that this lessened the chances of false interpretation of the torpedo's own sonar returns from the relatively shallow water.

"Unit One enabled," said the XO, who was substituting for Lieutenant Eckman, the weapons officer. The fire control crew enabled the torpedo via the trailing wire that unrolled from the torpedo tube as the weapon ran through the water.

"Acquisition!" said the XO quickly. A hush fell over the conn.

"Loss of telemetry on Unit One," said one of the fire controlmen. The XO's head swung around simultaneously with Worden's raising his eyebrows.

"Sonar reports detonation, bearing zero, six, three," said a phone talker.

The conn fell silent once again as the few eyes that didn't have to watch consoles wandered over to Captain Worden.

That was fast, thought Worden. It detonated only seconds after it was enabled.

"The torp must have been right on top of them when we enabled it," he said quietly.

Admiral Yi

The shock wave rolled over the boat, sending crewmen flying from their positions and sprawling to the deck. Captain Hong gingerly picked himself up from the deck as the lights flickered out for a few seconds, leaving them in absolute darkness, then bathed them in dark red as the emergency lights came on. Hong shook his head and looked about him, waiting for the rush of water that would signal his death and the death of his entire crew.

The rush never came. He staggered over to the intercom.

"Damage Control, give me a report," he gasped into the device.

Thirty seconds later, Damage Control responded. "Preliminary report indicates watertight integrity in all compartments."

Hong let out his breath in relief, but the question uppermost in his mind remained unanswered. Why were they still alive? He remembered a comment an admiral had made to him once as he had assumed command of the *Yi*. A British Royal Navy admiral had told him that once a Mark 48 torpedo had detected your boat you might as well kiss your ass good-bye. The Russians had some subs that could outrun a Mark 48, and maybe sometimes, if conditions were right, they could outdive it, but nothing the North Koreans had would be effective against it.

Damage Control came on the intercom and gave him a set of reports by compartments largely consisting of a few small leaks here and there. Hong's mind raced. The torpedo had exploded in front of them. Why?

The answer suddenly occurred to him, making his mouth pop open in an undignified manner. The wreck! He knew that the sunken ship was in front of them, how far he wasn't exactly sure. The torpedo must have gone after the wreck after he dropped the *Yi* to the bottom of the channel behind it!

The American sub probably thinks now that we're sunk, he thought. He could lay low and wait for the American to leave, then quietly steal away. That course of action appealed to him, but he quickly realized that it wouldn't work. The American would linger around looking for debris to make sure that Hong's boat was sunk. And they wouldn't be fooled into mistaking the sunken ship's debris for debris from a Kilo-class submarine. He had a small period of time before the American sub commander discovered that Hong and his crew were still alive, and Hong decided to make the most of it.

He gave the conn crew a fierce look. "Get back to your positions! Diving Officer, depth twenty meters! Load torpedo tubes one and two!"

Hong's orders had the desired effect. The crew reacted as if lightning had just struck, and frantically went into action. Orders were relayed over intercom and sound-powered phones. The entire boat came alive again.

"Activate sonar! Minimum number and strength of pulses to detect where the sunken ship is," ordered Hong. The order was instantly relayed to the *Yi*'s sonar room.

One thing is certain, thought Hong, I have to find the exact position of the wreck to carry out my plan of attack.

U.S.S. Topeka

A few of the conn crew expressed restrained glee at what they thought was the sinking of the North Korean submarine, but Captain Worden felt no satisfaction. He mentally asked for forgiveness for the death of Nancy Garrett. He wondered who she was and what she'd looked like. . . .

"Captain! Sonar says they have active sonar on bearing zero, six, three!" said a phone talker. "Half a dozen pings, then nothing."

The North Korean was still alive! His first torpedo had homed in on something, but what was it? The explanation of the strange behavior of the *Topeka*'s torpedo suddenly became clear. He had forgotten about the ship that had sunk in the pass! The torpedo must have hit it!

"Stand by to fire torpedo tube three!" ordered Worden. "Set Doppler gate at five knots." Once the Doppler gate was set, the torpedo would ignore anything that was moving slower than five knots, which would exclude the wreck. But anything faster would be fair game.

But where was he? Behind the wreck or in front of it? Worden bet that he'd be behind it.

"All right, this time we'll enable the torpedo when it's past the wreck," he told the fire control party. He turned to the young officers on the Geo Plot. "Distance to first detonation?"

The senior JO spoke up. "Eight thousand, five hundred yards."

"Program tube three to enable at eight thousand, eight hundred yards," ordered the XO. Captain Worden nodded in agreement.

"Number three programmed," said a fire control tech.

"Shoot!" ordered Worden.

Admiral Yi

"Ahead standard, make turns for eight knots," ordered Hong. He was sending the *Admiral Yi* through the disturbed water from the first explosion.

"Torpedo tubes one and two outer doors are open and ready to fire!" said a phone talker in a loud voice.

The tension in the crew and himself was almost unbearable. The conn crew fidgeted, waiting for the next order from their captain. Hong waited until he had heard from his navigation people that he was past the wreck.

"Tube number one, fire!" ordered Hong.

The crew heard the loud freight train–like noise as it echoed throughout the boat. With a final muffled thud, the torpedo left its tube and ran out Gea Pass.

"All stop," ordered Hong. "Diving Officer, set the boat on the bottom."

Hong was trying to stay one step ahead of the American sub captain. When the Americans heard the torpedo that he had just launched, they would know that Hong and his crew were still alive. The American captain would figure out that his torpedo's magnetic detonators had exploded on the wreck and not Hong's submarine. To prevent that from happening again, the American would program a Doppler gate in his next torpedo so that it would ignore the wreck and go after the *Yi*.

But he would be on the bottom near the wreck. With any luck the inevitable second American torpedo would not detect his stationary vessel.

U.S.S. Topeka

"Torpedo in the water, bearing zero, six, three!" shouted the phone talker connected to Sonar.

"Torpedo Room, cut wire on three!" ordered Worden. "Left full rudder! All ahead flank!" The *Topeka* rolled as the sailor on the control yoke threw it into the turn.

"Emergency Deep! A thousand feet!" said Worden to the diving officer. "Maximum angle on the bow planes!" He whirled to another phone talker. "Eject noise decoy!"

Worden's frantic actions left a "knuckle," or an area of disturbed water, behind him as he quickly got away from his earlier position. The best way to confuse a torpedo was to put maximum speed on the boat at a direction ninety degrees from the path of the oncoming torpedo. The acoustic decoy had electronics that swept through various audio frequencies and transmitted them through the water for the torpedo to detect and home in on.

"Come to course one, five, three," ordered Worden in a calmer voice. The sub leaned bow down as the vessel dove into the waters of the Pacific. A sailor announced the sub's depth at periodic intervals until they settled at the ordered depth. The hull groaned a bit in protest at the increased pressure, but that was all—watertight integrity was still maintained in all compartments throughout the boat.

"Sonar says they lost the enemy torpedo," said a phone talker in a quiet voice.

Worden cautiously let out his breath. It was a good sign. If they couldn't hear it, then the torpedo probably couldn't hear them. Worden suspected that between the enemy torpedo and his boat was an inversion layer which would reflect sound waves coming from either direction, thereby shielding his boat from the torpedo and vice versa. Worden ordered his engines at dead slow speed to make himself as quiet as possible.

Time dragged by. Worden and the conning crew fidgeted and began to sweat as they waited for sounds that would tell them what had happened to the enemy torpedo that was out looking for them. They hoped for a detonation far away which would signal that the torpedo had gone after the noise decoy. However, they heard nothing—not even the sounds which might tell them that the torpedo had run out of fuel and had dropped harmlessly into the depths of the Pacific. They all feared that they might hear its high-pitched whine again.

"Running time for their torpedo?" asked Worden.

Riley, the XO, glanced at the stopwatch in his hand, then turned and looked at Worden. "It's two minutes past their max. It must have run out of fuel."

Worden nodded. "We'll stay down a bit longer."

Riley nodded in return. "Aye, aye, sir."

"Running time for unit three?" asked Worden.

Another officer spoke up. "One minute to go before it runs out, sir."

Admiral Yi

Captain Hong gripped the handholds near him as he listened to the whine of the American torpedo's screws as the weapon rapidly approached his position. Questions roared through his mind. Was he close enough to the sunken ship to fool the torpedo? Had the American captain done what he had expected him to do? Had the American programmed the torpedo to ignore slow-moving objects? Would the magnetic detonators on the torpedo go off anyway?

Hong forced himself to be calm and look around the conn. His men glanced at him with furtive eyes as he stared at each one of them in turn. His message was clear—face death with stoic calm. With his electric propulsion plant shut down, his boat was extremely quiet. Hong had ordered the ventilation system shut down to prevent the Americans from detecting the sounds of the fans and had ordered maximum quiet throughout the boat. The air had rapidly become stale, and Hong wondered how long he could keep his people on the bottom in this state. His thoughts were interrupted by a sudden movement at the door to the conn.

Lieutenant Kim was through the doorway and staring into Hong's eyes before anyone could move to stop him.

"You fool!" hissed Kim into Hong's face. Kim's eyes were slits of rage as he confronted his superior. "Your failures have led us to this!"

The frantic whine of the onrushing torpedo pounded the hull and the crew's ears with impending death. The torpedo came on and on with nothing to stop it.

"This American weapon heads toward us while we lay with our feet in the mud at the bottom of the channel!" screamed Kim.

Hong could feel the rush of Kim's breath against his face. Hong reached up and grabbed Kim by the throat with both his hands to choke the life out of him. The officers and men in the conn stared unbelievingly as the two men struggled with each other. Hong forced Kim backward and bent him over the plot table, jamming his head against the American chart of Kwajalein Atoll. The whine from the torpedo's screws hit its peak as the torpedo ran directly above the *Yi*'s position.

Kim's hands flailed at Hong's face as Hong's thumbs pressed deeply into Kim's throat, cutting off his air supply. Kim's eyes went wide open, and he gripped Hong's forearms in a desperate attempt to break the captain's hold on him. Suddenly Hong's hold broke, and Kim gasped quickly for an immediate lungful of air. Hong grabbed him by the front of the shirt and dragged him to within an inch of his face.

"Listen! You son of a dog!" shouted Hong. "Listen!"

The conn fell silent as the captain and the lieutenant listened to the sounds coming through the hull. The piercing whine of the American torpedo had diminished, and they all distinctly heard the weapon's sound drop steadily in volume.

"It has gone past us!" said Hong. "You imbecile! It doesn't even know we are here! *That* is why we are lying on the bottom of the channel!"

Captain Hong held Kim with his left hand, then slapped him with all his strength using his right. Kim's head snapped around, blood seeping from his nose and mouth, and he started choking again from Hong's attempt to strangle him. Hong let Kim go, and the gasping lieutenant staggered, then fell to the deck. Two armed sailors appeared, called by one of the other officers. To Hong, they were a welcome sight.

"Get this piece of human filth out of here!" ordered Hong in a voice seething with rage. "And don't let him come back!"

Hong attempted to calm down and consider his next move, but his thoughts turned to his incredibly stupid lieutenant and what Hong would do to him when they got back to North Korea. Hong would take great pleasure in disgracing Kim and his family through a court-martial and execution. Hong rubbed his face in his hands as if to wash away Kim's contamination, then forced his thoughts to the situation at hand. The American torpedo had passed them and was now in search mode. It would search back and forth for a target until it ran out of fuel.

All Hong had to do now was wait.

U.S.S. Topeka

Captain Worden leaned over the shoulder of Sonarman Ernie Menago. Menago shrugged and looked up at the captain.

"Nothing, sir," he said to Worden. "Unit three must have run out of gas."

"No detonations?" asked Worden.

"No, sir, nothing like that at all," replied Menago. "We would have heard an explosion, sir."

Worden nodded in agreement, then scratched his head. "Any ideas where Master Three is at the moment?" asked Worden as he faced Chief Geller squarely.

"It could have gotten out of the channel while we were deep, Captain," said Geller. "That could place it anywhere."

Worden shook his head to convey what a problem it would be if the North Korean had escaped.

"Wouldn't he have to duck our torpedo?" asked Menago. "I mean, would he have time to get out after our torp died?"

"That's a good question, sailor," said Worden as he turned to face Menago. "Where do you think he is?"

"He's on the bottom, sir," replied Menago. "And real quiet."

Captain Worden considered his very young sonarman who had enough guts to say what he thought to the captain of his vessel. Worden wasn't about to immediately agree with the young man, but he wasn't about to immediately dismiss his opinion either. Worden had had an intermittent, recurring discussion with Chief Geller about Menago's training and the progress he was making. Worden was disturbed that the inexperienced Menago seemed to be on the phones at every critical point in the *Topeka*'s tracking of the North Korean sub.

However, it was Menago who had detected the enemy sub in the first place. And with the Doppler gate that had been programmed into the last torpedo, the situation suggested by Menago might make sense.

"All right. We'll assume that Master Three is still in the channel, so concentrate your search on that bearing," replied Worden after thinking for a moment. "You hear anything, anything at all, you let me know immediately."

"Aye, aye, Captain," said Chief Geller and Sonarman Menago in unison. When the captain left, Geller looked at Menago and raised his eyebrows. Menago smiled in return.

Admiral Yi

"Contact!" said a phone talker softly. Captain Hong took a step toward the man who was linked to the sonar room.

"Blade count indicates they are at a slow speed," said the phone talker.

Hong nodded. The American was traveling at a quiet speed and was listening also. Was another torpedo imminent? Perhaps the American didn't know where the *Yi* was. Hong had only one more torpedo—he normally would have had eighteen, but the extra personnel and equipment had demanded more space. How best to use this last torpedo?

The *Yi* sat on the bottom with its torpedo doors already open, therefore Hong could quickly fire a torpedo without the telltale sounds of tubes being flooded and doors opening. Perhaps he could surprise the American. Hong mulled over a plan to quietly drift off the bottom, fire the torpedo, and then head for the surface in an attempt to confuse the inevitable next American torpedo. He might evade it, then make a fast run for open sea while the American was eluding his last torpedo. After that anything was possible. The *Admiral Yi* could stay submerged for twenty days, less at any sort of speed. Hong shook his head. Quite a gamble, but it was a very large ocean, and he might just succeed.

"Captain! The contact is heading closer!" said the phone talker.

Hong's mouth dropped open with surprise. That was the first mistake the American had made. Hong modified his plan quickly. He would wait until the American was very close, then fire his last torpedo at them.

There would be no time for the Americans to get away then. His final torpedo would be all he needed.

Lieutenant Kim sat on the edge of his bunk and stared unmoving at the deck. His life and career had come to an end, he was certain of it. Captain Hong would take his revenge on him, and he would be shot for endangering the mission and the lives of the *Yi*'s crew. And on top of that, he'd had to endure the ultimate humiliation of nearly being strangled by Captain Hong. He could never face the conn crew again, and after the crew went back to normal operations the word of Kim's degradation would spread through the crew like wildfire.

The situation was made worse due to the crew's adulation of Captain Hong. Anyone he corrected, they despised. Anyone he disliked, they loathed. The crew's feelings for him would go beyond mere hatred.

Kim raised his hands and felt his throat, which still ached from Hong's attempted murder of him. He coughed quietly to ease the feeling, but it was to no avail. He was lucky that Hong hadn't crushed his larynx. He dropped his arms to his sides, and his right hand hit the butt of his pistol, which was still strapped to his waist.

Kim pulled the weapon out of its leather holster and coldly considered it. With it, he had killed some Americans today, just as his father had done years ago. *And what would his father think of him when told of his humiliation at the hands of Captain Hong?*

He gripped the weapon tightly and pointed it at his face, plunging the barrel into his mouth. One quick motion with his right index finger and it would all be over. No humiliation by his countrymen, no disappointment and rejection by his father. There would be nothing. Forever, just nothing.

His hands began shaking as he lost his resolve. He slowly lowered the weapon, then flung it disgustedly toward his small foldout desk. The gun hit the desk top and slid across to fall off the opposite side. The weapon hit the hull with a sharp metal-to-metal sound, then clattered to the deck.

U.S.S. Topeka

Ernie Menago squinted as the sound reached his earphones. The sliding, grinding noise of the wreck filled the background, but this noise was different, a definite metal-to-metal sound, as if someone had dropped something in a submarine.

"Sonar supe! I have a transient, bearing zero, six, three!" said Menago in a loud voice.

Chief Geller quickly called it into the conn. Seconds later, Captain Worden was at Menago's side.

"Anything else?" asked Worden in a breathless tone.

Menago shook his head. "Nothing, sir."

"What did it sound like?" asked Worden.

"Metal to metal. Very definite, not like background noise at all. Just one pop, then a bit of a rattle, Captain," replied Menago.

Worden nodded and grew serious with thought.

"Like somebody dropped a wrench or something," continued Menago.

"Play it back over the speaker," ordered Worden. Chief Geller got the tape set and pushed the Play button. The watery sounding metallic sound filled the area. The captain nodded and looked at Chief Geller.

Worden smiled and turned to Menago. "You did a damn fine job, sailor. Well done."

Menago smiled back. "Thanks, Captain."

Captain Worden made record time back to the conn. He quickly got behind the fire control party.

"Make torpedo tubes two and four ready to fire," ordered Worden. Lieutenant Commander Riley turned to glance at Worden.

"We've found Master Three," said Worden.

Admiral Yi

"Contact is turning," whispered the phone talker.

Captain Hong knew it was time to get moving before the American's range increased.

"Diving Officer, lift us slowly off the bottom," said Hong. The diving officer gave orders to fill a few buoyancy tanks with compressed air. Seconds later, the *Admiral Yi* floated free of the coral reef with some attendant groaning and scraping. Hong held his breath. He reasoned that the Americans would confuse his boat's noise with the noises of the sunken ship, which was still moving slightly and settling in the current that flowed through Gea Pass.

"High-speed screws, bearing two, four, three!" said the phone talker in a panic-stricken voice.

The American had launched a torpedo immediately! How could he have known? Captain Hong racked his brain for his next move. The Americans would not have a Doppler gate programmed into this torpedo, because they had launched it without hearing any screws. He had to get out of the area, and fast.

"Emergency surface!" ordered Hong. "Ahead flank! Launch noise decoy!"

The *Admiral Yi* surged ahead as her single screw bit into the seawater and thrust them forward. The diving crew flooded the buoyancy tanks with compressed air, and the vessel began its rush toward the surface. Captain Hong tried to gauge the motion and visualize the rapidly approaching torpedo. Next they would hear the torpedo screws, then, if it detected them, the torpedo's sonar would start to fill the area with pulses of sound. Once that happened, there would be no escape, thought Hong.

The whine of the American torpedo's screws suddenly

was heard through the hull. Captain Hong, along with the rest of the crew, held their breath.

Any moment now, the torpedo would detect them, thought Hong, and its sonar would start. Hong waited as the piercing sound of the onrushing weapon filled the inside of the conn with noise. Hong knew the sound—it was death.

Hong's mind froze with the thought of his imminent death. He had always thought that he would face his death with courage and go out in a blaze of bravado. Instead he stood transfixed by the sound of the approaching torpedo, his mind stopped with no thoughts at all occurring as a torrent of feeling surged through him.

The whine of the torpedo hit a maximum and seemed to stay level for an eternity. When the noise began to decrease in volume, Hong's mind refused to acknowledge it. Some trick of the mind, thought Hong in his first conscious mental process in the last twenty seconds. He and the crew strained their ears to hear any nuance in the torpedo's sound. Was it really going away from them?

The noise from the torpedo's screws decreased steadily until the men in the conn looked about, startled. They looked at each other, then at their captain, who began to breathe again.

The American torpedo had passed them by! But why? Its sonar hadn't been activated, thought Hong. Maybe the Americans hadn't enabled the weapon until it had passed them, thinking that the *Yi* was farther up the channel. Whatever the reason, my crew and I have a reprieve, he thought.

Hong's mind snapped back to the tactical situation at hand. He glanced at the depth gauge. They were at thirty meters and rising rapidly. Now was the time to fire his last torpedo.

"Prepare to fire number two!" ordered Hong. "Set depth to fifty meters." The crew rushed to comply.

Hong's eyes rested on the phone talker who was connected to the sonar room. Hong gasped a full two seconds before the phone talker's eyes grew wide open with fear. Hong knew what the young sailor would say before he said it.

"High-speed screws! Bearing two, four, three!" said the young man.

A second torpedo only seconds after the first! Hong's mind had been working subconsciously, anticipating the American's next moves, and had come up with the correct conclusion before he consciously knew it.

Hong's mind raced. His boat was speeding toward the surface with its ballast tanks blown clear of water. To submerge again, he'd have to vent the tanks, and that would take several minutes once he was on the surface. An eternity from now. He had to move now—in any direction.

"Left full rudder!" ordered Hong, his voice still firm with confidence and authority which belied what he felt inside. "Eject noise decoy!"

With wavering voices, the phone talkers repeated the orders into their sound-powered phones, then looked apologetically at their captain.

Suddenly the whine of the approaching torpedo was heard through the hull, followed quickly by the loud, repetitive pulses of sound which signaled to Hong that the torpedo had entered its terminal phase. The rapidly nearing torpedo pounded Hong's vessel with sound that never wavered or seemed tentative. The weapon had locked onto the *Yi* and would not be deterred. The noise decoy would be ineffective now that the torpedo was using its own sonar.

Hong found time to reflect that the sound of death could take many forms. In his world, the peculiar high-pitched near squeal of a torpedo's counterrotating screws was the sound of impending doom. Hong decided to face it squarely. There was nothing else for him to do.

"Torpedo's speed is increasing!" said the phone talker. He seemed amazed.

Yes, thought Hong, they increase speed just before—

The torpedo detonated twenty yards in front of and thirty yards below the bow of the *Admiral Yi*.

CHAPTER NINETEEN

Disaster and Deliverance

The force of the explosion from the *Topeka*'s torpedo slammed into the front of the *Admiral Yi*, shattering the bow and opening seams all along the North Korean sub's hull. Seawater immediately rushed into the open bow and trapped the remaining sailors who had survived the initial shock wave in the torpedo room. The water quickly filled the torpedo room and rammed its way through the sprung watertight door to the compartments beyond.

To the crew, the explosion felt like a huge fist had pounded into the front of the vessel. Anyone not securely strapped into a seat was thrown forward and hit the deck violently as the sub was thrown upward by the force of the detonation. In the conn, the entire crew was thrown forward except for the helmsman, who was strapped into a seat. Captain Hong struck his head on a protruding fire control console and fell to the deck unconscious.

Nancy Garrett flew forward and slammed into a nearby bulkhead, breaking the chair she was sitting in but banging her head on the metal wall. She fell into a tangled heap of broken wood. She rolled away from the bulkhead to get some room to maneuver, but only got herself further tangled in the pieces of wood from the chair. The sub, after its initial leap upward from the explosion, quickly leaned forward and started to go down by the bow.

We're going down, thought Nancy in a panic. She wiggled to free herself from the shattered wood of the destroyed chair, to no avail.

Lieutenant Kim gingerly picked himself off the deck and staggered to the doorway of his stateroom. The doorway had been distorted by the blast and had popped the door open. Kim went into the hallway and looked around at the two guards who had been there to keep him away from the conn as Captain Hong had ordered. They were crouched down and were quickly darting glances about, in a quandary as to their next move. They saw Kim come out of his room and moved to stop him, but the lieutenant halted them with a stare.

"Quickly, comrades, get back to the aft hatch," said Kim. The two guards glanced at each other, then obeyed Kim's order. They knew the lieutenant might have a way to save himself and them, and under the circumstances they weren't about to disobey any orders.

The lights flickered out and panic leaped within Nancy Garrett as she fought to stand in the shuddering vessel. She screamed out in frustration and jumped with surprise when the door was slammed open. Quickly a man entered and cleared away the broken chair, then yanked her to her feet. They both staggered out into the corridor and the meager red emergency lighting. Nancy glanced at the man who was saving her. It was Moon, the technical expert in the North Korean landing party.

Nancy alternately hated him for picking her to be kidnapped back to North Korea, and felt grateful to him for saving her life. He had shielded her when gunfire had erupted in the parking lot of the Range Command Building on Kwajalein. Now he was helping her get to safety—at least she thought it was to safety.

Moon pushed her along, chattering in Korean. They went along the impossibly narrow corridor with the sub tilting initially at a shallow angle, then at increasingly larger angles. When Moon yanked her to a stop, Nancy estimated that the deck was at forty-five degrees to horizontal. Moon went past her and opened the hatch at the top of a short ladder. He turned and waved for her to join him.

That was it, then, she thought quickly. Moon was trying to escape the sub by going out the hatch they had come in through. Nancy knew it was a double hatch with a chamber between. She thought it was to allow divers to exit and enter the sub while it was submerged, and now Moon was attempting to use it, but without diving gear. She hesitated. How far down were they?

The thunder of collapsing bulkheads pounded her ears with sound. She visualized the advancing wall of death as the sea smashed through bulkhead after bulkhead until it would penetrate the entire vessel, extinguishing all life in a random, vicious, but thorough manner. The submarine shuddered around her and seemed about to break apart. She scrambled up the ladder, her feet immediately sliding down to the intersection of a ladder rung and the vertical handrail as the vessel tilted beyond forty-five degrees.

Moon grabbed her arms and roughly dragged her through the lower hatch, then quickly slammed it and dogged it down. He hit the control switch that evacuated air from the chamber and pumped in seawater. The water swirled around her feet, and as it hit her ankles, she jumped at the wet feeling and in fear of what she would have to do next. Moon grabbed her by the arm to get her attention.

"Stop . . ." said Moon. His eyes reflected confusion as he sought to translate from Korean to English.

"Yes, I know. Stop breathing," she said while nodding her head. The water was up to her chest now and she began to breathe deeply to fully oxygenate her lungs. She knew she was a good swimmer and diver, having had much experience scuba diving in the Caribbean, but was she good enough for this? Another thought occurred to her, filling her with dread. She didn't know much about submarines. Were they breathing pressurized air, or was it at normal pressures? Would she get the bends from a quick ascent, fighting to get to the surface alive, only to die a horrible death from nitrogen bubbles in her bloodstream? The realization hit her that the air was being compressed by the water that was flooding the chamber. During her last breath she would inhale compressed air at the same pressure as the water pressure at their depth. She would have to exhale continuously all the way to the surface. In any event, there was only one course of action—out the hatch and up as quickly as possible to the surface.

The seawater gushed around her, filling the chamber more rapidly than she was prepared for, creating a deadline that was impossible to avoid. The water rushed in over her head as she took in a last, deep lungful of air while pressing her head against the overhead. There was only one thought on her mind.

How far down were they?

Ken Garrett's head spun around at the sound of the underwater explosion. The shock wave hit the hull of his boat with a thump, causing the old craft to creak and groan in protest.

"What the hell was that, Mike?" he asked his friend. Mike Sprague climbed out of the bilge, where he had been trying to fix the engines, which had stalled as they had approached the spot where the North Korean sub had submerged. Sprague looked around quickly. They both went topside to survey the area. Garrett was the first to the binoculars.

The disturbed water from the detonating torpedo was easy to find. Garrett gaped at the scene, not wanting to comprehend what he was seeing. As he stared through the glasses at the entrance to the Gea Pass, he saw the North Korean submarine's tail come out of the water, its screw suddenly increasing in speed to flail the air, only to sink quickly into the depths.

Ken Garrett dropped his arms as if they were made of lead. Mike Sprague gave him a quick anxious look and took the binoculars from him. He looked through them for a long minute, then looked at his distraught friend.

"Oh, God, they sank her," Sprague said in a low voice.

"How could they do that? Nancy was on board!" moaned Garrett.

Sprague put his hand on Garrett's shoulder. "They probably didn't know."

Garrett's insides quivered, and he felt as if he couldn't breathe. He had never faced death before today. Even his parents and grandparents were still alive. Now his beloved wife was gone.

* * *

Nancy Garrett cringed as the water crowded in around her face after Moon opened the upper hatch and let the remaining air escape to make its quick way to the surface. She felt a hand grab her by the crotch and shove her upward. Under any other circumstances, she would have been outraged that anyone would have touched her there, but she was only grateful that Moon was trying to save her life. She reached her arms upward and swept them back toward her sides in a powerful stroke, then raised her arms again while keeping them close to her sides to avoid breaking her momentum.

Exhale. *Exhale.*

The air bubbles streamed from her mouth and nose in a continuous flow as the urge to inhale increased. Just as she thought her lungs were exhausted of air, she found new reserves of air to exhale as the water pressure on her body decreased and the air in her lungs expanded. She opened her eyes and looked up at the surface. The light swirled and shifted as the water bent and occluded the sunlight in a random fashion, causing it to wave and bounce, seemingly beckoning her to come join in its merry dance.

How far away is it? How far down am I?

Her lungs seemed to run out of air again, but she tightened her diaphragm to squeeze out as much air as she could. The quicker she lessened the pressure inside her lungs, the more likely she would be to avoid the bends, but the more likely she would be to find the urge to inhale irresistible.

She tried to speed up her strokes and began a scissors kick in an increased effort to get to the surface quickly. Her diaphragm began to burn with the desire to inhale, and her lungs seemed on fire. The lights above dimmed as her brain sought oxygen and found less and less as the seconds ticked by. Inhale and drown; pass out, inhale, and drown; or . . .

Her upraised arms were poised for yet another down stroke but instead broke the surface and flailed wildly in the air. Nancy's body came out of the water up to her waist, then quickly sank back to neck level. She noisily sucked in air and settled into an instinctive treading of water to keep her head up and enjoying the sweet sea air. After a few

minutes, her head cleared, and she looked about to find the
nearest land. A low-lying bar of sand covered with swaying
palm trees caught her eye immediately. She judged it to be
about a thousand yards off, and immediately began a relaxed crawl in its direction.

Nancy stopped after a few minutes to rest and did a slow
side stroke to keep her head above water so that she could
get her breathing back to normal. A spot bobbed in the
corner of her eye. She looked over at several men swimming in the water. She realized with alarm that she wasn't
the only survivor of the sunken submarine and squinted in
their direction to count the men in the water. Half a dozen
at least, she thought with panic.

And they were headed for the same island.

"We got survivors!" shouted Sprague as he stared
through his binoculars. Ken Garrett nearly jumped a foot
off the deck. Sprague handed the glasses to Garrett, who
quickly held them to his eyes.

"There's seven or eight of them!" said Garrett with burgeoning hope. He strained his eyes to spot Nancy's red hair,
but concluded after several moments that all the people in
the water were men. Hope wavered in him as he frantically
searched the water for other swimmers. He lowered the
binoculars in a frenzy and whirled toward Mike Sprague.
Sprague had left his side, and Garrett yelled to make sure
his friend heard him.

"Mike, we've got to get over there!" Garrett turned
completely around and looked down into the cabin below.
He could see Sprague's backside protruding from the engine compartment as his friend continued to work on the
engines.

"How much longer?" asked Garrett anxiously.

"Don't know," came Sprague's muffled response. "If
you'd get off your ass and help me . . ." Sprague left the
rest unsaid.

Garrett was next to Sprague in an instant. "I don't know
much about boat engines," he apologized.

"You're an engineer, aren't you?" demanded Sprague.

Garrett shook his head. An engine mechanic did not have
much in common with a radar engineer.

"I'll do whatever you want," said Garrett plaintively. He turned to look in the direction of Gea Pass. "We've got to get over there," he repeated softly.

Lieutenant Kim Il Kwon broke the surface and gratefully sucked in much-needed air. He had done it! Kim congratulated himself on escaping the ill-fated *Admiral Yi*, which had sunk in three hundred and fifty meters of water with almost all of its crew and technical passengers, as well as the stolen reentry vehicles.

After Kim began to breathe less frantically, he took a quick look around. He had come to the surface near another group of men who were desperately swimming for a nearby island. Beyond them, closer to the island, was a second group. That was it, then, thought Kim. Only two groups had gotten out the escape chamber. A total of—he counted quickly—ten men, including himself. He wondered if Captain Hong was one of the men in the water. He peered at them intently, then concluded that Hong had gone down with his vessel. Knowing Hong, he would have been the last to get out, if he had a choice. Hong had had too much integrity, the stupid kind of integrity. Integrity had gotten Hong killed, whereas Kim was still alive.

New hope ran through Kim as he began to swim for the distant island. Could he hide from the Americans until he escaped from this atoll? There might be a way. Steal a boat in the middle of the night and set sail for the Democratic People's Republic. Yes, he concluded as he stopped to rest, with the remaining men he could do it.

Kim gasped for breath and glanced at the island, which didn't seem to have gotten any closer. Kim realized he was exhausted from his free ascent from the stricken submarine, and now he had to swim quite a distance to get to shore. He thought with increasing anxiety that he might not make it. He tried to call out to the other men in the water, but couldn't make himself be heard. He began swimming again, pushing his aching body with the sure knowledge that if he didn't keep moving, he'd drown.

A spot of white on the shoreline to the left caught his eye. What was it? Kim squinted and stared, trying to keep the water out of his eyes long enough to get a good look.

He suddenly realized what it was, and his discovery gave him new energy that propelled him toward the island with new hope.

With its bow just touching the beach lay the *Sea Dragon*, Mike Sprague's boat, which Kim and his men had used before.

Nancy Garrett swam all the way into the beach horizontally, trying to keep her feet away from the razor-sharp coral that lined the edge of the island. The staghorn coral that formed protrusions which reminded humans of antlers were the most treacherous. She gave thanks that she had kept her sneakers on during her swim, but also thought that her thin blue jeans would be no match for the dangerous coral that lay below.

Fortunately she was on the leeward side of the island, which meant that the ocean would be much more calm than the water on the windward side. However, there were other dangers as well. Stone fish, which look like their name when undisturbed, were a danger if stepped on, and cone shells would shoot a biological dart into an unsuspecting swimmer's foot or hand if they were picked up.

Nancy swam, keeping one eye on the rapidly rising sea bottom. She tried to stay over the white areas of the bottom, which she knew were sandy, and avoid the dark areas, which had the dangerous coral. She eventually made it without injury to the eastern side of Gea Island and let the mild surf shove her gently up onto the beach. She lay totally drained of energy and let the seawater surge around her as each new wave broke on the sand. She lay as if she were dead until a stronger surge sent sand and salt water over her head, causing her to raise her head and cough and spit the grit from her mouth.

She got up on her elbows and dragged herself farther up on the beach, then collapsed again as the last reserves of strength left her. The tropical sun bore down on her, and soon after exhilarating in the initial warmth, she crawled under the shade of a palm tree to escape the direct sun. After a half hour of rest, she lifted her head with the thought of locating the rest of the survivors of the sub. She had to avoid them at all costs until the people on Kwajalein could get out here to rescue her.

Nancy dragged herself upright, gagging quickly on the remnants of swallowed and inhaled salt water. She recovered and looked over the water for any swimmers. There were none. A penetrating look up and down the beach produced no results. Where had they gone? She rubbed her face in her hands to aid her thoughts. Could they have all drowned?

The answer came to her quickly, and she looked around, startled at its implications. The North Korean survivors had already made it to the island and were probably in the process of searching it for anything they could use to survive or to help them hide from the inevitable American search parties. Nancy immediately looked toward the interior of the island, which was filled with palm trees, vines, and seemingly every imaginable green growing thing on the planet. She shuddered at the dense vegetation and gave in with the thought that she feared the North Koreans more than she feared the jungle.

Nancy Garrett stood and resolutely began to pick her way through the brush.

Lieutenant Kim actually smiled to himself as he assessed his situation. He had escaped the doomed *Admiral Yi* with no injuries and had nine healthy men with him. And they had recovered the forty-foot boat that they had used to leave Kwajalein. The lower cabin was still filled with some of the top secret documents that they had taken from the Range Command Building. The boat itself had split a seam in the hull, and Kim thought the damage had been caused by the two underwater explosions coupled with a collision with the reef. He had three men below trying to patch it up and slow the entry of water into the boat. The boat was in good condition nevertheless, but had only a limited supply of gasoline. The gasoline supply would at least put some distance between himself and Kwajalein Island. Kim nodded to himself with satisfaction. He was back in control, this time without the interference of Captain Hong.

Kim would portray Hong as a good captain who had made a fatal mistake by sitting quietly on the bottom of

Gea Pass when he should have been attacking the American submarine. To paint Hong as a bumbling idiot would be unbelievable to the people who knew him, and they would attack Kim's credibility. Fortune had smiled on Kim many times over—none of the survivors with Kim had witnessed his humiliation by Hong. The guards who had escorted him from the conn and had accompanied him to the aft escape chamber didn't know why they were guarding Kim. Just that Captain Hong was furious with him. Even so, he'd have to make sure that the guards did not make it back to the Democratic People's Republic.

Both of those guards had taken their automatic weapons with them and were now busy cleaning them with a gun-cleaning kit found on board. They had also found an AKM that had been inadvertently left behind when Captain Hong had angrily ordered the men to set the boat adrift. It was pure luck that the boat had been driven by the wind to beach itself on Gea Island.

So they had three AKMs and one Beretta 92 FS, the kind used by the U.S. military, that the owner of the boat had secreted away. Kim had taken it and had shoved it into his empty holster. The guards had two clips each in addition to the fully loaded ones in the weapons themselves. The AKM found on board had a full clip as well. Kim's men had found four clips for the nine-millimeter Beretta which Kim had pocketed.

"Comrade Lieutenant," said a voice over his shoulder. Kim turned quickly at the familiar voice and saw the technical expert, Moon.

Kim nodded and grunted at him in greeting. "So, Comrade Moon, you have escaped as well. It appears that this is our lucky day. Praise the Dear Leader," he said in a sarcastic tone.

Moon's eyebrows went up slightly in surprise. "Yes, praise him indeed." Moon looked at him warily. "The woman escaped with me."

Kim arched an eyebrow. "The woman engineer? We are indeed lucky this day." Kim looked beyond Moon. "Where is she?"

"I don't know," replied Moon. "We were separated when we escaped the *Admiral Yi*. But she must be on the island." Moon took a step forward, and his voice became urgent. "We must look for her, Comrade Lieutenant."

Kim's eyes narrowed, and he looked at Moon with disdain. Kim did not like being told what to do. Still, Moon had a point. The woman engineer would make a very nice addition to the store of top secret documents on the U.S. missile defense.

"All right, Comrade Moon, we'll look for her," said Kim. "But when we are ready to go, we are going to leave whether we have found her or not."

Moon's face filled with relief, and he agreed quickly. Kim leaned over to the men who were busy trying to stem a leak in the hull.

"How much longer?" he asked.

"About an hour more, Comrade Lieutenant," answered the senior enlisted man.

Kim stood and looked Moon in the eye. "We search for her for an hour."

Moon's face now reflected disappointment. He nodded anyway and prayed that they would find her quickly. He eyed the thick jungle that she was hiding in and shook his head. Kim ordered five men to accompany Moon and himself on the search. Moon was heartened a bit—Kim was taking everyone except the men working on the leak.

Nancy Garrett stumbled for the tenth time in ten minutes as she tried to make her way through the dense jungle to get to a decent hiding place. The island was small, only about four hundred yards square, but the vegetation was extremely dense. She thought her chances of eluding the North Koreans were about fifty-fifty.

The ever-present wind across the Pacific seemed to have stopped at the edge of the jungle, and the heat and humidity began to take a toll on her. Her head throbbed from having hit the submarine's bulkhead when the torpedo detonated, and she was exhausted from her free ascent from the sinking submarine. At least I don't have any sign of the bends, she thought. All her aches and pains seemed to be related to her desperate swimming to get to the island.

She strained her eyes to see through the dense undergrowth and spotted a small clearing a few yards ahead. She headed for it, and after fifteen minutes of exertion, she managed to wiggle through the brush to get to the clearing. Several palm trees had been knocked over by the recent typhoon and formed a triangle below which was an area that was ideal for a hiding place. After glancing about carefully, she gratefully sank to the sand below the fallen trees. The area seemed clear of insects or any other living thing, and Nancy settled down in a dark spot and closed her eyes.

Waves of fatigue ran over her, and her body screamed for rest. She would rest, she thought, but only after the North Koreans had left the island. She tried to force her eyes to open, but to no avail. She began to doze.

A clacking noise jolted her awake. Her eyes flew open, and she stared straight into the face of a particularly mean-looking, two-foot-long coconut crab. She jerked backward and let out an involuntary yell. The crab was in a fighting stance with its claws extended and wide open. It took a couple of steps toward Nancy, causing her to scramble away quickly.

Moon's head jerked around at the muffled sound in the jungle. Kim gave him a quizzical look.

"Hear something, Comrade Moon?" asked Kim almost pleasantly.

"In that direction, sir," said Moon. Kim held out his hand and gestured for Moon to go in the indicated direction. Moon nodded and set off quickly through the underbrush.

Nancy Garrett crawled around the base of a fallen palm tree, then peered over it to see if the enormous crab was following her. She caught a glimpse of the crab retracting its claws, and she gave a sigh of relief. A quick glance around told her that this might be a better hiding place than her first one. The fallen palm tree had exposed a small cave. She peered in, wondering if she could fit, then crawled halfway in. Her hand hit a piece of fabric half buried in the sand. She rubbed the sand away and yanked on the fabric, which immediately ripped, exposing a flat object in the sand. Her curiosity piqued, she dug around the object, which seemed to be a long piece of rotted wood. She worked for five minutes to get it free.

Nancy stared at the artifact with fascination. It was an old rifle with a bayonet attached. The stock was almost entirely rotted away, as was the bayonet, but the barrel and the body of the rifle were still in good shape. She ripped the rest of what she thought was oilcloth off the ancient weapon and immediately speculated on its origin. World War II? But which side? She rubbed the grime away from the barrel and saw Oriental characters. Japanese, she thought excitedly.

I've found a old Japanese rifle from World War II, she thought. There's no way this thing could fire, but if the North Koreans show up maybe I can use it as a club. Or maybe . . . She considered the ragged edge of the corroded bayonet as the sounds of vegetation being shoved aside floated over to her. Nancy Garrett looked about in a fever to determine who was approaching. Through the under-growth, she saw a smear of the color of flesh. She squinted and stared at the form that seemed to hang suspended among the vegetation.

Lieutenant Kim Il Kwon's face hovered among the thick brush.

CHAPTER TWENTY

Chase

Gea Island

Captain Peter VanHoeven of the recently sunken ship, the *Pacific Belle*, pushed the foliage aside and gave the cabin cruiser a good look. Several men had climbed aboard and were obviously working on the vessel. He briefly considered going up to them and introducing himself, but something told him to wait. Maybe it was the green uniforms and their Oriental faces that gave him a warning that these men weren't supposed to be there.

VanHoeven lifted his binoculars to his eyes and carefully examined the boat, and especially the men. They seemed to be doing something below decks—he thought maybe there was a leak that they were trying to plug. Their uniforms were unknown to him, some sort of green fatigues, unmistakably military in origin, with belts and holsters that seemed to want to hold various weapons.

So what is it all about, he thought. Japanese marines conducting some sort of survival exercise? He looked at the faces again. They didn't look Japanese. Chinese, then? But why would they be so far away from their country?

He wished he and his crew had seen the craft first. They would be working on it to make it seaworthy instead of these mysterious men who had seemed to arrive out of thin air. He turned back around and glanced over his men. Only five including himself had made it to this tiny island. He hoped the rest had gone to one of the myriad small islands that popped up out of the sea on the edge of the reef.

They weren't in bad condition, a few coral cuts the worst wound among them. They easily could have all drowned in the storm when the *Pacific Belle* had gone down, but they had been lucky. VanHoeven knew he wouldn't get another ship again, not after his fatal miscalculation to try to get inside the lagoon before the storm hit. He should have known that typhoons are unpredictable and change track sometimes at random.

VanHoeven eyed the boat again and figured he had no choice. He had to make their presence known. He and his men had to get off the island somehow. But something made him hesitate.

Nancy Garrett dropped like a stone to the sandy earth and froze with fear. She strained her ears to listen to the sounds of the North Koreans and prayed that they would head in a direction away from her. The North Koreans kept coming as quietly as they could with only the brushing aside of vegetation and intermittent, muttered, unintelligible phrases to break the silence.

Nancy slid slowly under two fallen palm trees while still gripping the old Japanese rifle. Her blue jeans stood out against the sand, and she felt panic at how her clothes were so different from her surroundings. She carefully began to push sand over her legs and hips to conceal the bright blue material. With her legs covered, she lay back, trying to push her head as far under the trunks of the fallen palm trees as possible. She thought of her dark red hair and silently cursed it for the millionth time in her life. When she was a young girl, she hated the color of her hair and the millions of freckles that went with it. However, as a young woman, dark red hair had become fashionable, and she was suddenly very chic. She never would have guessed that the color of her hair might put her in extreme danger someday.

She laid her head down on the sand and cautiously shoveled some sand up around her head for camouflage. Something with a thousand legs crawled across her forehead, causing her whole body to twitch in revulsion. She closed her eyes and bit her upper lip to keep from crying out. Her heart pounded in her chest and her breath came in shallow, silent gasps.

Lieutenant Kim's eyes swept the small clearing. So many places to hide, he thought, and glanced at his watch. And not enough time to check them all. It was hopeless, he concluded. Even on an island this small, the density of the vegetation made a thorough search impossible. Kim sat down heavily on a fallen palm tree and brushed the sand and dirt from his disheveled uniform.

A foot below the palm tree, Nancy Garrett could feel the grains of sand hit her face. When the cascade was over, she cautiously opened one eye and stared in shock at the backs of Kim's legs. She slowed her breathing to keep from making any noise, however slight, and listened to the thumping of her heart. Kim rustled above and sent a smaller shower of particles down on her. Thankfully she got one eye closed in time to prevent being blinded by the sand.

Kim gazed at his men, spread out around the clearing, and decided it was time to go. The top secret documents would have to be enough. Actually, thought Kim, the documents represented an enormous intelligence coup. He stood quickly and summoned his men to his side. A thought struck him. He quickly communicated it to his men. The men smiled in return, and even Moon, who had given signs of disapproval of Kim's prior actions, seemed pleased.

Kim, Moon, and one other man crouched down at the edge of the clearing while the rest of his men moved noisily in the direction they had come. Their sounds rapidly diminished, quickly absorbed by the dense vegetation.

Kim and the others knew it was a gamble. She might be hiding at the other end of the island or perched up in a tree looking down at them. Kim gave the treetops an involuntary glance. He relaxed and decided they had to wait for at least ten minutes to be sure. Five minutes later, he heard a cough.

Kim strained his eyes in the direction of the sound, then saw movement out of the corner of his eye. The sand under the fallen palm tree he had used for a seat began to move. Moon started to stand, but Kim restrained him with a firm hand on his arm. Kim stared at the area under the tree and saw the white sand fall away from a dark reddish object. Then she was suddenly in full view not twenty feet away.

Nancy Garrett breathed deeply at her close call and fought to get the sand and whatever else out of her hair. She combed her hair with her fingers, then gave up and brushed the sand away from her jeans. The movement almost directly in front of her caused her to jump with alarm. Incredibly, standing in front of her, with an arrogant smile on his face, was the North Korean officer who had threatened to kill her a few hours ago on Kwajalein Island.

She gaped at him for an astonished second until rage at his deception overcame all else. She whirled and picked up the corroded Japanese rifle, pointed it at Kim's chest, and charged. Kim's expression changed immediately from one of condescension to one of complete seriousness. Kim braced himself to jump out of the way as she drew near so that he could grapple with her from the side as she went past him.

Nancy got within a yard of impaling Kim with the rotted weapon when another man stepped into her path. The rusted bayonet slid along his forearm, gouging a furrow in the man's flesh. He yelled with pain and grabbed her hair with his free hand, yanking back on her head with such force that her advance was halted in midstep. She frantically swung the rifle around and hit the sailor a glancing blow to his back. She felt a rough hand on her shoulder that savagely jerked her around.

Kim punched her on the jaw, snapping her head back and sending her reeling. She fell backward and, nearly unconscious, landed heavily on the ground. Moon was beside her in an instant, and just by his presence shielded her from further harm from Kim.

Kim looked at his man who had tried to protect him from the mad American woman. He had a deep gash the entire length of his arm and was bleeding profusely. Kim ordered him to catch up with the rest of the men and send two of them back to the lieutenant in order to transport the woman back to the boat. The man stumbled off into the jungle trailing a line of blood.

Kim gave Moon a disgusted glance. Was he concerned about her because of her intelligence value or because he hadn't been with any women lately? Kim decided not to wait for the rest of the men. He went over to the woman and grabbed her around the waist. He jerked her upright, his hand slipping across her chest and resting on one breast. Kim spun her around and slapped her to wake her up, then shoved her toward Moon.

He regarded her for a moment as Moon fought to keep her upright. He had expected her to surrender, or at least to run away in a panic. But she had done neither. Instead she'd charged him with an ancient rifle that wouldn't fire even if she had had the ammunition. A feeling bordering on respect ran through him. This was going to be an interesting American. He wondered if she would show as much courage under the inevitable torture.

Kim looked at his hand briefly with the memory of her breast on his mind. A pang of desire mixed with the embryonic respect and created a feeling that was unique to him. The thought of having a woman again filled his mind.

Yes, he thought, that would be nice, but it would come later, after they were on their way back to the Democratic People's Republic.

Kwajalein Island

Jack Pearson jogged into the helicopter hangar and saw with satisfaction that a helicopter was being readied for takeoff. He ran up to the crew chief, who was a skinny, balding man in his fifties.

"I need that helo right away," said Pearson in a breathless voice.

Harold Clayton turned and gave Pearson a quick glance. "Oh, really? Just who the hell are you?"

"My name doesn't matter. It wouldn't mean anything to you," replied Pearson. "I need that helo to pursue the North Koreans."

Clayton turned fully around and was about to give this intruder hell as only a crew chief can when he saw the rifle Pearson had in his hand. His eyes flicked back and forth between Pearson's face and the weapon, then settled on his face.

"You're serious, aren't you?" said Clayton, being careful not to offend a man with a rifle in his hand.

"Yes, we have to hurry," replied Pearson.

"Well, this aircraft isn't going anywhere for a while," said Clayton.

Pearson gave him a quick look, and his face changed from anxiety to confrontation.

Clayton rushed to explain. "Engine's out. We have to replace it." He gestured to the opposite side of the helicopter, the side hidden from Pearson's view. Pearson walked over to the other side and saw two mechanics laboring over the port side engine.

"Damn it! How long?" asked Pearson in frustration.

"Several hours. We have to check out the hydraulics and the starboard engine as well," said Clayton.

"Is there any other aircraft that'll fly?" asked Pearson.

"No, they were all damaged by the storm. This chopper will be the first one in the air," answered Clayton. The crew chief examined the other man closely. "You know, I'd like to take a crack at those North Koreans myself, but you're gonna need authorization to take this helo. You Security or something?"

"Yes, I'm Security," said Pearson quickly.

"Well, I need to see a written authorization," said Clayton slowly. He kept his eyes on the rifle. "The CO is right over there. You could talk to him."

Pearson gritted his teeth. "No, I can't. I was just over there. Colonel Descano was murdered by the North Koreans."

Clayton's mouth popped open with surprise. After a few seconds, he clamped his mouth shut and gave Pearson a long look. He made a decision and walked over to his two mechanics.

"Put a rush on it, guys," he said. He jerked his thumb over his shoulder toward Pearson. "This guy has got a date with the enemy."

Gea Island

The sounds of men approaching caused Peter Van-Hoeven to tense immediately. He looked carefully through

the foliage once again and saw several men dragging a
woman across the beach toward the boat. He quickly peered
through the binoculars and centered them on the woman.
Red hair filled his sight as he frantically tried to focus in
on the scene.

She's obviously no Japanese or Chinese, he thought
quickly. He looked through the field glasses again, now
unsure of what he was witnessing. A tall, red-haired woman
being dragged along a beach by Orientals, he thought. Am
I losing my mind?

The conclusion was unmistakable. She is being kidnapped, he thought. But by whom? And who is she?

VanHoeven lowered his binoculars and quickly looked
around. He had only one real weapon, a revolver that had
been included in the survival kit on their rubber raft. The
raft had been punctured by the coral and the repair kit lost
in the surf, but they had retrieved the survival packet, which
also included a few flares.

He looked back toward the boat. Could he stop them?
Should he stop them? He was in a quandary. Some of the
men had automatic weapons, and he and his men wouldn't
stand a chance if the intruders opened up on them.

The men dragged the woman on board, then started up
the engines. They're about to get away, he thought frantically. What do I do? The woman made up his mind for
him.

Nancy Garrett's piercing scream split the air around the
island.

Gea Pass

Ken Garrett heard the rumble of engines across the water
and jerked his head up to determine the sound's origin. He
scanned the area near Gea Pass for the source of the engine
noise again and spotted a familiar white boat near the beach
on Gea Island. Garrett felt a chill run through his body at
the sight. He gave Mike Sprague, who was attempting to
fix the reluctant engines of the old craft, a quick glance,
then ran to the wheelhouse and got a pair of binoculars.
The glasses shook with the beating of his heart as he focused in on what he knew he would see. It was Mike's

boat, the *Sea Dragon*. The last time he had seen the boat, it was in the possession of the North Koreans, and Nancy was aboard being taken to the North Korean submarine.

He bit his lip, trying to stem the surge of anxiety that rushed through him. Was Nancy still alive? Or had she gone down with that ill-fated sub? He cursed for the thousandth time the badly maintained engines on their appropriated boat which had caused them to float helplessly while the North Koreans were now getting away, maybe with his wife.

When he heard the scream, a surge of fear mixed with adrenaline rushed through him. It was a woman, he thought feverishly, but was it Nancy? He strained his eyes to pick out any details of the people on board the boat, but he could see nothing.

Peter VanHoeven took careful aim at the stern of the boat, making up a plan of attack as he went along in this highly unusual situation. The boat had inboard engines, but VanHoeven knew bullets would penetrate the hull easily. Could he disable the engines by shooting through the hull? He also knew he didn't have any other choice.

VanHoeven pulled the trigger, and the gun jumped in his hand. He immediately reaimed at the stern where he thought the engines were and kept firing until the gun ran empty. That's it, he thought. I'm out of ammo.

VanHoeven hunkered down quickly as he saw the boat crew look about to determine the source of the gunfire. Maybe they would come after him, he thought, and he and his crew would try to disappear into the jungle. They could keep out of the intruders' way and delay them until they were rescued. When would that be?

VanHoeven peered through the foliage again and was alarmed at what he saw. Two men were pointing their automatic weapons over the stern and preparing to open fire into the island's undergrowth. VanHoeven jerked his head down and gave the rest of his men a frantic whispered warning. They all lay down flat on the ground.

The AKM bursts filled the air above them with lead and pieces of shattered palm trees.

* * *

The cracking of small arms' fire floated over the water to Ken Garrett's amazement. Someone else was resisting the North Koreans! Hope rose in him. Maybe they would stop them or delay them until help arrived. They now had some allies in their battle with the lagoon's invaders. He held his breath as he watched the boat with the North Koreans slowly back off the island's beach.

The North Koreans began to fire bursts into the jungle, and Ken's hopes fell. How could anyone stand up to that kind of gunfire? The chattering blasts from the assault rifles suddenly stopped, and the area fell silent.

There was no return gunfire.

Captain VanHoeven gingerly picked his head up from the hole he had made in the sand in his effort to keep below the automatic weapons' fire. He brushed the sand away from his face and looked around at his men. They all had escaped the vicious gunfire. He breathed a prayer of thanksgiving, then inched his way forward to give the boat another look.

The men near the stern of the boat were moving about quickly and seemed agitated about something. One of the men pointed over the side and gestured frantically toward something on the water. VanHoeven got the binoculars up and squinted through them to discover what had upset the intruders. He trained the glasses on the water behind the slowly moving boat.

The water had a slick on it that reflected the light in faint streaks of color which looked like wavy rainbows stuck to the water. Gasoline! He had succeeded in hitting a fuel line or maybe the fuel tank itself, and the boat was leaking gasoline. There was a sudden frenzy of activity on the boat as the men sought to contain the damage.

VanHoeven whirled around to get at the survival kit. Now he had the means to stop them from getting away with the kidnapped woman. If he could set the boat on fire, they would have to abandon it. He prayed that he wouldn't hurt the woman in the process. VanHoeven grabbed some flares and leaped to his feet as he saw the boat start to move quickly away from the beach. He moved out from the undergrowth and ran a short distance down the beach.

VanHoeven got behind a large palm tree and pointed one of the flares toward the boat.

He pressed the actuator on the side of the short round tube, and the flare ignited, rushing away from him and arcing out over the water. The flare was taken wide of the mark by the stiff ocean breeze and fell harmlessly, sizzling into the water. He gave the men on the boat a careful look and saw that they were too busy with damage control to give the flare any notice.

VanHoeven pulled out another flare and set it off after compensating for the wind. The flaming device flew out over the boat, then was pulled by the wind aft of the vessel to fall ten yards astern. The gasoline lying atop the water was immediately set ablaze, the flames running outward, outlining the gasoline slick and rushing toward its source, the boat itself.

The North Koreans were caught by surprise as the stern of the boat suddenly caught fire. They immediately jumped to fighting the fire as the helmsman throttled back, then shut down the engines altogether. The *Sea Dragon*, its stern on fire, went dead in the water.

Ken Garrett stared, initially hopeful, then horrified, at the flaming boat. Someone on the island had fired flares at the boat and had gotten the North Koreans to stop to fight the fire.

And here I sit dead in the water with Mike fighting to fix these damn engines! Garrett propped his elbows on the wheel to steady the view in the glasses and concentrated on the people he saw fighting the fire near the stern. He saw green, the color of the North Korean uniforms, and a swath of Oriental faces above the green. The green uniforms seemed to jostle for a moment, then they parted and gave Garrett a clear view of the rear deck.

Suddenly Nancy was in view, and Garrett's heart skipped a beat at the sight of her. He was flooded with relief that she was still alive, then dropped into despair at the sight of her captivity. He scrambled back to where Mike Sprague was still working on the engines.

Mike heard him coming and started to complain. "The electrical system on this tub is a piece of sh—"

''She's still alive!'' interrupted Garrett.

Sprague turned and gave him a startled look. ''Are you sure?''

''I saw her! She's on the *Sea Dragon*! The North Koreans have it, but somebody fired a flare and set the stern on fire,'' replied Garrett with a shaking voice.

''What!'' shouted Sprague in indignation. He dropped a pair of pliers and ran to the upper deck to take a look in the binoculars.

''It's the *Sea Dragon* all right,'' he said slowly. ''But who the hell fired the flare?''

Garrett was ready with the answer. ''Someone on the island. Looks like we've got a chance now to stop them.''

Sprague turned and gave Garrett a fierce look. ''Yeah, if my boat doesn't blow up first. Of course, that would stop them pretty good, wouldn't it?''

''We've gotta stop them,'' said Garrett almost plaintively.

Sprague looked at Garrett again and seemed ashamed of his last remark. ''Yes, we have to get Nancy back.'' He immediately turned back to his repair of the engines.

Lieutenant Kim gritted his teeth against the heat of the flames that swarmed over the stern of the boat. He had to get this fire out quickly before the gasoline tanks on the boat exploded. One of his men came up with a hose and sprayed the fire to keep the heat from them as others got buckets and anything else that would hold water to douse the flames.

After ten minutes of dumping water on the flames, they had control of the fire, and quickly thereafter they had it completely out. The stern was weakened and the deck distorted, but the boat was still seaworthy. The bad news was that they had only one engine available; the other's fuel line had been cut and its distributor smashed by gunfire from the island.

Kim pounded his fist on the cabin wall. These Americans were all over the area and surprised them at every turn. When were they going to give up and just let him and his men leave?

* * *

Garrett watched Sprague run to work on the reluctant engines. Five minutes later, he heard one engine come to life. Hope rose in Garrett that they would be able to finally get under way to rescue Nancy. He looked in the direction of the *Sea Dragon* and saw with dismay that the boat was under way and slowly making its way north.

Sprague came out of the bilges cursing. "I can get only one engine to work. The other one is hopeless," said Sprague. "Ignition wires are falling apart. I had to take wires from one engine and combine them with the other to make one good set. Even so, I think we're only running on five cylinders. Why couldn't this piece of shit have diesels?"

Garrett's face fell with despair. "We'll never catch them on one sick engine."

Sprague looked at his friend and shook his head. He had done all he could and Garrett knew it. Garrett's mind raced with a solution, and an idea seemed to explode in his mind.

"Mike! We'll go back to Kwajalein and get another boat—" began Garrett.

"It'll take too long," protested Sprague.

"We'll steal the *Jelang K*!" said Garrett with barely contained excitement.

Sprague immediately agreed. The *Jelang K*, and its sister ship, the *Jera*, were very fast catamarans that were used for trips to other islands in the lagoon. And they were quite a bit faster than his boat, the *Sea Dragon*. They could get back to Kwajalein, take one of the catamarans, and still catch up to the North Koreans.

"If we can't get the *Jelang* or the *Jera*, we can get one of Security's cigarette boats," said Garrett. "Those things practically fly over the water."

Sprague frowned and shook his head. "Those security boats aren't any good in rough seas. We'd probably tip the damn thing over. We'll get the *Jelang K*. I know where they keep a spare key," he concluded with a grin.

Garrett turned the wheel and pointed their boat toward Kwajalein. There was hope. They weren't out of the game yet. He gave an anxious glance behind them toward the rapidly disappearing *Sea Dragon*.

Nancy and he were headed in opposite directions. But not for long.

Jack Pearson leaned over the helicopter pilot and stared at the lagoon water below. They were at five hundred feet and headed for Gea Pass. He and the pilot both spotted the small boat at the same time.

"Take her down for a look," shouted Pearson into the pilot's ear. The pilot nodded, and the helicopter rapidly dropped in altitude.

Pearson surveyed the boat as they went by slowly only a hundred feet above the waves. The craft was puttering along headed for Kwajalein at a slow speed. Pearson saw two men and pulled up his binoculars to get a closer look at them. One older, heavy man was steering the boat with his face turned away from him, but the other had walked out from under the cabin roof and stared up at Pearson's aircraft. He was younger and in good shape. The man gave a quick desultory wave, then went back toward his companion.

Nothing here, thought Pearson. He told the pilot to head toward Gea Pass. The helicopter gained altitude and sped off to the northwest as Pearson sank into thought. The man's face looked familiar. Where had he seen that face before? Probably bumped into him on the island, mused Pearson.

His thoughts were interrupted by the pilot, who grabbed his arm. Pearson looked at him, and the pilot just pointed ahead. Pearson immediately put the binoculars up to his eyes.

There was another boat ahead, and this one was headed away from Kwajalein.

"I am sorry, Comrade Lieutenant," said one of Kim's men. "I wish I could give you better news, but we cannot stop the leak."

Kim grimaced and waved the man away. He had just gotten a report on the fuel reserves. They had lost quite a bit from the gunfire near Gea Island, but they still had enough to get them to the other end of Kwajalein Lagoon. Then they would run out. So it was a race to see whether they would first go dead in the water or go under the water. Kim went to the cabin below and ripped open every cabinet he could find. In one he found a set of charts of Kwajalein Lagoon and he spread them out on the table. He quickly found his present location on the chart and searched the chart for islands that were far away from Kwajalein Island. The largest one immediately caught his eye.

The island of Roi-Namur, Kim knew, contained radars and tracking equipment that supply the Kwajalein Range Command with reentry vehicle data.

Kim rubbed his chin. This island was inhabited, but it would certainly have fuel for his boat, or if they were lucky, they might be able to steal another boat to make their journey to the Democratic People's Republic.

Kim glanced up and looked at Moon, who was holding a bag of ice to the American woman's lower jaw. The blow from Kim had caused a large lump on her face. She stared back at him with a mixture of fear and hatred. So, thought Kim, her spirit isn't broken yet. That would come later, when they were out of this cursed lagoon and far away from the Americans—and far away from any sort of rescue for her.

Kim went topside and gave the helmsman a course to follow to get them to Roi-Namur. A thrumming noise in the air around him made his head jerk around toward the sound's origin. He raised his eyes to the sky. There was a helicopter rapidly approaching them.

Kim's mind raced. A helicopter could blow them out of the water if it had the right weapons. He made an instant decision and shouted to his men to get below immediately, then he leaped down the short ladder to the cabin below.

"Get the woman topside now!" he shouted to Moon. Moon gaped at Kim for a moment, then quickly got to his feet while Nancy looked at both of them with a puzzled expression. Moon grabbed Nancy by the arm and yanked her to her feet, then dragged her up the ladder to the upper deck.

Kim ran to the sleeping compartment in the bow of the boat and rummaged through Mike Sprague's clothes until he found a shirt and a pair of pants. He put them on over his green fatigues and cursed the fact that the clothes were much too big for him. He pulled the shirt's excess around to his back and jammed it into his pants.

Kim ran through the doorway to the cabin area, then suddenly reversed his steps as his mind recognized another object he desperately needed for his imminent charade. He leaped back into the sleeping compartment and picked up a western-style floppy hat with a large brim. Kim jammed it on his head and noted that the hat fit better than the clothes.

He ran through the cabin, with his men staring at him in disbelief, and up the ladder to the upper deck. He ordered an incredulous Moon to get halfway down the ladder to keep out of sight and ordered the helmsman to set the wheel to the correct course and tighten the small hand wheel on the side of the helm to keep it from moving. The man complied and quickly went below. Kim glanced at the approaching helicopter and guessed that it was still far enough away so that its occupants couldn't see any detail on the deck of his boat.

Kim pulled the handgun out of his pocket and viciously jammed the barrel into Nancy's side. She cried out in pain and tried to pull away. Kim grabbed her arm and kept her next to him, then he turned to Moon, whose head bobbed in the hatch that led below.

"Tell the woman that I will kill her if anything goes wrong," ordered Kim. After Moon translated, Kim said, "Tell her to smile and wave at the helicopter, and to keep the left side of her face turned away from the helicopter." Should the people in the helicopter see the lump on her face, they might get suspicious, thought Kim.

Moon nodded and translated while Kim stared into her eyes. She looked back and forth between Kim and Moon, then gave Kim a look that clearly said that she understood. Kim let go of her arm and took a step back. He had a sudden thought and turned to Moon.

"Tell her that she will be dead before she can jump over the side," said Kim. Kim could see her shoulders slump a bit as Moon talked to her. So she had been thinking of escaping over the side, thought Kim. He gave the aircraft a glance and turned halfway toward the wheel to appear as if he were piloting the boat. He kept both eyes on his female prisoner.

The beating of the air grew intense as the helicopter drew up beside the boat.

Jack Pearson leaned over the pilot once again and stared at the boat a hundred feet below them. The stern was blackened from a fire and they were proceeding slowly due to the damage. The boat had obviously seen better days.

"Hey, get a load of her," said the pilot over the rotor noise. A woman appeared from under the cabin roof and stood with her head turned forward. She began to wave as Pearson stared at her, recognition forming in his mind.

"Look at that! She's giving us the finger!" exclaimed the pilot.

The woman had the middle finger of her right hand extended as she pleasantly waved with her left hand in the direction of the helicopter.

Nancy kept one eye on the helo and one on Kim while praying that he wouldn't see her obscene gesture, or that if he saw it, he wouldn't know what it meant. There were two men in the aircraft with one stretching over the pilot to give them a look. He had a thin face and was bald, maybe fiftyish with a gray mustache. She recognized him with a start. He had caught her and Ken's attention in the airport. They had speculated then that he was some kind of security officer. Hope ran through her. He must be after the rest of the North Koreans.

She dropped her hand, keeping her middle finger extended and wiggling it for emphasis.

Pearson gaped at the woman for a moment. How had Nancy Garrett gotten out here? The finger signal was the telltale sign that she was in danger, maybe she was still with the North Koreans. Pearson had thought that the North Koreans had rendezvoused with their submarine by this time. Maybe they haven't been able to locate it, he thought quickly. The orders given to him via his satellite receiver suddenly filled his mind. If he fulfilled them, he would shoot Nancy Garrett now. He shook his head and pulled on the arm of the pilot.

"Get on the other side," he said. The pilot nodded and gained altitude.

"Ask her what the extended middle finger means," ordered Kim in a suspicious voice. Moon translated.

Nancy's mind raced. "It's the Hawaiian Good Luck Sign," said Nancy with a half smile.

Kim listened to Moon's translation and got a puzzled look on his face. He had heard that expression somewhere before. He shrugged it off and looked with satisfaction at the helicopter that was rapidly gaining altitude. The Americans in the aircraft had been convinced that his boat was an innocent one. His ploy had worked.

The helicopter rotor noise faded as the helo went high above Kim's boat. The pilot headed to the left of the boat, then decreased altitude until Pearson could see under the main cabin roof. He pointed his rifle out the window and tried to steady it to get a good look through the telescopic sight at the man at the wheel.

The rotor noise suddenly increased, causing Kim's head to snap around to see where the helicopter was. He looked directly into Pearson's eyes. Kim jerked his head down a split second before Pearson's bullet shattered the Plexiglas window just above Kim's head. Nancy Garrett gaped in astonishment at the gunfire from the men in the helicopter, then saw her chance to escape. Kim was turned away from her and was hiding below the cabin side wall to escape the fire from the helicopter. At the moment, he wasn't paying any attention to her.

She ran to the railing and got one foot over the side when strong hands grabbed her from behind. She kicked and screamed, but the arms encircled her waist and dragged her toward the hatch that led below.

Kim turned and thundered at his men. "All of you get topside and open fire on this helicopter!"

Kim's men scrambled up the ladder, nearly trampling Nancy and Moon, her captor. They fanned out on the aft deck and pointed their weapons at the hovering aircraft.

Pearson squeezed off one more shot, which hit the cabin's side wall, then grabbed the pilot by the arm.

"Take 'er up fast!" he shouted.

The pilot nodded and rapidly increased altitude. Pearson risked a glance toward the boat below and saw muzzle flashes at the tips of the North Korean weapons. He heard some of the bullets slap into the side of the helo and held his breath as the interior of the aircraft was filled with pieces of Plexiglas and bullet fragments in an explosion of violence. The pilot cringed from the gunfire and increased altitude as fast as the helicopter would go. Pearson looked out the shattered side window and saw the boat drop far below them, then slip behind them as the pilot increased forward speed.

Pearson breathed easier and glanced quickly at the bullet holes in the windows around him. I was damn lucky I didn't get my ass shot off, he thought. Where did all those North Koreans suddenly come from?

So, thought Pearson, the North Koreans still had Nancy Garrett and they were going somewhere in the lagoon. To meet their submarine? If that was so, then why weren't they in the ocean? Where were the rest of the North Koreans? Pearson shook his head and let out another sigh as he looked again at the holes in the windscreen.

The constant humming of the helicopter engine suddenly was interrupted as the engine coughed, then continued on. The interruption in the smooth running of the engine caused a bolt of terror to run through both Pearson and the pilot. They both glanced about.

"We've got to get back to Kwajalein!" shouted Pearson.

The pilot shook his head as he frantically looked over his gauges. "We're nearer to Roi than Kwaj. We'll have to head for there."

Pearson nodded. He wasn't about to argue with the pilot under the circumstances. He grabbed the seat quickly as the engine coughed again.

CHAPTER TWENTY-ONE

To Roi

Ken Garrett looked over at his friend, Mike Sprague, and shook his head once again. I guess he really did know where the key was to the *Jelang K*, thought Garrett. If it wasn't for Mike, God only knows what would happen to Nancy. At least now they had hope.

The *Jelang K*, a very fast catamaran, was speeding along at twenty-five knots with Garrett and Sprague aboard. Garrett desperately hoped that they could catch up with the *Sea Dragon* quickly. Sprague had said that the *Sea Dragon* hadn't much gas in it when the North Koreans stole it, and Garrett allowed himself a burgeoning hope that they might rescue Nancy.

Mike Sprague staggered up to the wheel as the boat bounced and swayed as it pounded through the waves in the lagoon.

"I've been thinking," Mike said over the engine noise. "Those buggers are going to have to refuel someplace before they set sail for North Korea. They're going to have to take on a lot of fuel if they take the *Sea Dragon*. And the only place they're going to get it is Roi-Namur."

"Could they even make it to North Korea in your boat?" asked Garrett.

"Well, they might. Crazier things have been done," replied Sprague. "But I wouldn't recommend it."

"They may have no choice," said Garrett. He felt hope surging in him once again. He gave his friend an appreciative glance. Mike Sprague had always given him hope even in the blackest situation. And it didn't get any blacker than this, he thought.

When Garrett had told him of his marital troubles months ago, omitting the unholy incident in New York City, Sprague had expressed optimism and had given him new hope. And now it was no different. He's by my side, ready to put his life on the line for me and my wife.

He thought over what Mike had said about the North Koreans refueling before they sailed for North Korea. It made a lot of sense. Exiting the lagoon at a different spot than Gea Pass, where their submarine was sunk, made a lot of sense too. The American submarine that was still out there wouldn't know where they would come out, or even if there were any survivors. Garrett got a cold feeling. He and Mike Sprague might be the only ones who knew the North Koreans were still alive and had Nancy captive. We might be the only ones to stop the North Koreans now, he thought. The idea made his insides flutter, until a grim determination overtook him.

Roi-Namur is where we'll stop them, he thought.

Nancy Garrett cringed before one of Kim Il Kwon's fierce stares. Her jaw hurt terribly where he had hit her on Gea Island, and it had swelled until she looked like she was chewing on a basketball. However, Moon kept giving her ice, which seemed to dull the pain and limit the swelling up to a point.

Fortunately he hadn't laid a hand on her after the gunfight with the helicopter. Nancy suspected that Kim's successful defense of the boat had mollified his anger at not being able to fool the men in the helicopter with his hastily rigged deception. She wondered what had tipped off the men that the North Koreans were on the boat. Had it been her "Hawaiian Good Luck Sign"? She quickly suppressed a smile.

She had read a book long ago about the crew of the U.S.S. *Pueblo*, a U.S. spy ship that had been captured on the high seas by North Korea in 1968. The North Koreans had allowed the international press to take pictures of the American crew to prove that the U.S. sailors weren't being mistreated. The Americans each made the same obscene sign while the press snapped away. The North Koreans noticed the signal and inquired what it meant. One sailor told them that it was the Hawaiian Good Luck Sign. The North Koreans were delighted. Their American captives were finally beginning to see things their way.

Later, when the North Koreans found out the meaning of the American obscene gesture, they punished the U.S. sailors unmercifully. Nancy had gambled that Kim and Moon were too young to know what it meant. She had been right and had gotten the signal to the men in the helicopter. The men in the helo had obviously interpreted it correctly. She had been successful, although she worried that Kim was searching his memory for the real meaning of her Hawaiian Good Luck Sign.

Kim called Moon over to his side of the cabin and spoke with him briefly while continuing to glare at Nancy. Moon glanced quickly at her, then looked at Kim as he extended his middle finger briefly. Moon nodded and walked toward Nancy.

"He want meaning of this," said Moon as he jabbed his middle finger into the air.

Nancy swallowed nervously, then gathered up her courage. "As I said before, it's the Hawaiian Good Luck Sign."

Moon looked puzzled, so Nancy continued. "You go like this"—she gave both of them the finger—"and you say 'Fuck you!' "

"Fruck you?" said Moon as he mangled the infamous word.

"No, no," exclaimed Nancy as her bravery began to mount. "Fuck you!"

"What that mean?" asked Moon.

"It means 'Have a nice day' in Hawaiian," explained Nancy. A small smile crept across her face. These two either were really stupid, she thought, or they had led extremely sheltered lives and didn't know anything about Americans.

Moon turned around and looked at Kim, whose face was frozen with rage. Moon's mouth dropped open in shock. Kim leaped to his feet and was an inch from Nancy face in less than two seconds. She could feel his breath on her cheek as she turned to avoid him. Abject fear mixed with the dumb realization that she had pushed him too far. He obviously knew what the obscene expression meant.

Kim grabbed her by the throat and began to shout something incoherent at her while choking the life out of her. Nancy's face turned beet red in a moment. Suddenly Moon was dragging Kim away from her. He broke Kim's hold on her neck and dragged him a few feet away. Kim turned and punched Moon full in the face, then, screaming with rage, he pulled his handgun from his holster and pointed it at Moon.

Nancy grabbed her stricken neck with her hands and tried to press her trachea back into shape so she could take a breath. She gasped and wheezed and coughed until she got some air back into her lungs. Nancy glanced at Kim and saw his finger tightening on the trigger.

Moon stood a few feet away and stared back at Kim without flinching.

"Go ahead, Kim," said Moon. "Shoot me, then the woman. Then all the rest. And when you get back to the Democratic People's Republic—when you get back *alone*—how will you explain that only you survived and all the rest of your men died?"

Kim began to shake with rage, then he suddenly steadied, pointed carefully, and pulled the trigger twice in rapid succession. The two bullets passed an inch away from either side of Moon's face to hit the bulkhead behind him.

Moon jumped with shock at Kim's action and took a step backward. The fear on Moon's face seemed to mollify Kim—he knew he had made his point. Kim was still in control, and no one was going to tell him what to do.

"Listen to me, Moon!" began Kim as he pushed himself into Moon's face. "I will not endure any more insults from that woman, or from you! You will control her or you will be shot! She will then be brutalized as if she were a South Korean terrorist!"

Moon was familiar with the barbaric torture that suspected agents from South Korea were subjected to before they died. The North Korean government and military took out its frustrations at losing the Korean War and its inability to reunify the peninsula on the only people it could, captured South Korean intelligence agents.

Kim reached back and punched Moon again, knocking him to the deck, then he kicked him in the face, sending a spray of blood across the deck and up the wall. Moon groaned and didn't try to get up. His face was a mass of blood. Kim turned on his heel and went up the ladder to the main deck and began screaming at the other men.

Nancy started to breathe seminormally and looked at Moon through tears of pain and anguish. She sniffed and wiped the tears from her eyes and felt pity for Moon. This man has saved my life once again, she thought. How many times has it been? She unsteadily got to her feet and got a wet paper towel from the kitchen area. Nancy went over to Moon and began to wipe the blood away.

The helicopter pilot looked frantically over the control panel.

"This thing is getting really sluggish!" he shouted over the rotor noise. "We must be losing hydraulic fluid." He pointed to a gauge whose needle was near the extreme left side of the dial. "Pressure is dropping! We only have a few seconds left!"

Jack Pearson pointed out the right side of the windows toward the water and the small islands that dotted the meandering line of the reef.

"Head for the reef to get near the islands!" he said.

The pilot nodded. "I'll try."

Pearson looked to the north and studied the island of Roi-Namur and its irregular crescent moon shape. The smooth curvature of the island's north side seemingly had a notch taken out of it, and the southwestern end had an elongated tip due to the addition of a runway that extended the land out into the lagoon. The reef, which separated the ocean from the lagoon, appeared as a light brown line running from either end of Roi-Namur with a light green smear of color lining the reef on the lagoon side. The green and brown of the reef stood out starkly from the deep blue of the ocean and lagoon waters. The reef seemed to connect the small islands in a connect-the-dots fashion as it wandered over the surface of the water.

Pearson glanced back briefly at Roi-Namur. The island seemed to him to be a dark green oasis in a sea of blue. They wouldn't make it to Roi-Namur, but he hoped they would be able to get to a much smaller island to the southeast. Perhaps from there they could signal the people on Roi to send a rescue party.

The pilot tried one more time to raise the aircraft control tower on Roi, then gave up in disgust.

"The gunfire must have hit the radio. I can't send or receive," said the pilot. "Let's hope they have us on radar. I hope the rescue beacon works," he grumbled, and flipped the switch to start sending the distress signal.

The helicopter was only feet over the waves in the lagoon as the pilot shoved the throttle forward to get as close to their target island as possible before he lost all control of the aircraft. The engine, which was already running roughly, started to cough in protest.

Pearson fixed his eyes on the island ahead of them which looked like a small patch of dark green encircled by a thin line of light-colored sand. The water rushed by only feet below them as the reluctant engine barely kept them aloft. He glanced at the hydraulic pressure gauge and saw that it was nearly at its minimum, and he suddenly knew that they wouldn't make it. He pulled his harness straps as tight as he could. It would be only seconds now.

Pearson instinctively held his breath as the small island loomed closer than he had dared to hope. They approached the thin beach and Pearson began to hope that they would make the shallow waters at least before their wounded aircraft gave up on them. The pilot began to pull back on the collective to take forward velocity off the aircraft in preparation to hover, but at that moment, the engine died completely and the helicopter dropped like a stone.

The helicopter slammed into the water while still upright, sending the shock of the collision through the fuselage and into the seats of Pearson and the pilot. A quick piercing pain shot through Pearson's back, causing all his muscles to grow taut. He held his breath, afraid that just inhaling would cause pain. The aircraft immediately began to fill with water. Pearson took a few fitful breaths and endured the pain that accompanied them, then glanced out the window at the crystal-clear water, but he couldn't determine how deep it was. The bottom could be two feet or twenty feet down.

There's no choice anyway, he thought. I've got to get out and swim no matter how deep the water is. He looked at the pilot and made sure he was all right, then unbuckled his harness and forced the door open. Water immediately rushed in around his feet as he slid off the seat and into the lagoon waters. He began to tread water with his back pain at a tolerable level, but his foot hit something, sending a surge of pain through his back once again. He ignored it and swam forward a few feet, then discovered that the bottom was only about six feet down. He swam twenty yards, then stood and looked around to see the pilot swimming alongside him. He grabbed the pilot's arm and helped him to stand.

They looked at each other, then back toward the stricken helicopter. It hadn't had far to sink and sat with most of its fuselage still above water, but it was canted at a forty-five-degree angle. They turned around and walked through the water to the beach.

"Well, it could be worse," said the pilot.

"Yes, you did a superb job getting us this far," said Pearson. The pilot smiled.

They sat down on the sand and let the tropical sun dry their clothes as they rested.

"Did you get any of those North Koreans?" asked the pilot.

Pearson shook his head. "No, I don't think so."

"Damn shame," said the pilot in a masterful understatement.

Pearson's thoughts ran on. They were lucky to be alive, but they were on a deserted island about a thousand yards from Roi-Namur. With his back pain, he knew he couldn't swim that far, but maybe the pilot could. The helicopter crash had effectively taken him out of the battle to stop the North Koreans from escaping with the top secret documents and their female hostage. Should he have shot her when he had the chance, instead of going after the North Koreans? He shook his head at the decision he had had to make. All he knew was that he couldn't shoot someone who showed so much courage in the face of the enemy. Her obscene gesture had tipped them off that the North Koreans were on the boat with her. What would happen to her? He fervently wished that he could have rescued her.

And now the North Koreans would escape with no one to stop them.

Ken Garrett squinted at a dot on the horizon. On impulse, he swung the wheel around and headed for the boat. Was it the *Sea Dragon*?

"Mike, we've got something out there," said Garrett over his shoulder. Mike Sprague was at his side in an instant. He grabbed the binoculars and stared through it for a moment.

"That's it," Sprague said with certainty. "It's the *Sea Dragon*." He looked over the water as it flew by their boat. He guessed that they were doing twenty knots and that the *Sea Dragon* was about six or seven miles off. Maybe the North Koreans were traveling at ten knots. He performed a mental calculation and decided that it would take about a half hour to catch up to them.

"Listen, uh, Ken," Sprague began.

Garrett gave him a questioning look. He didn't like the tone of Sprague's voice.

"How are we going to rescue Nancy?" asked Sprague.

The simple question set off a storm in Garrett's mind. He had been putting off the question and especially the answer for the last hour or so.

"I saw at least seven or eight guys in the water after their sub was sunk," said Sprague. "That means that we have to go through that many North Koreans to get Nancy back."

Garrett could see where this was headed. "So, what are you saying? That we do nothing?" His voice was desperate.

"No, nothing like that," replied Sprague quickly. "I mean, they're going to Roi, right? So let's get to Roi before they do. We could get a lot of help from those Roi Rats."

Garrett knew that on Roi-Namur there were about three hundred people, mostly Americans like himself, some police officers, and a few Marshallese Islanders. The people on Roi-Namur humorously referred to themselves with the nickname Roi Rats. He and Mike could get a significant amount of help, and maybe some weapons from the police. It made sense, but he didn't like leaving Nancy in North Korean hands any longer than he had to.

"If we tried a boarding action out here, we could get cut to pieces," said Sprague in a depressed voice.

"Suppose they don't go to Roi?" asked Garrett.

Sprague pressed his lips together as if he didn't want to think about it. He looked through the binoculars once again at the boat containing the North Koreans which was drawing nearer every second.

"The boat's down by the bow," said Sprague in a surprised voice. "There's got to be a leak. They're taking on water." He lowered the binoculars and looked at Garrett.

"That settles it," said Sprague with finality. "They have to go to Roi now."

Garrett nodded, finally giving in to Sprague's logic. They would have to rescue Nancy there. After the North Koreans set sail again, they would have no chance.

CHAPTER TWENTY-TWO

Roi Rats

Roi-Namur

Ken Garrett and Mike Sprague approached the southern side of the island and pulled up to a large dock called Yokohama Pier. The pier was in the shape of an L with the top of the L connected to the island and the angular portion extending out into the lagoon. At the apex of the right angle in the L was a small boathouse, and tied up at the pier was a very large oceangoing yacht. At the stern of the yacht flew a white flag with a large red spot in the center, the Rising Sun, the flag of Japan.

Garrett quickly wondered about the last time the Japanese flag flew over anything in the Kwajalein Atoll. Was it 1945? He wanted to know how this yacht came to be tied up at a pier on Roi-Namur.

Mike Sprague pulled around the lower part of the L shape and got alongside the pier near to the beach. Ken Garrett scrambled up a small ladder to the deck of the pier and caught the rope tossed from Sprague. He slipped the loop in the end of the rope around a piling as Sprague cut the engine, then helped his friend up the ladder. They took a quick look around, and seeing that the pier was deserted, they jogged up the pier toward the beach.

"Got to get to a phone," said Garrett as his overweight friend caught up to him. Without saying a word, Sprague pointed to his right as he drew abreast of Garrett. Garrett followed his finger and saw some small buildings that comprised the rest of the marina. He quickly ran over to one of them and was in the door in a second. He immediately ran into one of the pier attendants.

"Hi, what can I—" began the man.

Garrett waved him silent with a desperate look on his face. "I need a phone!"

"Uh, right around the corner," he replied. Garrett was around the corner in a second. "Hey! What's the matter?" the man asked.

Garrett ignored him and feverishly searched the nearby phone book for the number of Security. He found it toward the back of the combined phone book for Kwajalein and Roi-Namur and dialed the four-digit number.

"Security," came the voice on the line.

"Listen, a well-armed force of North Koreans is headed this way in a captured boat," began Garrett. "They have my wife—"

"What?" said the incredulous security chief.

"Listen to me, damn it!" shouted Garrett. "The North Koreans that invaded Kwajalein are headed this way. They have kidnapped my wife and are probably looking for another boat to steal to get them back to North Korea." He stopped as he realized what the North Koreans would see first as they approached Roi-Namur. The biggest, most beautiful, and most capable yacht of their dreams. The North Koreans would steal it in an instant. It was ideal to get them back to North Korea.

"North Koreans have invaded Kwajalein?" said the sarcastic voice on the line.

"Yes!" shouted Garrett. "Don't you people know anything? Haven't you talked to Kwajalein recently?"

"I last talked to Security on Kwajalein thirty-six hours ago," said the security chief. "Communication with Kwajalein was somehow cut off by the typhoon."

Garrett groaned. Security on Roi-Namur had no idea what was happening at the southern end of the lagoon. Garrett quickly recounted the events of the past day, then pleaded for help in rescuing Nancy from the North Koreans. The security man couldn't seem to make up his mind whether Garrett was part of a practical joke or whether it was real.

"The yacht that's tied up to Yokohama Pier—" began Garrett.

"Yeah, it showed up yesterday," interrupted the security chief. "They pulled in here to ride out the typhoon and to make some minor repairs to their radar."

"The North Koreans are going to steal it," said Garrett flatly.

Mike Sprague stuck his head into the room. "We got company."

Jack Pearson squinted into the distance at the small boat that seemingly limped toward Yokohama Pier. Could that be the North Koreans? He had seen the *Jelang K* shoot by and tie up at the pier, but hadn't attached any significance to the event. Boats were always in the lagoon, and the two catamarans were used for travel to and from the islands in the lagoon. But this second boat was a dead ringer for the North Korean boat.

He looked around quickly until his eyes rested on the half-sunken helicopter. His rifle was still on board—he could see the tip of the barrel through the still-intact windscreen. He got up painfully from his seat on a convenient rock and began to wade into the water.

"Hey, where are you going?" asked the pilot.

"I've got to get my rifle," said Pearson over his shoulder. The pilot was next to him in a second.

"You think that's the North Koreans?" he asked as he gestured in the direction of the slow-moving boat.

"Could be," replied Pearson. "If I could look through the scope on the rifle, I'd find out."

The pilot put a hand on Pearson's shoulder. "I'll get it."

Pearson nodded gratefully. The pilot returned a few minutes later with Pearson's mostly dry weapon. He set up near a downed palm tree and popped off the lens caps. He steadied the rifle by resting the barrel on the tree and stared through the scope to determine the identity of the boat that was approaching Yokohama Pier. He looked at the fire-blackened stern and nodded to himself.

"Yeah, it's them," he said to the pilot.

"Think you can get a shot in from here?" asked the pilot.

"Maybe," mumbled Pearson as he stared through the scope.

Lieutenant Kim couldn't believe how lucky he was. Truly he was destined to succeed in the light of this incredible good fortune. The yacht tied up to the pier was thirty meters long at least and could easily go the fifty-five hundred kilometers back to the Democratic People's Republic. The boat looked in good shape, and Kim guessed that it was at Roi due to the recent typhoon. He resolved to seize it at once. He eyed the Japanese ensign at the rear of the boat. The Japanese, always the enemies of North Korea, would inadvertently help them to complete their mission.

Their boat pulled alongside the pier in front of the yacht with Kim's eyes greedily searching the vessel for any of its occupants. The yacht seemed deserted, and that made Kim all the more anxious to take possession of it. He ordered all but two of his men onto the pier and personally led them to the ladder to climb aboard the large vessel. The North Koreans fanned out once inside the vessel and thoroughly searched it for anyone who might be aboard. Several minutes later, Kim's men walked toward him pushing one hapless crew member out in front of them. Kim gave the prisoner a close stare. The Japanese man stared back and refused to be cowed by the arrogant North Korean.

"So, you will not be broken, will you?" mused Kim to himself. "Let us see how unbroken you remain." He looked around at his men. "Anyone know any Japanese?" They all shook their heads.

Kim gave them a disgusted look and seemed to give up on an especially good idea. "I have no time for this. Shoot him and throw him over the side."

"So, what will they do to my boat?" asked Nobuo Ohnishi, the owner of the large yacht, who spoke without much of an accent. He was a Japanese gentleman, about forty years old with a balding head surrounded on the sides by black hair. His wife looked on anxiously. They had been on a South Pacific cruise when the storm forced them to seek refuge in Kwajalein Lagoon.

Mike Sprague lowered his binoculars and gave them a quick look. "They're going to take it to North Korea."

Ohnishi let out an oath in Japanese which no one understood—except his wife, who looked at the floor in embarrassment. "It is not insured for that," complained Ohnishi. "I should have stayed and shot it out with them."

"They have AKMs," said Garrett. Ohnishi gave him a sharp look. The room fell silent.

The sound of multiple AKMs was heard through the half-open window. Sprague quickly put the binoculars up to his eyes. "They just shot somebody," he said calmly.

"Who?" asked Garrett in a panic. "Was it—" He couldn't bring himself to say it.

"It wasn't Nancy," said Sprague convincingly. He turned to Ohnishi. "Was any of the crew aboard?"

"Yes, just one—" replied Ohnishi, cutting himself short. "Did they kill my man?"

Sprague nodded solemnly and gave Ohnishi a look of sympathy. The yacht owner returned a devastated look and translated for his wife. She put her hand to her mouth in horror. Sprague returned to studying the yacht and its new de facto owners.

"They're moving Nancy aboard," said Sprague in an undertone, and handed Garrett the glasses.

Ken Garrett looked through the binoculars and saw his wife being dragged along the pier and shoved up the ladder to get on board the yacht. He clenched his jaws together and prayed that they could come up with some sort of plan to rescue her.

Sprague could understand the effect on Garrett of seeing his wife in North Korean hands and spoke to distract him from the emotion of the moment.

"So, when is Security supposed to show up?" he asked.

Garrett shook his head. "He said he'd send someone down here to talk to us. I don't think he believed a word I said."

Sprague shook his head. "Useless bastards. We'll have to do it ourselves."

"Yeah," said Garrett.

Sprague glanced at Ohnishi. "How much food and fuel do you have on board at the moment?"

Ohnishi shrugged. "Some fuel, but not much food. We were going to reprovision at Truk, but we didn't make it there yet. My crew is out now, escorted by Security, to get some food aboard."

"So they're going to have to come ashore to get more food," said Sprague.

"Yeah," replied Garrett. "And we'll get on board while they're gone."

"They will leave guards on board," protested Ohnishi.

"That's better than going up against all ten of them," said Garrett.

The door to the marina office opened and a stout man in a black security uniform walked into the room.

"I'm Ed Atkinson, chief of Roi Security," he said. "Who's the guy I was talking to on the phone?"

Garrett identified himself and pointed to Mr. Ohnishi. "The North Koreans have seized this man's yacht, shot one of the crew, and are preparing to set sail for North Korea." The Japanese gentleman bowed slightly to the security man, but Atkinson just gave him a sour look.

Atkinson took the binoculars offered to him by Garrett and looked through them at the yacht for a long moment. When he finally lowered the glasses, he had a decidedly different expression on his face than when he had entered the room.

"What do they want?" he asked in a subdued voice.

"My wife, for one," replied Garrett in a testy voice. "And do you see the stacks of documents they're carrying aboard?"

Atkinson looked again through the binoculars.

"Those are top secret documents that detail our missile defense system that has been deployed in South Korea," continued Garrett.

"How the hell did they get them?" asked Atkinson in an incredulous voice.

"Never mind about that," said Garrett. "How many men can you get here, and what kind of weapons do you have?"

Atkinson ignored the question. "Why would they want your wife?"

"She's a reentry vehicle penetration aids engineer," said Garrett impatiently. "She knows how to defeat the U.S. missile defense deployed in South Korea."

Atkinson turned around and looked them over in obvious indecision.

"If we don't stop them, all of South Korea would be threatened," explained Garrett in exasperation.

Atkinson shook his head. "I don't have many men, and the only weapons we have are revolvers. We're no match for a large force armed with assault rifles."

Garrett had seen it coming in Atkinson's facial expression. He had to admit that Atkinson was right, but he couldn't let the North Koreans take his wife with them without at least trying to rescue her.

"See what I mean, Ken?" said Sprague in disgust. "Useless bastards."

Atkinson, his face livid with anger, turned to Sprague. "Do you realize what one of those automatic weapons would do to you?"

Sprague tilted his head back and screwed up his face. "C'mon, Ken. We're wasting time."

Atkinson glanced down in an abrupt movement of his head and saw Sprague's rifle at his side. "Where did you get that? You have to surrender that to me. You're not allowed to have weapons on this island."

Atkinson reached over to grab it, but Sprague slapped his hand away. The security chief reached up to his hip, where his holster sat, and instead felt a steel lump in his back. He immediately froze in position while Ken Garrett ground the barrel of his handgun into the small of Atkinson's back. Garrett unsnapped the holster and removed Atkinson's revolver.

"You guys are in big trouble," said Atkinson.

"Just relax now, and watch us do your fighting for you," said Garrett in a voice dripping with sarcasm. He pushed the stocky security chief to one side and backed out the door with Sprague behind him.

Outside in the fierce sun, Garrett squinted at his friend. "I guess I never should have called him."

They heard footsteps behind them and saw some people from the small crowd that had been in the marina. Among them was the owner of the yacht. They ran to catch up to Garrett and Sprague.

"Hey, uh, we heard what you said back there," said a young woman of about twenty-five. "Need some help?"

Garrett couldn't resist a smile. "Know how to use one of these?" he said as he held up the captured revolver.

"Well, uh—" she began.

"I sure as hell do," said a gray-haired man of about sixty who reached around the woman and took the gun from Garrett's outstretched hand. The older man stared at Garrett. "Ex-Marine, Chosin Reservoir," he said in a simple statement that meant a great deal.

The man had fought in the Korean War in the early fifties in a famous battle against the North Koreans and Communist Chinese. Although greatly outnumbered, U.S. Marines had fought valiantly to get to the coast of Korea in an effort to avoid annihilation at the hands of the Red Chinese. During the two-week-long battle, the Marines kept their discipline and their dignity and successfully fought their way back from the brink of disaster.

"I fought for South Korea once, and I'd hate to see it threatened again," he explained as Garrett gave him a grateful look.

Garrett looked at the young woman again and she explained as well.

"You have to rescue your wife," she said, and smiled.

Garrett smiled again and looked over the ex-Marine's shoulder at a man with dark skin and the features of a native islander. He was a Marshallese Islander who worked on Roi-Namur for the Americans.

"I'm Amata Milne. This is my home," he said as he gestured all around them. "It's worth fighting for."

Garrett nodded gratefully and glanced in Mr. Ohnishi's direction.

"The North Koreans have always threatened Japan," he said. "Besides, it is my boat that they have, and my crewman they murdered."

Tears came to Garrett's eyes. These were strangers. He didn't know any of them, least of all Amata Milne and Nobuo Ohnishi, who weren't even Americans. And now they had all banded together to follow him in a desperate attempt to stop the North Koreans from kidnapping his wife.

He blinked his eyes furiously, pretending that it was the intense sunlight that affected him.

"So, any ideas?" asked Thomas Necker, the ex-Marine, who hefted the revolver taken from the security man. Necker looked trim and extremely fit for his age.

Garrett stood, momentarily at a loss, then snapped his fingers. All eyes went to him.

"There's a scuba shop right down the road," Garrett said, and pointed toward the eastern end of the island.

Jack Pearson stared through the telescopic sight at the side of the yacht. Above the main hull was a deck lined with cabins that had outside windows. Pearson could see through one of the windows, and to his surprise, he clearly saw Nancy Garrett. She seemed to be sitting down, and judging by her restricted movements, Pearson concluded that she was tied to a chair.

He licked his lips and looked around the island. Beyond the pier, he couldn't see anything but a dense line of trees and foliage. If anyone was moving there, he wouldn't see it. He carefully moved the rifle in an arc to survey the pier. Nothing was moving. A glance at the yacht confirmed his conclusion that the North Koreans were preparing to get under way. He might have only minutes to make a decision. Should he complete his mission as ordered by his superiors at Langley? Should he kill Nancy Garrett to keep her knowledge from the North Koreans?

He looked through the scope once again. Nancy Garrett was helpless. How could he kill a helpless woman? But the information in her head would be devastating to South Korea. If she was taken back to North Korea, would her knowledge lead the Communist regime to attack South Korea? How many would die then, because he couldn't do what was necessary? How could he *not* kill her?

He looked about carefully once again. There was no resistance to the North Koreans from the Roi islanders. In minutes, the North Koreans could be gone.

Pearson began to go through the mechanics of setting up for a shot. He looked through the scope and estimated thirty inches from the top of Nancy's head to where he thought her waist was. He increased the magnification to the maximum but couldn't get the two marks in the scope to line up on his estimated distance of thirty inches. He glumly concluded that the distance was greater than a thousand yards. It would be a tough shot. He elevated the crosshairs above her head to allow for the increased range beyond the maximum calibrated distance of his scope. He looked around and gauged the wind. The wind would be no problem. It was at his back. Now here it is, he thought. The decision was on him again.

God, forgive me, he thought. He took a breath, then began to exhale slowly.

He pulled the trigger.

CHAPTER TWENTY-THREE

Rescue and Entrapment

Jack Pearson closed his eyes and took a deep sigh. He didn't want to look through the scope and see what he had done. After several long moments, he opened his right eye and squinted through the rifle scope.

Nancy Garrett's head was the first thing he saw. Her head was tilted all the way back with her face pointed upward. Maybe it's better that I can't see her face, he thought. At least I won't have that memory for the rest of my life.

Then he saw movement. Nancy Garrett pulled her head upright, then shook it from side to side as if she were struggling against restraints.

My God, she's still alive! He asked himself what had happened. He quickly searched the window glass for a tell-tale hole made by his bullet, but there was none. Pearson moved the scope about slightly as he looked over the side of the yacht to see where his bullet had struck. He found a dark round spot near the waterline that he thought might be the entry hole for his errant round.

I was way off, he thought, and searched his mind for the reason. His eyes hit the silencer on the end of his rifle barrel. Yes, he thought, silencers are not supposed to affect the velocity of the bullet, they're only supposed to reduce the velocity of the outgoing gasses to below the speed of sound. But at a range of over one thousand yards, a silencer had to make some difference, and a small difference at the gunbarrel would make a large difference at the target.

"Get 'em?" asked the pilot, who had been looking at Pearson all the while.

"I missed," said Pearson in an impatient tone. He turned the rifle around and quickly removed the silencer. He got set once again, with the barrel resting on the trunk of a palm tree and lined up on Nancy Garrett's face. He decided to take one last look around before taking another shot. Pearson played the scope up and down the pier to determine if anyone was approaching the yacht. Nothing moved until he got the scope centered back on the yacht. Several North Koreans were on the main deck preparing to go ashore. Pearson thought of a shot at them, but as they went down the ladder to the pier, which was on the opposite side of the yacht from Pearson, they went behind the yacht and were lost to view.

Pearson picked them up again as they walked down the pier, but they were at extreme range and at an almost impossible angle for a clean shot. Maybe later, he thought. He could pick off a few of them, but he wouldn't get them all, and with no rescue imminent for Nancy Garrett, he had no choice.

The relief that he had felt when he had missed Garrett fought against his new resolve to fulfill his orders. His eye lingered on the backs of the North Koreans until they disappeared among the jumble of buildings and island foliage that obscured the end of the pier. He moved the barrel back to Nancy's window, then his mind registered something he had seen at the end of the pier near the beach.

Pearson quickly moved the scope back to view the end of the pier. He searched, hope rising in him that he could give in to the relief he had felt before when he had missed Nancy Garrett.

There it is again, he thought excitedly. He saw movement under the pier.

Ken Garrett and Mike Sprague held their breath while listening to the footsteps of the North Koreans as they walked down the pier above them. The footsteps increased in intensity, punctuated by intermittent, guttural Korean expressions uttered in low voices, then faded away as they went onto the island.

Ken Garrett exhaled slowly, then put the scuba mouthpiece between his teeth to test the air flow. It tested all right, and Garrett gave Mike Sprague a thumbs-up. Sprague repeated Garrett's actions and gave a thumbs-up in return. They both wore their shirts and borrowed swim trunks and had left their pants and shoes behind. Garrett pulled his face mask down over his eyes and nose and checked for water tightness. After being satisfied that the mask would not leak, he gave Sprague a half glance over his shoulder and slid under the water.

Scuba diving was familiar to both Garrett and Sprague, who had enjoyed many of the interesting underwater attractions, sunken ships among them, that Kwajalein Lagoon had to offer. Garrett easily got into the rhythm of underwater swimming and put hard, fast strokes into the effort. He was driven by the thought of Nancy's being held by the North Koreans and by the limited time they had to effect a rescue before the North Koreans returned.

After five minutes of strenuous swimming, he was exhausted and his breathing came in quick, labored pulses. He turned around while he rested and saw Sprague working hard to catch up. Neither of them had had anything to eat during the day, except a ham sandwich they had liberated from a convenient vending machine at the marina when they took the *Jelang K*. Garrett's stomach growled in protest, and his head swam with fatigue as he watched Sprague wallow his way through the exceptionally clear water.

Garrett looked up toward the surface and saw that they were under one of several small boats that lined the eastern side of the pier. About halfway, he thought. He reached down and felt the hard lump of the handgun that he had put into a waterproof bag that his newfound friends had appropriated from the scuba shop. He had taken the security man's revolver and given the nine-millimeter automatic back to Sprague, and Sprague, in turn, had given his rifle to the ex-Marine. Maybe the elder statesman of their group could pick off a guard or two if he and Sprague got into trouble.

His breathing settled down from his initial strained gasping, and he turned and set out once again for the end of the pier. His eyes locked on to the massive hull of the yacht, which hovered in his watery world, suspended from above as if by magic. He drove himself deeper to get below the yacht's keel and rapidly swam toward it, pushing himself to the limits of his endurance.

Garrett swam under the keel of the yacht, then turned and saw Sprague laboring to catch up. He waved his friend on, then looked up to the surface, fifteen feet above. He could see the side of the yacht shimmering and shifting as the light responded to the constantly moving water. To Garrett's relief, no one appeared to be looking over the side. In this crystal-clear water, anyone could see thirty feet without a problem, he thought. He drifted a bit more under the keel to hide himself from above until Sprague caught up to him.

His friend finally arrived by his side and Garrett immediately pointed to the surface. They slowly drifted up, hugging the hull all the way. They quietly broke the surface with Garrett's eyes riveted on the deck rail for any sign of the North Koreans. Sprague pulled his mouthpiece away from his face and gasped for breath. Garrett looked along the side of the yacht for a ladder, but there was none. The deck was about ten feet above them and it was too far to jump. There were no handholds on the smooth hull to climb up to the main deck.

Garrett pointed to the stern of the boat to let Sprague know that they should look for a ladder there. Garrett and Sprague dove back under the water and quickly worked their way to the stern. They saw a ladder on the port side of the boat's transom and immediately headed for it. The thought suddenly struck Garrett that he didn't know what to do with the scuba gear. Climbing aboard with the gear on was cumbersome, and taking it off on the boat would delay them and possibly make noise if they weren't careful.

There was only one answer. Garrett grabbed Sprague's arm to get his attention, then gave him hand signals to take off the scuba gear and drop it to the bottom. Sprague at first shrugged his shoulders, then finally nodded as he understood.

Garrett and Sprague unstrapped their tanks and let them go. The two men drifted slowly up to the surface amid the cloud of air bubbles from their discarded tanks. Garrett slowly broke the surface and grabbed onto the ladder as he took a deep breath. Sprague was right behind him. Garrett took off his mask and swim fins and let them sink to join their scuba tanks. He climbed halfway up the ladder, then crouched down behind the transom and fished out his revolver from its waterproof sack around his waist. He took off the safety and pointed the weapon out in front of him.

Garrett slowly peered over the stern of the yacht, his eyes frantically searching the open deck and the dark places under the aft canopy for any sign of movement. Nothing moved. Only the constant Pacific breeze stirred the late afternoon stillness. Garrett gingerly swung a leg over the end of the transom and wiggled himself onto the main deck of the yacht. He crouched down to await Sprague.

Voices floated over to him and sent fear through him. Garrett licked his lips and feverishly searched the main cabin windows and the upper deck for the owners of the voices. After a few moments, Garrett could sense Sprague's bulky figure next to him. They had already worked out the plan ahead of time. Garrett would search the main deck cabins while Sprague covered for him. Garrett glanced at Sprague and wordlessly pointed at the doorway leading to the corridor that ran into the main cabin and down the center of the main deck. His friend nodded silently.

Garrett, while still in a crouch, moved quickly toward the main cabin doorway.

Jack Pearson frowned as he stared through his telescope. It appeared that two men were trying to rescue Nancy Garrett from the North Korean vessel. He was delighted. But both of the men stirred recognition in him, although he couldn't get a good look at the heavier one of the two. Pearson had gotten a clear look at the lead man, but couldn't place where he had seen him before. He mulled over it for several moments until it hit him suddenly.

He was the third person on the list of people who could not be allowed to be kidnapped by the North Koreans. Nancy Garrett was first on the list, followed by her boss, Nate Jackson, and then by her husband, Ken Garrett. It stood to reason that Nancy's husband would try to rescue her. But that presented a big problem to Pearson.

If Ken Garrett wasn't successful and got himself captured, then he'd have to kill them both.

Ken Garrett approached the doorway that led into the main cabin from the aft deck. His heart pounded away in his chest as fear-driven adrenaline coursed throughout his body. He placed his hand on the doorknob, then took a quick look around. The foreign voices came to him again, but thankfully they seemed above them and up forward.

Garrett rotated the knob and pulled the door open a crack. He peered inside and saw only an empty hallway with cabin doors lining each side. His heart sank. He would have to try each door and hope that he would find Nancy before he found any North Koreans. And how many North Koreans were left on board? There was no way to tell.

He opened the door slowly and entered the corridor, which ended in the forward part of the boat with a ladder that led up to the forward deck. Daylight poured in from the open hatch at the top of the ladder and lit the forward end of the corridor. He stared through the hatch to see if there was any movement beyond, and saw nothing but a white patch of sky.

Garrett turned to his right and grabbed the lever, which substituted for a doorknob, on the nearest door. He attempted to turn the lever, but it wouldn't budge. Now what, he thought. Do I break down the door to see if Nancy is inside? He put his ear to the door's surface and listened for a few moments. He heard nothing.

Garrett went to the opposite side of the corridor and tried another door. This one opened—to his surprise and increased anxiety—but no one was inside. He moved silently down the hallway with Mike Sprague quickly looking up and down the corridor for any sign of the North Koreans.

Garrett tried the next door and found it locked, but this door was louvered and by bending down and looking up at an angle he could see into the room. There was a bunk built into the bulkhead and a desk with a chair in front of it, but otherwise the room seemed empty. He heard someone suddenly exhale.

Garrett froze with a mixture of fear and anticipation. Was it Nancy or a North Korean guard? He stared into the room and brought his revolver up in front of him, then stopped in indecision. Should he check out the rest of the cabins before he took a chance and broke into this room? Did he have time enough for that?

The sunlight that flooded the forward end of the hallway suddenly was interrupted, and Garrett and Sprague heard a loud foreign voice nearby. There's no time, thought Garrett. After the voice died down, Garrett heard a grunt from the cabin, and it definitely sounded feminine.

Good enough for me, thought Garrett excitedly. He quickly stuck the barrel of his revolver between the louvers near the door lever and twisted the gun upward. Two of the wooden louvers snapped with a telltale noise. Garrett repeated his action again and quickly pushed the four louvers inward to get his hand through the door. He frantically reached for the door lock and found it only after a few agonizing moments. Garrett flipped the button, unlocking the door, and then tried to yank his hand free from the door. The broken louvers, which were still attached to one end of the door, closed in on his hand, the jagged ends pressing into the skin on the back of his right hand.

"Oh, shit!" said Mike Sprague behind him as the light from the forward hatch was blotted out momentarily once again. Sprague pointed his weapon toward the hatch opening and fired, the noise thundering around their ears in the confined space.

Sprague grabbed Garrett and pushed him through the doorway, then whirled to face the forward hatch again. Garrett stumbled into the room with his hand still jammed in the door. He lifted his right foot and savagely put it through the rest of the louvers in the door. The wood shattered under the force of his blow, and his hand came free immediately.

Garrett looked at Nancy, who gaped at him in shock.

"Ken!" she gasped, and stared at him, afraid that he might be a mirage. He jammed his revolver into his belt and began to untie the ropes that held her to a chair. When she was freed, she came out of the chair like a shot out of a cannon. She threw her arms around her husband and began to shake.

"Oh, God, Ken!" she said with an emotion-filled voice.

He held her tightly and jammed his eyes shut. He forced her away from him to take a good look at her. Except for a black-and-blue lump on her chin, she was okay.

"Ken, I didn't know—" she began.

"We're not out of here yet," he replied seriously.

She hugged him again, and he wiped his eyes with his hands so that she wouldn't see his emotion. Sprague's gun spoke twice quickly and made them jump. Sprague glanced back toward the aft doorway that led to the aft deck and saw a North Korean peering through the partly open door. He snapped a shot at him and ducked back into the cabin.

"We got guys at both ends now," he said in a breathless tone.

Jack Pearson could see the situation clearly. There were two North Koreans with what appeared to be AKMs at the forward end of the main cabin, and two at the aft end carrying handguns. He could also see the inside of the cabin. Ken and Nancy Garrett were side by side with the back of the second man visible as well.

The Garretts were clearly trapped on board the yacht. His mission orders were clear. He now had the opportunity to fulfill his orders if he acted quickly. It was an opportunity that wouldn't last long or occur again. Both of them were in clear sight, and with the silencer removed from his weapon, his next shot would be much more accurate. Only one question remained, a question he asked himself over and over in a whirlwind of mental agony.

Can I kill these two innocent human beings?

Mike Sprague fired again down the hallway toward the aft deck doorway, then glanced quickly in the opposite direction, toward the forward hatch. A rifle barrel swung in his direction, and he scrambled backward and cringed before the expected blast. A burst from the North Korean automatic weapon slammed into the louvered wooden door, shattering it and sending splinters flying around the room.

"It won't be long now," muttered Sprague as he looked around at the destruction caused by the enemy gunfire.

Ken Garrett, who was covering Nancy with his own body, looked about in a panic. The only way open to them was to get out the windows. He leaped over to the large rectangular window and ripped the short curtains away from the sides. Garrett slid the window open and turned to the two others.

"Quick! Out the window!" he shouted. Nancy and Mike Sprague scrambled over next to Ken Garrett.

"Yes," said Jack Pearson to himself. "Get out the window!" He squinted through the scope and repositioned his body with excitement. The window route was their only chance, he thought, then moved the barrel of the rifle to view the North Koreans on the forward deck.

He gasped and held his breath. One of the North Koreans was coming around the corner of the main cabin. He was going to walk along the outside catwalk between the cabin wall and the deck railing and come up on the window that the three of them were using to escape the yacht.

Pearson made an instant decision, one that he would later know was the only one he could have made. Orders be damned, he thought. He moved the barrel to line up the crosshairs on the North Korean.

Ken Garrett put a restraining hand on Nancy's arm. She stopped next to him and looked at her husband. He leaned over and stuck his head out the window. He looked aft at first, then seeing nothing there, he quickly rotated his head to look forward.

Ten feet away stood a North Korean pointing an automatic weapon at him. He yanked his head back through the window in a frenzy just before the enemy sailor opened fire.

The automatic weapon smashed the window glass and shredded part of the cabin wall, sending pieces of debris flying into the room. The three of them recoiled from the unexpected blast and fell to the floor in shock.

Sprague grabbed Garrett's arm. "There's one less North Korean up forward," said Sprague. "We've got to charge up the ladder to the forward deck and take our chances."

Ken nodded and they all jumped to their feet. Sprague fired two rounds through the cabin wall to slow down the North Korean who was outside the window, then ran out the doorway. Ken was right behind him and fired a shot down the hallway toward the aft doorway to keep the North Koreans ducking.

Pearson lifted the barrel of the rifle to give it the right elevation and pulled the trigger. The rifle jumped, and the gunshot sounded unnaturally loud in the quiet tropical day. He immediately lowered the barrel to center his view in his sight on the North Korean. The bullet had hit the man in the lower right jaw, shattering the bone and sending pieces of the deflected bullet into his neck. The bullet fragments had dug into his neck and ripped open his jugular vein. The North Korean twitched and fell to the deck, leaving a mist of blood in the air.

Sprague ran the short distance to the foot of the ladder while keeping his gun out in front of him. The gunbarrel of a North Korean weapon appeared in the opening, but Sprague didn't hesitate. He fired a shot that hit the hatch edge near the gunbarrel and he began to climb the stairs, his thick legs pumping wildly.

Ken Garrett grabbed Nancy and shoved her after Sprague, then took careful aim and fired two more shots at the aft doorway to keep the North Koreans there pinned down.

Mike Sprague got to the top of the ladder and peered out the hatch. The North Korean had retreated from the hatch edge and had taken up a position fifteen feet away behind the capstan, which was in the center of the forward deck. The North Korean opened fire when he saw the top of Sprague's head, sending a burst of fire around the hatch. Sprague jerked his head down and cringed at the slugs flying around him.

Ken Garrett glanced up at Sprague and gasped in despair. Sprague couldn't get through the hatch, and they couldn't go back down the hallway to get into the room. The North Koreans at the aft doorway were going to open fire any second.

The three of them were trapped.

CHAPTER TWENTY-FOUR

Death

Lieutenant Kim Il Kwon turned quickly at the sound of gunfire behind him. The AKM noise was unmistakable. His eyes searched the line of trees and foliage that hid the pier from view. What was happening back at the boat? Were the Americans attacking the men he had left now that he had led most of his men away?

Yes, he concluded quickly. The Americans would do something like that. He ordered his men to double-time it back to the boat. Kim reviewed the situation in his mind. Only three of them were armed, and he wouldn't have even that many weapons if he hadn't found some handguns on the yacht. If the Americans were attacking the yacht with any size force, then he and his men could be overwhelmed quickly. If only he had gotten more weapons from the sub before it went down. He let out an oath as he thought of how well they had been armed when they'd landed on Kwajalein and what little they had now. He had left most of the arms with the guards on the yacht because the island had seemed largely deserted. Now he knew where the island inhabitants were.

They ran eastward along Copra Road, which went across the southern shore of the island. The huge skeletonlike antenna of the Altair radar loomed above the island's low-lying foliage, but Kim and his men gave it no notice as they hurried back to the pier to relieve their comrades. They made the right turn to take the road leading to the marina and the pier came into view.

Kim heard another burst of gunfire, then silence, then the nearby solitary crack of a rifle. He searched the area frantically with his eyes. Where was the gunfire coming from? The burst had come from the pier, but the single shot was from a different direction.

The man next to him staggered, then fell up against Kim's side. Kim turned to look at him and saw that he was clutching his chest and blood was seeping under his fist. Kim stepped to one side and let his man fall to the ground. He yelled to the rest of his men to take cover and ran across the road to the side opposite the only building in view. The North Koreans hit the ground and scanned the area for the shooter.

Kim's thoughts turned bitter. Again this is happening! The same as on Kwajalein, snipers hiding away and picking his men off one at a time.

Thomas Necker slid away from the window and pulled his rifle back into the room. Donna Nelson, Amata Milne, and Nobuo Ohnishi looked at him expectantly.

"I hit one of them," he said. "The rest took cover. There's about five or six of them."

"What do we do now?" asked Donna. She hefted a revolver they had found in the scuba shop when they'd helped Garrett and Sprague with their underwater gear. Milne and Ohnishi had machetes from a box of equipment behind the marina office.

"We're going to have to get out of here fast," said Necker. "The North Koreans will figure out where the shot came from and be all over us in a minute."

They all followed Amata Milne, who knew the island the best, silently filing out a back door. They crossed the road behind the marina building and went into the foliage beyond.

Just as they had gotten settled behind cover, they heard gunfire from the now vacant building. The North Koreans swarmed over it, and in seconds they were crossing the road to the underbrush where the foursome were hiding.

Kim had second thoughts about entering an area where

they could be killed one at a time. He ordered his men to halt, then sent two men to recon the underbrush. They entered the dense growth and began groping their way through it while keeping alert for any movement.

Nobuo Ohnishi stood immobile behind the lower trunks of two palm trees that were joined at the bottom. The double width of the trunks gave him good cover, but he heard with alarm the approach of one of the North Koreans. He slowly, silently, brought his machete up from his side and got ready to use it if he had to. He was equally prepared to just let the North Korean walk by.

Ohnishi looked around to see if he could spot any of his companions and his gaze locked on to Donna Nelson, who was only partially hidden under a large bush. He held his breath as the North Korean walked slowly up alongside the palm trees. The enemy sailor stopped and looked about, then turned his head toward the bush covering Donna.

The North Korean said something in a loud voice and pointed his handgun at the bush. Ohnishi, only three feet from the North Korean, stepped from behind the palm trees and swung the machete with all his strength.

Kim's head jerked up at the sound of screams coming from the underbrush. The man was clearly in extreme agony, but Kim couldn't tell if it was one of his men or one of their quarry. An intolerable few seconds later, three quick gunshots ended the screaming, leaving a peculiar quiet hanging over the island. The situation was unnerving to say the least.

Was it one of the Americans, or one of my men? Kim bit his lip with mounting fear. The Americans were at it again, and he had played right into their hands. He had given chase to this area of brush where the Americans could easily set up a trap and pick off his men one by one.

One of Kim's men suddenly came running out of the foliage with fear stamped on his face. Kim grabbed him and shook him roughly.

"Where is the other man?" asked the lieutenant.

"Dead," gasped his man. "They cut his arm off."

Kim winced and gave the undergrowth a second glance.

"They are all over in there," continued the man. "There's too many of them."

Kim let go of the man's arm and took a step toward the dense underbrush. He could lose many men by going in there to root out the Americans. He took a quick count. He had four men left with him and four on the boat.

The cracking of gunfire was heard from the direction of the pier. That was the American plan, he thought. Keep us from getting back to the boat so that their attack on the boat would succeed. Kim ordered his men to run as quickly as possible to the yacht.

Kim took the position at the front of his remaining men and led them down the road toward the pier.

Donna Nelson sat shaking as the impact of what she had just done to another human being rushed in on her. Her revolver suddenly felt like a ton of lead at the end of her outstretched arms. She dropped her hands, exhausted over the emotion of shooting one of the North Koreans.

Ohnishi had come from behind a palm tree as the North Korean pointed his weapon at her. She had frozen with fear, the barrel of the North Korean gun seeming much larger than it actually was. Nelson had expected a bullet in the next second, but Ohnishi saved her by chopping at the arm holding the gun. The severed arm flew away, gushing blood, as the North Korean's face quickly changed from intense concentration to extreme agony. He staggered toward Donna, dripping blood and body fluids, his face a mask of pain and rage.

Nelson had put the revolver out in front of her and begun pulling the trigger to keep the North Korean away from her. Three bullets slammed into the luckless sailor's chest, sending him sprawling to the earth.

Suddenly Thomas Necker was next to Donna, gently taking the weapon from her hands. His head swung around at the sound of yet another enemy coming, and he swiftly led her away into denser brush. He turned back around to view the clearing and saw Ohnishi quickly retire behind the palm tree once again. Necker took a brief look at the Japanese gentleman and could see the red stain slowly spreading down the length of the machete.

Another North Korean burst into the small clearing and quickly took in the death of his companion. He looked about in desperation, fear rolling over his face like a wave. The North Korean made a quick exit.

Necker let out his breath and looked down at Donna Nelson, who was still shaking.

"It's all right now," he whispered into her ear. "He's dead."

She looked at him with tears in her eyes and nodded.

"C'mon, let's get out of here before more of them come back," said Necker. He gently led her away.

Ken Garrett took aim down the hallway and fired twice, sending bullets in the general direction of the two North Koreans who were maneuvering to get a shot at them. His hands shook so much that he sent one bullet into the ceiling and the second into the floor in front of the door to the aft deck.

He grabbed Nancy's arm with his left hand and pulled her behind him. The North Korean bullets would probably go through him, but at least his body would slow them down before they hit Nancy.

Mike Sprague peered over the hatch edge and looked straight into the barrel of the North Korean AKM, which the enemy sailor had pointing at him from his position behind the capstan.

Sprague began to jerk his head down inside the hatch but had the instant realization that he was too late.

Jack Pearson whirled the rifle barrel around in a furious movement, searching for the second North Korean on the forward deck. He found him crouching behind the capstan, and in one smooth, swift movement, he lined the crosshairs up on the side of his head, then elevated the barrel to correct for the distance.

Pearson didn't hesitate. He pulled the trigger.

Sprague's eyes were locked onto the North Korean as he fought to get his head below the hatch edge. Normally jerking his head down a foot would take a second. Sprague fought with all his strength to cut the time in half. Just as his eyes were about to go below the hatch edge, he saw the North Korean's head suddenly slammed to one side and a spray of liquid fly from his head into the air.

Sprague got his head below the hatch opening and waited for the blast from the North Korean's automatic weapon. He quickly recognized what had happened to the Korean as his mind interpreted what he had just witnessed. Someone had shot the North Korean in the head.

He stuck his head cautiously above the hatch edge once again and saw a welcome sight. The North Korean was lying spread out on the deck in a pool of blood. He turned to Ken Garrett, at the bottom of the short ladder.

"C'mon, let's go!" shouted Sprague. He grabbed Nancy Garrett by the arm and tugged her up toward the open hatch.

Ken Garrett felt his wife begin to move from behind him upward to safety. One of the North Koreans set up and quickly aimed down the hallway toward the trio. To Garrett's horror, he fired two shots at them, sending one bullet into the ceiling and the second whizzing past Garrett's left ear.

Garrett aimed and fired two more rounds down the hallway and saw both of them go awry, then pressed the trigger three more times in a panic-stricken motion. The hammer fell on empty chambers. The gunfire from Garrett caused the North Korean to duck around the corner once again, and Garrett took the opportunity to turn and scramble up the ladder after Mike Sprague and his wife.

At the top of the ladder, Garrett felt a strong hand on his shoulder. He looked up and saw Mike Sprague yanking him up out of the hatch just as he heard a gunshot behind him. The slug hit the wood molding just below where Garrett's hand rested on the hatch, sending up a shower of splinters. Garrett yanked his hand away and threw himself through the hatch and onto the forward deck.

Garrett leaped to his feet and threw the empty gun aside as he looked about for a way out of their predicament. Mike Sprague had the obvious solution.

"Quick! Over the side!" said Sprague as he looked about hurriedly for more North Koreans. Nancy and Ken Garrett immediately took Sprague's suggestion and ran across the forward deck, leaping over the dead North Korean and heading for the deck railing on the bow.

Mike Sprague turned to run after them, then heard footsteps behind him.

Jack Pearson quickly lined up the crosshairs in his sight on the pursuing North Korean who had gotten to the forward deck by going up the side of the yacht away from Pearson. Pearson immediately saw what was going to happen and resolved to help this gutsy band of Americans in their war against the North Koreans.

Pearson raised the barrel of his rifle as he had done twice before and quickly pulled the trigger. The expected gunshot and recoil never came. His weapon was empty.

Pearson watched through the scope in horror as the North Korean aimed his handgun at the fleeing trio.

Mike Sprague was in midair over the fallen North Korean when he heard the gunshot and felt the bullet slam into his back. His back felt as if someone had hit him with a sledgehammer. He gasped and cried out, and stumbled forward, hitting Ken Garrett in the back and thrusting him forward into Nancy. The two of them somersaulted over the deck railing and fell clumsily into the water. Mike Sprague staggered to the railing and got one leg over, then took another bullet in his left side just under his armpit. The force of the second bullet had enough impetus to send him over the railing and into the water below.

Ken Garrett, acutely aware of how clear the water was, dove deep below the surface, then he stopped and looked around to see Nancy only a few feet behind him. They both looked up to see Mike Sprague hit the water with a resounding splash.

The Garretts knew he was hurt by the feeble motions he made in the water, and Ken Garrett's chest tightened at the sight of the inklike smear in the water near Mike Sprague's left side. They both swam upward to help him. Ken got on one side of him, Nancy got on the other side, and together they guided him toward the cover of the pier. Ken glanced upward and saw a North Korean leaning over the side of the boat and pointing a gun at them. He made a noise with

his throat to get Nancy's attention and tried to drive
Sprague deeper into the water. Nancy looked upward and
her eyes grew wide as she caught sight of the North Korean.

The enemy sailor fired, the bullet left a line of bubbles
as it parted the water inches from Ken Garrett's head. More
bullets drove through the water as the North Korean vainly
tried to stop the trio's escape. Ken looked Sprague over
and saw that his eyes were closed in pain and some air was
dribbling upward from his mouth. They had to get Mike
up to the surface to take a breath quickly before he tried to
inhale. Ken wasn't even sure that Mike knew where he was.
He and Nancy, dragging Mike Sprague between them,
swam madly for the shadow of the pier.

Lieutenant Kim ran up to the yacht as his guard on the
boat fired into the water. His man quickly filled him in on
what had happened. Kim shouted orders for his remaining
men to fan out around the edge of the pier and fire at any
swimmers in the water.

Ken, Nancy, and Mike broke the surface of the water
under the pier and noisily gulped air into their lungs. Mike
Sprague began to groan, then coughed furiously. Ken Garrett looked up at the pier and saw the shadows of more
North Koreans above them at the edge of the pier.

"There they are!" shouted Kim as he glimpsed them
through a crack in the pier deck boards. "Fire through the
deck!"

Two of his men ran over next to the lieutenant and began
to fire through the pier deck at the three Americans who
were treading water and gasping for air.

"Down!" shouted Ken, and he shoved Mike under, taking Nancy with them. Ken immediately caught sight of the
trail of air bubbles caused by the scuba gear that Mike and
he had let fall to the bottom of the lagoon just before they'd
climbed aboard the yacht. He grabbed Nancy's arm and
pointed at it frantically. She understood immediately and
nodded quickly.

He swam downward, estimating that the tanks were in
about fifty to sixty feet of water. He had never made a free
dive of that depth before and his lungs were bursting when
he was halfway there. He pushed himself, driving downward as he thought of how Nancy must be struggling alone

with Mike, trying to keep him under the water yet not allowing him to drown, and dodging bullets all the while.

His lungs were searing him with pain as he fought the urge to inhale. He was ten feet away. A thrust from a desperate scissors kick and he was three feet away. He reached out and pushed the water to the side and behind him, and suddenly he was at the two tanks. He quickly grabbed a bubbling mouthpiece and greedily took in the sweetest air he had ever known. Ken grabbed the other tank, and after just a few seconds to take in more air, he swam furiously for Nancy and Mike.

Nancy had surfaced again and had Mike Sprague by the shoulders while she stared up at the North Koreans with horror. Bullets took pieces of wood from the pier deck and sprayed them with splinters and bullet fragments. She got her left arm around Sprague's neck and swam toward the corner piling that supported the pier. Bullets slapped the water around them as she fought to get the physically larger man toward relative safety.

A shadow loomed ahead of her at the top edge of her vision. She glanced up and saw that one of the North Koreans was leaning over the side of the pier in an effort to locate them. She gaped at him in shock and felt panic as she saw his arm swing down from above and point a gun at her. She dove frantically, dragging Mike Sprague with her just a few seconds before the sharp sound of the inevitable gunshot. The bullet hit the water and shot by her ear while rapidly decelerating in the water.

A panic-stricken instant later, Ken was next to them and offering her his mouthpiece. She took it and breathed gratefully for a half minute as Ken shoved the other mouthpiece into Mike Sprague's mouth. He watched for a nervous second, then exhaled with relief, sending a small cloud of bubbles to the surface as he saw his wounded friend start to breathe using the scuba gear.

A burst of gunfire from an automatic weapon above sent myriad lines of death around the three of them accompanied by the ripping sound of bullets penetrating the water. One of the slugs came perilously close to Nancy, but hit Mike in the left hip. That bullet is probably the least of Mike's problems, he thought. At least it hit him in a nonlethal area.

Ken and Nancy quickly resumed their former positions around Sprague and swam frantically with him deep into the lagoon.

They stopped to rest and look around. The North Koreans seemed to have lost them for the moment. Nancy gave the mouthpiece to Ken and let him take a few deep breaths. She looked Sprague over and could see the wound in his back and the other wound under his left arm. The back wound appeared to be in line with his right lung, and the other bullet seemed to have missed anything immediately vital, but the bullet might have passed very close to his heart. It was a wonder he was still alive.

Sprague's body suddenly jerked as if hit by another bullet. He rolled to one side and his mouthpiece flopped out of his mouth. Ken grabbed it and placed it firmly in his mouth while Nancy wondered why he twitched so violently. She figured it out quickly. Sprague had tried to inhale through his nose and had gotten a slug of seawater. They both held him until his choking settled down. Ken hadn't gotten any of their face masks when he had picked up the air tanks, and Mike Sprague had involuntarily tried to breathe normally as he slipped into unconsciousness. Nancy grabbed Mike's nose and squeezed it shut, then nodded to Ken. He gave her back the mouthpiece, and they grabbed their wounded friend.

They turned toward the beach and swam ahead with their bodies straining to move the inert man between them. After swimming for several minutes, the shoreline was within sight. They strained their arms and legs to push themselves toward the beach, knowing that Sprague's life could hang on a lost minute or maybe even a few seconds.

Ken Garrett reached out with powerful strokes and swept them toward shore while watching the sandy bottom rise toward them. He reached down with his right foot and jammed it into the sand, then raised himself up vertically to shove Sprague toward the beach alongside the pier. They got him to shore and dragged him into the undergrowth that lined the south side of the island. Garrett took a quick look around for any North Koreans, then turned to Nancy.

"Quick! Go get the others," he said in a desperate voice. "He needs medical attention right now!"

Nancy nodded, then left in a rush with the foliage rustling as she ran back to get their newfound allies in their battle with the North Koreans. Ken Garrett gently took the mouthpiece from Mike Sprague's mouth and laid him down on the sand. Sprague had blood dribbling from the corner of his mouth, a telltale sign of internal bleeding. Ken unstrapped his own tank and dropped it on the ground, then knelt and tried to take off Sprague's tank.

He stopped and stared at his friend as he lay among the undergrowth. Sprague seemed unnaturally still. A feeling of dread filled Garrett as he reached for Sprague's neck to find a pulse.

"Oh, God, don't do this," he mumbled as his trembling fingers felt Sprague's neck.

There was nothing. Mike Sprague was gone.

CHAPTER TWENTY-FIVE

Tunnels

Ken Garrett heard the rustling of the brush behind him but didn't turn around to see who it was.

"Ken," said Nancy. She touched his shoulder, and he placed his hand on hers but didn't turn to look at her. He could hear the others as they tried to save Mike by giving him CPR, but after five minutes they concluded that it was hopeless.

Amata Milne put a hand on Ken's shoulder. "I'm sorry," he said in a simple statement of compassion.

They all stood around for a few moments and stared at the brush and the blue water beyond, until Thomas Necker suddenly tensed. They all looked at him except for Ken Garrett.

"They're coming for us," said Necker, and pointed toward the end of the pier. Their eyes flicked toward the pier and saw that several North Koreans were forming up in front of their leader. The officer turned and led them purposefully toward the beach.

"We've got to get moving," said Necker, and he looked at Ken Garrett's back.

"Come on, Ken," said Nancy as she gently pulled him to his feet. "We'll come back for him later." Ken Garrett turned and his eyes locked onto the body of his friend.

"Come on, son," said Necker, his eyes following Garrett's gaze down to Sprague's corpse. "You never get used to it. Believe me, I know."

Ken Garrett was led away with his mind in a whirlwind of shock and confusion. Is that all a life means? How can a bullet, such an inert, tiny object, erase the life of so dear a friend? Was Mike really gone? He turned and involuntarily glanced at his friend's body. Mike Sprague lay forever still, and Ken Garrett suddenly realized that he would never be able to talk with him again. Mike, who had always been by his side for the past year, would never be there again. The sudden finality of his loss rushed in on him and left him with a sense of unreality. Surely this couldn't be happening, he thought.

He glanced back again, but his view of the body was obscured by the dense foliage. He stumbled after the others, who kept a watchful eye on him. His reactions to everything, including being hit in the face by branches from the brush they traveled through, was highly diminished as he struggled to make sense out of the death of his friend.

Garrett's mind went numb, and he was grateful for it. All the feelings would be put off until later, until he had time to live again. Right now they had to evade the approaching North Koreans.

They came out of the undergrowth and went out onto Copra Road, which ran across the southern side of the island. Nancy handed him his shoes, socks, and blue jeans, which he mechanically put on.

"Let's head toward the air terminal building, where the security people are," said Necker. He looked around quickly and hefted Mike Sprague's rifle. "We're just about out of ammunition. The security guys at least have some weapons."

Everyone nodded, and Nancy Garrett looked at each of them in turn for any weapons they were carrying. In addition to Necker's rifle and the revolver that he had taken from Donna Nelson, there was only a machete carried by Amata Milne and Ohnishi's blood-stained machete. Nancy's stomach churned at the sight, and she resolved to be absent when he explained later how his machete had gotten that way. All in all, they were in a bad way, especially to stand up against several heavily armed enemy sailors.

They started off on a dead run westward on Copra Road, which took them across the road that led directly to the pier. As they crossed that road, they all glanced in the direction of the pier to check on the advance of the North Koreans. The North Koreans were only a hundred yards away and running as fast as they could to catch up.

The six of them started running frantically after giving out involuntary cries of alarm. They had misjudged the advance of the North Koreans and had thought that they were still near the yacht. They all ran down Copra Road, constantly looking for any place in which they could hide from the steadily gaining enemy. They passed the overhanging bulk of the Altair radar, which dominated the skyline to their right, and all looked hopefully up Tradex Road for some cover. Then they heard the cracking of automatic weapons behind them.

"Split up!" shouted Necker. "Get off the road!" He waved furiously to both sides, then he grabbed Donna Nelson by the arm. "Stop and let's slow 'em down."

She looked at him with a frantic puzzled stare. Necker stopped and turned to face the onrushing enemy. He pulled out the revolver he had taken from her previously and tossed it to her, then knelt down and pointed his rifle at the North Koreans, who fired quickly at this new threat in the middle of the road ahead. Donna Nelson imitated his action and knelt beside him.

Necker fired twice, then realized that he was out of ammunition. With bullets whizzing by their heads, Donna Nelson took quick aim and fired three rounds which all went wild. She pulled the trigger several more times and got only a dull click as the hammer hit empty chambers.

Necker jumped to his feet and dragged Nelson with him. They both threw their empty weapons to one side and ran full tilt off the road toward the beach. Necker heard more cracking of gunfire, then heard the dreaded sound of a bullet hitting flesh. Donna Nelson shouted with pain and fell to the ground. Necker came to a quick stop and ran back to his female companion. She had taken a bullet in the left hip and couldn't walk, much less run, another step. With the rapidly advancing North Koreans in his peripheral vision, Thomas Necker grabbed Donna Nelson by the blouse and pulled her to her feet, then he flipped her over his shoulder in a fireman's carry.

She cried out in pain at her rough treatment, but Necker ignored it and turned to run for both their lives.

Lieutenant Kim Il Kwon suddenly stopped and saw what was happening. Two of the Americans were trying to lure them away from the one he really wanted, the American missile engineer, Nancy Garrett. The group had split into three smaller groups, with two of them going left, one going up Tradex Road, and three, including the female engineer, going to the right into an area of light jungle where the normally dense brush was thin and spotty. Kim had to ignore the other groups and concentrate on this last one.

"Halt!" he ordered. His men obeyed and gave him a puzzled look. "This way!" Kim shouted, and he waved them toward the three fleeing figures that were headed inland. His men immediately formed up and they all ran in the direction of Milne and the Garretts.

Ken and Nancy Garrett and Amata Milne ran through the sparse growth and frantically searched for a hiding place. After a quick survey, no hiding places were evident, and they all decided that they had to keep going. Ken Garrett turned and glanced toward Copra Road and saw the North Koreans forming up and turning to follow the three of them.

Ken Garrett caught a flash of metal at the edge of his vision, turned, and saw that Amata Milne had thrown his machete aside. Ken glanced at the machete as it fell and almost stopped to pick it up. No, he quickly decided. Milne's right. This was going to be a footrace, and the machete not only would slow them down but it was also useless against assault rifles.

The trio ran at top speed and came out on an unpaved road called Caribou Trail that ran east-west in between the two former islands of Roi and Namur. A causeway linking the two islands had been expanded and filled in, creating one island after World War II. They ran toward the west end of the island and saw a welcome sight. Several buildings sat at the end of Caribou Trail. If they could disappear inside one of them, then the North Koreans would have to search for days to find them.

"Let's get into one of them!" said Nancy between gasps for air. She pointed to the buildings that lay ahead.

Amata Milne glanced over his shoulder and grunted in dismay. "It's no good. They'll see which building we enter."

"A truck!" said Ken Garrett, and he pointed toward the white vehicle in a parking lot. He sprinted for it in a burst of energy, leaving the others behind.

"It's no good without keys!" shouted Nancy as she struggled to keep up with her husband.

Ken Garrett got to the truck and yanked open the door. His hands flew to the ignition and found it empty. He jerked the sun visor down to see if a spare key had been kept there, but to no avail. He slid across the front seat and fumbled with the glove compartment button. The door finally fell open, and he frantically spilled the contents on the floor in an effort to find a key.

Nancy and Amata arrived, and Ken glanced in their direction as he sorted through the contents of the glove compartment. He could see the rapidly closing North Koreans over Nancy's shoulder. They were very close. A burst from an AKM and they were all dead. He yanked the passenger side door open and got out of the truck, and immediately ran through the parking lot with the others following close behind.

Ken glanced back toward the North Koreans and saw with horror that they were aiming their weapons at them. This is it, he thought. They are too close to miss now.

He heard a guttural command and winced at the expected blast that would slam into their backs. He ran on, holding his breath and getting closer to Nancy so that he could get behind her and shield her from the gunfire.

The blast inexplicably never came, and Garrett let his breath out in a burst of relief. They rounded the corner of one of the buildings, and Ken started to slow down. He was exhausted. He hadn't had much to eat, and the day's events were beginning to catch up to him.

"We've got to try one of the buildings," he gasped.

"No, I have something better," said Milne as he grabbed Ken by the arm to keep him going.

Ken Garrett gave him a quick look and forced himself

to keep running. The alternative was a bullet in the head, which was all the incentive he needed to push himself.

"What is it?" asked Nancy, who voiced the question that Ken was too out of breath to ask.

"Yamada's command post," said Milne.

Ken found the strength to nod in agreement as he fought to keep moving. Rear Admiral Michiyuki Yamada had been the ranking Japanese officer on the island during World War II. His command post, which existed largely underground, had three tunnels going from it to three other areas of the island. If they could get to the command post, and even if the North Koreans saw them enter, the enemy wouldn't know which of the three tunnels their quarry had taken. Amata Milne had come up with a brilliant plan on the spur of the moment. The plan gave him newfound strength.

Kim ran on, knowing he was being lured farther and farther inland. With his escaped prisoner in sight, all his hunter and warrior instincts were in full play to the point where he couldn't resist them. His men had just tried to shoot at the fleeing group of Americans, but he had stopped them. There was too much of a chance of hitting the female engineer who had the secrets that would save his country billions of *won*, the currency of North Korea, and decades of development.

Moon had convinced him to go after her, and it hadn't required a lot of effort on Moon's part. Kim had been convinced of the woman's worth some time ago, otherwise he would have shot her for her insult with her finger earlier in the day. He hadn't known what the sign had meant, but he was familiar with the accompanying obscene phrase. His plan for her, after the Liaison Bureau got all the missile secrets out of her, was to take revenge for that insult. As a national hero, his desire for control of her, after her intelligence use was expended, wouldn't be questioned. He would take great pleasure in planning her torture.

But first he had to catch her, and that looked to be imminent, judging by the way he and his men were catching up to the group of fleeing Americans. Koreans were in much better physical condition than these flabby Americans, he thought with a large dose of national pride.

Their capture should be only a matter of a minute or two. He would shoot the two men with her and drag her back to the yacht.

Ken, Nancy, and Amata ran across an open field and came out on Eleanor Wilson Road, which ran along the east side of the former Roi Island toward the northern coast. Both Ken Garrett and Amata Milne knew that the ramshackle remains of Admiral Yamada's command post were next to this road on the left.

Where are the goddamned security people? Ken asked himself. Even though they had only revolvers, they could make the damn North Koreans duck for a moment, and that would relieve the pressure on us.

He squirmed around and caught a glimpse of the closing enemy over his shoulder. They were coming on with vehement looks on their faces, determined resolution in every feature. They weren't going to give up.

Well, neither am I, Garrett thought, and tried to ignore the rasping in his chest and the pounding of his heart.

"There!" gasped Milne, pointing to a clump of palm trees to the left. He ran across the road and dove immediately into the line of trees. Ken and Nancy followed him closely, and the three of them burst into a small clearing. Ken was puzzled—Milne had approached the command post from the north by initially bypassing it, then circling around once they got through the trees.

Milne didn't slow up at all and headed directly for a small concrete structure, about the size of a two-car garage, which was largely overgrown with brush. The structure was built entirely of concrete and had thick steel shutters covering the windows and door. The building also had a porch around the outside, which was an incongruous addition to a building that was obviously meant to survive sustained bombardment. Concrete pillars that supported the outside roof were heavily damaged, with some of them hanging freely from the concrete roof, the bottom halves having been blown away during the navy's shelling of the island in World War II. Exposed reinforcing steel bars and flaking concrete marked the rest of the outside of the building. Bullet and shell scarred, Yamada's command post represented their only salvation.

Milne ran up to the building, and when Ken Garrett thought he would slow down to find a doorway, Milne jumped, going full speed through the partially open shutters covering one of the windows in the wall of the command post. Nancy followed suit after slowing down considerably, and Ken piled in on top of her.

They all landed in rotting palm leaves and some equally disintegrating coconuts. Nancy expressed revulsion in a grunt, but Ken was gasping for air and couldn't utter a sound. Milne jumped to his feet and shouted to them to follow him. Ken and Nancy scrambled to their feet and stayed on Milne's heels as he crossed the small room, his feet crunching on the thin concrete layers that had fallen from the ceiling.

Milne reached the other side of the gloomy interior and jumped out another window after shoving the steel shutters aside with a protesting squeak from the hinges. Ken realized that Milne's ultimate objective was the bomb shelter alongside the admiral's house and could see in a quick glance around that the concrete floor was solid across the entire expanse of the interior. There was no entrance to any room below ground. Ken also realized why Milne had gone past it to approach it from the north. He wanted to go through the house first instead of heading directly for the bomb shelter, which was south of the house. The North Koreans would slow down before entering the concrete house, unsure of whether they were entering a trap. The delay wouldn't be long—the first glance into the interior would reveal that they weren't there, but any delay, however slight, added to their chances of escaping these terrifying invaders. Ken Garrett felt burgeoning respect for his newfound Marshallese friend.

Milne entered the bomb shelter through what used to be the entrance, wading his way past rubble and jungle growth to get inside. Nancy followed after him, and Ken entered with a furtive glance over his shoulder. The North Koreans were on the other side of the house and couldn't see where Ken and the others were going. The North Koreans weren't

stupid—it would take only a few moments for them to figure out what had happened to the three of them. Ken could
hear them approaching with grunts and half shouts.

Suddenly Ken realized that Milne wasn't in front of them
as they ran into the murky darkness of the interior of the
bomb shelter. He was puzzled for a moment.

"Come on!" shouted Milne from what seemed to be
under the ground.

Ken knelt and stared in the direction of Milne's voice.
After a few seconds, Ken's eyes got used to the dark from
the bright daylight outside, and he could make out where
Milne had gone. The Marshallese man had jumped through
what could only be described as a ragged hole in the
ground.

Ken stood and touched Nancy's arm. "Through here,"
he said with the air still rasping in his throat. She looked
down at the hole and he couldn't see her reaction due to
the nearly totally dark interior.

Ken Garrett turned and took a step back, then jumped
through the hole into abject darkness. He hit the ground
and rolled to his right as he felt pain shoot through his left
ankle. Amata Milne grabbed his arm and led him away
from the landing spot in anticipation of Nancy's entrance.
Seconds later, Ken could hear her hit the ground. He moved
toward the sound, calling her name, then touched her and
encircled her with his arms.

"You all right?" he asked with concern.

"I'm okay," she said. "Oh, I'm really gonna love this,"
she mumbled.

"It's better than getting shot," said Milne. He got no
argument from his two companions. "Put your pants inside
your socks," he ordered. Ken and Nancy both did as they
were told. Milne reached out and grabbed Ken's hand and
placed it on his back.

"Grab my shirt and don't let go," he said to Ken. "Then
get the lady to do the same with your shirt."

Ken and Nancy obeyed Amata's instructions, and they
silently tried to get prepared to go on what they knew
would be a terrifying trip through total darkness.

"Why did we put our pants inside our socks?" asked
Nancy with a wavering voice.

"Rats," said Milne.

"Oh, God," mumbled Nancy. Ken's insides fluttered at the notion that they would be walking through a rat-infested tunnel. He gave sudden thanks for the sturdy hiking boots and thick white socks that Nancy had handed him near the pier. He tried to think of what Nancy was wearing, but a mental picture of her feet refused to come to mind.

"When we get in the tunnel, don't talk or make any noise at all," said Milne. "These guys will be listening to see which one we are in."

Ken nodded, then realized that Milne couldn't see him in the pitch blackness. "Okay," he said in a low voice.

"All right. Let's go," said Milne, and started off in a low crouch. Ken expected him to straighten up and walk normally, then remembered that a coworker had said that the tunnels were about half normal height. They would have to stay in that uncomfortable position for the entire trip. The crouched position further aggravated his already slightly sprained left ankle.

The trio went through a low tunnel that Ken judged to be going in the direction of the concrete command post. He could hear Milne's hand brush along the side of the tunnel as they duckwalked in the darkness. After a few moments, Ken sensed that they had entered a larger chamber even though he couldn't see a thing. Maybe my breath seems to go away and stay away rather than bounce off something close by, thought Ken. Amata Milne began to veer to the right, and they were quickly into another tunnel, which Ken judged to be headed east toward the beach.

They shuffled along in complete darkness. Ken doubted if there were a single photon present in the tunnel. He was careful to keep his free hand off the ground; he didn't want to give the rats any more opportunity to take a chunk out of him than they already had.

Something skittered past his left leg, and it sounded as if it collided with Nancy's foot. She gave a short, low yelp and tried to climb up Ken's back.

"Shhh!" admonished Milne. Ken could feel Nancy trembling next to him. At least he thought it was her trembling. He was shaking pretty hard himself.

They slowly moved down the tunnel as Ken wondered

how Milne could find his way in the absolute darkness. The frequency of the small skittering feet around them increased as they moved farther into the tunnel. Something fell onto Ken's back and seemed to scramble to keep a foothold on his shirt. Ken let go of Milne's shirt and swung wildly at the creature who was digging into his back. He hit something solid with his hand, and it came partially loose. He felt something sharp pierce his flesh and he jumped upright at the pain, striking his head on the concrete tunnel ceiling. A flash of light sped through his mind as he hit the ceiling and new pain spread through the crown of his head.

Ken swung viciously and hit what he thought was a large rat square in the side with all his strength. The animal squeaked and flew to one side away from the trio and hit the tunnel wall.

"Ken, are you all right?" asked Nancy in a trembling voice.

"Yeah," he said in a low tone.

Milne grabbed his hand and placed it on the back of his shirt as before. They began to move slowly down the tunnel once again. And then the noise came to them.

Milne stopped dead in his tracks and listened in horror. The floor, walls, and even the ceiling seemed alive, crawling with hellish things. The sounds of a million tiny feet as the animals scrambled in response to God-knows-what floated down the tunnel to them.

The tunnel ahead was filled with rats.

Lieutenant Kim looked about in astonishment. The three fugitives had completely vanished. He had sent his men around both sides of the concrete house so there would be no escape, but his men had met on the other side without seeing anyone. He sent some men into the house, and they quickly found nothing. Kim looked at the one other structure, the partially destroyed bomb shelter, with renewed interest. He quickly sent two men inside to investigate.

Thirty seconds later, one of his men came out and told them of the hole in the floor. They needed some source of light to investigate further. Kim took a quick poll—no one had a flashlight. Moon spoke up and showed his superior a box of matches. In a flash, Kim had his men making torches with dried palm leaves wrapped around sticks and tied with jungle vines. The makeshift torches won't last long, thought Kim, but the three of them couldn't have gotten far.

Kim led half his men into the bomb shelter and lit the first torch. The orange flame showed them the deteriorated condition of the shelter, and it also showed them the hole in the floor which had been the three fugitives' escape route. Kim looked down the hole and then ordered one of his men to jump down. His man obeyed and looked up to receive the torch handed to him by Kim. He looked about for a few moments, then pronounced it free of danger.

Kim jumped down and immediately focused his attention on the entrance to a tunnel with a low ceiling that led back toward the concrete house. He stuck the torch into the opening and walked bent over toward what he thought was a larger room at the end of the tunnel.

Kim approached the end of the tunnel with his automatic out in front of him. He peered into the larger room and immediately saw that it was empty. He moved out of the tunnel and stood to his full height, then looked the small chamber over. They were under the concrete house, and Kim realized that this was some leftover artifact from World War II.

Kim saw three doorways in the walls of the room. One doorway was the entrance to the tunnel that they had just left, and two other doorways led to what looked to be other tunnels. One led west of their location to an unknown destination, and the other led east toward the beach. Kim looked over the marks in the sand and debris around the tunnel doorways. The tunnel leading west was undisturbed, but the one leading eastward to the beach had definite footprints and grooves in it, indicating where their quarry had gone.

Kim took a fresh torch, lit it, and leaned into the tunnel.

Ken, Nancy, and Amata Milne gasped in terror at what lay ahead in the tunnel. They could see thousands of rats in their imagination, their bodies fat and dark with shining eyes and razor-thin tails.

"We've got to go back," said Nancy in a voice that was much firmer than before. "We can't go through that."

"Maybe they won't know where we went," whispered Ken to Milne. He could feel Amata's indecision through the darkness.

Suddenly Ken realized that he could see the Marshallese Islander's face. He looked around puzzled. Where was the light coming from? Milne raised an arm and pointed back the way they had come in response to Ken Garrett's unspoken question.

"We have no choice now," Milne said in a calm voice. "They are coming for us."

Ken looked down the tunnel, trying not to get distracted by the occasional rat that ran by. The light was indeed coming from the entrance to the tunnel. It also appeared to be getting stronger. They only had seconds before the North Koreans came into view.

The three of them turned simultaneously and looked at the source of the rustling noises that lay before their only path of escape. Their worst fears were confirmed.

The tunnel floor was a sea of rats, their swollen bodies jammed next to each other to form a living, heaving mass of horror.

CHAPTER TWENTY-SIX

Another Kind of Rat

Roi-Namur

Lieutenant Kim climbed out of the old bomb shelter and shuddered, and looked around quickly to see if anyone had seen his slight surrender to fear. He hated to admit it, but he had a touch of claustrophobia, and his short time in the tunnel had given him some unusual moments of anxiety. Fortunately, the two remaining men hadn't paid attention to his body movements, only to his words.

"The Americans are headed toward the beach," said Kim. "We must find the entrance to this tunnel and be waiting for them as they come out."

His men nodded and formed up behind him. Kim thought about the two men he had left in the tunnel to flush the American fugitives out. Were either of them claustrophobic? He dropped the thought. The men were there to obey his commands. If they had to swallow their fear as he had done, then so be it. He looked around once again. Two men left including Moon, another two in the tunnel, and only one left at the yacht. He shook his head. They had been over one hundred strong this morning. He turned back around, grimly determined to complete his mission.

The North Koreans started off at a quick march toward the northeast coast of Roi Island.

* * *

The dim light wavered and caused the shadows of their bodies to bob up and down at random. The North Koreans were almost on top of them. Ken grabbed Milne's shirt and turned to grab Nancy's wrist.

"No!" shouted Nancy. She tried to yank her arm free, but Ken tightened his grip until her arm went limp and she wimpered with the pain.

"Speed is the key!" said Milne. "We'll run as fast as possible!"

"Okay," said Ken in a breathless voice, and got up in a crouch to run through the hellish tunnel. He caught a glimpse of the hordes of rats, fat, evil rats that filled the tunnel just ahead, and his stomach churned with nausea.

"Now!" shouted Milne, and ran in a crouched position toward the living, wiggling mass of rodent bodies.

Ken yanked on Nancy's arm, feeling her resistance, then her surrender to the inevitable.

"Oh, my God!" Nancy shouted, her voice giving the Deity's name an elongated shriek.

And then they were among the living walls and floor of the tunnel, their feet crashing down on the thick, squealing rats, the rats squirming and reeling under the attack of their boots. The rat sounds filled their ears with an ever increasing high-pitched noise until it became a steady roar. The entire tunnel came alive as the rats swarmed over the three human intruders' legs and over each other.

Ken could feel a dozen sets of teeth jab into him, and he pumped his legs up and down as violently as he could to shake them loose, but to no avail. A rat leaped onto his back and grabbed at his shirt. Ken resisted the urge to slap at it—to do so would require him to let go of either Milne, who was leading them along the tunnel, or Nancy, who would be lost in the dark. It would take precious seconds to get in contact with them again, seconds with the rats gnawing at their bodies.

Nancy began to scream, a high-pitched wail of utter agony and revulsion, as the rats bit into her legs and feet. She had a half dozen of the ferocious rodents hanging from her lower extremities and ripping her skin in innumerable places. A rat crawled up her back and quickly got tangled in her hair. Her continuous scream was choked off as she gasped for breath and grabbed at the animal on her head. She grabbed the body of the rat and yanked ferociously at it, finally pulling it free. She attempted to throw it aside, but it bit her on the arm and held on with its teeth. Nancy thrashed her arm back and forth violently and finally succeeded in jarring the animal loose and sending it back into the dark from where it had come.

Ken felt a rat climb his leg and head toward his waist. This one wasn't content to take a piece out of his leg or feet. This one wanted either a piece of his genitals or to reach higher and go for his throat. Ken shifted to one side in a frantic effort to dislodge the rat, and as a result, he slowed their panic-stricken journey down the tunnel. He knocked off a few of the rodents, but the most dangerous rat wasn't deterred. He kept climbing with frightening speed past Ken's waist and ran toward his head.

Ken let go of Milne's shirt and swung at the offending animal, knocking him off the front of his shirt and sending him flying into the darkness. He reached out for Milne's shirt again, but his hand flew through the darkness without hitting anything. Panic seized him, and Ken bolted forward, dragging Nancy along under the viselike grip on her arm. She began shrieking again as the rats made a renewed assault on her legs and buttocks, shredding her pants legs and squirming in to bite her bare skin.

Ken's right foot came down directly on top of a rat's body, causing his foot to roll to the right while his leg remained vertical. His weight came crashing down on his right leg and further folded his right foot inward until his foot was at a right angle to his leg. His foot slipped off the rat's body and his ankle slammed into the concrete floor of the tunnel. He howled with rage and staggered, hopping on his left leg to keep from falling. He grimly pressed forward, hoping to quickly make contact with their savior, Amata Milne.

Ken and Nancy suddenly pounded into Milne's back, nearly knocking him forward on his face. Ken frantically grabbed Milne's shirt and yanked him halfway upright to steady him, then all three of them began to run at top speed through the darkness.

Only Amata Milne had both arms free to swat at the rats as they thundered along the black tunnel. He had been through these tunnels before, but the rats had never been this bad. Milne had one hand above him to brush along the ceiling to keep them centered in the tunnel, and he used the other hand to swing at the rats who leaped on him. A horrible thought hit him. Suppose the tunnel's exit was blocked? The U.S. Army command had taken some steps to keep people out of the tunnels to prevent just what they were going through now. A horrifying vision came to him of the three of them slamming into a concrete wall, then falling back to be swarmed over by thousands of rats.

Ken felt the rat that still clung to his back climb his shirt until it reached his neck, then fall inside his shirt. The rat immediately sank its teeth into Ken's lower back. Ken roared with pain.

Amata Milne's hand that he was dragging along the ceiling suddenly hit a rat, knocking it loose and sending it down onto Milne's head. The rat squirmed around and bit Milne on the cheek. Milne screamed at the top of his lungs.

Suddenly the trio were among undergrowth, the branches slapping them in the face and around their bodies. They struggled to keep up their forward progress but were slowed by the density of the brush. Milne yanked furiously at the rat that clung to his face and pulled it free along with a chunk of flesh from his cheek. Milne ignored the pain and took quick stock of his surroundings. He quickly realized that the tunnel had ended and that undergrowth had grown over the tunnel's exit. He began to swing his arms at the bushes and hacked a path toward the open air.

Suddenly the three of them broke free of the brush and staggered out into the open, crying, screaming, and moaning at the dozens of rats that still held on to them. Ken yanked his shirt off and pounded the rat that was still gnawing on his back. The rodent gave a squeal and fell away. The two men swatted the rats away one by one until they were free of rats, then began to work on Nancy. The rats had packed inside her ripped pant legs and were biting her ferociously. She screamed, her body quivering in revulsion of the attacking animals.

Ken ripped her pants legs further open and feverishly

knocked the rats away. When her legs were clear, he yanked up her blouse and checked the rest of her body. She was finally free of the detestable rodents, but her back, buttocks, and especially her legs were covered with rat bites. Even her feet hadn't escaped. The rats had torn through her boots and had attacked her. Ken could see blood and torn flesh between the holes in the leather. Nancy lay on the ground shuddering in reaction to their horrific journey through the tunnel.

Ken sank quivering to the earth and passed his hands over his body quickly in loathing to what the rats had done to him. His ankle was beginning to swell in reaction to the ankle-turning incident in the tunnel. He could see a dozen places where he was bleeding and saw the same on Amata Milne, who had led them through hell to relative safety. He squinted in the still-bright daylight in contrast to the totally dark tunnel, then looked about to see how far they had come.

Lieutenant Kim and his two men looked up and down the beach for the entrance to the tunnel. There were a few undulations in the earth and he had his men check out each one methodically and thoroughly but none were the entrance he sought. Perhaps I should just sit and wait, he thought. My other men will flush them out in a few minutes.

Screams came to him as he stood on the sand. He turned and smiled quickly. There they were, and making a great deal of noise as well. He motioned to his men to chase after them.

They were only a hundred yards away.

Movement in the corner of Ken's eye caught his attention and made him stiffen with alarm. He turned and saw the three North Koreans in full view running toward them from the beach. Ken, Nancy, and Amata had exited the tunnel about one hundred and fifty yards inland. The old tunnel had gone to the seawall back in the 1940s, but now it was considerably farther inland, man and nature having added to the coastline of Roi-Namur.

He scrambled to his feet. "Let's go!" he said in a hoarse voice.

Amata Milne gave him a surprised glance, then looked in the direction of the onrushing North Koreans. He gaped at them for a second, then leaped to his feet. Ken grabbed one of Nancy's arms, and Amata took the other. They hauled her to her feet and began to drag her away from the North Koreans.

Pain shot through both Ken's ankles, and he suddenly realized that none of them were in any shape to run from the North Koreans.

"Take her!" he shouted to Milne. "Get her to safety!" The choice was very simple and one of the easiest he had ever made. The North Koreans were going to get him anyway, so he might as well try to slow them down. He reached down and picked up some rocks, then turned to face the enemy.

The North Koreans were very close and hadn't opened fire yet. Ken stopped breathing. He figured he only had a few seconds to live. While they're killing me, Nancy and Milne will get that much farther away. He threw two rocks at the approaching enemy, hoping that the North Koreans would slow down, maybe take cover behind something.

His rocks went wide of the mark, and the charging North Koreans merely gave the rocks a glance. When they saw that the rocks were going to miss, they ignored their flight path and pressed on. Ken caught sight of one of the automatic assault rifles carried by the lead North Korean. Who am I kidding? he thought. Rocks against automatic weapons?

He braced himself for the inevitable, but couldn't resist a glance in Nancy's direction. His heart seemed to leap as he saw Milne struggling with Nancy as they staggered away. They hadn't gotten far. The North Koreans would kill him in the next few seconds. A few seconds after that, his newfound friend Amata Milne would die in a hail of bullets. Then they would capture Nancy, or maybe kill her also.

He turned and looked into the face of death. The lead North Korean was only twenty yards away. He stopped and pointed his weapon at Ken.

Ken flopped down on the sand and knew he had nowhere to go.

"Now! Fire! Open fire!" shouted Ed Atkinson to his five men who were lined up along the road behind two security vehicles. The security guards obeyed and sent a host of lead in the direction of the North Koreans. He and his men had barely caught up to the movements of the invaders and had just set up when the security chief ordered them to open up on the North Koreans.

One of them is in real trouble, thought Atkinson. Imagine throwing rocks at guys with assault rifles. He's either the dumbest guy in the world or the bravest son of a bitch I've ever met.

Lieutenant Kim's head jerked around at the sound of the unexpected gunfire. More Americans—and they were firing from the road! He watched one of his men twist and squirm to avoid the gunfire. The man hit the ground, then jumped up and ran back to Kim. The Americans seemed to be using handguns, and they would be no match for his men's automatic weapons. But only one of his men had an automatic weapon with him. The other AKM was with one of his men in the tunnel.

Kim and his men took cover behind a large rock as he looked the situation over. These few Americans could very well cut them off from the yacht. He ordered the man with the assault rifle to fire a burst at the two security trucks on the road. Maybe the Americans would run at the sound of a real weapon. Kim's man fired a long burst, sending slugs into and around the vehicles behind which the six men were huddled.

Silence reigned for a moment after the loud blast from the automatic weapon. Then the cracking of distant weapons came to him with the immediate pinging sound of the bullets ricocheting off the rock in front of them. So, the Americans had stood their ground after being peppered by automatic weapons' fire, thought Kim. His father had told him that Americans were basically cowards and that they would run at the first sign of resistance from their enemies. Kim grunted to himself in disgust. These Americans evidently came from a different part of America than the ones my father was talking about, he thought.

His gaze rested on Moon for a moment. As a combat soldier, Moon is useless, thought Kim. I have only one real man trained for combat to go up against six armed men. The course was clear to him. As much as he hated to do it, Kim decided to give up his quest for the woman engineer. He still had the hoard of top secret documents safely stored back at the yacht. It was better to get away with something than to not get away at all.

Kim ordered his men back to the pier.

"How are you doing, Nancy?" asked Ken tenderly as he cradled her face in his arms.

"Oh, God, it hurts!" she said in a whisper, and squirmed in pain to emphasize the point.

"I know, I know," replied Ken. His own body was racked with pain from the myriad rat bites he had received in the terrifying tunnel. The bites were beginning to swell and blood and clear fluid still oozed from the ripped skin. What sort of diseases did the rats carry? What poisons were now traveling through his, Amata's, and Nancy's bloodstreams?

Ed Atkinson strode up and looked them over breathlessly. His heart still pounded from the encounter with the North Koreans. He was grateful to see them withdraw.

"You people really got tore up," he mumbled under his breath. He turned and waved to a couple of his men to come over and help the three of them to a truck.

"Thanks," mumbled Ken Garrett. "You saved our lives."

Atkinson knelt down and peered at Ken for moment. "You the guy who stole my weapon?" he asked sullenly.

Ken nodded. "Yeah. Sorry, I—"

"Where's your friend, the one who said security guys were useless?" he asked belligerently.

Ken lifted his gaze and stared him directly in the eye. "Dead," he replied in a firm monosyllable.

Atkinson looked at him steadily for a long moment, then dropped his eyes to look at the ground. "Let's get you guys to the truck."

The security men helped Ken, Nancy, and Amata to one of their vehicles and gently loaded them into the backseat. Ed Atkinson climbed into the driver's seat and started the truck.

"The North Koreans, where are they?" asked Ken from the backseat. He sat upright and held Nancy in his arms. She was moaning softly from the pain.

"They took off, probably back toward the pier," said Atkinson.

"You've got to stop them," said Ken in an exhausted tone.

"Not a chance," said Atkinson in a tone that dismissed the subject completely.

"They have top secret documents stolen from Kwajalein Range Command Center that'll detail how our missile defense system works," replied Ken. "They'll be able to threaten South Korea, and our troops that are there as well, with missiles."

Atkinson licked his lips but didn't reply right away. He looked at Ken in the rearview mirror in indecision.

"The trouble is that we're almost out of ammo," Atkinson replied weakly. "We can't go up against those guys—they have assault rifles."

"There must be more weapons on this island," said Ken plaintively.

"If there are, no one will admit it," replied Atkinson. "It's against the law to possess a gun here."

Ken fell silent and looked over the three of them. Milne seemed to be in the best shape, with maybe a few less rat bites than either Nancy or himself. He owed Milne his life and Nancy's life as well. How could he repay this Marshallese Islander?

He lapsed into thought about the escaping North Koreans as the truck rumbled along toward the aid station. How could he stop them from taking the top secret documents? Another question caught hold of his mind and wouldn't let it go.

How could he take revenge on the North Koreans for killing Mike Sprague?

The truck came to a stop, and the men assisted the wounded trio out of the vehicle. Waiting nurses rushed up to them and began to assess their wounds. Apparently the security men had called ahead, thought Ken. The head nurse told the other nurses to get the three of them inoculations for rat bites immediately, then to get their clothes off and dress the wounds.

They laid the three of them down on cots that were side by side and quickly administered the shots from a series of seemingly massive syringes. Ken wondered how all that liquid could fit in his arm. Thoughts of the North Koreans weren't far away as he watched the nurses attend to his wife first. One nurse chattered away about the diseases carried by rats.

"They can carry typhus, you know, and tularemia, rabies, trichinosis, and let's see, leishmaniasis, spirochetal jaundice, leptospirosis, and let's not forget bubonic plague," said the nurse as she attended to Nancy.

"Oh, no, let's not forget the plague," said Nancy under her breath. She glanced in Ken's direction, but he was lost in thought.

Weapons, he thought feverishly. What weapons do we have on this island? Maybe there was a weapon that didn't look like one, or whose primary purpose wasn't to be a weapon.

An idea roared through his mind so quickly he jumped in reaction.

"What is it?" asked Nancy as the nurses washed her bites and applied sterile dressings over the broken skin. She eyed her husband past the edge of the screen the nurses had put between her and the two men.

"I know how to stop the North Koreans," he said, and gave her a fierce look. He dragged himself to his feet and limped across the room to get to the door. He turned to give Nancy a final look, and she questioned him with her eyes.

"Altair," he said simply.

CHAPTER TWENTY-SEVEN

The Weapon

Lieutenant Kim Il Kwon ran up the pier toward the yacht, then turned to look back at Moon and his other man, who struggled to keep up. He waved them aboard the boat, then climbed the short ladder to get on board himself. The guard that he had left on the yacht immediately presented himself and reported that all was quiet. Kim nodded absently and ordered them to make preparations to get under way.

He walked to the railing on the second deck and stared at the island. All seemed silent and peaceful. The green, lush growth on the island swayed with the warm wind and tried to calm Kim's nerves.

It all seems like such a paradise, he thought, but I know better. Behind any rock or tree lurked an American with a gun ready to kill any of his men who let up their guard for even a second. He looked about himself self-consciously. He had only three men left.

Kim walked toward the stern of the yacht while reaching inside his shirt. He fingered the piece of fabric that he had hidden inside, then pulled it out with a jerk and looked it over. In a solid field of red stood a circle of white with a single red star in the middle. He had intended to fly this small flag over the Range Command Building on Kwajalein, but he had had no time to think about it.

Now it will fly over this capitalist's boat, thought Kim. He strode to the stern and yanked down the hated flag of one of his nation's eternal enemies. The Rising Sun was hurled contemptuously to the deck, and the flag of the Democratic People's Republic was raised in its place. Kim snapped to attention and gave it a stiff salute as the island breeze picked it up and lifted it, in Kim's mind to ruffle once again in glory.

Movement along the end of the pier near the beach caught his eye. Two figures were running up the pier toward the yacht. Kim squinted and saw that one of them carried a rifle and that they both were wearing North Korean uniforms. They were the two men who had entered the tunnel. He had written them off, assuming that the Americans had killed or captured them. The men climbed aboard the yacht and reported to him. He told them to help the others in their preparations to get under way.

He suddenly sensed Moon at his elbow. He turned and gave the man a steady gaze.

"Comrade Lieutenant, we must refuel before getting under way," said Moon. Kim continued to stare at him. "There are fuel drums in the building on the pier."

"See to it," said Kim.

"Yes sir," replied Moon in a humble voice, and went back to the rest of the men. They began to set up fuel hoses from the large shack on the pier to the yacht's fuel tank.

Kim fingered the handgun in his pocket and slowly wandered down to the pier. He walked around the pier building, inspecting the fueling operation and surveying the trees along the beach for any movement. Kim walked over to the side of the pier building facing the beach and stood behind some fuel drums. He shook them to see how much fuel they had left. They were empty. He spied a ramshackle chair, pulled it over, and sat down, then let a wave of fatigue pass over him.

He was tired, deathly tired from this battle they had fought with the Americans. Thank the Dear Leader that it was over, he thought.

"You know what I think?" said Ed Atkinson as he steered the security truck around a corner to get onto Altair Road. "I think you're friggin' nuts, that's what I think."

"My wounds will wait, but the North Koreans won't,"

replied Ken Garrett. "They're going to get away as soon as they can."

"And you're going to stop them with radar?" asked Atkinson in an incredulous voice.

Ken Garrett looked out the window at the imposing bulk of the Altair radar antenna. The antenna dish loomed over everything on this end of the island. With its one-hundred-sixty-foot-diameter reflector, the antenna stood two hundred feet over Roi-Namur. The palm trees covered only the bottom supporting structure of the antenna, giving the impression that the massive antenna was floating above the treetops.

"Yes," he whispered in reply to Atkinson's question. There it was; that was his weapon.

Garrett snapped out of his thoughts and turned to the island security chief. "You'd better clear the area of personnel in the path of the antenna. We don't want to lose anyone except the North Koreans."

Atkinson gave him an awestruck sideways glance. "That bad?"

Garrett nodded. "Yeah, that bad."

Atkinson rolled his eyes around. "This I gotta see." He picked up the microphone and ordered two of his units to clear the marina and the intersection of Altair and Copra roads of personnel—unless, of course they were North Koreans.

Kim stiffened as he saw a security truck pull up to the end of the pier. He shouted orders for the two men with the assault rifles to take aim on the truck and its occupants.

Another attack, thought Kim. These Americans just don't give up. He told his men to open fire if they began to come up the pier toward them. Kim could see several people walking around the truck, then it appeared that they all climbed in, with some people getting into the open rear bed of the truck. The truck pulled away and disappeared into the trees.

Yes, of course, Kim thought. They were clearing the people away from his men to get the island's occupants to safety.

Kim quickly relaxed. The Americans weren't preparing

to attack them. They just didn't want any of his men to kill any more of them. He ordered his two men back to their refueling duties.

The Americans have given up. They are just going to let us go peacefully, he thought with relief.

Garrett and Atkinson pulled up to the Altair radar site. Atkinson quickly got out of the truck and opened the locked gate in the fence that circled the site. He flung the fence gate wide and hopped back into the truck, then quickly drove through the open gate. Atkinson screeched to a stop in front of the entrance to the main building and leaped from the truck. He came around to help Garrett from the vehicle.

Garrett hobbled through the doorway, giving the empty guard's desk a glance, then went down the hall toward the control room. He had the thought that Atkinson must have gathered up all the security guards from their normal posts just to save him and the others from the North Koreans. Atkinson held the control room door open as Garrett limped through. A man seated at a console looked up as they entered.

"Hi, uh, Ken?" he asked in puzzlement.

"Yeah, you're Dan Keating, right?" said Garrett.

"Yeah. Holy shit! What happened to you?" said Keating, and came halfway out of his chair.

"It's a long story," said Garrett. "Is it operational?" he asked with a gesture toward the console.

"Yes, but we're not radiating at the moment," replied Keating, who then gave Atkinson a questioning look.

"What azimuth is Yokohama Pier?" asked Garrett quickly.

"Geez, I don't know. One thirty, one twenty. Why?" said Keating.

"You got a map of the island?" asked Atkinson.

Keating jerked his thumb over his shoulder toward another room. "Map's in there."

Atkinson helped Garrett over to the map. Garrett studied it for a second, then looked around helplessly. Keating handed Garrett a piece of clear plastic with zero to three hundred and sixty degrees printed on it in the form of a circle.

"Yeah, that's what I need," replied Garrett. He placed the center of the circle over the mark on the chart that represented the Altair radar, then oriented the circle of numbers so that zero degrees was to the north. He mentally drew a line from Altair to Yokohama Pier and read off the azimuth.

"One, four, zero degrees," he said with his voice a somber whisper. Mike Sprague's image lurked at the edges of his mind. He would not try to fool himself—this was for Mike. This was for revenge.

He hobbled over to stand over Dan Keating.

"Azimuth: one, four, zero degrees," said Garrett as he stared Keating in the eye. "Elevation: zero degrees."

The words sent a chill along Keating's spine. His mouth dropped open as he realized what Garrett was going to do.

"Are you sure?" was Keating's timid answer.

"Do it!" ordered Atkinson in a growl.

Keating typed the commands on the keyboard, but his hand hovered uncertainly over the key that would initiate the command. He looked up at Garrett with a clear plea in his eyes. Garrett reached around him and pushed the Execute key.

The massive metal dish of the Altair radar began to move with a clunking sound as the motors accelerated the large mass up to a constant speed. Red lights sprinkled around the area came alive to indicate that the servomotors were engaged. Inside the control room, a tone was heard indicating that the huge antenna was in motion. The pitch of the tone was proportional to velocity, and the sound started low in pitch then increased as the antenna began moving faster, then it finally leveled off as the antenna hit a constant speed.

Ken Garrett nodded to himself, then gave Keating a piercing look.

"When the azimuth gets to one forty, radiate at both frequencies," he said in a grim voice. "Max power, max rep rate."

"Are you nuts?" asked Keating, who looked from Garrett to Atkinson, then back again. "We have to declare 'RF

Hazards.' You know that. That's supposed to be coordinated with KCC.''

Keating referred to the Krems Control Center on Kwajalein Island, which controlled the operation of the various radars on Roi-Namur.

"We have already swept the area," said Atkinson. "And right now"—he jerked his thumb in Garrett's direction—"he *is* KCC.''

Keating shook his head in consternation. "I can call KCC and confirm that?'' It was more a plea than a question. He looked at both of them again. When they stood silently, he reached for the phone, but Ken Garrett's hand clamped down on it with sudden violence, causing Keating to jump involuntarily.

Garrett put his face within a inch of Keating's nose. "North Koreans have invaded the island,'' he snarled at the hapless radar operator. "We're trying to stop them.''

Keating's mouth dropped open. "You guys are shittin' me. Right?'' He looked at Atkinson, who returned a fierce look. "God, Almighty,'' he mumbled to himself.

All three of them looked at the azimuth readout. It read one hundred twenty degrees, and it was increasing rapidly. Dan Keating got busy and typed in commands to radiate at the maximum power level at one hundred fifty-five point five and four hundred fifteen Megahertz simultaneously. The transmitter radiated seven million watts at the lower frequency, and four and a half million watts at the higher frequency.

The audio tone indicating that the antenna was in motion began to decrease in pitch when the antenna slowed as it neared its commanded position. The tone grew lower in pitch, then stopped altogether, creating a seeming vacuum in the control room. They all looked at the antenna position indicator. It read: "azimuth—140 degrees; elevation—0 degrees.''

Keating's hand hovered over the Return key on the keyboard in hesitation.

"You guys are sure about this?'' he asked. "I mean KCC is only going to call me up and ask me what the hell is going on. If I don't give them a good enough answer, they'll only hit the emergency switch that will kill all the radar radiation on the whole island.''

''Communications are cut off with Kwajalein,'' said Atkinson. ''With KCC on Kwajalein, they're never going to know what went on here.''

Ken Garrett reached around Keating once again and pressed the necessary key, sending the command for the radar to radiate its deadly field.

The three of them watched the status display change to show that the radar was following the commands of its human masters. Silence fell over the room.

''I calculated once what the maximum near field power flux density would be,'' said Keating in a low voice. Garrett and Atkinson shifted their gaze toward him with the obvious question on their faces.

''Transmitting at both frequencies simultaneously, it's about a thousand times the safe level,'' said Keating.

Moon Si-Bok touched the small Japanese flag he had stuffed into his pocket. Lieutenant Kim, in a fit of emotion, had thrown it onto the deck when he had put up the North Korean flag. Moon had seen it and had picked it up, after looking about to see where Kim was. The Japanese flag would make good cover for their journey back to North Korea. Moon decided that he would try to convince the stubborn officer of its practical use. Would the Americans attack a boat flying the flag of Japan? The small flag would be useful if only to create doubt in the Americans' minds.

He looked over the array of shipboard electronics with satisfaction. Even though the labels on the controls were in Japanese, the functions were fairly easy to figure out. The Global Positioning Satellite receiver was giving what seemed to be accurate position on the earth, and the radar was in operation, giving him returns from their surroundings. He eyed the radar console and nodded to himself. In an hour or two, it would be dark, and they would need the radar to get outside the reef to open waters. With the GPS receiver, it would be very easy indeed to navigate back to the People's Republic.

He turned on the radio and listened to some of the chatter on the HF bands. Yes, even the radio works, he thought to himself. He looked out the bridge window toward the dock and saw that the men were just finishing their refueling task. And the Americans were nowhere to be seen.

Moon thought of the tall, redheaded American woman who had been his prisoner for a large part of the day. She was an engineer as well. Americans were such a curious people. Beautiful, elegant women like that doing what was traditionally a man's job. She must have been a good engineer, Moon mused, or she would not have had such a position of responsibility on such an important program. He had been looking forward to working with her and finding out just how good an engineer she was. He sighed. All that was behind them now.

The chatter on the radio suddenly ceased, and the noise level increased until it began to hurt Moon's ears. He walked over and quickly turned down the volume. The GPS receiver caught his eye. The display was blank. He tapped it a few times to resurrect it, but to no avail. He glanced at the radar screen and saw that it was solid white. Concern rose in him. Something was wrong.

He looked around the bridge quickly to discover any clue to why all the electronics on the yacht had suddenly died. His eyes wandered around and he eventually looked out the window toward the pier. The metal skeleton caught his peripheral vision.

His eyes flicked up over the building on the pier to take in the huge radar dish that loomed in the distance over the tops of the island's palm trees. The antenna had been pointed to the east when he had arrived on the yacht's bridge. Now it was pointed straight at their vessel.

Moon's mouth dropped open as he suddenly realized what was happening.

Lieutenant Kim Il Kwon sat slumped in the rickety chair behind the sheet of steel that he had propped up against the fuel drums. He had wanted a shield from any American gunfire they might want to send his way. Five feet behind him, leaning against the wall of the pier building, was another piece of sheet metal left over from a repair project on the island. Kim sat quietly reflecting on his father's heroism years ago as electromagnetic energy from the Altair radar flooded the area around him. The waves of energy from the radar reflected off the metal behind Kim and traveled toward the sheet of metal in front of him. The energy that reached the front piece of metal was in turn reflected back to the metal behind Kim. This action set up a standing wave and had the effect of concentrating and nearly quadrupling the power in the electromagnetic field around Kim's body.

Kim closed his eyes and tried to envision his father's actions on that fateful day almost twenty years ago. His father had attacked furiously, and the Americans had cowered before him. At least that was what his father had told him. As a youngster, Kim had devoured his father's stories of that day and had dreamed of becoming a hero as his father had in the mid-1970s. And today he had had the chance of fulfilling that boyhood dream. The Americans had other ideas, of course, and had fought him and his men every second of the day. He had been attacked by snipers, helicopters, submarines, and civilians. But he was still alive and able to make his escape.

He realized that the chance of a lifetime, the chance of becoming a national hero, was gone now. Things had gone badly, and now it was up to him to salvage something from the day's disasters. He still had the documents which would be a boon to his nation's intelligence community, and with them he would fashion his claim to heroism. Relief flooded him as he thought of how soon they would be departing. Yes, he would be glad to get away from this hellish place and these damnable Americans who didn't know when to give up.

A sensation of heat seemed to crowd around him, and he guessed that it was the final vestiges of the tropical sun just before it dropped below the horizon. He opened his eyes and received the shock of his life.

He looked seemingly through a mist which totally obscured his peripheral vision and left vision only in the centers of his eyes. He could see only in shades of gray.

Kim's mouth dropped open, and he blinked his eyes furiously to clear them, then rubbed them harder and harder in a futile attempt to make his vision normal. His eyes flicked to his left toward the sun, which was low in the sky. The expected red-orange ball was sickly white and gray.

Kim issued a plaintive moan from his lips and slowly rose from his chair. What was happening? he thought feverishly. How could this happen? What sort of magic did the Americans use on me to do this? He closed his eyes tightly for a moment, and the other sensations in his body suddenly were noticeable. He felt an aching, and somehow he knew that this was a harbinger of enormous pain to come later. Panic filled him and forced his eyes open with the hope, in vain, for his vision to return. Instead his vision failed completely, the mist seemingly closing off even the narrow range of vision he had had seconds ago.

He was now totally blind.

Moon jumped down below the window edge, his mind racing at what the Americans were doing with the large radar antenna that loomed over the line of trees. Were they radiating? He glanced in the direction of the radar screen and the GPS receiver. The equipment had died, and he was suddenly sure that the island's inhabitants were doing all they could to stop them . . . or kill them.

Was the radar powerful enough to kill? Moon shook his head. He didn't know. Even if he knew what the radiated power was, he would need to know how to calculate power levels in the near field of the antenna. Even though he was a technical expert, he didn't have that kind of specialized knowledge at his mental fingertips. He shook his head again. The Americans were using a totally unexpected weapon on them. The radar's use was quite brilliant.

Moon slithered across the deck to find a megaphone he had seen in a cabinet at the rear of the bridge. He opened the door and picked it up from one of the shelves. He flipped on the switch and slid over to the starboard side window. Moon opened the window, being careful to keep his head below the window ledge, and stuck the megaphone through the opening.

"Find Lieutenant Kim and get aboard immediately!" he shouted. The megaphone amplified his voice and sent it echoing around the island's southern coast. Moon heard two of the men acknowledge his order, and he nodded to himself.

Moon knew that the energy would flow through the window even if it were closed and bounce off anything metallic on the interior of the bridge. Moon knew that his best chance was to get as close to the bulkhead below the window as possible. The electromagnetic waves would diffract over the edges of the window and create regions where the energy added and null regions where it canceled, but he had no way of knowing the location or size of the null regions. He did know that the bulkhead below the window created a shadow of energy just behind it. Would the shadow be filled in by the reflections of the radar's energy from the metallic objects and opposite bulkhead? There was no way to tell, but at least the reflections had less energy than the incident waves.

He sagged to lay on the deck of the bridge, his mind thinking about the damage electromagnetic fields can do to the human body.

The field of energy set up by a radiating antenna changes in intensity at radio frequencies, millions of times a second. This causes the water molecules in a person's body to flip back and forth at the same rate due to the molecule's slight positive charge on one side and slight negative charge on the other. This extremely rapid movement at the molecular level creates friction and produces heat. This is the same principle by which microwave ovens cook food.

Moon's stomach churned. The Americans were trying to cook them.

A shriek split the air very close to the yacht. Moon jumped and resisted the urge to look out the bridge window. The sharp sound faded away and silence again reigned over the island. Then another jagged scream was heard, and another, and another. Soon the screaming became continuous.

Ken Garrett stood at the door to the Altair radar control building and listened to the screams of agony that floated over the treetops from Yokohama Pier. He squirmed around, ignoring the pain shooting up his legs, and stared at the brilliant colors of yet another spectacular sunset. He wished Mike Sprague was here to see it.

The screaming went down in volume, as if something

had come between him and the screamer. Yes, thought Garrett, he's going on board the yacht. A feeling of satisfaction ran through him. He had done all he could do to stop the North Koreans . . . and to revenge Mike Sprague's death.

Garrett cocked an ear and caught the continuous agonized shrieking of his victim muffled by the boat's structure and the intervening trees.

Garrett's thoughts turned cold. The North Koreans might leave the island, but at least one of them would never get away.

CHAPTER TWENTY-EIGHT

The Journey Back

The Pacific sun was just an orange memory on the western horizon when the yacht with the six remaining North Koreans set sail from Yokohama Pier on Roi-Namur. Moon Si-Bok gave the wheel a hard left to put as much distance between them and the huge radar antenna as quickly as possible. He held his crouched position below the window level until he estimated that the radar antenna was directly behind them, with the superstructure of the yacht between them and the antenna to block the radar's energy.

Moon stood on rubbery legs and looked behind him. The antenna couldn't be seen due to the intervening structure of the boat. Moon knew that they were still being irradiated, but at lower levels. Electromagnetic energy had the unnerving characteristic of reflecting and diffracting around corners even when there was no line of sight to the source.

Moon could still hear the intermittent whimpering and screaming of Lieutenant Kim Il Kwon, who had been, until recently, the leader of their ragged band of survivors. The other members of the crew must have locked him in one of the rooms. Moon mumbled a prayer and shoved the throttles wide open. The engine noise increased to a throaty roar, drowning out the agonizing noises from the stricken officer, and the yacht sped away to the south.

Moon eyed the string of small islands that lined the edge of the lagoon to his right. He would have to pick what looked to be the deepest passage through the reef between the islands to get to the open sea, then navigate somehow to get back to the People's Republic. He leaned forward and glanced at the sky. It looked to be a clear night. Maybe I could use the stars, he thought.

He swung the yacht around to the west and headed toward a gap in the ring of islands which he hoped was deep enough to let the large yacht through. As he approached the passage through the reef, he slowed down, with the engine's roar dropping in level and unmasking the frantic shrieking of Lieutenant Kim. He tried to ignore the painful sound, but found himself wondering about the rest of the crew. Two of the men had complained about impaired vision, and they all wondered in awe how Lieutenant Kim had been affected. None of them had the technical background to come to the same conclusion as Moon had, and Moon wasn't about to tell them the truth, that all of them had been irradiated and that the effects might not show up immediately, not for a few hours at least. What about the long journey home? How many of them would be left to get this boat to its destination?

He shook his head and stared at some of the items around the bridge. His vision seemed to be unaffected. Possibly he had escaped the last American assault on them. Moon shook the thoughts from him and concentrated on the job at hand. He glanced over the now useless array of electronics that lined the bridge and uttered a low oath. The Americans had taken care of any electronic help he might have had.

The fathometer suddenly came to mind. Would that have survived? It had no antenna, as the radar, radio, and GPS receiver did that had received the island radar's enormous energy. He looked over the electronics again and studied the titles of each piece of equipment. The Japanese words were only partially intelligible to him, but he found the depth meter without much problem. He turned on the meter and got a normal display and almost instant readings of the depth of the water.

Moon let out a deep sigh of relief. With this depth meter, he would be able to safely navigate the passage.

With the last vestiges of sunlight in the western sky,

Moon negotiated the reef passage and sailed into the open sea.

"We have got to call Kwajalein!" said Ken Garrett in a determined voice.

"You're going back to the aid station and get those wounds looked at," said Ed Atkinson as he gunned the truck's engine to cross the island at breakneck speed.

"You don't understand," replied Garrett in a weak voice. "We've got to tell the sub that the North Koreans are leaving in the yacht."

Atkinson's head swung around to stare at Garrett. "What sub?"

Ken told him about the U.S.S. *Topeka* and its brave landing party. Atkinson gave a low whistle.

"I have a radio at the security station that I can use to contact Kwaj Security," said Atkinson. "I was trying that link when you showed up with your cockamamie story about North Koreans invading Kwajalein." He gave Garrett a brief grin.

Ken Garrett couldn't help but like the big man. He smiled back. In some ways Atkinson reminded him of Mike Sprague. His smile faded as he thought of the loss of his friend. Gone, but never forgotten. He told Atkinson where Sprague's body was located and asked him if he could get someone down near the marina to pick him up.

Atkinson nodded and readily agreed. "But now you're going back to the aid station," he said gently. "I'll take care of everything from here. You've done enough already today."

Garrett felt the strength go out of him. It had been a long, horrifying day, and he was totally exhausted.

"Okay," he whispered. He longed to see Nancy again.

Minutes later, Atkinson pulled up to the aid station, then got out to help Garrett inside. His eyes went immediately to Nancy's bed. She was asleep, and on the other side of the room, Milne was also sleeping. The painkillers must have taken effect, he thought. Ken longed for sleep as well.

Atkinson deposited him on the bed next to Nancy's, then prepared to make his all-important call to Kwajalein. The

North Koreans had a head start, but an American nuclear attack sub could catch up easily if it only knew about it.

Atkinson gave the Garretts and Amata Milne, who had a large bandage over the side of his face, a quick look to see that they were all right, then turned to go.

"Ed," said Ken Garrett. Atkinson turned back around and questioned Garrett with his eyes. "Kwajalein might not be able to contact the sub directly. Tell them to call Vandenberg and get them to call the Pentagon. They'll know what to do."

Atkinson nodded. "Right. You take care." In a second he was gone.

The nurses suddenly arrived and busily began to attend to his wounds while berating him for leaving earlier. They bustled over him for about a half hour, wiping him, injecting him, and making him swallow an odd assortment of pills. Then they were gone, leaving him to get some rest. Ken glanced at Nancy, who lay with her eyes closed on the bed next to him.

A swell of emotion rose in him. He had almost lost her a half dozen times today, and he knew that that would have been the devastation of his life for as long as he might live. Tears came to his eyes, and he furiously blinked them back, then gave in and let them roll unimpeded down his cheeks. He got out of bed and knelt down next to her.

Nancy rolled toward him and sleepily opened her eyes a crack. She looked at him for a few seconds, then her eyes opened wider but not quite all the way. Ken gently took her face into his hands.

"Ken. Oh, Ken," she said softly. She put her arms around his neck and pulled him close to her.

"I almost lost you forever," he said in a shaking voice.

"I'm here, Ken," she whispered. "I'll always be here."

The Pentagon

General Stephen Barnes, U.S. Army, Chairman, Joint Chiefs of Staff, looked at each man around the table in the conference room in the National Command Center in the Pentagon.

"All right. Let's get to it," he said, and the others squirmed in their seats slightly in impatience.

"As many of you know," began General Barnes, "the army command at Kwajalein has had its communications cut with the States due to the recent typhoon. We have had more contact with the U.S.S. *Topeka* than with anyone in the area. The *Topeka* has destroyed a presumed North Korean submarine as it headed out of the lagoon toward the open sea."

There was a murmur of excitement around the room. Admiral Albert Kern spoke up.

"Do we know if they had retrieved any RVs from the lagoon floor?" asked the admiral.

General Barnes shook his head. "Not for certain, but the crew of the *Topeka* said that some civilians believed that that was the case. Just how they knew this is anybody's guess at this point. I have just received a call from General Talbot at Vandenberg, and he has been in contact with USAKA at Kwajalein."

They all leaned forward in their chairs for the update to America's latest military crisis.

"Apparently there is an unconfirmed report from Security on Roi-Namur that some survivors from the North Korean sub have made off with top secret documents relating to our missile defense system," continued General Barnes.

"How did they do that with their submarine sunk?" asked Admiral Kern.

"They apparently stole a yacht owned by a Japanese industrialist who had put into Roi-Namur to escape the typhoon," replied Barnes.

Admiral Kern gave the general an incredulous look and shook his head. "I think we have to confirm that report before we start blowing Japanese yachts out of the water."

General Barnes nodded. "Agreed. But we do have to stop these documents from getting back to North Korea. They are potentially devastating to our missile defense effort. Incidentally, Kwajalein is determining which documents were taken, and we should have that information to begin an assessment in a few hours."

"And we have to tell the *Topeka* to stop and board any

boats flying the Japanese flag which are in the area," said Admiral Kern.

"When is the *Topeka*'s next communication window?" asked General Barnes.

Admiral Kern grimaced. "Eight hours from now."

"Keep trying to contact them in case they go to communications depth for some other reason," said Barnes.

"Aye, aye," replied Admiral Kern.

"We'll scramble all available aircraft from Pearl and Hickam, also Guam," offered another officer.

"Don't forget about Okinawa, and let's find out what we might have on Wake Island," said Admiral Kern. "That'll be the closest."

"I wish we still had Clark in the Philippines," said an aide. They all agreed.

"Carrier aircraft?" asked General Barnes, and looked directly at the admiral.

"None for quite a while yet," said Kern. "We'll get the *Independence* moving out of Japan, but the rest are tied up in the Indian Ocean and the Persian Gulf."

"We have to work the space assets as well," added General Barnes.

"Yes, it looks like White Cloud will have a new priority," said Admiral Kern, referring to the three low-flying satellites that were specifically designed to find ships at sea. "It found the North Korean sub the first time, and it'll find this damn yacht as well."

"Let's cover all the bases," said General Barnes. "I'll formally request Keyhole coverage of the area with the CIO as soon as we're done here." The Central Imagery Office controlled requests and determined priorities of the United States's spaceborne imagery assets, specifically the KH-11 satellite, which provided near-real-time optical imagery and electronic intelligence through which radio frequency emissions of targets on the surface of the earth were identified.

Admiral Kern looked around the table. "There is one other asset." They all looked at him expectantly.

"Aurora," he said.

Moon Si-Bok looked over the calm ocean and stared mesmerized at the sparkling light from the slowly rising moon that seemed to hang just a few degrees above the horizon. The sea was peaceful even though he ripped through the water at over twenty knots. The sea rushed by the sides of the large craft with a continual noise, sometimes slapping the sides of the yacht with an errant wave.

Moon looked at the old mechanical chronometer that was mounted to one side of the bridge. The American radar had left that piece of equipment unaffected. He had been at the wheel for about ten hours now, putting increasing distance between them and the Kwajalein Atoll.

Lieutenant Kim's screaming had gratefully ceased about an hour ago. Moon had sent a man to check up on him. Kim was still alive but in excruciating pain and all but in shock. He had finally passed out from the pain, which seemingly increased as time went on. Moon suspected that Kim's brain had swelled due to the heating caused by the electromagnetic radiation from the American radar. The rest of Kim's body would also have suffered a similar fate, thought Moon, causing the joints to swell to the point where they were immobile. Hollow viscera within the body might have captured some of the radiant energy, causing resonances and an exacerbation of the heating effect.

It all came down to one thing, thought Moon. The Americans had partially cooked Kim, unleashing incredible agony within him. Moon could think of no worse way of dying.

He shook the thoughts from him and noted that the only sounds reaching him at the moment were the thrumming of the engines and the sea sliding by the sides of the yacht. He became increasingly grateful for those sounds which had replaced the agonizing shrieks of Lieutenant Kim.

Even as he grew exhausted by the lateness of the hour and the events of the previous day, he felt a new confidence building in him. They were in the middle of the Pacific Ocean over two hundred miles from the nearest American forces. Even the Americans with all their vaunted technology would have a very hard time finding them. The yacht was made almost totally of fiberglass and wood, which did not reflect radar signals well. While the yacht wasn't exactly a stealth vessel, any American radar would have to get much closer to detect it than if it was made of metal.

Even the American submarine that had sunk the *Admiral Yi* would have to know where to look to find this boat.

The Pacific was a big ocean, thought Moon with a smile. A very big ocean indeed.

CHAPTER TWENTY-NINE

Aurora

Groom Lake, Nevada

Major Mike Tallant, USAF, settled into the cockpit and rocked back and forth a bit to get his orange-colored space-suit into the creases of the seat. The ground crew helped him plug in the various cables and lines to the sides of the cockpit: one for communications: one for suit environmental control, and one for oxygen.

He heard his RSO, radar systems officer, climb into the seat behind him by conduction of the sound through the seat and his hard helmet. Captain Erwin Jansen settled into his seat, plugged in his cables, and immediately went on the intercom between pilot and RSO.

"Comm check," said Jansen matter-of-factly.

"Read you five by five," replied Tallant.

"And I read you five by five," said Jansen.

The ground crew checked out the aircraft with the help of the two crew members, then they cleared the area for engine ignition. Tallant hit the switches to enable engine start while the ground crew started the engine remotely from a protected shelter.

The engine started with a low growl, then rapidly increased to an unbelievably loud roar accompanied by a low-frequency pulsing sound which fluctuated in intensity about once a second. The pulsing sound was caused by the buildup of pressure as the air was compressed by the curved underside of the fuselage and its subsequent sudden release as it flowed out the exhaust.

The ground crew quickly retracted, by remote control, the wind-making device that sent a stream of air into the intake to start the combination cycle ramjet. Part rocket and part ramjet, the aircraft's engine would lift them to well above one hundred thousand feet and propel them at above Mach 6 in velocity. Ignition cables separated from the aircraft body, also detached by remote control from the ground crew shelter.

The aircraft was nicknamed Aurora due to the persistent mistake made by a number of media writers in dubbing any potential SR-71 follow-on aircraft with the name. Actually Aurora was a name given to B-2 bomber funding during that program's competition phase. The Aurora had gone through a succession of other names, including Senior Citizen, until the official name became the RS-90. The name was similar to the name of its predecessor, the SR-71, SR standing for Surveillance Reconnaissance. Originally the aircraft was named RS-71, but a mistake by President Lyndon Johnson, who announced the existence of the legendary aircraft, inverted the order of the letters and sent government officials scrambling to rename the plane to be consistent with the chief executive.

Major Tallant nudged the throttles forward a hair and the throbbing sounds grew in intensity. He felt the aircraft slowly begin to roll forward. The Aurora moved out from underneath the hangar, and Tallant and Jansen got a good look at the night sky. The windscreen was tilted upward, giving them a good view above them but a severely restricted view directly forward. To create good viewing conditions forward, the designers would have had to put a bubble over the pilot's head, which would have caused extreme drag at six times the speed of sound and would have melted any sort of transparent material used for the windscreen. So they settled for a small window which conformed to the streamlined shape of the Aurora's fuselage.

Tallant swung the secret aircraft out onto the taxi strip, sending waves of sound across the flat air base. The sound reflected off the hills that ring Groom Lake and added to the noise that inundated the installation. He steered the sleek aircraft out onto one end of the six-mile-long runway.

"Romeo Sierra niner, zero, niner, ready for takeoff," announced Tallant into his microphone.

"Romeo Sierra, you are cleared for takeoff," said a familiar voice in his earphones. "Mike, Ed, good hunting."

"Roger," replied Tallant, and shoved the throttle fully forward. The aircraft responded by sending liquid oxygen to the rocket nozzles that were in the aft end of the aircraft. The Aurora sent an ear-shattering roar across the dry lakebed and began its takeoff run down the runway. Tallant examined the displays in front of him and noted the position of each of the bar gauges that told him engine inlet temperature, exhaust temperature, fuel pressure and temperature, and a host of other parameters that showed the status of his highly advanced aircraft.

Tallant could feel the lift building on the delta wings and suddenly they were airborne. He yanked back on the stick, and the Aurora sped into the night sky. They proceeded smoothly through Mach 1 up to Mach 3, leaving the characteristic round pulses of light in the flame from its tail, described by some in the media as "doughnuts on a rope." They flew in silence, all the while checking their instruments for proper operation of their aircraft, until they heard another familiar voice.

"Romeo Sierra, this is Kilo Charlie one, three, five, Bravo Tango," said the voice of his refueling tanker pilot. "I have you on two, seven, zero, range seven, fiver."

"Roger, Kilo," said Tallant. "Two pepperoni pizzas to go."

"That'll be the day, Mike," said Major Frank O'Donnell.

"Well, if you don't have any pepperoni pizzas, then forty tons of liquid methane will have to do," replied Tallant with a chuckle.

"The methane I got," said O'Donnell. "So where is it this time, Mike? Kamchatka? China?"

"Maui," quipped Tallant. "They think we're overworked and undersexed."

"I volunteer to refuel you when you get airborne," said O'Donnell with a laugh.

Tallant backed off the throttles and slowed below Mach 1 to subsonic speeds to approach the KC-135 tanker. Standard procedure was to take off with a minimum load of fuel, then top off while airborne to get enough fuel for the mission. Should there be a crash during takeoff, then they wouldn't destroy all of Groom Lake.

Tallant mentally calculated the time it would take to get to the target area in the South Pacific traveling at Mach 6. It was two thousand, one hundred forty-two miles to Hawaii, and two thousand, one hundred thirty-six miles beyond Hawaii to Kwajalein Atoll. Yes, he thought, just a bit under an hour. Then he would head in a line northwest of the atoll and photograph everything below. From a height of one hundred thousand feet, he would be taking pictures of a huge swath of the Pacific.

In the event of cloud cover, the Aurora had a side-looking, synthetic aperture radar that constructed opticallike pictures and used transmission frequencies that could "see" through the clouds. As the aircraft passed by an object, the radar continued to receive reflected pulses from the target. The angle to the target changed with each received reflected pulse and was used to construct an image of the target with much higher resolution than could be had with conventional radar imaging techniques.

Tallant approached the refueling aircraft and kept his eyes on the end of the boom and its blinking red light. He could feel the familiar buffeting as the Aurora went into the wake of the much larger aircraft. Tallant hit the switch to extend his fuel intake and slowly maneuvered the intake nozzle until it entered the cone-shaped tip of the fuel boom.

"Contact," said a voice from the KC-135. Tallant knew it was the refueling officer.

"Ready to take on fuel," replied Tallant as he eyed the green light on his control panel.

"Beginning to pump . . . now!" said the refueling officer.

A half hour later, Major Tallant and Captain Jansen were on their way. They dropped in altitude, then increased speed to get in front and above the tanker.

"See ya, Frank," said Tallant to the tanker pilot. "I'll bring you back a grass skirt."

"Good luck, guys," said O'Donnell. He sounded serious.

Moon surveyed his handiwork with some satisfaction. He had gotten some scrap aluminum from the engine compartment, that he guessed was to be used to repair the hull if any leaks developed, and had fashioned a shield to cover the two exhausts for the yacht's powerful diesel engines. The shields would spread out the heat the exhausts radiated and might be enough to help him escape detection by the infrared detectors used by the Americans to locate them.

The metal shields would be good reflectors for radar waves, but stealth technology from the United States had shown that rounded plates would reflect radar waves back to their source. Flat plates however, would reflect radar waves at oblique angles away from the radar. That was the reason the F-117 stealth fighter had flat segments making up its fuselage. Moon had therefore taken a piece of flat aluminum and just bent it once, turning it into an inverted V, then fastened it over the exhaust ports.

Moon looked at the curved metal plates that made up the stern of the yacht and bit his lip with worry. He wished they had been made of fiberglass instead of aluminum. The designers had put a slight bow in the transom in an effort to add some style to the craft. An idea struck him, and he excitedly ran below to see if he had the materials. He needed fiberglass body filler and a large file, along with another piece of aluminum. Below, in a small compartment filled with tools, he found what he needed. The fiberglass body filler was carried on board to fix holes in the fiberglass hull.

While on his way topside, he latched onto one of the other men and enlisted him to help in his campaign to make the yacht less detectable by the Americans. He ordered the man to file the piece of aluminum and save the filings in a cardboard box he had scrounged from below. After the man had half the piece of metal filed into slivers, Moon mixed the fiberglass body filler. He grabbed a handful of the metal filings and mixed it in with the fiberglass paste. Moon began daubing it over the metal parts of the stern in a random pattern.

An hour later, Moon nodded to himself. The metal filings in the now hardened fiberglass would reflect radar pulses in myriad directions, in effect lowering the strength of the reflected pulses received by the radar. He went over to the hoses he had prepared when his man was filing the metal and drooped them over the rear of the yacht. He set them to spray water over the two exhaust shields, which would further lower their IR emission.

Would it be enough to escape detection? Moon shrugged and looked at his watch. It was already several hours into the next day. He had a good man at the wheel who had not been affected by the electromagnetic radiation from the island's radar. Moon knew he had done all he could. He shuffled off to get a few hours of sleep.

The Aurora thundered through the thin atmosphere at one hundred fifty thousand feet, its fuselage glowing red under the bright moon. Major Tallant glanced over his gauges and noted that the position of each was within nominal limits. His aircraft was functioning well as its engines swept in the scarce air and guzzled liquid methane. He glanced at the gauge that told him the outer skin temperature. It hovered at around a thousand degrees Fahrenheit.

The heat in Tallant's cockpit came at him in waves. He reached out and placed a thickly gloved hand on the windscreen, feeling the heat seep quickly through the layers of insulation in his glove. A stray thread from one of the seams in his glove suddenly started to smoke, nearly set afire by the heat on the inside of the window. Tallant pulled his hand away and rubbed it with his other hand to put out any embryonic flames which might appear. No sense in setting off the fire alarm, he thought.

"Point XRAY in sixty seconds," said Jansen in the intercom.

"Roger," replied Tallant. The aircraft automatically went to a slower speed and a lower altitude so they could make the next scheduled turn. Point XRAY designated Kwajalein Atoll, and the mission called for a turn to the northwest. They would then increase their speed to Mach 3 for their sensor run. A turn and another run on the way back, then off to home to catch the refueling plane, which

was racing across the Pacific to meet them near Hawaii.
Tallant glanced at his fuel gauge. Less than half remaining,
which gave him a nervous moment. The brass wanted them
to get to the target area quickly which the Aurora was em-
inently capable of doing.

"Satellite contact in ten seconds," intoned Jansen. The
signals from their various sensors would be instantly transmitted to a satellite in geosynchronous orbit and relayed
back to the United States for processing. Tallant looked into
the darkness around them. They wouldn't get any optical,
but they would give them infrared and radar imagery.

"Sensors are up," said Jansen. The aircraft's computer
was programmed to control the plane's sensors and automatically turned them on at the proper location.

The aircraft automatically went into its preprogrammed
turn, then settled up at Mach 3 and one hundred thousand
feet. Tallant's eyes flew nervously over the control panel
as the aircraft turned, then he relaxed as the aircraft settled
on a straight and level course. He had always gotten anxious when one of his aircraft did something on its own. He
supposed he'd never get used to these fully programmed
flights.

National Reconnaissance Office
Northern Virginia

Commander Clifford Harmon, U.S. Navy, squirmed
around in his seat to view the rest of the large room in one
of the NRO's new office buildings near Dulles Airport in
northern Virginia. There were plenty of people from NPIC,
the National Photographic Interpretation Center, with their
booklets, titled "Joint Imagery Interpretation Keys Structure," showing them what different ship types would look
like from a hundred thousand feet up, or from space and
magnified a few hundred times.

Harmon turned back toward the mammoth screen in the
front of the room. NRO's logo with its colorful depiction
of the earth encircled by a single satellite dominated the
screen. A deputy director from the NRO stepped to a po-
dium to one side of the screen.

"Gentlemen, we have imagery from an RS-90 mission

over the western Pacific,'' he said, then looked at the NRO's director, who nodded as a signal to proceed. He pushed a button, and the NRO logo disappeared, to be replaced by a wide-angle shot showing points of light spread over what Harmon thought to be a large area.

Controllers at a table near the screen in the center of the room began to enhance each point of light using a joystick which in effect zoomed in to view each target with great resolution. The pictures were from an infrared camera and showed heat sources from each of the ships as fuzzy bright areas. The NPIC people busily classified each one. Sailboats, freighters, oil tankers rolled by on the screen. Then one image came up that was markedly different.

The heat sources thought to be from engine exhaust were faded in intensity and spread out behind where the vessel was thought to be. The NPIC people thumbed quickly through their booklets and shook their heads. It looked significantly different from anything in their library.

''Maybe we can superimpose the imagery from the Aurora's radar,'' suggested the supervisor of the controllers at the front table. They immediately got to work, and in a few minutes they had the radar image and the thermal image on the same screen. The radar image only appeared as a few disconnected lines in a background of shading that was suggestive of a boat.

The controllers played with the size of the images with their joysticks and put them over each other in various arrangements. Suddenly the images clicked in everyone's mind. The lines from the radar image outlined perfectly the fuzzy blobs from the thermal image. Commander Harmon would have bet a month's pay that one of the lines was the metal railing running along the side of the boat.

''What do you think?'' the deputy NRO director asked the senior NPIC evaluator.

''Seventy percent probable,'' replied the man from NPIC. They both turned and looked at Commander Harmon, who had stood in preparation to walk over to an adjacent table and use the phone.

''We'll check it out,'' he said, and headed for the phone that would connect him with the National Command Center at the Pentagon.

"We'll have coordinates in a minute," said the supervisor, and typed the required commands into a nearby console. The system computer took data from the Aurora's GPS receiver, which gave the aircraft's precise location, and coupled it with range and angle data from the spy plane's radar and infrared detectors, calculating the location of the target on the surface of the earth.

"Any optical yet?" asked Commander Harmon.

"Not yet. Still dark out there," replied the deputy NRO chief.

"KH-11 data?" asked Harmon.

"Not for another six hours," said the NRO executive.

Harmon nodded. The satellites were in fixed, predictable orbits and could cover only the area of the world that they could see below them. NRO had to wait for the KH-11 satellite to get around to the area of the western Pacific where this potential target was located. Therein lies the advantage of the aircraft nicknamed Aurora. It could go anywhere, anytime, and apply its sensors to anything.

Commander Harmon got the National Command Center on the line quickly. The NRO supervisor read off the latitude and longitude from the display in front of him and the time at which the data was taken. Harmon repeated it into the phone.

The *Topeka* will get its sailing orders, thought Harmon.

U.S.S. Topeka

Captain Fred Worden's eyes went wide as he read the flash operational message from the National Command Authority. The message detailed the escape of the surviving North Koreans from their sinking submarine, their seizure of the yacht, and their escape with many precious top secret documents. When he got to his orders, they were brief and to the point. He was ordered to sink and destroy the yacht in such a way as to insure that all top secret documents were destroyed as well. They gave him coordinates of the last probable contact with the yacht. Worden looked at his watch. The data was three hours old.

He quickly assembled his XO and navigator and filled them in on their latest orders. The officers were flabbergasted at the tenacity of the North Koreans. The navigator plotted the coordinates of the yacht given in the message and drew a circle with the yacht's location in the center. The circle represented where the yacht could be if it had sailed in any given direction at the estimated speed that it must have traveled to get that far from Kwajalein.

"Two hundred and fifty miles from here, Captain," said the navigator.

"And in a direct line to North Korea," added the XO.

"Assuming we go to flank speed," began the captain, "and they continue along with their present course and speed, how long before we intercept?"

The XO punched the numbers into a fire control computer and eyeballed the result.

"Six and a quarter hours, sir," replied Lieutenant Commander Riley.

Worden looked at both of them. "Let's do it, then."

"Aye, aye, sir," replied the officers in unison. The XO turned to give the OOD instructions as Worden gazed at the chart of the wide-open Pacific. The North Koreans were literally in the middle of nowhere. There were no combat assets the U.S. could bring to bear in this vast part of the western Pacific. Worden knew something about intelligence estimates after having served in the Pentagon several years ago. The intel people were never sure about anything. He looked at the message again. The contact was seventy percent probable that it was the yacht they were looking for. So he would take his boat racing across the sea to check out this contact and cross his fingers that this was the one they wanted. Another thought struck him, and he suddenly knew he had a severe problem on his hands.

After he visually sighted the contact, how was he to know if there were North Koreans aboard, or if they had top secret documents belonging to the United States? If he tried to stop and board them, they might try to run. Then what? Do I shoot first and ask questions later?

Captain Fred Worden brooded over the problem as he felt his ship increase speed.

CHAPTER THIRTY

Secret's End

U.S.S. Topeka

"Transients," said Sonarman Ernie Menago, and pressed his earphones hard against his ears. The sonar supervisor, Chief Stan Geller, stepped up behind Menago and listened in on another set of earphones. The sound settled down into the definite pattern of screws beating the water.

"What is the designation?" he asked.

"Sierra Four Five," responded Menago.

"What's the prelim classification?" asked the chief.

"Preliminary classification is surface noncombatant," said the sonarman. Geller picked up a microphone and informed the OOD in the conn.

Geller set up the spectrum analysis to evaluate the sound coming from above. He studied the screen and looked at the book of commercial vessels to see if he could match up the sound signature with one in the book.

"Okay, I've got one that's close," said Geller. "Ocean-going yacht, U.S. design and manufacture." He picked up the microphone and informed the conn.

Captain Worden nodded at the call from Sonar. "That must be it," he mumbled to the XO, Lieutenant Commander Riley.

Riley nodded. "Suggest we close to ten thousand yards, then go to periscope depth to make a visual."

"Sounds good, XO," replied Worden. The captain

hadn't solved the problem he had been struggling with earlier: how to positively identify this vessel as the one stolen by the North Koreans.

"Conn, Sonar. Blade count indicates that Sierra Four Five is doing ten knots," said Geller over the intercom.

"Conn, aye," replied the XO. He turned toward Worden. "He's slowed down. He did twenty knots from Kwajalein to open up some distance from us, but now he's probably worried about his fuel supply."

"If that's him," said Worden with a worried look.

Fifteen minutes later, the XO turned again to the captain. "We're at periscope depth, Captain," said Riley.

"Up periscope," ordered Worden. The scope slid noiselessly upward until the viewpiece was at Worden's eye level. He flipped the handles down and quickly turned three hundred and sixty degrees to view what was around his vessel. He settled on the white ship to the north of them. Worden increased magnification and got a good look at the ship.

"Yacht, maybe one hundred feet long, no other significant markings," said Worden. He stepped back to let the XO take a look.

"Let's get a picture," said Worden. "I can use it in my defense at my court-martial." He gave a wry smile.

The XO pulled back from the eyepiece and gave the captain half a smile in return. The XO took a second look and the expression on his face changed to one of concentration.

"You know, Captain, the yacht is flying an ensign on its stern," said Riley.

Worden's eyebrows went up in mild surprise. "The message said that the owner was Japanese. It's the Rising Sun, right?"

Riley didn't answer right away but increased the magnification to the maximum. He turned back around to his superior with the half smile back on his face.

"I think you should take a look, Captain," said Riley with a mysterious tone in his voice.

Worden peered through the eyepiece and couldn't believe his eyes. The expected white flag with the red circle in the middle was not what he saw. The flag had a red background with a red star inside a white circle.

It was the flag of North Korea.

Moon Si-Bok was jolted out of his bed by the sound of screaming. Lieutenant Kim was at it once again, with excruciating pain racking his body. Moon rubbed his face and looked around him. The stateroom was spacious, befitting a decadent capitalist, as he imagined the owner to be. The accommodations were quite a departure from his room on the submarine, *Admiral Yi*. Moon had the curious sense that the submarine and all its crew, including Lieutenant Kim, had been in his experience a very long time ago, that he had been on this boat for months, even years, and was surprised to remember that the *Admiral Yi* had been sunk only yesterday.

Moon slid from the bunk and walked out into the passageway, intending to go up to the bridge to check on the status of their journey back to the Democratic People's Republic. The rest of the crew, except for the one man on the bridge, were asleep, giving in to the exhaustion of the horrendous day before.

"Comrade Moon," said a voice behind him. He turned and saw one of the other men whom he had assumed was asleep.

"Comrade," said the man, "what are we to do with Lieutenant Kim?"

Moon eyed him closely. "What do you suggest we do with him?"

The man evaded Moon's question and instead asked a question of his own. "Are we to leave him in agony for the entire trip home?" The question left no doubt in Moon's mind what the man was suggesting.

"It is my understanding that we have given him all the painkillers we have, and that none of it did any good anyway," replied Moon.

The North Korean sailor's face grew hard, and he stared Moon in the eye. "We can take the pain from him," he said in a low whisper as he hefted a handgun. "This is what he would want anyway."

Moon was tempted. He'd like to see Kim get a bullet

and watch the arrogance and the life seep from him. Moon recalled vividly how Kim had brutalized him while on the cabin cruiser during their trip from Gea Pass to Roi-Namur. He touched his cheek where Kim had struck him with the automatic and found it still tender with a scab forming over the cut, and his nose was still swollen from the kick he had received from the nearly deranged officer. Yes, thought Moon, it had been only yesterday. He would like to take revenge on Kim for that, but what would a bullet do? A flash of pain, then the nothingness of death. Much better to let Kim live a while longer in agony, thought Moon.

"No, we will not kill an officer in the Republic's navy," said Moon with finality. The man started to voice frustration, but Moon turned from him and walked to Kim's door.

He opened the door and peered in and gaped in shock at Kim, who was lying on the bed.

U.S.S. Topeka

"Captain, we have a firing solution," said the *Topeka*'s XO.

"Ship ready?" asked Worden.

"Ship ready!" replied the XO.

"Solution ready?" asked Worden.

"Solution ready and loaded into tubes one through four," replied the XO.

"Weapons ready?" asked Worden.

"Weapons ready!" answered the XO.

"Select torpedo tube number one. Open outer doors," ordered Worden.

The opening of the torpedo tube outer door echoed throughout the boat.

"Outer doors open," said the XO.

"Stand by to fire," said Captain Worden.

A fire control technician grabbed the firing switch and shoved it over to the standby position. "Ready," said the XO.

"Shoot!" ordered Worden. The fire control tech shoved the handle over to the firing position. The torpedo launch noise filled the air around them as Worden's thoughts turned grim. He'd never thought he would ever have to sink an unarmed ship. His training was mostly for antisub operations, not blowing yachts out of the water.

He ordered the periscope up and regretted the masochistic tendency in him that urged him to watch the yacht go down. The reports from fire control floated to him on the incredibly still air in the conn. The torpedo was performing perfectly.

"Ten seconds to detonation," said the XO. The crew held its breath.

"Five seconds," continued the XO.

The yacht's last seconds to be whole ticked off, and the sonar operators braced themselves for the sound of an underwater detonation.

The sound never came.

Moon stared in horror at the sight of Kim in the throes of unbelievable agony. The men had tied him to the bed to prevent him from injuring himself, and Kim's writhing had pulled the ropes taught to the point where the circulation in his wrists was cut off. His hands were purple and flopping uselessly as he squirmed in a futile attempt to lessen the pain.

Blood flowed out of his mouth and down his front to splash on the bedsheets, staining them dark red. Kim had bitten through his tongue and upper and lower lips, his teeth working away gnawing at the ragged flesh around his mouth. Kim's eyes were rolled up inside his head, giving him a zombielike appearance with just the whites showing as his eyelids fluttered with the waves of pain racking his body.

The sounds coming from him were not full-fledged screams as they had been all through the previous night, but rather were growling whimpers. Pity welled up in Moon. Maybe I should let the men shoot him, he thought. The suffering Kim was enduring was beyond imagination and far outside any conceivable torture invented by the human race.

How much longer could he last? Moon thought of his treatment at the hands of Kim and decided once again to let him die naturally. When they got back to the Democratic People's Republic, it would be very difficult to explain why they'd had to kill a military officer. Would the authorities understand how electromagnetic radiation affects the human body? Would they even take the time to listen to what he had to say? Like it or not, he apparently was in command of the survivors, and he would be held responsible for their actions. The men seemed to gravitate to whoever had the most knowledge about how to get back home. They would follow his lead until a real naval officer arrived, perhaps when they finally tied up at the dock in Wonsan. At least the men thought he was in command, which was a de facto appointment to be their leader. And he had made his decision: he would let Kim live.

Moon closed the door quietly and faced the man in the corridor.

"Make him as comfortable as you can," said Moon to the frustrated sailor.

U.S.S. Topeka

Captain Worden stared through the periscope with mounting surprise.

"Plus ten seconds," said Lieutenant Commander Riley. The conning crew looked at each other with raised eyebrows.

"It missed?" asked the OOD.

Worden shook his head. "Was it enabled?" he asked the XO.

Riley nodded. "Yes, sir."

Worden shook his head and looked through the periscope once again. The yacht continued on the same course and speed. They hadn't seen the torpedo speed by under the boat.

"Not enough metal to set it off?" asked Worden of himself. The torpedoes were designed to go below the hull of a target ship and detonate in order to break the keel and make the ship sink as fast as possible. The torpedo had done just that, but hadn't detonated because it needed to detect more metal above it than what was on the yacht.

Riley offered a solution. "We could set the next one for contact detonation."

Worden's mind raced. Send another torpedo and the

North Koreans were sure to see it. If it didn't go off, they would race away. Surface and try to get them to come to, and they would surely make a run for it. He could easily catch up, but what weapon would he use to sink the yacht? He could use a Harpoon antiship missile, but he would have to open up a large distance between the *Topeka* and the target. Suppose the Harpoon's signal processing was set for larger ships? Would the Harpoon be effective against a relatively small fiberglass yacht? If he opened up the required distance and the Harpoon didn't do the job, then the North Koreans might be able to outrun them to Korean waters. They'd probably run out of gas, but could he take that chance? Were there any North Korean subs there to escort the yacht home?

"We're going to ram the yacht," said Worden to the XO.

The crew's eyes went wide open.

"Aye, aye, sir. I understand," said Lieutenant Commander Riley. His mind had been working on the problem and had come up with the same conclusion.

"OOD, I have the conn," said Worden. "Down scope." The periscope slid downward.

"The captain has the conn. The OOD retains the deck," said the OOD to the conning crew.

Worden turned to the junior officers at the plot board. "Give me heading at twenty-five knots to put us a thousand yards in front of her and a thousand yards off her port beam at her present course and speed."

The JOs got busy, then looked up. "Course zero, two, one. Time to intercept is four minutes."

"Left standard rudder," ordered Worden. "Come to course zero, two, one. Ahead two thirds. Make turns for twenty-five knots."

The *Topeka* surged forward, pulling them along to a destination that Worden dreaded. He had never rammed anything before and had never been on a boat that had. He basically had a choice of hitting the vessel with his sail, the superstructure that sat above the sub's hull, or hitting it with the bow. It wasn't much of a choice. The bow had the boat's powerful sonar and the diving planes, which were finlike surfaces that changed the sub's attitude under water.

The sail had an upward-looking sonar used for ice detection and had periscopes and antennas on its top. If it were a choice of losing their bow sonar or the ice-detection sonar, Worden would pick the latter, especially since they were about six thousand miles from any ice. He had to pick the depth just right so that the sail's main body would hit the yacht's hull and the bow would pass under the yacht's keel.

At two minutes to go, Worden gave his next orders. "Ahead one third. Make turns for ten knots. Come up to thirty feet."

The diving officer gave the appropriate orders and the sub pushed upward until its sail was just under the surface.

"Up periscope," said the captain. Worden leaned down and took a look through the periscope with the top of it still submerged, and was able to get a view of the yacht through the clear water. The yacht was still on its original course and apparently hadn't seen them yet. The *Topeka* made a low lump in the ocean as the sub's sail pushed the water in front of it, and the hull forward of the sail made the sea bulge upward as the submarine knifed through the water.

Worden had some bearings taken to the yacht as the two vessels ran alongside each other. He ordered both periscopes lowered until they hit the stops. He wanted to have nothing sticking above the upper edge of the sub's superstructure.

"Range to target is fourteen hundred yards," said a phone talker.

"Right standard rudder, come to course zero, four, five," ordered Worden. He was now at one tip of a triangle, the yacht at the other. If they both kept the same course and speed, they would meet at a right angle at the third tip of the triangle. At the last minute, Worden would increase speed to get the maximum impact on the yacht that was possible. He did a quick computation in his head.

They would collide in just over one minute.

Moon walked aft, intending to look over once again his handiwork in crafting shields for their exhausts. He passed through the now bullet-scarred doorway to the aft deck and walked to the stern. A glance told him everything was in place where they had constructed it last night, although the edges of the shields were getting black from the engine exhaust. He reached his hand up and casually placed it on the railing. It was warm to the touch, and the sensation prodded his mind into action. Could the Americans detect a warm railing with their infrared equipment? He smiled to himself. Everything was warm. But what about radar? The railing was metallic.

The thought unsettled him. The radar would have to be very sensitive, but the Americans had a knack of coming up with such equipment. He promised himself to mix up some more of the fiberglass and aluminum filings and paste it over the railings on the yacht.

The ensign on the short boom made a snapping sound in the stiff breeze. Moon looked idly up at the small flag. He had wanted to convince Lieutenant Kim to replace it with the Japanese flag which he had saved after Kim had discarded it with contempt the day before. He now no longer needed to convince the officer, and he made up his mind to replace it before forgetting about it again. That was another detail that he had to attend to. He left the side of the boat and let his eyes sweep the sea as he walked slowly to the doorway that led into the cabin.

There was something in the water on the port side, something very large and headed toward them at a very high rate of speed.

U.S.S. Topeka

"Ahead two thirds," said Captain Worden. In a few moments, the *Topeka* was traveling at twenty-five knots straight at the yacht.

"Sound collision alarm!" he ordered, and seconds later the panic-inducing warble was heard throughout the boat.

Worden and the rest of the one hundred and twenty-three men of the *Topeka* grabbed something solid and held on, waiting for the impact.

They are going to hit us, thought Moon with alarm. The object was just below the surface, and it hurried toward his yacht with frightening speed. The water bulged in front of the dark mass, and Moon knew what was heading for them after only a quick moment. It was an American submarine!

Moon raced across the aft deck and up the starboard side with his mind a jumble of thoughts. How had the Americans found them so quickly? The railing came to mind in a fraction of a second. How did they know who was on the boat? The blood-red North Korean flag flashed across his consciousness. Yes, the Americans knew, he thought in a rush.

Why wasn't the yacht turning to avoid the onrushing submarine? he thought desperately. He had the answer in an instant. The man at the wheel had been affected by the radar radiation on Roi-Namur. He was in intermittent pain and had tunnel vision. The young man couldn't see the submarine unless he looked straight at it.

Moon scrambled along, his legs feeling like lead. He shouted to his man at the wheel, but to no avail. The sound of scraping on the underside of the boat came to him just before his world exploded.

He heard a massive thud, and the yacht jolted sideways, slamming him against the starboard side windows. Moon bounced off the windows, then rebounded off the railing. He heard a loud crunching sound that drowned out the sound of the water rushing past the hull.

The sub's titanium sail ripped through the yacht's fiberglass hull like a machete going through cardboard. The port side of the luxury craft buckled around the curved front of the sub's superstructure and disintegrated under the massive impact of the rapidly moving submarine. The sail gouged its way to the other side of the hull, ripping a huge hole through from port to starboard. Moon fell into the sea as the starboard side of the yacht separated from the rest of the boat and fell flat to the water. The stub of one of the retracted periscopes hit Moon full in the chest and flung him aside like a piece of driftwood. The precious top secret documents scattered, their pages fluttering among the violence, only to become water-soaked and eventually to give up their secrets to the sea.

The two halves of the yacht immediately filled up with seawater and sank quickly, taking the sleeping crew and their agony-filled former leader with them.

The sub kept going, its engines ordered stopped by the captain, but with the screw still churning the water, chopping up debris and an occasional body that got sucked in from the surface.

Captain Worden ordered the *Topeka* to surface, and they immediately began to search for survivors. Worden surveyed the still-agitated water where the yacht had once been and saw only a few pieces of wooden furniture, some ragged pieces of the fiberglass hull, and other unidentifiable debris. The red covers of the top secret documents littered the sea along with the white pages that were stamped with the words *Top Secret* on top and bottom and on both sides.

I'm going to have to pick up as many of those documents as I can, thought Worden. I may have to prove that the North Koreans had them in their possession. He had another thought and searched in vain for the North Korean ensign that had been flying from the stern of the vessel. Then he spotted movement in the water, as did two other men on the *Topeka*'s bridge. An arm extended out of the water.

There was a survivor.

EPILOGUE

Reconciliation

Kwajalein Island

"I just thought I'd stop by and see how you folks were doing before I took off," said Jack Pearson after introducing himself.

Ken and Nancy Garrett eyed him curiously from the doorway of their trailer in Silver City.

"Exactly what was your function on the island?" asked Nancy.

Pearson's eyes narrowed a bit, then he recovered quickly. "Security," was his simple reply.

Nancy nodded. "I saw you on the plane when I arrived. You look the part."

Pearson nodded, somewhat in resignation. He had been told that many times. Ken invited him in, and they sat down across from him at the kitchen table. Ken studied him for a while until Pearson started talking.

"I heard you were bitten by some rats in one of the old Japanese tunnels," said Pearson. Ken and Nancy nodded. She winced just thinking about it. "I hope you're feeling better now," said Pearson.

"Yeah, we're almost done with our rabies shots," said Ken. "Thank God, they developed those new ones, only five shots in the arm instead of the three weeks of shots in the stomach."

Pearson nodded in sympathy, then eyed the two of them.

"I think you two are the bravest people I've ever met," he said in an even tone.

Ken wasn't surprised, but Nancy's eyebrows went up.

"You were the guy picking off the North Koreans," said Ken with certainty.

Pearson gave him a steady look, then nodded quietly.

"You were in the helicopter?" asked Nancy. Pearson nodded again.

"You saved both our lives," said Nancy.

Pearson's gaze broke, and he stared at the tabletop. "You know I had orders to kill you both if you were being taken by the North Koreans." His voice was quiet and firm.

Ken's and Nancy's mouths dropped open in surprise. Ken choked out one word as anger welled up in him.

"Why?" he asked as his face flushed red.

Pearson looked at Nancy. "Your wife knows why."

She looked at him, her eyebrows raised to question him, then she closed her mouth abruptly as the reason surfaced in her mind. "It's the missile defense system, Ken," she said, her voice bordering on disgust.

"I don't know if you will believe this," said Pearson. "But I had a chance to do you both when you were on the yacht . . ." His voice trailed off.

"What stopped you?" asked Ken in a belligerent tone.

"I decided to shoot North Koreans instead," replied Pearson. He wasn't smiling.

Ken's anger began to dissipate. The news that he and Nancy had been targets for this hit man was too much to assimilate. Still, he had to know what had happened in the end.

"The yacht," said Ken. "Did it get away?"

Pearson shook his head. "Sunk by an American sub."

Nancy gave him a concerned look. "Any survivors?"

Both men looked at her with surprise. She explained, "One of the North Koreans was almost kind to me. He protected me several times against a crazy officer."

"There was one survivor, a seventeen-year-old kid who was nearly blind," said Pearson. His face reflected bewilderment. "No one, not even this kid, can figure out how his vision failed. He also had some crazy story about the North Korean officer screaming in agony for hours on end.

He and the one other survivor of the fighting on Kwajalein will probably be repatriated back to North Korea after a while."

Nancy gave Ken a meaningful look, then looked at Pearson, who was studying them intently. "I was hoping the man who helped me would have survived," she said to explain. She didn't tell him that she knew how the North Korean youngster lost his vision, and how the officer had been injured so grievously. Ken's face showed the debate that had been going on within him for the last few days.

They all sat in quiet for a while as the Garretts digested the incredible news told to them by the mysterious man who sat across from them.

"Who do you work for?" asked Nancy. "I mean, who do you *really* work for?" She didn't expect an answer.

Pearson raised his eyebrows and said nothing. He moved to go.

"I don't know whether to punch you in the mouth or shake your hand," said Ken as he stood to see Pearson out.

"Take the nonviolent way, my friend," said Pearson with a short smile. "Believe me, it's always the best way." He extended his hand.

Ken grasped it, and they gave each other a surprisingly warm handshake. Pearson walked to the door, then stopped and looked over his shoulder at Ken.

"The man with you on the yacht," said Pearson. "Was his name Mike Sprague?"

Ken was surprised. "Yes. Did you know him?"

"I knew of him," replied Pearson.

"He was my best friend," said Ken with emotion. "He laid down his life to get Nancy back from the North Koreans."

Pearson turned and gave Ken a close look, then let his eyes wander around the room.

"Mike Sprague was an agent for the Red Chinese," said Pearson carelessly. "He helped you attack the North Koreans because he had orders from the Chinese to stop them from stealing missile secrets from the United States."

Ken's mouth dropped open in astonishment. He wanted to reply with some devastating fact that would prove Pearson wrong about Mike, but the CIA man continued, his voice conveying a certainty to his surprising statements.

"Sprague had been an agent for the old Soviet KGB. After the Cold War was over, Russia began to bring its so-called illegals home, and Sprague was one who was ordered home. But he had acquired a taste for all things American and opted to stay. The Communist Chinese contacted him a few months later. It was too tempting to resist: just keep doing the job he was already doing, only send the information to a different destination. We intercepted some of the messages that were sent to him via satellite channels from a man whose code name is Shifu, which is Chinese for 'master craftsman.' Sprague's code name was Guairen, which is the Chinese equivalent of 'weirdo.' " Pearson gave another short smile. "Apparently someone in the Chinese intelligence service has a sense of humor."

Pearson took in Ken's and Nancy's shocked faces and regretted his lecture. He had figured that these two heroes would have wanted to know who Sprague really was, but he was wrong. He had only made the two of them sadder than they had ever been. Pearson mumbled a good-bye and was out the door a second later. Ken slowly walked over to the kitchen table and sat down with a puzzled look on his face.

"Mike was a really good friend, wasn't he," said Nancy in a soothing manner.

Ken nodded as if in a daze. "The best," he said. He closed his eyes and rubbed his face.

"Pearson was wrong about Mike," he said. The desperate charge across the road to rescue Nancy from the North Koreans, as the officer held his weapon to Nancy's back, roared through his mind. Was that just to stop the North Koreans?

"I know he's wrong about Mike," said Ken with conviction. "He might have been a Chinese agent, but he was still my friend."

"Then he's my friend too," Nancy whispered into his ear.

Ken looked at her with surprise. How things had changed over the past few days, he thought. They had finally had a meaningful talk about their relationship, and they had learned some things about each other. He remembered his question from two days ago.

"Did you mean it? Will you always be there?" he had asked, referring to her statement when they were both in the aid station on Roi-Namur.

"Yes," she had said. "I'll always be there for you. Now that you've proven your love for me—"

"How have I done that?" he snapped back. "By killing someone? By acting like some fairy-tale hero? The murder in New York showed you that I wasn't some kind of fanciful action hero, that I wasn't going to race in and save the day like they show in the movies, and that's why our marriage has gone down the drain. Is that all a man means to you? Why should I have to always prove my love for you? Why don't you prove your love for me by loving me unconditionally?"

He remembered the mortified look on her face. The words had come in a rush, venting his frustrations and emotions of the past year and especially the past few days.

"You love me now that I'm a killer," he had screamed at her. "That killer is not me. It's someone I invented to get you back from the North Koreans. I became someone I had always hated because if I had lost you, I would have hated myself even more."

Nancy had burst into tears, and he immediately regretted his words, but they were all true. They had talked for a long time afterward, exploring their feelings and admitting to each other things that they had kept hidden. Nancy had realized that she had underestimated how dangerous the world was, but most of all she had realized that she had underestimated him. She knew how he had abhorred violence, and she had marveled at what it had taken for him to attack the North Koreans. She came to the stunning conclusion that she was really getting to know him for the first time.

Hours later, they sat peacefully on Emon Beach, on the northeastern tip of Kwajalein. The bench they were sitting on faced west, and nature was treating them to a spectacular sunset. Ken picked up the bottle of champagne he had taken from the refrigerator and popped the cork, then poured each of them a glass.

"You never told me about *The Lady N*," said Nancy. She smiled at him, knowing now that he had named his sailboat after her. She felt a little guilty as well. She had refused to follow him down to this island, and he'd named his boat after her anyway.

"Well, she is okay," he replied. "She was run up on the reef near the western end of Kwajalein. A couple of friends pulled her off late yesterday and anchored her in deeper water. They said there were no leaks, so I guess she won't sink anytime soon. We'll check her out tomorrow."

"So what's the *N* stand for?" she asked innocently, a wide smile giving her away.

"Well, there was this girl named Natalie—" he began, but was cut off by Nancy's tickling him so hard he lost his breath. He responded by laughing out loud and surprised himself with how good it felt. They both settled down, he with a wide smile on his face and she giving him a comical, piercing look. She rested her head on his shoulder once again. A few minutes went by as he waited for her inevitable question.

"So, who is Natalie?" she asked. She couldn't resist it.

He had supposed he would laugh at the expected question, but when she asked it with more than a semblance of seriousness, he was touched. Nancy was jealous. Jealous of a name he had made up on the spur of the moment. The smile on his face disappeared. He put down his glass of champagne and took her face in his hands as he had done when they were in the aid station on Roi-Namur.

"The *N* is you," he said tenderly. "It has always been you."

Nancy began to blink her eyes quickly, then she put her head on his chest so that he wouldn't see her cry. She dried her eyes in a minute as some of the island's inhabitants approached.

A few people came up to the Garretts and shook their hands to congratulate them on their defense of Kwajalein. Ken and Nancy both were heroes on the island, and their story spread quickly among the inhabitants. Ken was careful to give credit to Amata Milne, Nobuo Ohnishi, Donna

Nelson, Tom Necker, and Ed Atkinson. And Mike Sprague was at the top of the list and closest to Ken's heart.

Amata was recovering nicely from his injuries at the hands of the tunnel rats on Roi, and Donna Nelson would completely recover from the bullet she'd taken in her left hip while fleeing the North Koreans. Mr. and Mrs. Ohnishi and their yacht crew, along with the body of one of their crew, had left to fly back to Japan after taking an emotional farewell from the group that called themselves Roi Rats. Ken grunted in amusement. He had come to know two kinds of rats—Roi Rats, who would forever be regarded with affection, and the other kind of rat on Roi-Namur, the tunnel rats who would forever be in his nightmares.

The rest of their resistance group had been uninjured in their battle with the North Koreans, except for the landing party from the U.S.S. *Topeka*, which had lost three men and suffered eight wounded. It was a different story for the island's civilians, police force, and U.S. Army personnel. Over fifty people had been murdered by the North Koreans, and the United States was moving more forces into the area near the border between North and South Korea as the two countries hurled threats at each other. He had heard that the current U.S. administration didn't want to go to war over the invasion of Kwajalein Atoll by the North Koreans. Why kill more people over an incident that was a failure by the North Koreans? Ken and Nancy agreed completely.

There was one group he and Nancy hadn't met. The shipwrecked crew of the *Pacific Belle*, who had fought the North Koreans on Gea Island, had left Kwajalein before the Garretts had a chance to thank them or say good-bye. Ken resolved to look them up when he got back to the States.

Ken thought of all the brave men and women who had joined together to fight the North Koreans and to rescue Nancy. How can I thank them? What do I say?

Nancy nestled in Ken's embrace and rested her head on Ken's shoulder as they took in the colors of the sunset. Ken's thoughts shifted to his relationship with Nancy, and all the walls that can be built up between two people. The incident in New York had built up a big one. Did the battle on Kwajalein just tear it down?

No, he thought after a while. *We* tore it down, the two of

us. It wasn't the battle with the North Koreans. It was Nancy and I. And that was just the first step. He knew that it might be a long road back to the relationship they had had before the incident in New York, but now they had found out some things about each other. He especially had seen how easy it was to slide into violence. He had become like his father, aggressive and belligerent, both foreign and repulsive feelings to him. But how else was he to deal with a stubborn and intractable enemy like the North Koreans? Above all, he had taken revenge on another human being just as his father had done. But his father hadn't had his best friend murdered. The entire incident would be one of the great paradoxes of his life.

The colors of the sunset deepened, with the sun lighting the edges of the clouds with red fire and giving their undersides a slight purple hue. The entire western horizon was lit up with a spectacular light display as the clouds and the raw natural colors gave form and substance to the day's fleeting light.

"God, isn't it beautiful," mumbled Nancy.

"Mike loved sunsets," Ken said in a low voice. He clamped his mouth closed, afraid to let the emotion come out, afraid to expose his inner feelings to Nancy. Maybe that's the problem we've been having between us, he thought. He had already said more to her in the last few days than he had ever wanted to. And now I've lost my best friend, and I'm afraid to mourn.

In the end he gave in, the emotion pouring out, but he modulated it with a macho tone to his voice.

"Here's to you, Mike, wherever you are," said Ken, and with tears welling in his eyes, he raised his glass to the sunset.